"A great novel as well as a superb thriller, Doubling the Penny serves up a smooth blend of personal angst mixed with a potentially devastating attack on the U.S.

24 meets *Homeland* in Mark Shaff's relentless and riveting take on the mindset of a hero as well as an equally tortured nation. A splendid addition to the triumvirate of Brad Taylor, Brad Thor and the late great Vince Flynn."

-Jon Land,
USA Today bestselling author

"A terror plot so ingenious and plausible, it will keep you up at night."

- Leslie H.

Author Mark Shaff has done it again. **Doubling the Penny** is every bit as good as its prequel – his spectacular debut novel, **Redemption Road**. Every page leaves you gasping; you can't wait to find out what happens next in this chilling Age of Terrorism thriller. It's as modern as the latest high tech science.

In **Doubling the Penny** there's something for everyone: action and intrigue; daring heroism and depraved villainy; stirring romance; even a touch of the paranormal.

Shaff, a master storyteller, builds a story in such a way as to grip your emotions from the get-go, then keeps drawing you in until you feel part of the story. He creates characters who are larger-than-life, yet relatable. His hero, Marcus Diablo risks his life in one agonizing, catastrophic incident after another, yet his family is always foremost in his heart.

There's no way you won't enjoy **Doubling the Penny.**

-Carol P.

It's a fast read and you really get into the characters. You want to keep reading because you feel like you're there. Buy it!

-Dennis D.

Definition of writing

The written word is the foundation upon which all other forms of communication are based. Through words the future is speculated upon, the present is chronicled and the past recorded. Words paint pictures, put voices to music, create images, vivid and raw of all things that are, were and what might be.

-Anonymous

Force Ten:
Doubling the Penny

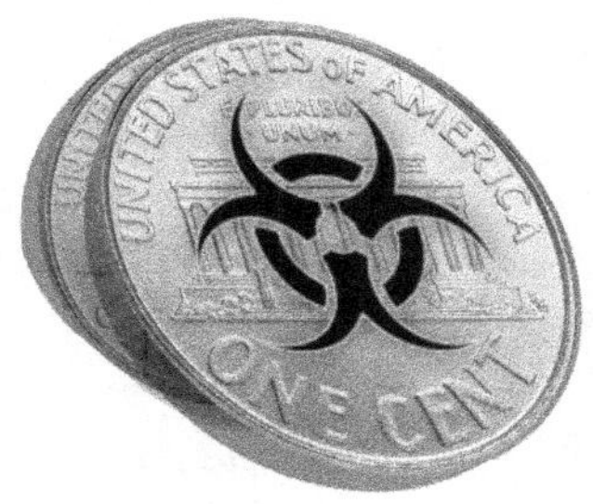

By Mark Shaff

LeRue Press, LLC
Reno, Nevada
www.lrpnv.com

For information or additional copies, contact LeRue Press, LLC, 280 Greg St., Reno, Nevada 89502

Cover design by: shebangdesign.net in partnership with MAC Creative Management

Library of Congress Control Number: 2016960817
ISBN: 978-1-938814-12-9

First Edition, December, 2017
10 9 8 7 6 5 4 3 2 1

Printed on FSC paper, responsibly sourced

Dedication

To my sons, Lucas and Colton: In so many ways you are responsible for me finding my writer's voice. There is this level of emotion, this depth of love that I tap into when I write and when I find myself struggling to see that path all I have to do is think of you. That our lives have provided me with so much material to write about is a testament to the family we are and the love we have for each other.

Acknowledgements

For me writing is a "me time" pursuit: Me, alone with the words and the pictures in my head. But the truth is that to convert writing to something not only tangible but viably marketable takes a team. To all those who read the many drafts and offered free advice and critique, as always you have my love and appreciation.

To my editors: Michael Carr, once again you mentored me. Your encouragement, prodding and the many, "I have no idea what this means," allowed me to take another step toward becoming a better writer.

To Carol Purroy: Wow, I never really grasped what a copy editor did. As a writer, I get caught up in the rhythm and the flow of the story. I spend my time sculpting characters and painting scenes and not nearly enough on the foundation: spelling, grammar, and punctuation. Your keen eye has made what I know to be a good story so much better.

Lastly, to my publisher, LeRue Press, LLC: Well ladies, especially Janice Hermsen, I would not be here if not for you. The quality of this book, from the writing to the cover is due to your consideration and appreciation for my work. How many times did I say, "The manuscript is ready?" With patient understanding you guided me, put up with me, and most importantly stuck with me. I am proud to have *you* on my side and to be a part of *your* team.

Author's Note

In reference to time and distance: I have used the 12 hour and 24 hour clocks, as well as miles and kilometers. This is a distinction between civilian and military terminology, also it is a distinction between the U. S. standard of time and measurement and that, which is used in many parts of the rest of the world.

CHAPTER ONE

November 29, Black Friday,
Beginnings Ranch, British Columbia

Shop or shovel shit.

Just give me a shovel, thought Marcus Diablo as he stood on the flagstone patio in the predawn and stared out across the main compound of Beginnings Ranch. Here, the busiest shopping day of the year didn't mean squat.

Two hundred yards away, in the long shadows of the setting moon, the Coldwater River moved like a thick black snake, its smooth skin glistening as it undulated through meadows and coniferous woodland. On the bank stood a man, his breath making small vapor clouds in the cold air.

With his hands stuffed into the pockets of his canvas work jacket, Marcus headed for the river. The gravel crunched under his boots as he passed one of the steel maintenance buildings and the lit-up bunkhouse, alive with get up and get to work activity.

As he approached the river's edge the man didn't turn. Marcus stopped next to him. This morning, the smell of wood smoke rising in lazy plumes from the chimney flues filled the air. Along with sounds of moving water, cattle complaining, and spur rowels clinking, the entire scene reminded him of some long-ago time. He felt nostalgic for *what used to be*. At the same time, he harbored a deep-seated hope that *what was* would be a safe, happy place for him and his sons.

"I wondered when you might show up," Marcus said.

Colonel Samuel Webb spoke, his gaze still on the river. "You and I have been here, what, almost four months, and every morning 'bout this same time you come and stand right here. Figured I'd leave it be for a while, give you and the boys some time. Well, times up!"

Marcus shifted from foot to foot. In the darkness he contemplated, as he did every morning. What purpose waited out there for him and his sons? He glanced at his friend. Although, about the same size, the colonel had ten years on him, but it hardly showed. The years of field command, especially with groups of younger officers, kept him youthful in body and mind.

When Marcus spoke his voice had an edge. "In the last sixteen months my boys lost their mother and moved away from the only home they had ever known. Then there's the matter of their father, who was once just a regular dad..."

The colonel interrupted, speaking in the refined Southern drawl that Marcus always found both soothing and disarming. "I've known you long enough to realize that there is very little about you that is 'regular'."

"Maybe so. But how can I expect Bodie at 13, and Garrett, only 9, to wrap their heads around the idea that their dad is a member of Force Ten—an elite private military contracting firm—when I can't even do that?" Marcus stared into the dark water. "On top of that, for the past few days I've had this feeling. Call it a premonition, or maybe just paranoia, but I've got this nagging sense that something big and bad is coming, and soon. Probably just paranoia!" Marcus shrugged.

The colonel looked at his watch, just after 5:00 in the morning. He turned the collar of his jacket up. "Well...I don't put much stock in paranoia." The colonel slapped Marcus lightly on the back. "I'm freezing my ass off out here." The colonel began walking up the gravel drive toward the barn. "Why don't you join me in Ops this morning."

As the colonel and Marcus passed the massive log house the back door to the kitchen opened. Norma Jean Rea, the house manager, head cook, and self-appointed all-around boss at Beginnings, stood there in a flour-dusted apron. In her hands she held a thermos and a brown paper lunch bag. "Well, fancy that! Two of my favorite men."

The colonel stepped up to the door and took the offered thermos and bag. In the warm glow coming from the lit-up kitchen, the aroma of fresh bread wafting out into the cold morning air, Marcus watched as Norma and the colonel exchanged a conspiratorial look. Norma laughed as she brushed back a wisp of silver-gray hair, leaving a smudge of white across her forehead.

"I'll forgive you missing breakfast, just this once." Norma's eyes never left the colonel. With a girlish twirl she turned back into the kitchen. Before shutting the door she called out, "I'll expect you for lunch." Marcus never knew just how to take Norma. But if she had her sights on the colonel, well, good on him.

The two men continued on toward the big barn that sat on the bluff above the main house. As they approached, Marcus considered how odd it was that this building played such a big role in why he, his sons, their large extended family, and Force 10, were here on this ranch.

* * *

AFTER THE LAST MISSION, MARCUS'S first with Force 10, finding a safe place to regroup and lay low was a top priority. Force 10 had a training facility deep in Australia's Simpson Desert. But it was on the wrong continent, not to mention too isolated and remote for families and children. Wherever they went, besides being reasonably close to schools and a decent sized town, a ready-made location for an operations and command center was critical. This ranch, and specifically this barn, solved that dilemma.

According to the story the original owner had picked this land to build his ranch on because of what lay behind the barn: a large natural limestone cavern. Here he protected his livestock from the cold, harsh winter until he built a barn. And until he put up a small cabin it served as shelter for his family as well. The ideal place for an operational command center was buried deep underground, but a cave would do.

The colonel and Marcus entered the barn through the side door into the dim glow from steel-caged lights mounted on posts. Though the colonel came here every day, this was only the second time Marcus had been inside the barn since his arrival at the ranch.

Breathing in the smells of livestock and hay, they walked past the stalls toward the back. A brighter light shone from beyond where normally there would be a wall. Over the years, as heavy equipment became available, the cavern had been enlarged so that today it was over two hundred feet long and, in places, nearly a hundred feet deep, with a high, solid rock dome above.

Stepping into the vast space they moved toward the concrete building tucked into the back corner. Within days of the ranch purchase a Canadian specialty construction firm began building the components for the thirty-by-thirty-foot *wine vault* for the eccentric new owner. At the concrete bunker the colonel entered a code on the keypad. The four-inch-thick steel door whooshed open and they stepped inside.

CHAPTER TWO

INSIDE THE OPS BUNKER, J. T.—Jonathan Tiberius—stood in front of a wall where an arced steel frame held four rows of five sixty-inch TV screens. With a touch pad, he posted information onto the wall of high-resolution monitors, which could show multiple applications simultaneously or could be merged to provide larger views.

Without words the colonel and J. T. began their well-established morning review. On the monitor wall pictures of men, some with heads covered and scraggly beards, others impeccably groomed and in expensive suits, began appearing. Each had a brief synopsis of which terrorist group they were affiliated with, their status in that group and their current location. Other images showed current terrorist-related attacks and conflicts, of which there were dozens every day. That only the high profile attacks made the U. S. news went to the general lack of understanding about just how terrorism works.

Without looking away from the monitors, J. T. said, "Nice of you to join us, Marcus. I was beginning to think you didn't like me anymore."

Marcus appraised the young Force 10 tech wizard. At a buck-twenty dripping wet, thick-framed glasses, a pocket protector, and a baby face, "nerd" described him to a tee. He looked like a 20-year-old college kid, not a 38-year-old-genius who had been working for America's top intelligence-gathering agencies since he was 18.

"I've got to say, when you show them like that," Marcus cocked his head at the screen, "It's like jihadist poster boys side by side with the successful next door neighbor. One group to fundraise and promote an agenda, the other to incite, radicalize and train—specialized talent for specific jobs. Sounds a bit a like Force Ten?"

It pleased the colonel that Marcus fell naturally into the review process. Questioning, commenting, and making assumptions as only he could. The colonel's stomach grumbled, the wall clock read just before 11:00 A. M. They had been at it for almost four hours and he needed to eat. Besides he had a lunch date he dared not miss. Although the colonel stuck to a routine in all things, J. T.'s sense of time when it came to sleeping and eating seemed immune to any type of regular schedule.

This typified why he had been the colonel's *first* Force 10 recruit. When he left the Army to start his own private military contracting firm, finding "kick-ass and take-names" types wasn't the problem. To be successful, he needed someone who could keep his new firm on the cutting edge of intelligence gathering, mission communications, logistical planning, and data analysis, as well as someone who could handle the technical end of managing all manner of complex information, gadgets and hardware. These tasks required an exceptional mind and a dedicated focus. Two things J. T. had in spades.

J. T. spoke. "The *Takbir* is making good time."

A real-time satellite view of a sleek, black, six-hundred-foot super-yacht powering through the ocean showed on the screen.

The *Takbir* had just completed a weapons retrofit in its homeport at the head of Russia's Golden Horn Bay in Vladivostok.

"What's up? Why is she at sea?" asked Marcus.

"A couple of weeks ago, I decided the time had come to get the ship closer to home."

The colonel and Marcus shared a look.

"You're not the only one whose sixth sense is pinging," the

colonel said.

"I'll be uploading a new software upgrade into the God's Eye Satellite operating system over the next few days," said J. T.

The colonel had no idea what the software did, but J. T. knew and that's all that mattered. Just the concept that a private organization, in this case, Force 10, controlled the most sophisticated spy satellite currently in existence seemed like science fiction, but it wasn't.

"Do you guys want an update on the money? The colonel's stomach grumbled again.

"You okay, Colonel?" J. T. asked with a smirk.

"Well some of us have to eat real food, not..." The colonel pointed at the collection of chips, soda cans, and beef jerky bags on a counter against the wall.

"I take it we still have money, right?" said the colonel.

J. T.'s face was part *Are you stupid?* and part, *Who do you think you're talking to?*

For thirty years the colonel ran black ops for the U. S military, during which time, he had access to the latest in information and weapons technology. It took a lot to surprise him. The fact that Force 10 controlled a floating palace, now equipped with military-grade weapons, a spy satellite, and a sum of money nearing a trillion dollars, boggled his mind. Combined with operating out of a five-hundred-thousand-acre working cattle ranch in British Columbia's Nicola Valley went beyond anything he could conjure up in his wildest imagination.

But none of it surprised J. T., or Marcus, for that matter. For J. T., like a kid in a candy store, there was no such thing as too much. And for Marcus, his unrestrained imagination simply refused to recognize anything as impossible.

"Okay, before we go get something to eat, dazzle us with the results of your exceptional money management."

As the men scanned the information, all the screens except the God's Eye view of the *Takbir* went dark.

"What the hell just happened?" asked Marcus.

J. T. didn't answer. Instead, he moved to what he called a "console," really just an expensive high-tech recliner. He sat, put on a wireless headset, flipped up an arm-mounted keyboard, and feverishly began typing in commands. "Vanessa, run a systems check," he said aloud.

J. T. had programmed the ops computer with a voice command and interface program. The colonel made a mental note to schedule the most socially-and normal-life-challenged person he knew a vacation, preferably with a flesh and blood companion.

There was a momentary pause, then the sexy voice: "Yes, Jonathan, a substantial portion of the United States Internet system is off-line. Without more data, I cannot determine how extensive."

"How is that possible?"

"Well, Jonathan..." Vanessa's programmed sultry drawl lingered on his name.

J. T. interrupted, uncharacteristically self-conscious. "Vanessa, call me J. T."

"As you wish. J. T., one or more of the Internet interconnectivity hubs has been subjected to a disruptive event that has caused an interruption in the feed. There is redundant backup to protect the storage of critical data. However, there are reports of failures in essential power grids, security, like air traffic control, and widespread cell phone network overloads. I have prepared a map."

The colonel and Marcus studied the map of the United States. Red dots, each with a brief summary of the issues, indicated trouble spots. J. T. brought up live news feeds on several of the monitors. Scenes of looting, police in riot gear, and traffic-clogged streets and highways filled the screens.

"What the hell is this all about?" the colonel said.

"This is the one of the busiest days of the year for the Internet!"

The colonel's look of confusion deepened.

"The day after Thanksgiving. Stores open at 0-dark thirty.

People camp out, wait in line all night. Not to mention the billions of dollars in online sales. How don't you know this?"

A ringing phone startled them. The colonel looked around. He couldn't remember how long it had been since he had heard that ordinary ring of an analogue telephone.

"Oh, shit!" J. T. said.

This was the secure line. He called it the "Bat Phone." Only two people had the number: General Walter Kittredge, the colonel's long-time friend and head of the Joint Chiefs of Staff, and Nathan Reynolds, Deputy Director of the FBI. This was the first time it had ever rung.

The colonel crossed the concrete floor to the wall of desktops and picked up the handset.

"Sam, that you?'

"Yes, General."

"Damn glad to hear your voice. I guess you know what's happened."

"Well, General, I'm aware that the Internet is off-line, and it ain't pretty. Beyond that, not much."

"That's right, and I don't claim to be an expert on what that means exactly, but I do know that three of the country's primary Internet hubs, New York, L.A., and Seattle have crashed. Apparently, just about the whole goddamn Internet operates through them. And from what my people tell me, today is one of, if not the busiest, day of the year for the Internet.

"Okay Sam, you know the drill. The 'powers that be' start demanding from those of us with stars on our shoulders, and we in turn, chew our way down the food chain. So consider yourself my main course."

The general sighed then continued. "I got a bad feeling. We're still picking up the pieces from the last attack. For God's sake, there are small, remote pockets, mostly out west, where citizens are in charge, running the show like militias of the old days. And, truth be told, I can't blame 'em."

"You wouldn't be talking about me and Force Ten, now,

would you, Walt?" the colonel asked, his tone as breezy as if they were discussing the weather.

"Shit, Sam, I didn't consider you, honest. Now that you mention it, though, I believe you'd fall into the category, but then, you don't currently reside in the land of the free and the home of the brave, do you?" The general's voice held not a hint of disdain. "You get yourself a dog yet?" A laugh reverberated in the colonel's ear. "Here's what I need, Sam. I'd consider it a personal favor. You're going to get another call soon after you and I are done here. Give the folks a sit-down and the benefit of your wisdom. I know that Force Ten's contract with the U.S. Army is up, but from the intelligence rumor mill, I understand that making money may not be a motivating factor in the jobs you and Force Ten consider."

"I should've known I couldn't just drop off the face of the earth. I'll take the call and we'll see what I can do. Beyond that, we're launching an in-depth analysis of the attack as we speak. We have access to some unique intelligence-gathering tools."

Another chuckle. "When this is over, my friend, you and I need to sit down and you can enlighten me over a bottle of single malt. But right now we need to get out in front of this thing 'cause, as bad as it is—and we're not even an hour into it—the real fireworks are still to come. I just know there's more. Find out what that *more* is!"

"All right, General, I'll get on it. And, hey, when I do get that dog I'm gonna name him after you."

Hanging up the phone, the colonel said to Marcus, "Told you, I don't put much stock in paranoia."

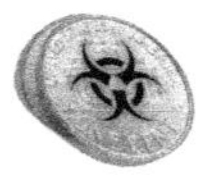

CHAPTER THREE

FBI headquarters, Washington D. C.

Deputy Director Nathan Reynolds sat in his corner office inside the J. Edgar Hoover Building going over the day's threat assessment analysis. Sitting back in his chair, he rubbed his eyes. Determining a credible threat from some disgruntled rant often felt like going all in with a pair of twos and no face card.

The red light blinked on his intercom. Hitting the button, he heard the voice of his secretary, "Sir, turn on the TV." Reynolds hit the remote and on came CNN. "A secure, encrypted email transmission just came in from General Kittredge, I'm sending it to you now. Also, you are needed in MTAC. Ten minutes."

The deputy director brought up his internal email as he watched on the TV scenes of mayhem play out in one shopping center after another. As he used the keyboard he said a silent thank you that the FBI used its own secure *intra*net. He read the email.

Picking up his phone, the deputy director hit a series of numbers. A shrill buzz, then a clear dial tone told him he had access to a secure outside line. From memory he punched in a phone number.

"Colonel Webb."

"Deputy Director. Seems like we are back in the shit."

"Yes, Sir. I'd like to get your—Force Ten's—take on what's going on. I have a meeting in a few minutes. Over the next hours the picture of what is happening will begin to take shape. Think you might consider sharing your insight?"

"I promised the general I would. When and where?"

"I'll let you know, but soon. And Colonel, don't feel like you have to come alone."

* * *

INSIDE THE FBI'S MULTIPLE THREAT Alert Center, Deputy Director Nathan Reynolds listened to the briefing being delivered by Cyber Crime Specialist, Agent Sonja Stanwick.

Standing with her back to the large display monitor, which showed pictures of three buildings, she spoke. "Today at 11:00 A. M., Pacific, 2:00 P. M. Eastern, three of the largest and most important interconnectivity hubs in the United States were attacked."

Turning to the screen she pointed. "One Wilshire Data Center in Los Angeles, the Westin Building in Seattle, and 60 Hudson Street, New York City. These facilities provide data management and storage services for a diverse array of private sector businesses. We're talking everything from tech to toilets. Because all this data is transferred via the Internet, these locations also serve as critical Internet transmission centers." She fidgeted with the remote in her hand. "We don't know the extent of the damage, but we believe only some of the servers have been affected. As a precaution, all systems at these locations have been taken offline. As to the cause, we are working on that."

"What actually does that mean, agent?" Demanded the Director of the FBI, Edward Pinehurst.

"Sir, we are having difficulty getting teams to these buildings," she said with a hint of, *Aren't you aware of what's going on out there?*

Agent Reynolds broke in. "Director, teams are en route and the buildings are locked down. This is the busiest shopping day of the year. The Internet is necessary for inventory management, credit and debit card transactions." News footage showed on the monitors. "These scenes are playing out at stores and shopping centers across the country. Riots are erupting, streetlights are out, and city, highway, and freeway traffic is at a standstill. Until some calm is restored we won't be able to conduct proper onsite investigations."

Turning his attention to the room of agents, "We are all familiar with the recent events in Ferguson and Baltimore, this..." he motioned to the screen behind him, "is much more dangerous. This is not isolated. It's happening in every city and town across the country. We're talking rampant looting and vandalism, and..." One of the news programs showed a view from a helicopter as it zoomed in on a man attempting to lock the door of an upscale jewelry store. Something hit the glass storefront, maybe a rock, as a man approached and shot him point blank with a pistol. "That! This is going to get ugly fast. All agents are to work in teams, and anybody who goes out there is fully geared up." Tuning back to agent Stanwick, "Please continue."

Trying to shake off the being-in-the-spotlight jitters, the young agent swallowed hard. With her short bobbed hair, navy pantsuit, and black flats, she looked like she'd stepped out of an FBI recruiting video.

With renewed confidence Agent Stanwick continued. "What we do know, Director, is that as of now, for most Americans, the Internet has been turned off. And that's not the worst of it. There are redundant protocols for such an incident. Stored data is backed up to more than one source in more than one location. In fact, there are dozens of interconnectivity hubs. And if we were talking about storage only, the redundant protocols are sufficient. What we must keep in mind is, these facilities, referred to as 'the cloud', house the conduit, the hardwiring, that provides each of us with the data we are so dependent on." She held up her smart phone.

"This is not about the stored data, it's about the data we access every minute of everyday: Email, GPS directions, restaurant reviews and reservations, Facebook, YouTube. It's about systems, like transportation networks, including traffic lights. Also, air traffic control, financial markets, I could go on, that rely on an Internet connection for part of their operation. So, even though nearly all the data that the attack destroyed is backed up to servers in other locations, no one planned for the sheer demand that instant access to information would place on the redundant systems. Simply put, these back-up systems cannot support both the data storage demands and the volume of Internet traffic. As long as these three locations," she looked quickly back at the monitor, "remain offline we are going to see a cascade of failures within the redundant network, which by the way," she held up her phone again, "means these may not even work to make calls."

Edward Pinehurst stood. "So you're telling me Agent Stanwick, that…"

"Yes sir." She took a step forward. "Things are going to get a whole lot worse, before they begin to get better."

CHAPTER FOUR

Los Angeles, California

BRANDON FRANKS LOOKED AT THE time on his phone and shook his head. A couple of minutes to eleven in the morning and it had already been a long day. Well, no shit. The store opened at 1:30 A.M. and he had been here hours before that. But what did he expect as the manager of a large electronics store in Century City Shopping Center on the busiest shopping day of the year—Black Friday. God, he hated those two words.

There'd been a crowd when he opened the doors. Some people had camped out on the sidewalk for a few days to be first in line for the highly advertised, very limited killer deals. *Don't these people have jobs?* Last year, across town at a competitors' store, a lady got trampled...to death. All for a chance to buy one of only three 48-inch, $150 flat screen TVs. It gave the term *addicted to TV* a whole new meaning. His store had hired extra security. They had everyone working overtime, and so far so good. The screaming deals—those carrots that everyone dangled—were long gone. But they had a ton of inventory and plenty of *good* deals and, most importantly, a huge captive audience.

Walking around the store, he kept an eye on his people. In the TV aisle a women stood in front of an empty self where 54-inch flat screens had been. "Excuse me, ma'am, can I help you?"

"I thought you would still have some left. I promised my kids."

Her frustration was not the exception this day. "Tell you what." He nodded his head for her to follow. "These 60-inch models are also on sale and with the manufacture's rebate, only twenty bucks more."

With a customer calmed and a sale made, he approached the front checkout station. The six registers each had long lines. He watched as first one clerk, then another, stared first at their monitors, then up, looking for him.

At the first station Brandon looked at the register. It had power, but where he should have seen data, it read, *Unable to complete transaction at this time. Please try again.* At each register it was the same story. Brandon pulled his cell phone from his back pocket and hit speed dial for the company's IT department. Holding his phone to his ear he expected to hear a reassuring voice on the other end. Instead, he got a recorded *All circuits are busy.*

Then the grumbling began.

"What the hell's going on? I've been in this damn line for almost thirty minutes."

"What's the matter; you all forget how to use a cash register?"

"You don't want to honor your special pricing, so you're pretending your credit card machines don't work? That's bullshit."

Brandon sensed things getting ugly. He jumped up on the counter of station three.

"Please, please." He held his hands in the air. "We are experiencing some kind of technical glitch. Just give us a few minutes. We'll get it figured out."

Hopping down, he tried his phone again with the same result. Finding one of the security men, he whispered, "Calmly and carefully, let's get people moving to the front exit. Tell them we are working to resolve the problem, but until we get it figured out we need to clear the store, as a precautionary measure only. All pricing will be honored."

As the security staff gathered Brandon looked out the glass storefront to a commotion in the parking lot. People frantically pushing full carts while looking back over their shoulders, others ran by with arms full of clothing still on hangers. Some had boxes of what appeared to be kitchen stuff—pots, pans, and blenders.

Turning back, Brandon looked at the growing unrest in his own store. He knew a shit storm when he saw it. He'd been taught at management training that in case of an emergency, and only as a last resort, he should lock the doors, even with customers still inside. Taking the keys from his pocket he moved to the doors. He got the first pair of five locked. As he moved to the next, a man, a good ten years older, fifty pounds and five inches bigger, stood there with a box that contained a sixty-inch flat screen on the floor leaning against his hip.

Before Brandon could say a word the man slugged him. As Brandon lay on the floor blood gushing from his nose, the man hefted the box up with meaty hands and walked out the door. Brandon got to his feet. His face hurt like hell. As he staunched his bleeding nose with his shirttail, he noticed a female reporter step inside the automatic opening door. She pointed at Brandon, and the man standing next to her trained his camera on his smashed and bloodied face as she thrust a microphone toward him. "Sir, Brandon..." She read his name from the badge clipped above his shirt pocket. "Can you tell me what's happening? Do you know what's going on?"

Brandon ignored the questions. He had bigger problems. He stood and watched as what had been a reasonably calm crowd minutes before, morphed into a raging, looting mob.

He motioned for the register clerks to follow him. As the group made their way up the aisle toward the back of the store, gathering sales staff as they went, two men fighting on the floor blocked the way. The bigger man sat astride the other and hit him again and again in the face, as he yelled, "Push me, will you? You son of a bitch."

A girl of maybe ten stepped out from behind a fallen headphone display and screamed, "Stop Daddy, stop!"

His bloody fist cocked for another blow, the man turned to the yelling girl.

Brandon looked from daughter to father. One face held the expression of unadulterated fear, the other, pure hate, and for what, a $600 television?

Brandon led his group around and down a side aisle. They dodged shoving and pushing people as merchandise fell from high shelves and smashed to the floor. A gang of people, and that's what they were, thought Brandon—a gang—ripped, tore and smashed model TVs, computers, and cameras attached to theft-proof tethers. The stores only 98" big-screen exploded when it hit the floor. Shards of thin sharp glass flew through the air like mini-spears. Brandon felt the projectiles cut his face and arms. Looking to his group he saw droplets of blood form on exposed skin, and crimson stains spread on clothing.

"Come on, we have to get to a safe place," Brandon said, as he led the way to the back of the store.

One of the clerks tapped him on the shoulder and pointed. "Look."

Two guys, sales associates of the store, each pushed carts over-filled with merchandise. He shook his head. There was nothing he could do to stop them, or the hundreds of thousands of dollars in merchandise walking out the door. He felt like the little Dutch boy with his finger in the dike. And like that situation, there were just too many holes and not even close to enough fingers to hold back the coming flood.

Brandon and his group reached the back of the store. "Inside the break room, now!" he yelled. Taking a last look out at crazy land, he saw that instead of people fleeing the store, scores were flooding in. As he shut and locked the door he prayed his decision to ride it out was the right one.

CHAPTER FIVE

Union Station Shopping Mall, Washington, D. C.

Jodie Chin and her cameraman stood under the domed ceiling of the Union Square Mall—one of the most popular shopping and dining destinations in Washington D.C. She drew the afternoon assignment to capture the crazed shopping event as it began to wind down. Although, from the hordes of shoppers, some moving like zombies, others on anxiety and caffeine overload, it didn't look like the frenzy had slackened.

"Excuse me," Jodie said to a woman with two small children in tow and her arms loaded with bags. "I'm Jodie Chin with Channel Eight. Can you tell me, was the day successful?"

Before the woman could answer, the noise from shattering glass and yelling voices echoed through the once grand train station lobby. Heads swiveled trying to locate the source. Her journalistic instincts suddenly on high alert, Jodie spoke loudly. "Be ready!" she said to her cameraman as people began moving. No more zombie shuffle or energy drink strut. "Zoom in on their faces, their eyes." The camera panned the lobby: The hunting and the hunted, thought Jodi.

When Jodie looked back the woman and her children had left. The crowds poured out of stores, off escalators and staircases into the lobby. The noise of a coming riot echoed throughout multi-storied rotunda.

Her cameraman touched her shoulder and yelled, "We need to move, now. Back over there." With his camera on his shoulder, he cocked his head toward a space under a wooden stairwell that went up to a mezzanine.

Jodi and her cameraman stood under the stairwell, their

backs to the wall, and shot footage. Everyone was in either "fight or flight" mode. Some ran by, panicked, looking for an exit. Others had their arms loaded with merchandise. A man stopped in front of them, a crazed look in his eyes, his hands filled with jewelry. Twenty feet away, Jodie watched two groups of young men confront each other. They argued over cartons that contained Xbox and PS4 game consoles. Her gut told her to run, but there was nowhere to run to. Quickly the confrontation escalated. In the next instant, she saw guns—lots of guns. Jodie and the cameraman huddled back farther under the stairwell. When the shooting stopped, bodies littered the floor, pools of dark red blood forming Rorschach inkblots on the white marble.

Prairie Island Nuclear Power Plant, Red Wing, Minnesota

JUDD SWAN SAT BEFORE THE twenty-foot long control console inside the Prairie Island Nuclear power plant. He'd been here since 6:00 A. M. and he was glad about it. This morning, his wife and two teenage daughters had left the house before 4:00 A. M. They had a big day of shopping planned in Minneapolis. He hated shopping. Besides, he got double time working today.

For the most part, his job was to watch the screens, gauges and dials that monitored the operation of the plant. He often imagined this room to be like NASA's Mission Control. It certainly had the sophistication. The advanced digital technology that the IT guys regularly upgraded meant he just had to sit on his ass and watch. The automated systems took care of everything. Sometimes, he thought the only reason to have a human being here was to hit the manual shutdown, which in his five years had never happened.

Looking up at the row of clocks on the wall that showed the time in the different time zones this plant provided power to, he saw it was almost 1:00 P. M.

He rolled his chair away from the console to a section of the desktop and opened his lunch box. As he ate his turkey sandwich he noticed the monitor that showed a series of side-by-side fluctuating bars. The automated systems received a digital signal as power demands from one area to another fluctuated and made the necessary adjustments. According to the bars the system wasn't doing this.

Across the room, his colleague talked on the phone. Hanging up he said, "Something's happened to the Internet."

Not quite comprehending, Judd stood and walked around the monitoring console to stand before the wall of gauges, dials, and digital readouts that showed the status of the cooling system for the nuclear reactor's core. Everything appeared good there. Ironically, the loss of an Internet signal improved the plant's operational security. However, it meant that the digital signals required to make the adjustments in the power grid distribution, as demand shifted from region to region, weren't getting through.

From the readings, in a few moments there was going be a power outage in parts of northern Minnesota in the U. S., and southern Saskatchewan and Manitoba in Canada.

CHAPTER SIX

Mexico City

PETER REVANT SAT INSIDE A suite at the Gran Hotel in downtown Mexico City. He neared the end of his allotted fifteen-minute audience with don Eduardo Gutiérrez and his wife, la señora Isabel Santiago Valdez de Gutiérrez.

Casually he looked at his watch. As if scripted, someone knocked loudly on the door, then one of the guards who had searched him when he arrived came into the room, apologizing profusely for the interruption. As the guard stood at the entrance to the sitting room, Isabel rose and approached him.

Peter watched his hostess. In black jeans and a white blouse, from raven hair to full red lips, every curve and swell screamed temptation. She embodied all he loathed about western infidel women—overtly sexual, brash and aggressive. No wonder those perching strict adherence to the Quran and Sharia Law demanded that women, when in the presence of anyone but their father or husband, be covered. But he kept his thoughts to himself, smiled, and admired the view.

The guard whispered in her ear and then, walking backward a few steps, turned and left the suite. Isabel came and spoke a few hushed words to her husband.

In his late fifties, with stylish, casually long salt-and-pepper hair and a thick mustache, don Eduardo looked tan and fit. To Peter, definitely a man who enjoyed the fruits of his labors and realized that to truly enjoy the splendors of his much younger wife he had to put forth some effort. Eduardo reached out and picked up a remote from the coffee table.

Don Eduardo pointed it at the flat-screen TV mounted on the wall. They watched as an American newscaster, a woman, *go figure*, reported that the Internet in the United States and parts of Canada and Mexico had crashed, and that cell phone networks still working couldn't support the volume of traffic. The newscast bounced from location to location. People appeared frantic and angry. From a mall in Los Angeles, a picture of man with a bloodied face filled the screen. The badge on his shirt read BRANDON, MANAGER, and he stood just inside a big-box electronic store. The female reporter said she had just watched him be assaulted by a customer. The camera panned on a big man as he walked out of the store with a very large box in his hands. The footage shifted to an aerial view that showed freeways gridlocked.

Rising, Peter thought to himself, *If this is what happened in just minutes, give it a few more hours and then see how civilized people behave.* Looking at his hosts staring at the TV, then to their smart phones, then back to the TV, Peter imagined what must be running through their minds: *How much money is this going to cost the Gutiérrez Cartel? Plenty,* he hoped. It would make his proposal all the more attractive.

Without the slightest indication that what played out on the screen bothered him in the least—a sign he hoped would not go unnoticed—Peter said, "Thank you, don Eduardo and señora Gutiérrez, for your gracious hospitality. I will give you some time to consider my proposition." Reaching into his inside jacket pocket, he took out a plain white business card with nothing but an address on it. "I can be reached here day or night. I will be staying on in your beautiful city for another week. I hope we can do business." With a slight bow, he finished. "I will show myself out. Thank you both again."

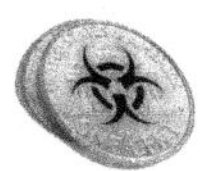

CHAPTER SEVEN

National Microbiology Laboratory, Winnipeg, Manitoba

DRESSED IN A STERILE, WHITE biohazard suit with a hood that stretched tight over his straight black hair, Dameer Maro sat on a rolling stool inside the Level 4 biological safety containment laboratory. Through goggles he peered at the fifteen white rats caged in groups of five, inside a self-contained isolation chamber.

Adjusting his goggles, Dameer rolled his chair closer. One cage held five rats, shaved along their backs and halfway down both sides. Transdermal patches on their skin, similar to those worn by smokers, administered the selected infectious agent. In another cage, the rats received the agent via a series of daily injections over a five-day period. In the last, the rats inhaled the agent from an aerosol spray.

Through a set of flexible articulated arm slots, he flexed his fingers to get a good fit in the stiff, bite-proof gloves. He prodded the cage holding the rats wearing transdermal patches. They responded lethargically to the jolt. He clearly saw that the rats wearing patches were the sickest.

"You boys got hold of a nasty little bugger," he said softly in his Indian accent as he nudged the cage again.

"How do the test groups look?" a female voice asked over the speaker from outside the primary containment chamber.

Dameer pulled his arms out and swiveled in his chair. On the other side of the glass-walled entrance to the BSL-4 containment lab stood his colleague, Adriana Leher.

Smiling, Dameer said, "Even though the rats we have been injecting are sick—some quite sick—it seems, from observation, that the timed delivery method using the silicate crystalline microneedles attached to the transdermal patch, is more effective and certainly much simpler to administer. But the bloodwork will tell."

"Well, we knew that before we started the test," Adriana said, throwing a mock punch at the glass as if giving Dameer a playful poke on the shoulder. "So you think the pathogen's protective silica coating is effectively broken down by the oils and amino acids in the skin?"

Pretending to contemplate Adriana's question, Dameer rubbed his hand over his chin, which sported a thin but passable goatee. "From as sick as the rats are, I would say yes."

Just then the lights went out and a loud beeping from the lab's computer harddrive drew Adriana's attention. She looked at the screen, hit a few keys and saw with relief that the computer had switched to battery power and all the data had automatically backed up to the lab's onsite server. A few seconds passed until the backup generator kicked on.

"What is the problem?" asked Dameer as he left the containment chamber.

"Not sure."

A yellow light above the exit door flashed meaning the facility's systems had suffered a breach or failure. Adriana and Dameer quickly followed protocol and secured the containment lab, shut down the computer system, and exited the building.

* * *

AT THE RESTAURANT, BETWEEN BITES of pad thai, Dameer said, "Do you know what this means? We have proven that it is possible to suspend a bacterium or virus for months or possibly years, then reactivate it simply by putting it in contact with living flesh. And now, when we are on the cusp of the biggest epidemiological breakthrough in decades, how could the Internet just be turned off? How will we let the world know?"

Adriana smiled at her companion. Dameer always acted like this. One minute, surfing the wave of intellectual discovery and the next, thrashing about under the crushing weight of that same wave. All agitated over things he had no control over. Like ambiguous results, unreasonable deadlines, or… the Internet crash.

* * *

DAMEER BROUGHT HIS FORK TO his mouth and smiled at Adriana. With her carefree air of confidence, radiating from an emerald gaze upon a lightly freckled face—she was perfection. For the past nine months they had been lovers, and Dameer had never been happier.

They had worked together the past three years. Both held PhD's from the University of Wisconsin, Madison—he by way of New Delhi, Adriana from South Africa.

Dameer had never worked with a more gifted microbiologist. Just 28, Adriana had an inner drive to understand the contagions and infectious diseases that plagued the impoverished parts of the world, especially Africa, that he found inspiring.

"You shouldn't worry so much. The power outage only lasted a few hours. I'm sure the Internet thing will get worked out soon enough. You should be thankful we aren't working in Atlanta at the Center for Disease Control (CDC). From what I hear, the city's a mess, locked down."

"Of course, you're right." And like that, Dameer was back on the crest of the wave. "With your lab skills and my talent for using technology to address the critical problems of economical manufacturing, packaging, and storage, we're going to be famous. I know other biologists have already proven the science of suspending a contagion inside a silicate coating, but we have discovered a way around the one thing that most often prevents the inoculation of large, widespread populations—refrigeration. Our patch design is cost-effective, and will allow vaccines to quickly be delivered to needed parts of the world."

Dameer put his hand on hers. "And by varying the lengths and diameters of the crystalline microneedles we should be able to adapt the process to any number of medicines. It's brilliant!"

* * *

After dinner, Adriana made excuses about needing some time alone to digest the enormity of their discovery. Dameer was clearly expecting some victory sex, but Adriana knew his dreams of a Nobel nomination would lessen the slight. She had her eyes on a different sort of prize.

Slogging through a cold drizzle to her two-story row house five blocks away, she imagined what this discovery would mean. With a simple alcohol swab of the skin and the application of a Band-Aid-sized patch, lifesaving immunity could be delivered or, she reflected as she walked up the steps to the front porch, life-ending sickness.

Inside, Adriana took off her damp coat and hung it on a wall hook below a mirror. Staring at her reflection she felt a glow of satisfaction. The picture of an introverted, slightly plain lab geek pushing thirty had worked out better than she ever imagined. Necessity dictated she become Dameer's lover. To achieve *her* goal, she needed him to trust her, to need her in ways that went beyond a professional relationship. And that he did.

Kicking off her low-top boots she padded over the wood floors. In the kitchen she put the box of leftover Thai food in the refrigerator. Turning, she crossed the tile floor. She entered a series of numbers into a panel mounted on the wall and heard the click as the electronic lock on the basement door deactivated. Opening the door, the lights came on.

Downstairs, she moved through her small lab. Although nowhere near a safety-level 4, it had everything she needed. She gazed through the glass of the refrigerator door at racks of neatly labeled sealed vials. The vials contained live samples of some of the bacteria and viruses she and Dameer worked with in the National Microbiology Laboratory. She had samples of plague, cholera, tuberculosis, and leprosy, as well as the polio and smallpox viruses. Biologists called these ROTM's—run-of-the-mills—bacteria and viruses you could find scattered throughout nature, and many, in miniscule amounts, living in the human body.

She opened the door, removed one of the racks and put it on

the stainless steel counter next to a Light Microscope. Taking a key from her pocket, she unlocked the cabinet over the counter, and took one of two shoebox-sized packages off the shelf and set it next to the rack of vials.

It was wrapped and addressed with official NML markings, identifying it as a priority emergency medical package. She would put it, along with two similar boxes stored in the refrigerator, in the mail in a few days. Even though the attack on the Internet had commercial air traffic at major airports shut down, emergency flights to deliver critical medical supplies and specialized personnel, especially from labs like the NML, would receive the highest priority.

This box and the one still in the cabinet each contained five hundred patches similar to the ones she and Dameer had been working with. Using a manual press like the first scientists working on transdermal patch technology did, Adriana made microscopic depressions in the patches. Then one by one she applied the silicate-suspended concoctions to the thousand patches and packaged them so that to even the trained eye, they appeared like the real deal. Between her day job and Dameer, it had taken her six months and many very late nights.

As she sat on the high stool working, her eyes strayed to two pictures taped to the wall above the counter—the only personal photos in the entire house. One showed her standing on a porch in front of her family home in the Limpopo Province, in South Africa. Her father, Hans, mother, Eva, and her big brother, Ernest, stood on either side of her. She was only 9-years-old. She brought two fingers to her lips then reached out and touched the old photo.

The other picture showed her as an 18-year-old. A bit scruffy, she thought, in her khaki shorts and shirt. With her hair bobbed and white teeth beaming from a weatherworn face, she stood next to a 24 -year-old Peter Revant against the backdrop of a Tanzanian bush camp. Dressed in the khaki of a big game hunter, he had his arm around her. She grabbed the photo from the wall and studied it. The thought of him brought on a rush of heat. It had been four weeks since they were last together, and only for one night. Today, he had broken their 'written in stone' rule about phone contact and left her a voice mail message, the first one ever.

Admonishing herself to stay focused, she pulled on a pair of rubber gloves and donned a facemask. Then from a drawer she removed a glass microscope slide. She prepared the slide with a small sample from the vial and placed it under the microscope. People assumed you needed a specialized facility to culture such things as bubonic plague, cholera, *E. coli,* anthrax, smallpox, or any of the various flu viruses. Hah, she thought! Any competent microbiologist could do it in an apartment kitchen.

Organizations such as hers and the CDC didn't focus so much on *producing* bacteria or viruses, but on containing and controlling them. If neither of those issues bothered you, laying your hands on any number of deadly contagious agents just wasn't that hard. And now that she and Dameer had solved the refrigeration issue . . . She smiled as she turned the knob and brought the microscope into focus.

CHAPTER EIGHT

November 30, Mexico City

Peter Revant walked through the yard of the modern glass and steel villa, in the exclusive gated-neighborhood of Bosques de las Lomas, only minutes from the city center. At five grand a day it came fully staffed and supplied. Standing at the yard's edge, he found it a bit disconcerting that in a city known for earthquakes, an entire backyard, lawn, and infinity pool would be built on a massive trestle-supported platform hanging fifty feet high off the hillside.

He stared toward downtown at the sound of sirens and plumes of thick black smoke rising into the already smog-filled air. What was it with rioting people and fire? He wondered. It seemed to be a universal trait. It heartened him to see that the effects of the Internet crash had expanded beyond the United States.

Peter returned to the covered patio. He glanced at the television that hung above the outdoor gas fireplace and resisted the urge to turn it on. It had been less than twenty-four hours, and all speculation surrounded the financial costs and attempting to determine which group of "evil doers" to blame. Peter knew the finger pointing had just begun.

A maid quietly took his teacup and saucer and disappeared into the house. Servants in Mexico knew their place. He reached into his shirt pocket and removed a small object. It amazed him that this small black dot the size of a nickel and as thin as a paper made it possible to bring down the Internet. With no worry about intrusions Peter sat back, closed his eyes, and reflected on the results of his handiwork.

He had traveled nearly nonstop the last six weeks. First he

secured office space for his information technology company, Visionary, in the three most prominent U. S. interconnectivity hubs—60 Hudson Street, New York City, The Westin Building, Seattle, and One Wilshire, Los Angeles. Then he squeezed in a one-night rendezvous in Winnipeg with Adriana Leher before flying on to Bangalore, India, the home of Visionary headquarters.

* * *

Three weeks earlier, Visionary Headquarters Bangalore, India

Peter stared at the collection of steel, titanium, and glass components spread over several tables in Visionary's lab, three stories underground. He watched as two-men teams of engineers with cordless screwdrivers assembled the components. In ten minutes each table held a pair of torpedo shaped devices that with odd protuberances of bright metal—some round, some flat, others twisted or bent and curved at seemingly random angles—looked like some teleportation experiment gone awry.

"Strange looking, yes. But I assure you they are quite proper functioning electromagnetic pulse generators," said Visionary CEO and lead engineer Agni Kannan.

Turning to the demure Indian, Peter thought that Agni, with his slight build, leather sandaled feet, and unassuming, respectful manner, was the perfect face of Visionary. Peter said, "You and your staff have exceeded my expectations. These components will be displayed prominently for all to see in niches and pedestals throughout the public spaces in our U. S. offices. A collaboration of engineering and art, they will be the centerpieces of the 'Form to Function' marketing campaign announcing our presence in America."

Peter ran his hand over the shiny, bizarre-looking generator. "I take it you have solved the directional antenna issue?"

Smiling, white teeth against dark skin, Agni held out his hand and showed Peter the small black dot in his palm. "It has a self-stick backing. We designed them in black to mimic the color of electrical tape—also in white, red, yellow, green, and blue, to coordinate with the colors of the most common electrical wiring."

Peter took the dot.

"Considering that only a few months ago the smallest directional antenna was about the size of a TV satellite dish, I would say this is a vast improvement," Agni said.

Peter nodded. "You and your three teams of engineers will need to leave for the U. S. tomorrow."

"Yes, sir. All is ready. As we comply with the requirement of the tenant improvements to supervise the installation of the sophisticated fiber optic wiring bundles that connect our office computer networks to the data storage servers located on entirely different floors, it will be no problem for us to discreetly place these dots around the necessary wires. As soon as we sign off on the wiring, all will be hidden behind wallboard and paint. No one the wiser."

Agni instructed the engineers to begin disassembling the generators and pack the components in already-prepared egg-crate foam. "Each location has an office where, at the prearranged time, the generators will be assembled and parallel-connected."

Peter gave Agni a questioning look.

"To produce a pulse with enough power to cause a significant disruption we will need two generators running in tandem. It will take only a few moments to laser-sight the transmission ports on the generators to the locations inside the walls. Another thirty seconds to build up the charge and only a fraction of a second to discharge the electromagnetic pulse. Then the generators will be disassembled and the components returned to their respective display positions. Our data storage servers will be among the many that are compromised, which will deflect suspicion."

As the two men walked out of the lab, Peter said, "As we have discussed, in respect for American tradition we will give all but critical staff that Thursday and Friday off. Thursday, after you have confirmed that the generators are set up, you will fly out of New York to Bangalore. It is important that you are back at headquarters. In a matter of days, the richest and most powerful people in the world, who, thanks to Allah, are Muslim, will be rushing to have Visionary as their information storage and technology provider."

"What about the three teams of engineers? Certainly they cannot remain in America," said Agni.

"Quite right. By Saturday the six will be on their way home. I have arranged for each team to board a private fishing charter out of its respective city. They will rendezvous in international waters, with merchant freighters en route to ports where they can then board flights to Bangalore.

A muffled sound, like a distant explosion, shook Peter from his reverie. He set the dot on the table. Probably car gas tanks exploding he thought with a tinge of sadistic satisfaction, as he closed his eyes again.

* * *

Two weeks earlier, Amman, Jordon

As Peter readied to leave India for Mexico, an unexpected summons arrived from Sheikh Nazir al-Mohmoud to immediately come to him in Amman, Jordon.

As a young teen, while living with his family in London, Peter attended the same prep school as the sheikh's son, Adad al-Mohmoud. Quickly they formed a bond and became best friends. When Peter's parents died in a car accident, Sheikh Nazir took him in and became like a father. Peter owed this man everything.

From that time on, Adad, one year older, became his brother and mentor. They grew into manhood together. Adad taught him about the perseverance and the commitment required from the faithful to ensure that Islam take its place as the world's one true faith. After college Peter went to work for the al-Mohmoud family. It was because of Adad that Peter owned Visionary. They had been partners in the venture, but at their last meeting, nearly a year and half ago, Adad signed over his majority holding in the company to Peter. Adad insisted that Peter view his sole ownership as a vehicle by which *he* might further the reach of Islam. It was the last time Peter had seen or spoken to Adad.

Peter flew from Mexico City to Amman, Jordan. Between the Assad regime and ISIS, the sheikh's ancestral home of Damascus had become a dangerous, lawless land and like millions of others, the sheikh and his household had been forced to flee. As he drove into the foothills of the Kursi Mountains, through the gate of the exclusive community of multi-million-dollar homes, Peter prayed that the sheikh had news of Adad.

A bodyguard met Peter in the driveway and led him into the house. Sheikh Nazir, dressed in a simple white robe and a matching *kaffiyeh* held in place with a double circlet of dyed-black camel hair, stood with arms outstretched. Peter approached the sheikh, bowed his head, and said without looking up, *"Al salamu alaikum,"* using the formal greeting "Peace be upon you."

The sheikh reached out and gently lifted Peter's chin. In heavily accented English, he said, *"Kadir,"* using the name that meant "Friend and confidant," which Adad had given to Peter when they were boys, "My son, you and I shall not stand on formality." Stepping forward, the sheikh pulled Peter into an uncharacteristically emotional embrace and whispered in his ear the informal greeting between friends and family. *"Marhaban."*

With his arms wrapped around the man who, from their first meeting, was bigger than life it struck Peter how frail and old he seemed. To Peter, the sheikh had always been the alpha wolf, his gray hair and beard vibrant and healthy, his brown eyes alert, constantly on the watch. There was never a doubt about the control he held over *his* pack. His command was absolute, his rebuke beyond question.

"Come sit with me. There is much for us to discuss," The sheikh said releasing Peter from his embrace and motioning to doors open to a patio where a table sat arranged with platters of food.

Peter followed the sheikh who, with his shoulders hunched, his steps short and shuffling, looked now, like the old wolf, gaunt and life-worn, soon to be turned out from the pack. They both sat. Peter took a fava bean dipped it in a small clay saucer of cumin, then salt, and put it in his mouth.

"Kadir, you have news of Adad?"

"No *alab*," Peter replied using the Arabic word for father. "I had hoped you did."

The sheikh looked away, into the distance. "I have prayed that I was wrong. That possibly my fears that Adad is dead were somehow mistaken."

Peter watched the sheikh's face. Whatever small vestige of hope that still lived inside of one of the richest and most powerful people in the world flickered out before his eyes.

The sheikh fixed his dull gaze on Peter. In Arabic, his voice weak and hesitant, he said, "I must tell you a story."

The sheikh told him about meeting Marcus Diablo at the Syrian oasis of Palmyra. Peter couldn't hide his shock at the mention of Diablo. The husband of the woman, he had executed for the cause— for Adad—Annie Diablo. How could that be? And why hadn't he heard of it before?

The sheikh said Marcus came to him as a simple man of the desert. He looked, dressed and spoke as a Bedouin. He relayed how Marcus told him that he had taken control of nearly 800 billion dollars of al-Mohmoud family assets and that if the sheikh agreed to leave Marcus and his family alone he would return half it. Diablo also told the sheikh that Adad was dead. That Adad's life and the other 400 billion were the price paid for the death of his wife. Peter looked at the sheikh's trembling hands and silently hoped age and despair were causing his surrogate father to misremember.

As the sheikh finished his story a young boy came running out of the house, stopped at the table and looked at the sheikh, then at Peter. "Jabril, you will greet our guest properly," the sheikh said, switching to English.

With his jet-black hair, swept back, and big, golden-brown eyes, the boy's resemblance to Adad was unmistakable.

His palms pressed together, Jabril stood with feet together and bowed. In a voice innocent and small, with a hint of British accent, he said, "*Sa'eeda Kadir.*"

From the other side of the courtyard, Peter heard a woman's voice calling Jabril. His grandfather patted him on the head and the boy skipped back into the house.

Peter sat, stunned, again. He had known nothing of the boy—Jabril al-Mohmoud—Adad's son. Why had Adad kept it from him? For what reason would he hide such a thing?

Over the next few days Peter got to know Jabril. The boy talked incessantly about an upcoming trip to America. Something Peter, at first, dismissed as a young boy's fantasy. However, he learned, the sheikh did plan to send his grandson, along with the boy's mother and two bodyguards to the United States. Peter found it unbelievable that a man who would never himself consider setting foot in America, would allow his grandson to visit a nation caught up in a wave of anti-Muslim xenophobia. A nation, which if the sheikh was right, spawned the man who had taken from him his only son. And just to see a mouse named Mickey?

As Peter pulled out of the driveway, the sheikh stood, his hand resting on Jabril's shoulder. Both waved. Peter waved back and thought this man was not the hard lined Islamist who had always insisted he and Adad live a life committed to fundamental Quranic principles. The loss of Adad had caused the sheikh to become nothing more than a very, very rich grandfather content to spend all his time and energy doting on his seven-year old grandson.

On his way to the airport Peter considered how he might get the sheikh back in the game. His plan to continue the fight to make Islam the world's one and only faith needed the sheikh's support, as well as his considerable influence and money. To make that happen something very drastic would have to take place in the sheikh's personal life.

In that moment Adad's admonitions from their last meeting resonated in his head: *"You must plan on many fronts simultaneously. This will mean that you cannot rest and that you must seek unlikely allies. When in need, seek out those who are committed to their cause in the same way we are to ours. That these causes often have no relation is of no consequence. All that matters is that they provide a means to **our** end. In our struggle, all else is secondary—even family and friendship. A time may come when one or both will become your most valued and important weapon."*

Peter adjusted his sunglasses and wondered if those words

from Adad were not specifically intended for this very moment. Peter smiled. He knew just the people to help him.

CHAPTER NINE

"Señor Revant?"

Peter opened his eyes and looked up to the doors that opened to the marble-floored living room. "*Sí, Mauricio. ¿Qué tal?*"

"You have visitors," Maurcio said in accented English. "Don Eduardo Gutiérrez and la señora Isabel Santiago Valdez de Gutiérrez."

Rising from the table, Peter picked up the dot and put it back in his pocket. "Please show them in and bring fresh coffee."

Don Eduardo and señora Gutiérrez, flanked by two bodyguards, walked down the steps from the foyer to the main living room.

"Don Eduardo, señora, how nice to see you again," Peter said in Spanish.

With a hard stare, Isabel said, "We must speak, Mr. Revant. In English!"

Peter looked at the woman whom he had found so disconcerting at their meeting the day before. Today she wore white jeans with a black blouse and stilettos. He liked this combination better. Extending his hand to don Eduardo, Peter said, "I am honored to have you in my home." With a slight bow and a sweep of his arm, Peter gestured to the open patio doors. "Shall we? The day is so pleasant."

They followed him. At the door, Isabel nodded at the two bodyguards who took up stations on either side.

Peter stood as don Eduardo pulled out a chair for Isabel then sat next to her. Under a linen sport coat, he wore a starched blue shirt open at the collar so that the thick gold chain holding a simple but elegant cross was clearly visible. *Chalk one up for the Christians,* Peter mused as he took his seat.

"So, my young friend," don Eduardo said. "You have gone to great lengths to put this meeting together. Yesterday everything was so vague. A business proposal, worth millions, you said. But you offered no details."

Reaching into a purse that cost more than the salaries of the entire staff, Isabel took out the unmarked white envelope Peter had left with them at their hotel and set it on the table.

Don Eduardo picked up the envelope and waved it. "I think, Peter, that someone has mistakenly added an extra zero." His tone was dismissive, as if certain an error had been made.

"Don Eduardo, I assure you no one has made a mistake."

"Why would anyone offer this kind of money?" Isabel demanded. "You must think us fools. You throw out a number that is patently ridiculous and just expect us to enter into business with you?" Her voice held a hard but controlled edge. "Mr. Revant, we will not do anything without full disclosure as to the particulars. Your explanation that you needed our expertise with a few matters is far from sufficient."

She spoke as if she were the CEO of a major multinational company—which she might very well be, thought Peter, trying to look confident. He had put a lot into this arrangement. It was an integral piece and he had no plan B.

"I would expect nothing less. I am prepared to make a nonrefundable deposit of ten percent of the sum written on the paper inside the envelope, just for you to explore my proposal. I am certain that when you hear the details you will agree, the service I would like to hire you to provide is more than covered by the deposit alone. Exploitation is your business—drugs, snuggling, human trafficking . . ." Eduardo started to interrupt, but Peter held up his hand. "I know that you also have many *legitimate* business interests, but none of them are as profitable as . . . these ventures. This could be a nice, shall we say, bonus to add to your coffers."

"Yesterday, when the news of the Internet crash in the United States came on television, you were not surprised." Isabel stated.

"Much of our business is conducted via the Internet and our biggest source of income is in America. I don't know how you are involved but, Mr. Revant, we are not people you would want as enemies."

He had her worried and worried people made bad decisions. "Believe me, señora Gutiérrez, having you as an enemy is the last thing on my mind. We have a common goal." This got him an inquisitive look from Eduardo. "Profit . . . and keeping prying eyes out of our business." Peter paused. "And who is it that believes they have the right, and sacred obligation, to be the world's watchdog?"

Eduardo's eyebrows rose.

"Without question, it is the ***United States***," Peter said, perhaps a bit more emphatically than he intended.

Uncrossing his legs and setting his coffee cup on the table, Eduardo appraised his host. Then he shifted his attention to his wife. "Isabel, is not Peter a citizen of the United States?" He posed the question as if Peter were perhaps a young schoolboy about to be reprimanded by the teacher.

Isabel got up and stood behind her husband's chair. "Yes, he is an American citizen. Born in Oak Ridge, Tennessee, in 1976, to Syrian parents—now deceased—who were granted political asylum and citizenship." Her clasped hands rested on Eduardo's chair back. "He spent many years being educated in England and graduated from the London School of Economics. He is a Muslim. He speaks several languages fluently." A disdainful smile crossed her lips. "Including Spanish. He travels extensively, especially throughout Central and South America and the United States, as well as occasional visits to South Asia and the Middle East. In fact, he most recently arrived in Mexico from Amman, Jordan."

Isabel put a hand on her husband's shoulder. "He worked for many years for Global Equities, a privately held company controlled by Sheikh Nazir al-Mohmoud of Syria. Rumor has it the sheikh fled the civil war in Damascus and, at the invitation of King Abdullah II, has taken refuge in Amman."

How could she possibly know all this? Peter wondered and hoped his face didn't betray his shock.

Isabel continued. "It is the sheikh's son, Adad al-Mohmoud,

who is suspected of being the mastermind behind the attack on the U. S. almost a year and a half ago."

Peter could tell Isabel liked being in charge.

"It appears, however, that Peter is no longer with Global Equities. Now he is the sole owner of Visionary, an information technology and data storage firm headquartered in Bangalore, India that caters to those of the Islamic faith. Visionary recently opened three offices in the United States: in New York City, Los Angeles, and Seattle. It seems though, they have suffered from the Internet attack." Her accusatory tone lessened a bit.

Eduardo held up a hand and she paused. "You see, Peter, I am a careful man. It is an absolute necessity in the world I live in, as, I am sure, it is in yours. Please do not assume that because we come from a country that the world sees as lawless and corrupt, we are ignorant or without *resources*. You have done business in my country for many years. You are certainly aware that the Chinese, Koreans, Russians, as well as the big players from the Middle East, the Saudis, Iranians, and... the *Jordanians* are all here. Eager and ready to dump billions of dollars into an economy they see as underperforming, starving for hard currency, rich in resources and cheap labor, and ripe for exploitation."

Isabel took over in what Peter recognized as a well-practiced dance. "We have decided to explore your business proposal. However, before discussing the details, we will need a nonrefundable... fifty... percent deposit."

Peter flinched. He'd offered ten. Fifty was outrageous.

Seeing his host's surprise, Eduardo said, "What is it the Americans say? Take it or leave it. To me it does not matter. However, if you leave it, remaining in Mexico would be...unwise."

Peter reminded himself he was facing the reigning champions, playing before a loyal home crowd. He, the decided underdog, would have to leave *everything* on the field.

"No, don Eduardo, I accept your terms."

"Very well. Shall we say, by the end of the day?"

"If it's all the same to you, can we take care of this matter now? Then we can get down to business."

Eduardo now had the surprised look.

Peter stood. "Give me just a moment."

Peter went inside and returned with a satellite phone.

"Do you have the wiring instructions?"

Isabel handed him a piece of paper.

Sitting, Peter laid the paper out in front of him. He dialed a number and waited, then gave instructions in a language neither Isabel nor Eduardo understood.

After a few awkward moments, Peter slid his phone across the table. "Would you care to check with your bank?"

Still standing, Isabel reached into her purse again and removed a phone much like Peter's. "Do not think you are the only person who is prepared." She dialed and put the phone to her ear. Less than a half-minute later she ended the call without ever having said a word. "My compliments. That is a record. Now, as you say, we can get down to business."

Peter grabbed his briefcase from the floor, removed a file, and slid it across the table. Isabel stepped around her husband, picked it up, and sat.

Eduardo looked at Isabel. "Peter, would you give us a few moments?"

"Oh course." Peter rose and went inside.

* * *

PETER RETOOK HIS SEAT AT the table.

"We have decided to explore your business proposal." Isabel had the file open in her hands.

Eduardo leaned forward in his chair. "The time has come to speak plainly and get to the specifics, or I'm afraid this meeting is at an end." His tone made it clear he believed he was in charge. And with Peter's fifty million wired to some offshore account, he was.

"My proposal is simple," said Peter. "I need someone kidnapped."

"You offend me, Peter. Do I look like a kidnapper to you? Or even someone who might consider such a . . . *barbaric* enterprise?"

"I would not presume to think that you dabble in such disreputable activity, but you did ask me to speak plainly. We both know that the Gutiérrez Cartel has a wide reach spread out among a diverse number of enterprises, legitimate and otherwise. Your success has been built on providing certain goods and services that are…quite specialized and not readily available."

While they continued to peruse the contents of the file, Peter said, "As you see, the job should not be too difficult. The subject will be in that location for three days, and it would be hard to find a place better suited for creating a distraction. He will be with his mother. They will have only two bodyguards and, although well trained, they will be completely out of their element."

Isabel looked up from the file. "This seems too simple . . . too easy. What's the catch? And how do you imagine they will get from Amman to LA with the airports closed?"

"First, no catch. I need this to appear as extortion, plain and simple. For that perception, I am willing to pay what we all know is a ridiculous sum. Once you have the subject, get him to Mexico. He is not to be harmed," Peter said in a soft but commanding tone. "Second, I imagine the airports will open to limited commercial traffic within a week or so. And if not, the very rich with private jets can always find a place to land."

"Don't you have all the answers? So what happens if this place of distraction is closed? You know how paranoid Americans are."

"Señora, after the terrible inconvenience the American people have been put through, the one thing we can bet on is the government making sure places of distraction are open for business," Peter said sarcastically.

"Okay, so if all goes according to your plan, what are we to do with this *subject*?"

"I will need you to hold him and keep him healthy for perhaps several weeks. I do not know how long it will take me to extract what I need from his guardian. Again, señora, for the fee I am paying, it is not much to ask. Additionally, once I arrive to retrieve him, I will need a safe house with helicopter access for one week at most. I will leave the choice of that location in your capable hands. I suggest that we use simple, prepaid phones to communicate. I know that for the time being, cell phone service"—he held up his sat phone—"is a mess, especially in the United States, but also in parts of Mexico, but that will quickly be resolved. In the file you will find a schedule of dates, including communication windows."

"Is that all?" Isabel asked.

"There is one additional service I would like to discuss."

Isabel glared at him.

Peter needed to proceed carefully. This was the most important part of the plan but it needed to appear secondary.

"Before I explain, I will pay half again what I am paying for the kidnapping for this additional arrangement." Peter was banking on the one fault shared by nearly all people, whatever their race or religion: greed. In his mind, he thanked Allah that he answered to a much higher calling.

Eduardo looked uncomfortable. Obscene sums of money often had that effect on people, Peter reminded himself.

"I would like you to arrange for five hundred of *your* people to move across the border into the United States. I have some specific requirements, the first being that I want all five hundred inoculated with the flu vaccine."

Isabel mouthed, "*¿Qué?*"

"Besides the fact that the coyotes who operate most of these smuggling operations are unscrupulous, greedy pigs, the reason many groups of 'passengers' are abandoned is because they get sick. I will supply the vaccine and everything else for the inoculation. I want people who are looking for opportunity and who have the ability to blend in and stay a while. This service, like the first, must be done within the same three-day window."

Isabel started to say something, no doubt to balk about the time frame, but Peter charged ahead. "I know it is a short window, but your network is vast, and for me to make the point of how vulnerable America's borders truly are, despite the political posturing, as many of the five hundred as possible must be in the United States in three days. Greasing palms is your specialty, so make it happen."

Isabel closed the file and clasped her hands on top of the table. "I don't know what your game is, Mr. Revant, but crossing the Gutiérrez cartel would be much worse than merely a fatal mistake."

"I take it then we have moved beyond exploring my proposition?"

She looked at her husband.

Eduardo spoke. "I believe we can help each other, Peter."

"Less than three weeks remain before your window. When will you have the vaccine?" Isabel asked.

"In four days. The day after, I will go through everything with whomever you assign this task."

They all stood. "It has been a pleasure to do business with you don Eduardo. I will take care of the additional deposit straight away." The two men shook hands. Peter walked them to the front door.

On the front stoop Isabel turned and fixed a hard gaze on Peter. "I will pray to *my* God that you and I never see each other again."

CHAPTER TEN

Beginnings Ranch, British Columbia

His hunger and his obligation to Norma sated, the colonel needed to wrap his head around the implications of the Internet crash. To do that it was always best if he spent some time with J. T. before briefing the rest of the team.

"Okay J. T., what d'we know?"

J. T. talked as he posted information. "The only event that could disrupt the Internet on this scale, without blowing the buildings to bits, is an EMP—an electromagnetic pulse."

"Like what happened back in the 60s, some nuclear test out over the Pacific, near Hawaii?"

More data popped up on the monitors. Another reason J. T. had been the colonel's *first* Force 10 recruit. He maintained and regularly updated, a comprehensive database, downloaded on a secure server, that held information on all manner of armament, explosives, and delivery systems, past and present. Not to mention that he held dozens of patents, nearly all classified, for some of the most advanced communications, tracking and drone technology in existence. Add to that an eidetic memory, and the guy was the colonel's personal, real-life search engine.

"Yeah, code named Starfish Prime, they inadvertently fried all the telephones and radios in Hawaii. It started a race of sorts between the Soviets and us. The notion that you could attack your enemy without killing people or destroying buildings really excited the war mongers."

The colonel gave J. T. a scolding look.

"Sorry. I'm just sayin'." J. T. shrugged.

"But this wasn't caused by a nuclear explosion."

"Right." On the screens J. T. posted several pictures of some torpedo-and rectangular- shaped devices. "This had to be done by some type of electromagnetic pulse generator. These Internet hubs are shielded. Surrounded by what's called a Faraday cage."

"A what?"

"A Faraday cage. It's an enclosure that's impervious to radio waves. In simple terms, that's all an electromagnetic pulse is, a radio wave. Behind the interior walls, this bunker has a skin of aluminum sheeting, making it a Faraday cage."

J. T. walked over to a set of shelves. "A microwave oven is in essence a type of Faraday cage. I keep several analogue cell phones and batteries inside this old one."

"Well, aren't you the doomsday prepper?" said the colonel.

"Maybe a bit, after all, I do hang out with people who seem to be always pissing off some of the craziest people on the planet."

"Okay, you might have a point. So what does all this mean?"

"This attack came from inside the buildings. Maybe you could get me into one of those interconnectivity hubs? Let me dig around for a few hours."

The colonel considered that and how he might make it happen. "I'll see what I can do. Let's gather the team and get them briefed, then Marcus and I need to make a little trip. We will be gone less than twenty-four hours. When we get back we need to have a comprehensive threat assessment in the works. You start digging into this generator theory. We need to find out the who, how, and why."

CHAPTER ELEVEN

November 30, McLean, Virginia

MARCUS AND THE COLONEL LANDED at U.S. Military Joint Base Andrews, east of Washington, D.C. Although commercial air traffic had been shut down, military operations still remained online. That the colonel had clearance to land their private jet at the same airfield that served the president meant Sam still had friends in high places.

The colonel had not shared with Marcus or the team anything about the meeting. Marcus surmised that if he had told him who they were going to meet, he would have opted to stay home.

Two other members of Force 10 accompanied them. Bronson Daughterly was the pilot. The rangy Texan, an ex-Air Force Special Operations Officer, could fly anything from a Cessna 182 to a Boeing 777. The other member with them, Jamie Marsden, served as co-pilot. They would stay with the jet.

The colonel and Marcus walked across the tarmac to a waiting Sikorsky UH-60 Black Hawk helicopter.

Once seated and strapped into the backseat, they donned headsets that muffled the rotor noise and allowed them to speak to each other and the pilot.

"It's an honor to have you aboard, sir."

"The honor is mine, Major. It's a privilege to fly with HMX-One."

"Thank you, sir. Sit tight, and we'll have you gentlemen on the ground in about fifteen minutes."

With that, the Black Hawk rose smoothly and, with nose down, sped away from the lights of the nation's capital.

"HMX-One? Isn't this the squadron responsible for

transporting the president?" asked Marcus.

The colonel merely smiled.

The chopper landed somewhere in Virginia. Horse country, from the look of the place. In the glow of ground lighting, Marcus could make out barns and three-rail fences that surrounded acres of frost-covered pasture. In the cold night, Marcus, the colonel, and a Marine escort walked twenty yards to a single-story brick house that looked as though it belonged in the English countryside. His breath forming clouds, Marcus reminded himself that despite the whole *let's share tea and scones* appeal, he'd arrived in one of the most cold-hearted, self-serving places in the world.

The pair of marines flanking the entry did a quick pat-down of them both. Then one of them led the way down a wide hall to a set of double wood doors.

"The directors are expecting you, Colonel." The lieutenant held the door.

The room they entered occupied the back of the house. In the middle of the outside wall a fireplace blazed. Floor-to-ceiling bookshelves, walls paneled in dark walnut, and wide plank floors, made the place look like the library of a retired political Brahmin. From leather chairs surrounding a table three men rose.

Marcus instantly recognized one as FBI Deputy Director Nathan Reynolds. Reynolds had been the special agent in charge of Annie's case when she went missing. He'd screwed up big time, but in the end redeemed himself some.

The smaller of the two older men stepped forward. Thin and sixty-ish, dressed in charcoal corduroys and a light-gray cardigan, he looked like Mr. Rogers without hair.

"Sam, it's good to see you again." The man extended a hand.

"Edward. I'd like to introduce Marcus Diablo. Marcus, please meet Edward Pinehurst, Director of the FBI."

Marcus got a perfunctory handshake.

"I thought you were coming alone," Pinehurst said.

"I hope it's not a problem, Ed. If it is, Marcus . . ." he paused for only a second ". . . and I will take our leave."

Now the third man walked around the table. Well over six

feet, he easily weighed 250 pounds. His navy suit and white shirt looked slept in. "Roland," the colonel said, grasping the man's meaty hand.

As the big man shook Marcus's hand, the colonel said, "Roland Hanover, director of the CIA."

Roland said to the FBI director, "Edward, I don't see what harm there is. If Colonel Webb wants the man here, then . . ." Without finishing, he returned to the table, where he sat down heavily in one of the padded leather chairs, picked up a glass containing amber liquid and ice cubes, which he brought to his lips.

Marcus shifted his gaze to FBI Deputy Director Reynolds. "Well, well, Nathan, funny how you and I should meet when, once again, everything's running off the rails."

Reynolds stayed in place. "Marcus, Colonel Webb, as always, it's good to see you."

"Likewise," the colonel said.

Marcus eyeballed Reynolds, but said nothing.

"Please, come have a seat," the CIA director motioned from the table. "Can I get you something to drink, Sam? I have a wonderful bottle of single malt." Hanover raised his glass.

The colonel nodded, and a few moments later, the young marine who had escorted them in entered from a side door and handed the colonel his drink. Neither director asked Marcus if he wanted anything; in fact, it seemed they had decided to ignore him altogether—which was fine with him.

"Marcus, how about you—can I get you something?" Deputy Director Reynolds asked, which earned him a dark glance from his boss.

Reaching for one of the glasses on a wood tray along with a pitcher of water, Marcus said, "This'll do fine. Something tells me I'm gonna need a clear head."

The colonel set his glass of scotch on the table. "I have come here as a professional courtesy. Marcus is here at my invitation, and that's the end of it."

"It's good to see you haven't lost your strut, Colonel," Hanover said before draining his glass.

FBI Director Edward Pinehurst gave his CIA counterpart an annoyed glance. "Okay, Sam, have it your way. It's at the recommendation of General Kittredge and the deputy director that we've asked you to come. They seem to think you and your team—what do you call yourselves?" The question was purely for dramatic effect—no way the director of the FBI didn't know about Force 10—so the colonel remained silent. "That you might have a...perspective on this most recent situation. Nathan, will you bring the colonel up to speed?"

Marcus thought how typical of the FBI to refer to the breakdown of basically all Internet activity, as "this most recent situation," as if it were no more consequential than the neighbor's dog shitting on his lawn.

All eyes shifted to FBI Deputy Director Nathan Reynolds. Picking up a remote control from the table, he stood. "With a little help from NSA, we've been combing through flagged communications from before this latest attack."

Marcus said, "It's good to see that the whole Snowden thing hasn't slowed anybody down."

"Be that as it may, Marcus, most of this data mining is nothing more than running everything through a voice recognition program." He fiddled with the remote. "Earlier today, the analysts came up with this." Reynolds pointed the remote at a cabinet against the wall, and a man's voice filled the room.

"My business is almost concluded. Hope your travels go well. I can't wait to see you."

At the first word, something in Marcus snapped. His mind instantly flashed to the memory of the voice of the man who had held Annie—his wife.

Looking directly at Marcus, Deputy Director Reynolds said, "We've checked and rechecked. The voice is an exact match for the man who spoke on the 'proof of life' Internet feed, the one that came almost two months after Annie Diablo was abducted from the mountains north of Yosemite. It's also a match to the second, the last one, that came just before...her murder."

"Who . . . is . . . he?" Marcus asked.

"We don't know, but we believe he may have been part of Adad's inner circle."

"What's that supposed to mean, Nathan?" Marcus stood up from the table, almost toppling his chair. Cold anger made him shiver. Ignoring the looks of the men at the table, he walked to the fireplace and stood in front of the blaze, extending his hands toward the heat. In that moment, Marcus closed out everything around him and stared deep into the flames.

At the periphery of his consciousness, Marcus heard his name being called: "Mr. Diablo . . ." Then louder: "Mr. Diablo!"

Tuning to face the table, Marcus looked at the seated men. The colonel showed no sign of discomfort, but the two directors stared at him as if he had grown an extra head. "Mr. Diablo, are we boring you?" the director of the FBI asked.

Marcus gazed at the smallish man in the cardigan, and all the disdain he had for the Bureau's arrogance and ineptitude, for their failure to save his wife, flooded through him. "Mister Diablo, I'm talking—"

"Let it be, Edward," the colonel said.

Marcus looked at Nathan Reynolds, who said, "We interrogated all the people we apprehended after the attack, and those Force Ten turned over when they took control of Adad's ship, the *Takbir.* We retrieved no information concerning another attack. But I'm just saying it wouldn't be out of the realm of possibility that Adad had another plan.

"For the past month, we've been monitoring a lot of chatter that indicated something was in the works. Everything we deciphered pointed at primary transportation hubs as likely targets." He pointed the remote at a cabinet again. The large flat screen came to life, showing a detailed map of the U.S. eastern seaboard.

Marcus looked at the screen. Symbols of airplanes, trains, buses, and subway cars indicated the transportation centers. Turning back to the table, he said, "And you don't consider bringing down the Internet an attack on a primary transportation hub?"

FBI Director Pinehurst spoke in the tone a teacher might use when his authority was questioned by a fourth-grader. "Everything indicated that an attack was imminent and that the target or targets were those you see in red."

Marcus looked at the TV. Red symbols highlighted five areas: D.C., New York City, Boston, Chicago, and Philadelphia. He stared at the man making excuses for why the FBI hadn't considered the attack on the interconnectivity hubs a possibility.

"Marcus, what is it?" the colonel asked. "What are you thinking?"

Still standing with his back to the fire, Marcus said, "I was thinking about this offense I've been teaching to my sons' basketball teams."

"Really, this is . . ."

The colonel turned away from Marcus and looked hard at the CIA director, then back at Marcus.

"Anyway," Marcus rubbed his hands, one massaging the other, "it's called 'false motion,' and if you do it right, it creates all this confusion, and the next thing you know, the basket's wide open." He paced as he continued. "The whole idea is to have guys running this way and that . . ." Marcus began to relax a little, his speech and gestures becoming more animated. "When you watch a team execute it right, like a good college team, the defense is totally confused. The purpose of the offense is simple: get the defense looking here and there, and then, *bam!*"—Marcus clapped his hands, making the two directors jump—"the hoop's wide open for a backdoor dunk."

"Well, that's all very interesting," said Pinehurst. "Thanks for the basketball lesson, but I fail to see the relevance." He turned to Colonel Webb. "Sam, I have always had the greatest respect for you, but it seems that maybe you've lost your touch."

Marcus stepped closer to the group, placed his hands on the back of a chair, and leaned in. Then he smiled.

"Is there something funny about all this, Mister Diablo?" the small, shiny-headed director of the FBI said.

Marcus's blue eyes narrowed. "You know, this is the reason my wife died: because men too small-minded to see the possibilities ran the show." The FBI director seemed about to speak, but Marcus barreled on. "I stood by for days, weeks, months, as you and that bunch you have working for you sat with your thumbs up your asses." Marcus's fingers dug into the seat back. "And by the time you figured it out, it was too late—not just for my wife but for the whole country. So rather than sit there and tell me what you think, let me tell you what I think. Yeah, these people are terrorists, and they may still attack an airport, blow up a plane or a train, or set off a bomb in a subway. But that's not *the* plan. Those possibilities are just distractions to draw your attention away from the real target. And you know why it works? Because you are so . . . fucking . . . predictable."

On a roll, Marcus charged ahead. "You know, you spend all your time profiling, trying to figure out what makes these people tick, but what you don't realize is your organizations, your agents, are the most profiled of all. These people know exactly how you operate, how you're going to react. But, of course, you're way too smart to see that." Marcus finished, his face a mask of contempt.

Roland Hanover stood up and stared at Marcus for a few seconds. "You know, Mister Diablo, there is no statute of limitations on murder."

Marcus grinned back. Hanover was talking about the two men Marcus and the boys had found ransacking their campsite when they returned from their day of fishing. Once he sent the boys out of the mountains, Marcus went a bit crazy, and in his desperation-filled effort to find his wife Annie, he killed them. To Marcus's knowledge, the FBI official report listed the deaths as self-defense, but he also knew that for the FBI what was "official" one day could be thrown out the next.

"You know, we might just arrest you right here and now. What do you think about that?" Hanover asked through gritted teeth, clearly unaccustomed to being lectured, let alone accused of incompetence.

Marcus glanced quickly at the colonel. If the man felt any hint of agitation or concern, it didn't show. Reaching into his shirt pocket, Marcus fished something out. He thought he saw a flash of panic in the CIA director's eyes.

He set a USB drive on the table. CIA Director Hanover looked at it and reached out. Marcus brought his left hand down with a thump, covering the drive, before Hanover's hand could touch it. "Why don't you relax and sit, Director?" he said. The big man looked to his colleagues, then at the colonel, and sat.

"That's better. Now, I think it would be best if you and I . . ." Marcus made eye contact first with Hanover, then with Pinehurst, ". . . came to an understanding." He slid the hand covering the USB drive across the table as far as he could and leaned heavily on it. "You don't get it. These guys have you figured out. They know when and where you are going to spend your time and resources. All they have to do is spoon-feed you enough information to keep you looking exactly where they want you to look. This isn't about blowing shit up or killing people. No, it's all about making folks feel unsafe in their homes, making them question their government's ability to keep them safe. It's about *fear.*"

Marcus paused and took a deep breath, dialed back his anger. "I'm pretty enlightened about how you work—a lot more than your average Joe. You see, I don't really care what kind of freaky shit either of you does in the privacy of your own home. I couldn't care less where you keep your money or even how you made it, or what little backdoor deals you've struck over the years, but if you come after me or my family—and, gentlemen, it's a big-ass family—I'll burn your fucking houses down." Marcus's gaze landed on each of them in turn. "Make no mistake. We have information that, if it became public, would rock the very foundations of your organizations. You would quickly have every Congressional member on the Hill crawling up your ass with a microscope. Every news organization in this country would be tearing like piranhas into you and everyone in your families. This thumb drive is just a taste of the hellfire we will bring down on you."

Both men looked at Marcus, then at the colonel. But Marcus wasn't finished. "Now, you may want to talk to your young colleague." He nodded toward the deputy director, who hadn't moved from his position by the TV. "Because he's, hands down, the most intelligent of the intelligence officers in this room. He knows what I'm talking about, and although he doesn't know for sure, my guess is, he's got a pretty good idea of the resources at Force Ten's disposal. That is the real reason we're here, right? You see, we are, as they say, at a crossroads. The key is figuring out which way to go. Trouble is, you two don't have a clue."

Staring at the directors of the FBI and CIA, Marcus had no confidence in their ability to keep him or any other American out of harm's way. He lifted his hand from the USB drive. "Now, if you don't mind, I'm going to get some fresh air."

* * *

STANDING ON THE FLAGSTONE PATIO, Marcus welcomed the seeping cold of the damp night air. It had been a long time since he'd felt so worked up. He had known that the day would come when he must either get back on the horse or walk away, but he had done his damnedest to ignore it. Besides, walking away had never been an option. He had come too far and sacrificed too much. He had asked people for help, and they had stepped up. Now he needed to take his place in the team and begin repaying that debt.

Letting the cold air bathe his lungs, watching the plumes of breath condensation dissipate, Marcus heard footsteps. "Well played, Nathan," he said, as the Deputy Director of the FBI walked up. "That was quite the little performance you set up in there."

Deputy Director Reynolds stood beside Marcus, looking out into the night. "Well, there were things that had to be said—things that, if they came from my mouth, would certainly have landed me in the hinterlands of FBI purgatory. And as I recall, someone once threatened to make sure that if things didn't work out right, that was exactly where I would end up."

Marcus glanced over at Reynolds, who, tall and broad shouldered, was the archetypal FBI agent. "Yeah, I think someone also said that if you played your cards right you might find yourself running the whole show someday. And from what I just saw, you're a lot more qualified than the guy doing it now."

"I don't know about that, Marcus, but we all work within certain sets of . . . restrictions."

Marcus gave Reynolds a look that said, *You sure about that?*

"It may not seem like it, but you, too, work within a certain set of guidelines. That those guidelines aren't the same as what the rest of the world operates on, well . . ."

"Well what? That's why we're here, right? You know what's going on in there?" Marcus nodded at the French doors. "The colonel's in there agreeing to put the resources and expertise of Force Ten to work, looking into the situation. Meanwhile, those two bureaucrats are tossing you under the bus. Making this whole thing your responsibility—all of it on your shoulders. But you knew that already."

"Well, Marcus, not to sound like a broken record, but someone told me once that I had had my turn to fix things and now it was *his* turn, and that I had best stay the fuck out of his way. I've had a fair bit of time to think about that, and you know what?" Nathan smiled. "I figured, if it worked for him, it just might work for me."

Marcus shoved his hands into the front pockets of his jeans. "You like baseball?"

He knew that Nathan had been a pitcher in college—a very good pitcher. If he hadn't thrown his arm out, there was a good chance he would have been soaking up the sun in Florida, making a ton of money, instead of freezing his ass off here in the Virginia countryside with one of the most exasperating men he had ever known.

"Yeah, you know damn well I do."

"What's the magic number for any baseball player?"

Nathan shuffled from foot to foot and tucked his hands up under his armpits to hold in some warmth. "Three hundred."

"Three hundred. A guy hits that over the course of a decade or so, and hell, he's probably Hall of Fame bound. So is it the fact that he hit three hundred that makes him so special?" Marcus shook his head. "No, it's that he figured out how to mitigate and manage failing seven out of ten times. Those two bozos in there . . ." He nodded toward the doors again. ". . . they think it's possible to bat a thousand. Now, I don't have a clue what's coming next, but whatever it is, it's already in play. This isn't about prevention, Nathan; it's about mitigating and managing."

Just then the door opened and the colonel stepped out onto the patio, handed Marcus his jacket, and pointed toward the chopper.

As Marcus and the colonel walked down the brick pathway, Marcus turned back to the deputy director of the FBI. "You need to be a baseball player, Nathan. A very, very good baseball player."

CHAPTER TWELVE

Winnipeg, Manitoba

DAMEER FOUND AN ENVELOPE ADDRESSED to him on his desk. It looked like Adriana's handwriting. He hadn't spoken with her since last night. He had hoped he would wake up with her this morning, but he did understand her needing some time alone to grasp the significance of their breakthrough. He opened the envelope and removed a single sheet of paper. In Adriana's precise print, the note read:

> *Dameer, my love, I'd would like to make up for last night. So tonight meet me at 6:30 at the Fort Gary Hotel. When you arrive, the key will be waiting. You know how you like to play. Well, you have been a very, very bad boy. I expect that when I arrive, you will be waiting and prepared to receive your punishment. No one must know of this. Now take this note to the incinerator.*

DAMEER WAS ECSTATIC AS HE walked into the lab, tore the note into little bits, and tossed it in the incinerator used to destroy discarded biological samples. He loved to role-play, especially if he might be the one tied up and wearing a dog collar. Adriana encouraged him to explore his sexual fantasies. At first he'd felt self-conscious, but Adriana had showed him that with her, he needn't be embarrassed.

* * *

Somehow Dameer got through the day. Besides the anticipation about his evening with Adriana, the Internet crash had the NML in a rare panic. All data from the over four hundred employees needed to be backed up onto the NML's secure servers. The events playing out, especially in the States, had escalated beyond the Internet. Yesterday's power failure that affected a large block of Winnipeg and the potential for additional outages had Canada on high alert. This morning, the New York Stock Exchange had suspended trading. Never before had Dameer been so glad that he lived in Canada.

* * *

When Dameer entered the room, the drapes had been drawn. Scented candles and a rose petal- scattered bedspread rounded out the ambiance. On top of the petals he saw with delight, a pair of padded handcuffs, a ball gag, and a Roman slave whip. Attached to the headboard with a short leather lead was a spiked dog collar. A black hood rested on the pillow next to an envelope. Dameer removed the note.

> *Are you ready to fulfill your fantasy? You've earned it. Now undress, lay on your back, put on the gag, then the dog collar, and finally put the hood over your head. No matter what happens, don't look, or you'll ruin the surprise.*

Dameer could barely contain himself. Frantically, he undressed and lay naked on the bed. With the short leash on the dog collar, he had to prop pillows under his back to get it on, forcing him to sit at an incline with his head midway up the backboard. Already fully aroused, he slipped the black hood over his head.

* * *

ADRIANA WATCHED FROM INSIDE THE closet. She knew Dameer would be so excited he wouldn't think of searching the room. They had experimented with bondage and discipline, though never to this extent. But Adriana had seen some of the porn sites Dameer visited and knew he would be willing. Besides, he trusted her completely.

She'd rented the room yesterday, over the phone, using Dameer's credit card. The Internet outage made her plan more complicated, but as she watched Dameer put the gag in his mouth and fasten the strap, she realized, it made it safer. Electronic trails had become so easy to track.

Adriana had a voice change app on her phone, but with the Internet crash it didn't work. She found a device at a local spy shop that altered her voice. She used it to make the hotel reservation. She also bought a pre-paid cell phone with a local provider whose small regional network was still in operation. Then she posted a typewritten note, with tear-off phone number tabs, on the community bulletin board outside the student services building at The University of Winnipeg.

The note said:

```
Getting   back   at   my   scumbag   of   a
boyfriend.   Need   four   volunteers
willing to spend a few hours in a five
-star hotel room with champagne, mini-
bar,   and   snacks,   of   course.   Looking
for folks who want to make full use of
the   room,   if   you   know   what   I   mean.
This guy is a real tool. Call to win.
                Nobody's Bitch
```

In less than an hour Adriana had her room crashers. One couple checked in first, got two keys, gave one to the second couple. Per instructions they returned to the university and left their key in an envelope on the same bulletin board before returning to join their friends.

To ensure that they left the rooms by five P.M. Adriana made dinner part of the deal with a reservation at a popular restaurant. A three-hundred-dollar tab, prepaid. When she arrived at the hotel, her head covered with a scarf, heavy clothes that made her look a bit plump, and dark glasses, she found the rooms in perfect shape. The beds were a mess, sex for sure, open bottles of champagne, dirty glasses, and a few dozen empty mini-bar bottles. The roaches in the ashtray and residue of something they snorted on the coffee table, a bonus.

As a biologist Adriana understood the science of forensics. The probability that evidence of someone's presence existed was a near certainty. In the bathroom, standing inside the shower on a sheet she had brought with her, she removed a HAZMAT suit from her suitcase and put it on before cleaning the room. With years of experience working with deadly virus and bacteria, Adriana knew how to keep herself to herself.   It took an hour. She made the bed, bagged the bottles, glasses and drug evidence, and waited inside the closet for Dameer to arrive.

* * *

ONCE DAMEER PUT THE HOOD over his head, Adriana quietly came out of the closet. She pointed a remote at the nightstand and one of Dameer's favorite songs, *I Gotta Feeling,* came blaring from the MP3 player.

Adriana picked up the whip and hit Dameer across the stomach. Not too hard. Then she took his hands and cuffed them above his head to the leash that held the dog collar. He squirmed at bit, not panicked, not yet. Next she put lengths of soft rope, which she had attached to the bed frame while cleaning, around each ankle and pulled the slipknots snug.

When she tightened the dog collar two more holes Dameer thrashed and tried to kick his feet. With the gag and the hood, his breathing came in wet, sucking gasps. Adriana pulled one of the pillows out from behind Dameer's back, which put more tension on the dog collar, then one more pillow.

Looking down at Dameer as he thrashed, struggling for breath, she felt nothing. She had been raised in the African bush where only through death could there be continuing life. And often man, not nature, decided who died.

CHAPTER THIRTEEN

December 1, U.S. airspace

THE PLANE TOOK OFF FROM Andrews Field nine hours after it landed. Marcus was tired. Dealing with powerful, self-important assholes exhausted him.

Once they reached cruising altitude, the colonel said, "That was quite the stunt. So what was on the thumb drive?"

Marcus looked at him—the bald head with high-and-tight gray sidewalls, the dark brown eyes that could see more in a man than that man could see in the mirror. "I don't really know. J. T. just said that if they started 'getting up in my shit'—his exact words— I might want to throw out the thumb drive. I'm assuming since they didn't deny anything or get all indignant, some of my bullshit hit home."

The colonel raised his eyebrows.

"Now, don't blame J. T. He was only looking out for me."

The colonel reclined in his seat, pulled a blanket up over himself and hit the switch on his chair arm to turn off the overhead light. "Marcus, the only thing I would ever hold against J. T., or any of my people, is if they *didn't* look out for you. Now get some rest."

* * *

A VOICE ROUSED MARCUS AWAKE. Rubbing the sleep from his eyes, he looked at his watch. *Still almost two hours left in the five-hour flight.* Focusing, he saw the colonel at the table mounted against the side bulkhead, a satellite phone to his ear.

Then he heard, "Okay, we'll deal with the situation as it

arises, but there's no doubt, our location's been compromised."

Marcus stood and stretched. He flexed his stocking-footed toes in the thickly padded carpet and gave the colonel an inquiring look.

Standing, the colonel said, "There's been a attack at the ranch, up by the line cabin." The calm, matter-of-fact tone that he always used when he was in mission mode had an edge that Marcus couldn't recall ever hearing before.

"What happened? Are the boys okay?"

"Sit down, Marcus."

"Tell me what's going on, Sam," Marcus said as he plopped into the sofa.

"Garrett's hurt. The Hide got blown up with him in it. He's in the ER at the Nicola Valley hospital in Merritt."

Marcus jumped up. The boys had discovered the cave, what they called "The Hide," behind the line cabin near the summer range meadow, and had turned into a fort of sorts. " Hurt? How bad? It's thirty miles to Merritt from the ranch, further from the cabin. With Bronson flying our jet, there's no one at the ranch to fly the chopper. How did they get him there?"

"They got a local helicopter charter to transport him to the hospital. It couldn't have happened much faster even if *we'd* been there. Garrett is stable but he's still unconscious. From what I know, he's in remarkably good shape, considering. No internal bleeding, no broken bones. Chaya's with him, and you know as well as I, there not a better critical care doctor."

"What about Bodie?"

"Looks like he killed two men. Beyond that he's unharmed. Pete killed two others. A third man, he took alive. We'll see what he can tell us."

Marcus stared at the colonel. Pete—Pyotr Petrovich—was in charge of the hand-to-hand combat training for the team. Of all the members of Force 10, Marcus knew the least about him. Although his training techniques had left Marcus with plenty of cuts and bruises, Pete didn't talk, smile or socialize much. He did know Pete had been with the colonel since 2000. A former Spetsnaz with the Russian special-purpose regiment, what he could do with his hands and a knife would make your everyday badass seem like a Cub Scout.

"Now sit back down!"

Reluctantly Marcus did, his anxiety on the verge of full-blown rage.

"This morning, before sunrise, the boys went up to the cabin in that old Jeep. Seems they were out at the wall talking with their mom . . ."

It still surprised Marcus that everyone—all his family and every member of Force 10—talked about this relationship that he and the boys had with a dead woman as if they had no shred of doubt it was real.

"Anyway, as the sun came up, they spotted a group of men at the edge of the big meadow below the cabin. Ranch hands are in that area often so they didn't think anything of it. As they watched and the men didn't move out of the trees, Bodie got the monocular from the cabin. That's when they realized these guys didn't belong there. Bodie called Sit. He had them go to The Hide while he got people headed toward them."

"Who are these guys?"

"We think they're Russians."

"Russians? And they specifically came for the boys?"

"It appears that way. But trust me, Pete's gonna find out."

"What the fuck, Sam? I know we pissed off half the crazies in the Middle East, but the Russian's? What would've happened if...?"

"It didn't! Now you need to pull it together. Because right now we're thirty thousand feet in the air, and no matter, we can't do shit about what's *already* happened."

* * *

MARCUS STRUGGLED TO CONTROL HIS emotions. He had one job, take care of his sons, and he couldn't even do that. The thing he and the boys had with Annie made no sense. Before Marcus arrived at the ranch, Bodie and Garrett had built a rock cairn on top of the stone wall that ran along the bluff separating the cabin from the meadow below. They placed the OLD PEACH can that held Annie's ashes inside. This had become his and the boys' special place.

But there was more to it. Since the day Annie went missing a year and a half ago, Garrett claimed he communicated with his mother. And when they recovered Annie's body and found the place she had been held for nearly three months, it fit Garrett's description down to the smallest detail. Then Marcus's dreams started. Annie would come to him, especially when he needed direction or he found himself in deep trouble. _Though he hadn't had a single dream of her since arriving at the ranch. But call it whatever you like, the power of heaven, spirits from the great beyond, whatever, Annie was with them.

The colonel had also been right about Chaya Lanyer. The Force 10 doctor was the best. She'd saved Marcus' life for sure. And to say that *their* relationship was complicated wouldn't even begin to cover it. But she loved Garrett and Bodie, and would lay her life down for either of them.

The colonel had recruited her while still serving in the Army. She had been trained by the most deadly intelligence agency in the world—the Israeli, Mossad. On top of being a critical care doctor and first-rate at battlefield triage, she also possessed serious language skills that included Hebrew, Arabic, Farsi, and more than a dozen others. She offered the colonel a special set of talents. As a woman, she had an ability to get under a fundamental Islamists' skin, which came in handy when interrogating insurgents— especially male insurgents. As a doctor, she had an intimate knowledge of the human body. Inflicting pain while keeping an enemy conscious could be valuable, especially when the need for information was immediate. And just like Marcus, a personal tragedy had led Chaya to the colonel.

Of course Bodie had called Sit. As designation F-2, in the colonel's (F-1's) absence, he would have been in ops. To Marcus, Sit seemed like a lame call sign, even with a given name of Stanley Ignatius Thorn. When Marcus had first questioned the Force 10 sniper and weapons expert about it, Sit, in a Tennessee-hills drawl, explained it to him. "Sit be short fo' *Sit-yew-a-tion.* You be gettin' in one, I be gettin' you out." And he had done exactly that for Marcus, more than once. Besides, Marcus figured, how many Mavericks and Vipers could there be?

Combine his habit of sounding none too bright with being a six-eight and well over three- hundred-pound black man, he was perhaps the most unlikely-looking sniper anywhere. A decorated Army Ranger, the colonel found him relegated to Firearms Instructor at the Army Ranger Maneuver Center in Fort Benning, Georgia. That was sixteen years ago.

* * *

THE COLONEL WATCHED THE MASK of an anguished father on Marcus' face fade, as he processed what had happened to his sons. What he'd come to recognize as the, *Look the fuck out, there's gonna be hell to pay* expression began to replace it.

Even though all the members of Force 10 had multiple skill sets, each had a special talent. The colonel knew that Marcus believed his talent to be his ability to speak any language he heard. And not just speak it, but match inflection and dialect. Plenty of ongoing debate still raged about how he had acquired the skill—too much time in the harsh Australian outback sun, a good bump on the head, or maybe an encounter with aliens. However it happened, Marcus wouldn't say. The colonel only knew he didn't have it when he arrived at the Force 10 Australian compound, and did before he left. To be sure, his language skills had proved valuable. But his true talent, one he didn't yet recognize—his ability to cut through the emotion of a situation while still remaining personally attached, especially when it involved the most important people in the world to him. He had a way of seeing things that defied logic. A roundabout approach to getting from point A to point B that usually included landing on several other letters of the alphabet first. But the end results spoke for themselves. He was right. A lot. That's why the colonel wanted him to be part of the FBI/CIA meeting.

* * *

Several minutes of silence passed.   "You good? Ready to continue?" asked the colonel.

Marcus nodded.

"Okay. As the boys came up to the rock outcropping where the hide is, they spotted two more men approaching from the backside. Once they were inside the hide, Bodie radioed Sit again."

Marcus looked hard at the colonel. "How could these guy have known about the cave? Hell, by the time I found out, they already had it stocked with water, food, and supplies. I thought Jamie and the boys were just...playing fort...like boys do."

"Yeah, I know. I don't think it had anything to do with the cave. Somehow they tracked 'em. Anyway, and this is where things get a little sketchy, it's pretty crazy at the ranch. One of the men Bodie killed, it looks like he blew up the hide just as Bodie shot him."

Marcus took a deep breath and let it out in a huff and willed his imagination to drop out of warp. Just then Jamie Marsden came out of the cockpit. Marcus had never seen the young man look so... afraid.

At 28, Jamie was the youngest and most hotheaded member of Force 10, although Marcus often gave him a run for his money in the hothead department. He had developed a big brother relationship with Bodie and Garrett. The three spent a lot of time exploring the vast ranch, hunting and fishing. They had discovered the cave together, provisioned it, and named it The Hide. It had been his suggestion that the boys learn about guns. After all, they did live on a ranch with a whole range of hunting opportunities. Not to mention that the ranching culture had as strong a tie to firearms as it did to cattle. So, with Sit's help, Jamie taught the boys to respect, handle, and shoot rifles and pistols.

Marcus stood. "Hey, Garrett's gonna be okay."

"How the fuck do you know that, mate? Those bastards brought the whole thing down on his head. For Christ's sake, I'm the one..."

"Jamie," Marcus yelled. "If there hadn't been a place for them to go, what do you think might have happened?"

The look on his face was all the answer Marcus needed.

"Exactly. Instead of us worrying about him regaining consciousness, we might be contemplating something a whole lot worse. And I for one refuse to go there. So you get your ass back in the cockpit and get us on the ground. Then we can start dealing with this."

Jamie looked to Marcus and then the colonel, turned, and went back to co-piloting the jet.

Marcus turned his attention back to the colonel. "Sorry about that Sam, sometimes I forget...."

"Don't you ever apologize to me for doing what comes natural. You need to know something. Over the years I've led teams that have followed me right to the very gates of hell. But this team, these people, not only would they follow you through those gates, they'd stay there with you, no questions, no regrets. Now that's a loyalty I've never seen. I know you said you haven't quite wrapped your head around being a member of Force Ten, well, you got less than an hour to come to terms with it."

Marcus started to stand.

"No, you sit tight. I've got to make some calls. When we land I need you composed and focused." The colonel stepped to the desk and retrieved an iPad. He scrolled through it and handed it to Marcus. "Maxim Gorky, being read in Russian, of course. I have a feeling you're going to need it. What is that you're always saying? *Find strength in the struggle.*" The colonel sat at the desk and before Marcus put the earbuds in he said, "You can count on this, whoever is responsible, long before they answer to *their* god, they're damn well going to answer to us!"

CHAPTER FOURTEEN

Beginnings Ranch, British Columbia

Sɪᴛ ᴡᴀɪᴛᴇᴅ ᴀᴛ ᴛʜᴇ ʀᴀɴᴄʜ runway as the jet came in. In contrast to spring and summer, the stands of birch, tamarack and aspen stood naked, which is exactly how he felt.

He stood on the tarmac as Marcus exited the jet.

"Marcus, I'm so sorry. I never should have let the boys out of my sight."

Marcus looked at the big man. Sit was the member of Force 10 closest to his age, just two years younger. From the day they'd met, nearly a year ago, Sit had taken him under his wing, providing not only training but friendship.

Marcus reached out and patted an arm the size of most people's legs. "Hey, you didn't do anything wrong. Annie and I raised the boys to be independent. I can't take that away from them. You got him out and got him the help he needed, that's what counts."

"Marcus, he could've been..."

Marcus looked up into the deep pools of Sit's root beer-colored eyes. "Listen to me. I trust you with my life, with their lives."

"Yeah, but you don't understand, Marcus. The whole cave came down on him. There's no way anyone walks away from that. Red, the ranch foreman, had a crew up at the summer range meadow, just above the hide. Moving troughs or something. They had a backhoe. I got them moving toward the hide before the guy blew it up."

"How did you...?"

"Later about that. Anyway, they started digging within a few minutes of it blowing up. I had GPS tracking on both the boys. Chaya had Bodie, but Garrett, his signal came from inside the pile of rock and dirt.

"I rode up in the chopper. Red and his boys were just ready to bust through when I got there. The risk of the backhoe hitting Garrett concerned me. So I took a shovel and dug by hand. When I broke through, there was a space just big enough for him. Like he had a cage around him. He lay there curled in a ball, like a sleeping baby. I picked him out of there and put him on the chopper with Chaya. Marcus, what I'm saying is that space…shouldn't have been there."

Marcus had never seen the man so worked up. As a sniper he always maintained a level of composure and calm. "I understand things that can't be explained, believe me. You did everything right. Now, I need to go. You and the colonel start figuring out what the hell's going on. We'll do a complete debrief when I get back." Marcus turned and headed toward the powering up chopper.

* * *

THE COLONEL APPROACHED SIT JUST as Marcus walked away. He'd known Sit a long time and couldn't remember him ever being visibly distressed over anything. He would keep it bottled inside, but never wear it on his sleeve. Well, Marcus had brought that to the team too. For him, *all in* meant just that—skills, emotions—the whole gamut of what it meant to be human. In addition, he had the talent that defined all true leaders. He could give you a perception of complete control, even while inside he was on the verge of exploding.

"You good?"

"How does he do that Colonel? I mean Garrett should've died."

The colonel gave Sit a questioning stare.

"We'll go though it in Ops."

The colonel could tell Sit needed a few minutes. As they headed for the barn, he said, "Old soldiers like us, we made our mark by being methodical and detached." He poked a thumb back over his shoulder. "Those two words don't exist in that man's vocabulary."

72

* * *

AT THE CHOPPER, BRONSON WAS finishing his preflight check. Jamie stood by the door looking lost. Marcus tilted his head and mouthed, *"Come on. Let's go."*

On board, Marcus donned a headset and looked at Jamie. He had been an Australian Special Forces commando whose knack for tracking man or beast was a talent that went way beyond reading signs. Jamie had a sixth sense when it came to tracking. He walked in his quarry's shoes, felt the weight of their load and the effects of their injuries.

He was born and raised on a remote cattle station in the middle of Australia's Simpson Desert. His mother died during childbirth and the task of raising him fell to his mean, nasty drunk of a father. One morning his father didn't wake up. Jamie was ten. A few days later, Jamie was found by the grandfather of a young aboriginal boy he went to school with. The man happened to be Killara Wanganami, chief of the Arrernte. From then on, Jamie was raised as an Arrernte. When he left at 18 to join the Australian Special Forces, he took with him something magical—something beyond the world of mere men. The Arrernte are some of the oldest and most mystical people on earth. As Marcus looked at the young man, his face painted in guilt, he knew they shared something only the two of them would ever understand.

Jamie had been Colonel Webb's *second* Force 10 recruit. With his operational wizard secured, he then needed a base of operations. It had to fit a very specific set of parameters: somewhere dry and inhospitable, like most of the Middle East, since that's where they would be working, yet far from the United States. The young man he had commandeered to help track down insurgents in the Army during the Iraq war had the perfect connections to make that happen.

Over the com Marcus said, "Hey. He's gonna be all right."

The look Jamie gave him said, *God, I hope so.*

Marcus had a different relationship with each member of Force 10. Peer to peer with Sit, more like father and son with Jamie.

Marcus slapped him on the knee. "If I never told ya, I really appreciate how you've looked out for the boys. We'll figure this out and whoever did this...is gonna pay."

Jamie bit his bottom lip. Though he didn't have control over his emotions quite like the older and more experienced members of Force 10, this thing with Marcus, the boys, and the whole Diablo clan, had the entire team in uncharted territory.

CHAPTER FIFTEEN

Nicola Valley Hospital, Merritt, British Colombia

WHEN MARCUS ENTERED THE SMALL hospital he saw Chaya talking to a tall man in a white coat. With only eight beds, the lobby served as check-in, waiting room, and conference area. Chaya stepped away from the man and came up to Marcus.

In dirty jeans and her curly brown hair pulled back in a bandana, her hands looked like she'd been in a bare-knuckle fight. No friendly meet and greet, just all business. "Let me introduce you to Doctor Johnson."

In his early forties, Doctor Johnson had an easy, confident manner. "Mr. Diablo, I'm Doctor Eric Johnson."

"Just Marcus, doc. So how's my boy?"

"Well, Marcus, that's a bit of mystery. We're a small hospital and don't have all the fancy diagnostic equipment, but I'll be damned if I can find much wrong with him. He has barely a scratch; all his vitals are stable, and his EEG is normal."

Marcus looked at Chaya.

"I can't explain it either. It's like he shut down, like he's in a deep sleep."

"I need to see him, now." Marcus said.

* * *

AT THE DOOR TO GARRETT'S room Marcus paused. Bodie was at the bedside holding his brother's hand and talking to him. He saw Marcus and came running into his arms.

Marcus held Bodie. His long blond hair matted with dirt and

twigs. Between sobs Bodie said, "I'm sorry, Dad. I shouldn't have left him alone."

Marcus pushed Bodie back, his arms on the boy's shoulders. "Look at me! This is not your fault. Right now, though, we need to get your brother back. Then we'll figure everything out. Okay?"

Bodie wiped his face on his dirty shirtsleeve and nodded.

At the bed, Marcus sat and took Garrett's hand. On his side, curled into a fetal position, Garrett looked angelic—if angels can be covered in dirt. His cheeks had good color. His breath came slow and even. Marcus caressed his forehead. "Hey buddy, Daddy's here. Can you wake up for me?"

* * *

"Hey, baby."

"Mom? I can't see you."

"That's okay, honey. You don't need to see me this time. How you doing?"

"Okay. I did what you asked and moved up to the place where the rock we use as a shelf sticks out of the wall."

"I know. You did real good. Now you need to do something else for me. I need you to wake up. Daddy's waiting for you."

"What about Bodie, Momma? A little while ago, I thought I heard him talking to me."

Garrett heard his mother laugh. "Yeah, Bodie's waiting too. Everybody's worried about you."

"Even the colonel?"

She laughed again. "Especially the colonel. Now it's time to open your eyes. Come on, you can do it..."

* * *

MARCUS LOOKED TOWARD THE DOOR and saw that Bodie had gone out into the hall to stand with Chaya, Bronson, and Jamie. They looked on through the big window. The squeeze of Garrett's hand startled him. Marcus squeezed back. "Hey, buddy. It's time to wake up. Can you open your eyes for me? Come on."

Garrett opened his eyes and smiled at Marcus. "Hey, Dad."

"Hey to you too. How you doing? Do you know where you are?"

Garrett shifted around and sat up. "Looks like a hospital. Do you know where you are?"

They both laughed.

"Do you remember what happened?"

"Yeah, sort of. Bodie and I went to see Mom. There were guys down in the meadow, not anybody who works at the ranch. Sit told us to go the hide, but when we got there, we saw two other men close by." Some of the color faded from Garrett's face.

"Dad, Bodie had to go and stop them. He had the rifle we keep at the cabin. The one Sit taught us how to shoot. He had no choice. He had to go or those men would have taken us. That's what they said. If we just came out, they wouldn't hurt us, just take us on a little trip."

Marcus brushed some crusted dirt from Garrett's forehead. "Hey, buddy, we don't have to talk about this right now."

"Yes we do," Garrett said pushing his dad's hand away. "It was Mom. She came to me, told me to move up under the shelf rock. I couldn't see her, but she told me to tuck up underneath it and curl up in a ball. Then she covered my body with hers, and whispered, 'Close your eyes, and everything will be okay.'"

Marcus pulled Garrett into his arms, and thought, *Not a cage, Annie.*

CHAPTER SIXTEEN

Beginnings Ranch, British Colombia

"Okay, people," the colonel said to the team assembled in the barn command center bunker, "You've all been at this long enough to know the drill, so let's get to it. Weathers and Liam are en route with the *Takbir.* They'll be in Vancouver late tonight. Ham is on a military transport out of Saudi Arabia and will also be here very early tomorrow. We'll continue developing a comprehensive threat assessment as well as an action plan. Okay, J. T., let's see what you got."

Standing in front of the monitor wall, touch pad in hand, J. T. said, "The first part is audio only; then we have video."

Marcus sat in one of the reclining consoles, closed his eyes, and listened to what had happened earlier that day.

* * *

"Papa Bear, Papa Bear, you read me?" Bodie's voice spoke.

"I'm here, Fox. What's up?"

"Me and Rabbit are at Mom's. We got three guys at the big end of the meadow, dressed in what looks like full battle gear."

Sit made a slash motion with his hand across his throat, telling J. T. to mute the audio.

"Get eyes on those boys and the meadow, now!"

J. T.'s hands where flying over the touch screen. One of the biggest challenges with security on a property of nearly eight hundred square miles was surveillance. The main compound wasn't the issue—it was wired and camera-equipped every way from

Sunday. It was for the rest of the sprawling ranch that J. T. had had to come up with a way to get visual monitoring fast, especially in the places where Marcus, the boys, and the rest of the family liked to hang out. So, using the latest in drone technology, he had positioned various sizes of remotely controlled planes, some the size of seagulls; others, with greater range, the size of a child's wagon if it had wings; and a few even larger ones, kept at the main compound, that could stay up for hours and had enough range to cover the whole ranch. He also had short-distance helicopter models positioned around the most frequented areas.

J. T. didn't worry about legal restrictions on the private use of drones. Like Marcus, he saw rules as flexible and thus, meant to be interpreted, changed, or ignored altogether if necessary. Besides, J. T. held dozens of drone patents, all classified, and he still had connections.

"In five, four, three, two, one," J. T. said.

Flying three hundred feet above the ground, the electric-powered helicopter, painted flat black, was unrecognizable and silent. Its high-resolution cameras mounted on the nose and belly brought the meadow into view on the wall monitors. Sit stood in front of the giant screen. One side showed the boys leaning over the wall. Bodie had a monocular to his eye and it looked like Garrett was talking to him.

"Papa Bear . . . Papa Bear . . ."

"I copy, Fox. You and Rabbit get your gear together and prepare to bug out."

Just then Pete and Chaya walked into Ops. J. T. motioned toward the screen.

Pete walked up and stood next to Sit, took a couple of steps forward, cocked his square head, and squinted at the big screen. Then he motioned and said in his shorthand English, "More, more," meaning he wanted J. T. to go to a full-screen view of the men in the meadow.

"Russians, see?" He pointed his finger.

Sit stared at the screen, wondering how Pete knew.

"Russians! See?" Pete pointed at the body armor the men

wore. "Kazakh vest. Russian. Make in China. No good."

Sit still didn't have a clue, but he wasn't about to question the only Russian he knew, a man he had served with for over fifteen years.

"Show boys?"

The screen divided again and showed the boys still leaning on the wall, their attention focused on the men below.

Sit spoke. "Fox, you copy?"

"Copy, Papa Bear."

"Fox, you and Rabbit head to The Hide. Now!"

"On our way, Papa Bear."

The view showed the boys each grab a small daypack from the ground. Then they went up the steps to the cabin. Bodie ducked inside and came out with a rifle in his hands. They headed for the trail that ran behind the cabin. It would take them to The Hide a quarter of a mile away and continue on to the summer range meadow above.

Sit and Pete shared a look. Pete said, "You help boy not do anything stupid. Like father, head is rock." He tapped the side of his crew cut with his knuckles. Turning to Chaya, who was staring at the screen, he said, "You come with me. No time for worry. Time to go. Now!" Turning back to J. T., Pete said, "Find helicopter!"

With that, he took Chaya by the hand and left Ops.

J. T. gave Sit his, *What's he talking about?* stare.

"A helicopter... with a pilot, unless you can fly the one parked outside."

Sit took a quick moment. In all the years Sit had worked with Pete, he had never heard him speak so many words at one time.

The drone followed the boys through the trees as best it could. An early dusting of snow helped provide a good contrast.

"J. T., give me a view of The Hide."

As the rock outcropping came into view Sit saw two men coming in from the back side. They must have circled around the meadow. His instinct told him to call the boys but he checked himself. The squawk of the radio might give away their position. He needed them to get inside The Hide first.

"Zoom in on them."

As the camera focused Sit could see that these men, like the ones in the meadow, were combat equipped, but it wasn't the AK 47s, or the body armor that had his attention. However, the row of dark gray explosive charges in pouches across one side of the vests they wore did."

"How long till the boys get there?"

"Less than two minutes."

"What's that?" Sit pointed at some movement at the far edge of the camera view.

J. T. panned the drone camera in on three men working with a backhoe. They had some metal object chained to the bucket. "It's Red, the ranch foreman and a couple of hands. Looks like they're moving troughs around."

"Get him on the radio; tell him we got trouble. I need them to move up to the gate, there." Sit pointed at the barbed wire gate at the meadow entrance. From there it would put them only a few hundred yards from The Hide.

"They sit tight and if I give the go, they haul ass to The Hide with the backhoe."

J. T. didn't need an explanation. Anticipating a worst case scenario is what they did, and what they planned for.

J. T. moved toward Sit. "I got a chopper inbound to pick you up. Be here in five." Sit glanced at J. T. "You need to get up there. I'll deal with Ops."

The radio squawked. "Papa Bear, we're in The Hide. Now what?"

Sit watched the men. One approached the area near The Hide's brush-obscured entrance. Sit couldn't figure it out. How did these guys know where the boys were?

J. T. said, "I see it too. I have no idea, but there's no doubt that somehow they're tracking 'em."

Sit cocked his head at the Force 10 genius. First Pete talking up a storm and now J. T. saying, "I have no idea." How many more firsts was he in for today?

The man at The Hide bent over and looked at the ground. It

wouldn't take him long to find the boys' tracks. Once he did, the makeshift plywood door would be as big an obstacle as a tent to a Grizzly Bear.

"Fox, you copy?"

"Here, Papa Bear."

"Listen carefully. Move Rabbit to the back and then get your rifle."

J. T. mouthed to Sit, "*What the hell?*"

"Copy that."

Sit said to J. T., "Vitals."

In the bottom right corner of the screen, two words with numbers appeared: "Fox 95" and "Rabbit 102."

Everyday every member of Force 10 and of Marcus's family took a small sugar tablet about the size of an allergy pill. Just one of J. T.'s many ingenious inventions. Inside each tab a microscopic ceramic chip, undetectable by even the most sophisticated body scanners sent out a low frequency burst every ten seconds. Powered by the body's own electrical micro currents, using a nanotechnology that only J. T. understood, they even worked for ten or fifteen minutes after the person who ingested them died. Using God's Eye or some other satellite J. T. could hack into, the pulse provided not only a GPS location, but also real-time heart rate.

"Fox, check your rifle. Take me through it."

"Five in the mag, safety on."

"Is Rabbit in the back?"

"Yes, sir."

"Okay, I need you both to calm down a little," Sit said in his soothing, southern drawl. "I've got tracking on you and eyes on the bogies. Now, Fox, I need you to go out the back tunnel. Slip the earpiece in and plug it into the radio so I can talk to you without anyone hearing. I'll have eyes on you as soon as you pop out. You need to do exactly as I say. Can you do that for me?"

"Copy that."

Both Sit and J. T. watched as Bodie's head popped out of some dense scrub brush on the backside of the rock outcropping.

"Slowly now, Fox. Make your way up around those rocks in

front of you. Then come in from behind through that gap in the boulders so you have a clear view of The Hide's entrance."

Sit heard the approach of a helicopter.

J. T. handed him a touch pad. "You'll be able to see everything on this. The audio feed is patched into it as well. Go."

The chopper never set fully down before Sit was onboard.

When he looked at the pad he could see Bodie coming up over the top of the rocks. "Good, Fox. Nod if you see him."

Bodie looked up like maybe Sit was floating around above him and nodded.

"Okay. That rifle's sighted dead-on at a hundred yards. You're about fifty out. Put the crosshairs in the center of his chest."

Bodie looked up to the sky again.

"Don't worry about the body armor you're shooting a thirty-aught-six. You hit him, he's going down, and he'll stay down.

"Fox, I need you to bring your heart rate down. Breathe deep, boy." Sit watched the screen as the numbers started to fall off: 90 . . . 83 . . . 70. Sit shook his head and wondered, *How in hell can a thirteen-year-old boy focus like that?*

"That's good. Now I'm still a few minutes out, and I need you to buy me some time. Can you see the other man, off to your right?"

On the screen Sit saw Bodie scoot up a little and crane his neck over the top. He shook his head yes.

"Good. As soon as you fire at the first man, picture the second guy in your mind and move the rifle. Remember, *smooth is fast.* Just like shooting balloons."

Sit was referring to a drill he had taught the boys, shooting balloons tethered by strings. Even in a dead calm, the balloon always moved, and a proficient sniper needed to always anticipate a target's movement.

Sit stared hard at the screen, as if imposing his will on Bodie. He could hear the teenager's breath, easy and calm. His heart rate was hovering right at sixty-five, but his little brother's was even lower. Which didn't make any sense. The boy should be seriously scared, especially being left alone in The Hide.

The reality of the situation hit Sit. What the fuck was he

doing, letting Bodie . . ? He shook it off. These men whoever they were, had clearly come for the boys, to take them or kill them, probably both. Either way, they had to be stopped now.

Bodie had his com channel locked open so Sit could hear him. Slowly and quietly he chambered a round, sighted in on the man who now pounded on the door to The Hide. Sit heard Bodie say in a soft, calm voice, "For my mom."

On the screen Sit saw the man's feet come out from under him as he landed in a thud on his back. Bodie repositioned and sighted on the other man, who was already moving. He fired again, but missed. Sit lost sight of him for a moment. When he came back into view he had something in his hand, it wasn't a gun. That's when Sit saw his vest no longer had the black wrapped rectangular shaped charges of plastic explosives attached to it. Oh shit!

Sit noticed that the screen now showed two views—The Hide, and the other man. Bodie located the man and fired, missed again. Sit heard the bolt slam another round in the chamber. He looked at Bodie's heart rate, 70, not bad. Garrett's, however, had fallen to 50—what the hell? The man outstretched his arm and as The Hide exploded, so did his head.

* * *

PETE AND CHAYA RODE FOUR-stroke, 250cc dirt bikes up the road toward the line cabin. Where the road headed up toward the bench, they turned off onto a game trail that ran up through the brush and aspen-dotted ravine. In a mile, it dumped them into the stand of trees at the south end of the meadow. When the trees came into sight, they stopped and turned the bikes off. A hundred things ran though Chaya's mind. *What if the boys . . ?*

"Boys good," Pete said as if reading her thoughts. "In two minutes you take bike and go to The Hide, take care of boys. Me take care of Russians."

As Pete headed toward the meadow, it struck her that she couldn't remember Pete ever being so vocal. It seemed she wasn't the only one who had grown attached to Bodie and Garrett. She made a mental note to talk to the rest of team about getting Pete to take some personal time. During her time as a member of the colonel's U.S. Army team, before Force 10, downtime was mandatory. Team members could go home to see their families or take a vacation. But in the five years she'd been with the colonel, Pete, to her knowledge, hadn't gone anywhere. Did he even have any family? Chaya knew that the ranch's unique characteristics hadn't been the only reason for choosing it. The colonel wanted a location not too far from a decent sized town. They needed schools for Marcus's boys and all his nieces and nephews, as well as a place where the team members could get a drink and perhaps a bit of companionship. She smiled to herself. Maybe she needed to start a dating site: *mercenariesonly.com/alovetodiefor*. She shook her head, chagrined at how much like Marcus that kind of thinking seemed.

* * *

PETE MOVED THROUGH THE TREES. Before the clearing, he stopped and scanned the meadow. It took only a moment for him to find the three men. He saw cigarette smoke. These guys weren't worried. Well, he'd take care of that.

Pete made good time circling around the meadow. When he was twenty yards behind the men he threw a rock as far as he could back into the trees. One of the men left to investigate. Just what he wanted; even the odds a bit. Pete waited about thirty seconds, then walked in the direction of the two waiting men. Thinking it was their friend returning they paid little attention. When they finally noticed, it took Pete just seconds to cut one man's throat and break the other's neck. Pete moved away and waited. The third man returned, knelt down to the bodies of his comrades, and out went the lights. Pete trussed him up like calf ready to be branded. Then he heard the explosion and took off running in the direction of his motorcycle.

* * *

THE CHOPPER SET DOWN JUST as Chaya arrived at The Hide. Red and his crew had been there a few minutes and had started digging through the rock and dirt. Bodie was beside himself. He knew where Garrett had been but wasn't sure he'd stayed there.

J. T. had the GPS tracking signal transmitted to Sit's touch pad. It showed that Garrett had moved, but not much, about four or five feet. His heart rate still hovered right around fifty. How could that be, unless...

The backhoe moved the dirt and rock. The GPS tracker put them within inches. Sit held the backhoe up and grabbed a shovel. Carefully he dug. In less than a minute he had uncovered a small opening into what appeared to be an air space. With a flashlight, he peered in and saw Garrett rolled into a ball with a clear space of just a few inches around him. Working carefully, so as to avoid bringing tons of rubble down on the boy, Sit and Chaya created an opening big enough so that Sit could drag Garrett out.

Chaya quickly did a triage check. With his airway clear, and no visible signs of explosive trauma, she loaded him on the chopper with Bodie.

Pete arrived as the chopper lifted off en route to the Nicola Valley Hospital some thirty miles away.

"How boys?"

Sit didn't know how to answer.

"How boys?" Pete demanded again.

"Bodie shot these two, both dead. They blew The Hide up with Garrett in it. He's alive. Beyond that I don't know. Who the fuck are these guys?"

Pete turned and looked at Red. "Bring tractor and them." He pointed at the two men Bodie had shot. "And meet me at lower meadow."

To Sit, Pete said, "Gonna bury some Russians, then going to take one Russian and find out what they doing in our house."

As the bike roared off Sit thought, *That's one man I don't ever want interrogating me.*

* * *

MARCUS STAYED QUIET FOR A moment. The code names had been Sit and Jamie's way of teaching the boys to never go anywhere on the ranch without a radio. For them it had been like a game, that is, until today.

Chaya broke the silence, speaking to Marcus. "Garrett doesn't remember much about the explosion. I can't explain it, but he seems fine. Now, Bodie, you need to talk to him."

Sit broke in. "Marcus, he hasn't said a word about what happened up there."

Marcus got up out of the chair. "Look at all of you, everybody guilty about something. You did what had to be done. The boys are all right, and the bad guys aren't."

"But Marcus, he killed two men, and he hasn't said one word about it to anybody," Sit said again.

Marcus looked at Sit, then Chaya, then Pete, the only one of the three who didn't seem bothered in the least. "Listen, I've done plenty of things that wouldn't win me any 'Father of the Year' awards. But the one thing my boys do know is they are surrounded by people who love them. When they need to talk, they will. We all knew this day was coming. It's because of me they've had to grow up this way. If we're gonna do this—go after monsters—well, they need to be prepared."

"Back on task, people," the colonel said. "I want everybody to take a little bit of time. Tomorrow at O-six hundred we go into tactical mode. I want to know who these guys are and how this connects, if it does, to the Internet attack. Oh, I forgot. Does anyone object to Force Ten taking this on?" He looked around the room. "Good."

* * *

WITH NOTHING MORE TO DO right then in Ops, Marcus went to find Bodie. Other than a brief, "You good?" at the hospital, they had not spoken about anything but Garrett.

Walking down the hill from the barn, Marcus saw his older son by the river, throwing rocks. As Marcus approached, Bodie glanced over his shoulder and let the rock drop from his hand. Marcus walked up and stood beside him. "Hey, you all right?"

Bodie stared into the dark, swirling water. "Yeah, I guess." He turned toward his dad. "I thought it would make me feel...you know, better. Like somehow it was payback for Mom."

Marcus placed a hand on his son's shoulder. "Yeah, but you've got to admit, in the moment it felt pretty damn good."

Bodie slapped his arm away and took a step toward the river. Marcus stayed put. He knew the struggle going on inside his son.

When Bodie turned back, tears were welling in his eyes, and his upper lip quivered. "That's the problem: it felt good. *Too* good. I was so mad, and worried about Garrett, all I wanted was to kill." He took a step closer to his dad. "What does that say about me?"

Marcus wanted to tell Bodie everything would all right, but that would have been a lie, and he had promised his sons he would never do that to them.

Tears streamed down the boy's cheeks. "We've done okay, right? I mean you, me, and Garrett—Mom would be proud, wouldn't she?"

"Oh God, Bodie." Marcus stepped up to his son and pulled him into his arms. "Of course, she's proud."

Sobbing now Bodie said, "I miss her so much!"

Marcus hugged him tightly. Unable to hold back his tears, he choked out, "I know, buddy. Me too." And for the first time since Annie's death, father and son truly grieved.

* * *

ON THE PATIO OF THE main house, Chaya and Garrett watched as Marcus walked up to Bodie. When Marcus embraced the boy, Chaya started to walk down to them, but Garrett grabbed her hand.

"Leave them."

She looked down at the nine-year-old boy who had just been buried alive. Yet he showed no signs, physical or emotional.

"They have to do things like this. Mom says it's because they're so much alike."

Chaya knelt and brushed her finger through Garrett's wave of light-brown hair. "How is it that you watch over them?"

"It's my job."

Chaya tilted her head.

"We each have our jobs. Dad's is to make sure Bodie and I are okay and that we pull our own weight. Bodie's is to give Dad a bad time." Garrett chuckled. "And me, I'm the glue that holds us together." Sadness clouded his face. "That used to be my mom's job, and I was her helper. Maybe you . . ."

As hard as she tried, Chaya couldn't keep the tears from her eyes as she hugged Garrett. "I would *love* to be your helper."

CHAPTER SEVENTEEN

National Microbiology Laboratory, Winnipeg, Manitoba

ADRIANA SAT IN THE OFFICE of the director of the NML. Holding a wad of tissues, she dabbed at her eyes, sniffled, then blew her nose. Dr. Loren gave her a moment.

"I know how difficult this must be, Adriana. We are all shocked, none more than you."

Although Adriana and Dameer had been discreet about their relationship, their close colleagues knew.

"The police say it appears to be an erotic asphyxiation gone wrong. Did you have any idea?"

Adriana sobbed and buried her face in her hands. "No-o-o. We never..."

"There, there, Adriana. I understand. It seems quite the party had been going on, alcohol, and possibly drugs. The authorities are going through Dameer's personal laptop to see what it may tell them."

After Dameer stopped convulsing, Adriana put all the evidence she had collected back on the coffee table and dresser top. She removed and packed her HAZMAT suit. Put on her disguise and left.

"I know how hard you and Dameer have worked. I have spoken with human resources and we feel you should take some time away."

Adriana looked up, her eyes bloodshot and her nose running.

"No, no, Adriana. This is not punishment. Quite the contrary."

Adriana made a show of composing herself. "I think I would like to go home. It's been a long time. Perhaps I could go and work in a clinic for a month or so."

The NML had an active presence in Africa. Most recently helping to contain the Ebola outbreaks. Beyond that Dr. Loren served on several non-governmental organization (NGO) advisory boards, helping to formulate long-range management strategies for preventing deadly outbreaks of any number of diseases that plagued Africa and other impoverished parts of the world.

Dr. Loren leaned back in his chair, his hands clasped in his lap, and smiled. "Yes, that's a splendid idea, and I have just the connection. The African Medical and Research Foundation (AMERF), an organization we provide support to, has a clinic in Loliondo where you grew up. It so happens we have a shipment leaving tomorrow for Cape Town. I take it your passport is in order?"

"Yes, it is." Adriana said, hoping her pretend relief sounded sincere.

"Good. Then I will get the paper work in order. You contact your family and let them know you are coming."

Adriana rose to leave. Before she turned, Dr. Loren said, "I'm so sorry Adriana. But we will overcome this. I want you take whatever time you need, and come back renewed."

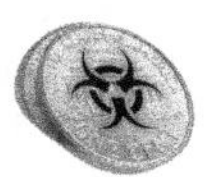

CHAPTER EIGHTEEN

December 2, Beginnings Ranch, British Columbia

COLONEL WEBB ARRIVED AT OPS early. He knew J. T. would already be there. The guy only slept three or four hours a night, and as far as the colonel knew he did that sleeping in Ops. J. T.'s ability to collect, sort through, and collate data was unequaled. It helped for the colonel to go through a review with him before he discussed an action plan with the full team. It always amazed the colonel how well they worked together, mostly because the guy was the least military person in the bunch, including Marcus. But they had clicked since day -one, over ten years ago.

J. T. spoke. "Like I said yesterday, I'm sure an electromagnetic pulse caused the Internet crash. My problem is, there are dozens of companies that produce some version of an EMP generator. Hell, you can download step-by-step video instructions from the Web showing exactly how to do it. Although not today, and maybe not for the next several weeks."

"What does that mean?" asked the colonel.

Live news feeds showed the continued chaos, especially in big cities.

"No one figured on just how dependent people are on the Internet. It's like a drought."

The colonel furrowed his brow.

"You know how, when there is an extended drought, and it's compared to dry periods in the past?"

"Get to the point."

"The point is, you can't compare a five-year drought that happened ten years ago to one that's happening now, because the demand on the resources is so much greater today. With the Internet, the demand increases exponentially, not year to year but day to day. The simple fact is the redundant systems can't keep up."

J. T. raised the volume as a newscaster reported regional power grid failures in parts of the northeast and upper Midwest. A cold fall had hit both regions and even parts of Canada were being impacted by the outages. Nationwide, trains, subways, and bus systems that relied on digital signal automation for operation and routing were either shut down or working in a very limited capacity. The worst of the collateral damage was the traffic. The footage showed city streets and highways clogged with abandoned cars. Nothing could move and that meant essential supplies, like water, food, and medicine couldn't be delivered, even if the ransacked stores could have opened for business.

"Jesus, how long before things come back online?"

"It's happening as we speak, but it will take a few weeks, at least, before we see it begin to trickle down to the everyday family. Until then, the animals are out of the zoo. I hacked the Pentagon and CIA databases in search of potential suspects." J. T. said it nonchalantly. "Just about every country on the planet is exploring EMP technology, including more than a few nut jobs, like North Korea, Yemen, and Chechnya.

"I've also torn into the companies with offices in the three locations. Many big tech and finance companies, as well as lots of businesses heavily into R and D, like pharmaceutical conglomerates, have a presence in each location, not to mention several other offices in the United States and around the world. Thousands of companies utilize the servers in these three locations, but so far I haven't managed to narrow it down much."

"What about the FBI? What do they know?"

J. T. pointed at the screens. "They've pretty much got their hands full just keeping the peace. Right now it's nearly impossible to execute a comprehensive physical investigation." J. T. played with his pad and showed the colonel satellite views of the three Internet hub locations.

"Just look. Not the FBI or any other law enforcement agency is getting safely through that mess. Not for a while. Guess I'm not getting there either."

"All right, we need to look at the attack on the Internet and the attack here on the ranch as two separate events. It seems the Internet thing is going to have to play out a bit before we can start to deconstruct it, so let's focus on the ranch attack. We need answers. First and foremost, who the fuck are these guys, and who sent them? And how in the hell did they track the boys?" The colonel glared at J. T. as if any seemingly impossible tracking technology had to be something he knew about.

"Hey, I'm not the only really smart person on the planet. There are one, maybe two others."

The colonel let it pass. He'd poked the bear, and knew J. T. wouldn't rest until he had the answer. "We know that the *Takbir* drew a fair bit of attention while in Vladivostok. After all, we spent . . ." He paused, waiting for J. T.

"A billion, give or take."

The colonel turned and stared in amazement as J. T dropped his scrawny body into one of the console chairs.

"The weapons systems we bought are as sophisticated as they get, and that means expensive. Besides, since they're illegal, we couldn't have laid our hands on them anywhere else. Russia's black market is the best when it comes to military munitions."

"So tell me, is there a Russian or any group of Russians that we've pissed off?"

J. T.'s fingers moved over the touch screen. The image of a man, with short hair, and a square Slavic face shaded with black stubble started at them. He looked to be in his mid-to-late- forties. He stood on a dock surrounded by expensive yachts. Wearing a white polo shirt, the man had his head slightly turned toward an attractive brunette as if in conversation. A rich couple on holiday?

"Yakov Anatoly Dementyev," J. T. said. "One of the 'new Russia's' oligarchs and one of the very few people on this planet with as much money as us."

"So how does Yakov play into this?" the colonel asked.

* * *

GLEN DIABLO, MARCUS'S BOTHER AND best friend, sat at the counter along the back wall of Ops. He'd come in unnoticed while the colonel and J. T. prepared for the morning team meeting. The attack on the ranch had upset and scared him, and not just because of Bodie and Garrett. The Diablo clan, twenty-seven strong, all called Beginnings home. A tough, opinionated bunch, they went about family matters a lot like Force 10 went about a mission. Each of his brothers and sisters and their respective wives and husbands, as well as their children, each brought a special talent to the family table when it came to dealing with a problem or issue. They deferred to each other, and more often than not they came up with a plan that served the greatest good. For Glen, getting back to what he knew was the best way for him to contribute, especially when his anger threatened to get the best of his common sense.

For Glen, his wife Ellie and their two children, Renée and Charlie, the last sixteen months had been—terrible and—incredible. When Annie went missing, Glen and his family lived in Sydney, Australia, where he ran the Pacific Rim division of the world's largest gaming machine manufacture. Of course, they came home to be with Marcus and the boys. And who would have thought that Annie's disappearance was just the beginning of a much larger attack on the United States, and that they would find themselves stranded.

But the horror and the craziness didn't stop there. After the world watched Annie's murder, Marcus somehow convinced the FBI to send him, the boys, and Glen and his family back to Sydney. Glen hoped new surroundings would help them all grieve and heal. But how could Glen have known that Marcus had an ulterior motive. And that motive, Colonel Samuel Webb, stood in Ops right now talking to the smartest man Glen had ever met. It had been Marcus's idea to bring him in to help J. T. manage a sum of money fast approaching a trillion dollars.

Glen recognized immediately that although J. T. had an inflated view of his own importance, he could deliver. For his part, Glen was equally accomplished, but whereas J. T. was a tornado of unrestrained thought, Glen had made his living and reputation taking the J. T. wannabes of the world and getting them to be vital and effective parts of a much bigger team.

In front of Glen, a series of monitors displayed world stock exchange and currency markets. The Internet attack had led the U. S. to suspend all trading at the New Stock Exchange, but the world's other markets hadn't followed suit.

It still blew Glen away that they had their own *satellite.* It did give him and J. T. real-time access to any financial, currency, commodity, or futures market in the world. But beyond that, Force 10 had, at its disposal, a surveillance and intelligence-gathering tool that was better, according to J. T., than that of any country in the world, including the United States.

After the Internet crash, J. T. hacked into the Secret Internet Protocol Router Network (SIPRNet). Although, far from secret, just ask the Army private serving thirty-five years in Leavenworth; it still worked. With more money than some small and some not so small countries, it required daily tending. The task should have required a team of financial analysts, accountants, and lawyers, but between the two of them and the most sophisticated information and analytic network in the world, they were doing all right.

Over his shoulder Glen saw the silhouettes of the colonel and J. T. against the light coming from the monitor wall where there was a picture of Yakov Anatoly Dementyev. Then he heard the colonel ask J. T., "So how does Yakov play into this?"

* * *

"Well . . . ," said a voice from the back of the room.

Glen walked toward the monitor wall. From the day they decided that the Force 10 Ops center should double as the financial hub for managing the resources at Marcus' and Force 10's disposal, there had been an implicit understanding that because of Glen's integral knowledge and expertise in dealing with billions in cash and assets, there might arise a situation where he would be in Ops at the same time Force 10 was working on a mission.

Glen had the floor. "As we sorted through the assets Force Ten appropriated from the al-Mohmoud family, we came across billions invested in Russia and throughout the former Soviet republics. You name it: oil and gas, timber, mining, precious gems, shipbuilding—and that's just the tip of the iceberg. Anyway," he said, cocking his chin at the giant picture, "it seems that our friend, Yakov Anatoly Dementyev, and Adad were business partners, in a very big way. As we dug, we discovered—big surprise—that Yakov does not feel especially bound by national or international law.

"Over the past several months we have been distancing our money from Yakov. We even orchestrated hostile takeovers of a few of the companies. I could see where we might have become a royal pain in his . . ."

Glen paused, looked at the colonel...and blanched. "Oh, Jesus, did I cause this? Is it my fault those men came to the ranch?"

The colonel considered his response. "We all knew what we were getting into—us certainly more so than you. No, not your fault. If they hadn't come now, it would've been tomorrow, next month, next year. Besides, we're not doing business with people who pursue personal gain at any cost. It's a fine line to walk, and I trust that I can count on you to make sure we keep to that line. And besides," he said, smiling, "when I need to cross over to the dark side, when walking the 'fine line' just isn't cutting it, I've got your brother. Now, you were saying?"

Glen went on using his pad to post information. "One of the

companies we found ourselves heavily invested in was Wide World Employment." The company logo and its headquarters in Moscow were on the screen next to Yaakov's picture. "On its face, it's an employment agency specializing in placing trained professionals and tradesmen for Russian companies doing business all over the world. But when you peel back the layers, you start to find other things."

J. T. took over. "Human trafficking on a scale that is unbelievable: child labor, from sewing to sex. Men, women, and children literally sold into slavery. We're talking over a hundred thousand victims a year. The system is complicated and decentralized. It took some serious work to trace it back to Mr. Dementyev."

The baton went back to Glen, seamlessly, as if the two of them had been doing this for years. "We've been systematically selling off our interest in Wide World Employment." Glen looked to J. T.

"While at the same time anonymously notifying law enforcement agencies all over the world. Over the past eight weeks there have been hundreds of arrests, offices closed, and assets seized." Pictures began to pop up on the monitor. "Throughout Eastern and Western Europe, Canada, and the United States, including over a dozen major seizures in Russia," J. T. finished.

"Good," the colonel said. "Let's focus on Yakov. Pete will have IDs on the men who attacked the ranch soon. Then we'll see what the connections are."

"I'll delve deeper into Yakov's finances," Glen said as he headed back to his desk.

"I'll get with Pete and dig into the guys who attacked us," said J. T.

The colonel considered the two men: one near his own age, conservative and introspective—exactly the opposite of his brother—and the other an egotistical renegade, in many ways just like Marcus. It could be that, in Glen, he had finally found the right hand to help him keep the brains behind Force 10 focused and on task.

CHAPTER NINETEEN

When Marcus entered Ops, he saw everyone else already there. Since his arrival at the ranch this was the first time the entire Force 10 team was in the same place. Weathers and Liam had arrived late last night aboard the *Takbir* into the Port Metro, Vancouver, BC. The colonel had reached out to contacts in the Royal Canadian Navy, and a contingent of Maritime sailors had been assigned to keep watch on the ship.

Hamal Kamal—Ham— arrived from Saudi Arabia, a few hours behind them at the Kitsap Naval Base on the Kitsap Peninsula, northwest of Seattle. As the only Arab-American member of Force 10, he'd been assigned the task of handling the transition to a new protective detail for the royal Saudi family. Ham looked and spoke the part of a native, making him ideal for the job. During the mission to find Adad al-Mohmoud, Force 10 had ruffled more than a few feathers in the Middle East. Consequently, for Force 10's only client other than the U. S. military, the House of Saud, providing adequate and focused security services had become untenable. Due to the colonel's personal relationship with the royal family, he agreed to help find a suitable replacement and oversee the transition. The colonel built and maintained, but never burned bridges.

Bronson flew the Gulf Stream 5, Force 10 kept in a hangar at the ranch, that picked them up. Even though they had only been at the ranch a couple of hours they looked fresh and ready to go to work.

For the last forty-eight hours there had been much debate and plenty of finger-pointing, especially among Marcus's family, about the incident with Bodie and Garrett at the line cabin. Most of it concerned how Bodie should never have been allowed, let alone helped, to kill another human being. But Pete had interrogated the lone survivor. When he confirmed that the boys had definitely been the targets, everyone took a step back.

Pete had the floor, which seemed unusual.

"I find high altitude parachute gear there," he pointed at the monitor wall. A drone camera showed a clearing a few miles north of the big meadow. "These guys experienced. Jump at night, from twenty thousand feet, maybe more."

Marcus watched the team. From the looks on their faces, Pete's participation surprised them.

"Also find camping gear. Enough supplies for a few days. Plan was to wait for boys to go to cabin. Show men, J. T."

J. T. stared at Pete.

"Earth to J. T," said the colonel.

"Sorry."

At the top of the monitor wall appeared a big picture of Yakov Anatoly Dementyev, and beneath it photos of the five men who had attacked the ranch.

Marcus studied the pictures of the men who had tried to kill his boys as he listened to J. T.

"All five have dual citizenships: Canadian, and either Russian or Ukrainian. Two are brothers from Toronto. They are the ones who blew up The Hide. The others are from Alberta, Saskatchewan, and Vancouver respectively. The one from Alberta is the one Pete interrogated. They are between the ages of 37 and 42, and, like Pete said, they all have extensive Russian military special-forces backgrounds. They've been living in Canada for five-to-ten years. Seems they all immigrated around the age of 32. All of them are businessmen. They own restaurants, bars, strip clubs, laundromats, payday loan operations, and construction companies. Pete just got the names an hour ago. We'll know more about them soon."

"Okay," said the colonel. "What do we have on the Internet attack?"

"Still not much." J. T. brought the team up to speed on his EMP generator theory. "We are seeing some regional power outages, one in Minnesota yesterday that effected parts of south central Canada. Lasted a couple of hours. It's got the energy providers with nuclear reactor plants more than a little nervous. In fact, some companies are taking a number of their facilities off line.

"The big cell phone providers are also experiencing widespread systems failures. But the worst is, people are plain freaked out. Anybody in a uniform, law enforcement or not, is in real danger. The FBI did get teams into the New York City and Seattle locations. LA could take a few more days."

"All right. We are in full mission mode and will meet every

morning. Make sure your coms are charged and with you at all times.

As the team left Ops the colonel stared at the pictures. Usually when they tracked down terrorists it was your classic follow the breadcrumbs. But so far they couldn't find any connection between the attacks on the ranch and the Internet, and although the Internet being shut down was wreaking havoc, nothing else had happened. That had him worried.

* * *

THE COLONEL SPENT ANOTHER HOUR going over the information they knew. When he left, J. T. and Glen had financial information all over the wall. The money they managed never took a day off and had no concern about the Internet.

As J. T. worked on the latest acquisition—a gold-mining operation in Peru—Glen came and stood next to him.

"Over the next few days you might need to take over most of the money stuff."

Glen looked at the dorky little man. Only someone with an IQ north of 160 would refer to over one hundred billion in cash, forget the hundreds of billions in assets, as "money stuff."

"No problem."

"I've programmed your voice into Vanessa, so just ask her and, she'll…you know… tell you things."

"Fine, as long as you are the only one she's attracted to."

J. T. gave Glen an offended stare. "If you haven't noticed, the ratio of women to men is a bit on the thin side up here in the wilderness."

"What about…?'

"Cows and sheep don't count."

"Well, not yet anyway."

"You know, you sound just like him."

Glen cocked his head at J. T.

"Him…as in your brother. That's a comment I'd expect from him."

Glen put his hand on J. T.'s shoulder. "Listen, calm down. I'll make you a deal. Soon as things settle down, why don't I help you plan a vacation? A place where you might find some kindred spirits."

J. T. didn't respond but did what he always did when he felt out of his element, changed the subject. "Marcus ever tell you how we came to control God's Eye?"

Glen shook his head.

"Dude, he was surfing the conspiracy blogs. I mean, this is where fat guys with poor hygiene who live in their mom's basements spend their time. These nuts see shadows around every corner and boogeymen under every bed. Anyway, he starts connecting the dots, like only he can do." J. T. glanced at Glen.

Glen gave him his *Ya think?* look.

"Long story short, your brother pitches this crazy notion to the colonel. He figured that if the Cheeto-eating, Red Bull drinking kooks were right and such a satellite did exist, and it was being financed by the world's wealthiest Islamic families, a guy like Adad al - Mohmoud would have a piece of it. So I do some poking around, and sure as shit, Marcus was spot-on about all of it, and then some."

There was a definite tone of respect in J. T.'s telling and Glen knew that when it came to imagination, J. T. and Marcus were wired the same way: more than a little tweaked.

"Can I ask you something?" J. T. said. "Why is it Marcus never asks about the money? I mean, it seems like he doesn't care."

Glen shifted his attention away from the currency-market information displayed on one-third of the monitor wall. "It's not that he doesn't care. It just that he's not equipped to deal with it."

"But how does he know we're doing . . . you know, a good job?"

"You've got to be kidding me, Mister I-can-do-what-a whole-team-of-financial-gurus-can-do, and still find time for a whole bunch of spy shit. Okay, let me give you a little insight. You see, for him, it's about trust. When there's something he can't do or something he's not good at, he finds someone who is. But here's where he's different from most people I've known: once that task is handed off, he doesn't think about it again. But *someone* does—like you and me—and he knows that.

"Someday, he's going ask you if you've done something. He'll ask in a way that implies the two of you have talked about it, even though you haven't. And the weirdest part will be, you will have done it. And at that moment, you'll understand."

Glen went back to his tablet but continued talking. "There's not a weapon Force Ten has at its disposal that is as powerful or dangerous as this money, and Marcus knows that too. From that moment on the *Takbir,* over a year ago, when he had us divide the eight hundred billion into halves, he gave the responsibility to us"— Glen swung his finger first at J. T., then at himself—"and unless we're flat broke, he doesn't want to know."

CHAPTER TWENTY

THE COLONEL STEPPED OUT OF the barn and headed down the hill toward the main house. As he thought about Norma and a hot cup of coffee with a slice of apple pie, Marcus entered the maintenance barn. The colonel followed him into the large steel maintenance building where tractors and other equipment stood in various states of repair. Marcus leaned against the wall at the open door to a room in the back of the building.

The room had once been for spare-parts but now served as Pete's gym, with heavy bags, weights, and pads—lots of pads—on the floor and walls. Pete trained the team in hand-to-hand combat. He made sure every member of the team grew ever more proficient in close-quarters defense and attack skills. An expert tactician with blades, garrotes, sticks, staffs, and bare hands, combined with a lack of English language skills, which made him nearly impossible to argue with—he did the job to perfection.

As the colonel approached, Marcus pointed into the room. Pete stood in the center of the padded floor with Bodie and Garrett on either side of him, each holding a wooden knife. With his hands outstretched, palms up, Pete beckoned them to approach.

* * *

MARCUS OBSERVED THAT THE BOYS held their knives properly, in an underhand grip with the sharp edge turned up—not the way he had held the knife the first time Pete took him through this drill.

The boys circled Pete, feinting and backing off. Small and fast—another advantage they had over their dad.

"You play, but this is not game," Pete said, eyes locked on his "attackers." "You think you take me? Okay. Show me."

As the boys closed in, Pete moved so fast and with such fluidity that Marcus couldn't quite decipher it. Pete had the boys pinned to the mat, Garrett on top of Bodie, and Pete astraddle both of them. With their wooden knives in his hand Pete grinned. Marcus couldn't recall a time he had ever seen the man smile.

Marcus shook his head and whispered, "You think this is a good idea? I mean . . ."

The colonel placed his hand on Marcus's shoulder and moved him back from the doorway and out into the middle of the barn. "Didn't you just say that this is their life now and they need to be prepared? You do know they've been working with him for months, right?"

Marcus stared openmouthed.

The colonel shook his head. "For a guy who can be so perceptive, I'm coming to find out there are some things you have no clue about."

Marcus took a deep breath. He felt overwhelmed and hopelessly at sea on how to address what his sons had just been through.

"If you and the boys were in the mountains and something happened—say, an avalanche —and everybody reacted exactly as they were supposed to, and everybody came through it physically fine, would that be the last time you ever went into mountains?"

Marcus thought a moment. "As soon as we could—right then, if possible, but certainly the very next time we were there—I'd take them right to the spot where the avalanche let go."

"Why?"

Marcus looked at the colonel and laughed. "Thanks, Sam."

The colonel turned out of the barn.

Marcus followed. "Of everybody on the team, I've been able to figure out at least part of their stories, but not really anything about Pete. So tell me, what's his deal?"

"If you want to hear that, after the day we've had, I'm gonna need a drink."

* * *

MARCUS SAT IN ONE OF the leather-covered chairs that faced the stone fireplace in the colonel's cabin, one of six near the river.

The colonel came from the kitchen holding two-pint Mason jars in one hand and a bottle of Tennessee sour mash in the other. He set them on the table between the two chairs. "You pour." He walked to the bookshelf just left of the fireplace. Returning, he handed Marcus a book, picked up his glass, and sat in the other chair.

"Page sixty-eight."

Marcus thumbed to the page. He was looking at a series of pictures of round glazed terra-cotta reliefs of swaddled babies, mounted in a row along the top of a wall in what looked like a very old building.

"Some call them 'the ten bambini.' They're on the wall of the *Hospital of the Innocents* in Florence. It was built in the early 1400s as a home for abandoned children. Anyway, there's been a lot of debate about the bambini—what they mean, and all. Look at the seventh one from the left. See how it's the only one with unwrapped feet?" The colonel took a sip of his drink.

"Yeah." Marcus wondered what this had to do with Pete.

Leaving the book open on his lap, Marcus picked up his glass, took a sip, and gave the colonel his attention.

"Among the black-ops crowd, there have always been rumors about assassins, men who have never been seen or photographed. Mostly fiction, or so I thought. Anyway, for as long as I've been doing this, there've been these stories about a group of Russian assassins." The colonel rose, picked up a log from the hearth, and put it the fireplace. Standing with his back to the flames, he went on. "As the tale goes, the Russians went about finding and training these assassins just like they did with gymnasts, ballet dancers, and chess players. They created a profile and developed a series of tests, then went out into the countryside in search of very young children who would become the next gold medalist, prima ballerina, grand master, or, if you believe the legend, the next ghost assassin."

The colonel threw another log on the fire and returned to his seat. "Those pictures of the swaddled babies, they are symbols of abandonment."

"The Russians call it *otkazyvat'sya,*" Marcus said, surprising himself.

"Good to see you haven't lost your talent. Now where was I? Oh, yeah, symbols of abandonment. Supposedly, this group, which was mostly men—although I'm certain now that there are some women—each wore the mark of the abandonment as a tattoo on some inconspicuous place on their body. To be honest, I never gave the story much credence—that is, until I was in the Chechen capital, Grozny, in 2000. Sit might have told you some of this.

"We had to come up with a plausible cover story just to be there. The whole situation was a mess—a thousand times worse than what's going in Crimea and Ukraine, at least so far. As you might imagine, it's pretty hard to take Sit along and not have him draw some attention. So we decided to make him the centerpiece of our little visit. We went in on the pretext that Sit was an up-and-coming, albeit unknown, super-heavyweight, and we were looking for bouts. Some of the best superheavies come out of that part of the world, and besides, the Russians love a good ass-whup, even more so if they can beat up on an American. A *black* American is just frosting on the cake."

The colonel paused and rattled the ice cubes around his empty glass. "We'd been in country a couple of weeks. Our real purpose was to monitor the Russian response to the Chechen uprising—not to interfere, just to observe. Things were escalating by the day, and even though the country was coming apart at the seams, we still managed to get Sit a few bouts." The colonel raised his glass in a mock toast. "The big man throws a left hook that'd kill a steer. You don't grow up the way Sit did, with that kind of size, and not have every bad-ass on the block wanting to take a shot at you.

"By February first, we knew our days in country were numbered, and on the fifth, the Ichkerian regime, which controlled Chechnya, fell. We were right in the middle of downtown Grozny when the shelling started and the tanks came rolling in. We had a two-hour window to get our asses out. On foot. We had to get to a prearranged exit point where we would hitch a ride out via a Red Cross supply convoy. As we were making our way through streets full of panicked people, the air choked with smoke, Sit notices this pair of boots sticking out from a pile of rubble. He moves the debris, and there, unconscious, is this young man in a Russian military uniform. Other than a nasty head gash, he looked pretty good, except that his shirt was almost completely torn off. I knelt down to check for a pulse, and when I lifted his arm, that's when I saw it."

The colonel stopped talking, reached for the bottle of whiskey. He refreshed his glass, then Marcus's, then leaned back and stared into the fire.

After a few moments, Marcus said, "Saw it?"

The colonel motioned with his head to the book still in Marcus's lap. "It—the bambino, the one with bare feet. It was a tattoo, crude and faded, under his arm, almost in the armpit. I made an on-the-spot decision to take him with us. Sit picked him up, and we made our rendezvous.

"We kept him sedated. Three days later, when he woke up in Landstuhl Medical Center in Germany, and someone explained—in

Russian, of course—what had happened and who I was. All he said when we met was, 'I work you now.' It's been almost fifteen years, and Pete and I have never discussed that day.

"So here's his deal: if you were to ask me which member of this team has been most affected by you and your boys, I would say it's him. And that's saying a lot, considering that you have managed to have a damned profound effect on everyone. So if something were ever to happen and you had to pick someone to watch over the boys, pick him."

CHAPTER TWENTY-ONE

December 3, Loliondo, Tanzania

IT TOOK ADRIANA LEHRER NEARLY a full day to get to Cape Town, South Africa. Dr. Loren had arranged a position for her with the African Medical and Research Foundation. She had no time to take in the city that was to have been her family's refuge twenty-one years ago. And it would have been had they been ready to leave their farm a few hours earlier.

No sooner had she been processed through customs when she boarded an AMREF-chartered plane to Loliondo. The flight was over 1700 kilometers and would require two refueling stops. The second stop, at the Eastgate Airport in Hoedspruit, put her only an hour's drive from what used to be the Lehrer farm, in Limpopo Province. She convinced the pilot to give her a few hours so she could take care of a personal matter. She hadn't been back to her childhood home since the day Dr. Koch found her hiding, terrified, in her fort. As she drove in a hired car, an unfamiliar sense of uncertainty and trepidation fell upon her.

* * *

ADRIANA PULLED ASIDE THE ACACIA branches and peered inside. The rough canvas tarp that once served as a door was long gone. She crawled in and sat on the dirt floor. The fort was so much smaller than she remembered. She peered through a gap in the old piano crate slats her father had used to make walls. In her mind she could still see the eyes of the men who attacked and murdered her family—eyes filled with raw hatred.

Coming out of the fort, Adriana looked around. This farm had been so alive and vibrant! She remembered standing with her father and watching as a soft breeze blew through the maize, making it sway like ripples on a green sea. Now the once-lush fields stood bare, nothing but sere, brown bushveld. She walked up the broken and rotting wood steps to the front porch of her girlhood home—it too tumbledown and neglected.

Adriana paused at the door-less front entrance. She hadn't set foot in this house since that terrible day, when through the same crack in the fort's slat wall she had moments before looked through, she had watched her family murdered. Her father was killed in the driveway, her bother on the porch, and her mother inside the house. But not before . . .

She stepped through the doorway into what had been the parlor, with the staircase to her right, the dining room on the left. When she lived here, this home had been filled with antique furniture, lace curtains, the aroma of the next meal, and love. Now it was an empty shell. The paint and wallpaper faded to a mold-colored gray. Frayed wires stuck out where light fixtures had hung, and the once polished wood floors lay splintered and buckled. She stopped and stared into the dining room and imagined the long wooden table where they ate every day. It was on that very table that her mother had been repeatedly raped and then killed.

As Adriana walked out of the house, even though the day was warming up, a cold shiver ran through her, leaving goose bumps on her bare arms. Her father had insisted that she and her brother Hans be tough. He made sure they understood the life of a farmer, especially the life of an Afrikaner farmer. And over the ten years she had lived with Dr. Koch out on the East African savannah, working as his assistant, moving from camp to camp, that toughness had been reinforced and had become as much a part of who she was as the air she breathed. She had learned to be dispassionate about death, often seeing it as a means to a greater end.

* * *

THE SINGLE-PROP PLANE SET down on the packed dirt airstrip, kicking up a trail of dust. As the plane taxied Adriana saw a small crowd gathered outside one of the mud-brick buildings, among them Dr. Koch standing next to Mama Bulala. They made quite the pair: he in his khaki shorts and shirt with worn leather chukka boots, she in a colorful sarong tied behind her neck, with a matching head scarf and bare feet. Not to mention he was white and barely sixty kilos, while she was ebony black, six feet tall, and twice his mass.

Stepping down from the plane with her backpack slung over her shoulder, she smiled at the two most important people in her world. She had made only two trips home in the past ten years, the last five years ago, just after graduating college. Oh, they'd talked occasionally, but mostly they wrote letters to each other—"the lost art," they joked. Dropping her pack, Adriana stood in front of Dr. Koch and lightly touched his hand. He had gotten older and although a man of slight build, he still had the look of a rough-and-ready bush guide. He also had the not unpleasant man smell of hard work and dirt that always reminded her of her father.

She turned to Mama Bulala, who stood with her hands resting on her ample hips. The black woman, with a wry smile, spread her arms wide. "Now, child, it is about time you come home."

Stepping into her embrace, Adriana was transported back twenty years, when, as a frightened little girl, she had found these warm arms, with the sweet smell of curry and spiced yams, the safest, most comforting place in all the world. Although she had promised herself she wouldn't cry, the tears came, and for the first time in as long as she could remember, she felt . . . vulnerable.

* * *

ADRIANA STOWED HER PERSONAL GEAR in the hut she and Dr. Koch had first moved into so long ago. Only one room then, now it had a separate bedroom, a proper bathroom, and an adequate, though basic, kitchen. Loliondo had changed a lot, but especially since 2011, when a retired Lutheran pastor claimed he had a miracle cure for everything from HIV/AIDS to cancer. Since then, hundreds of thousands of sick people from across East Africa and beyond had been flocking to Loliondo to drink a cup of Babu wa Loliondo's magic concoction.

Dr. Koch came in with one of the boxes of medical supplies. As he made room in the refrigerator he said, "Not really that different from when you were last here. Just a bit a larger."

Adriana began to speak, to apologize for not having visited more often, but before she could get the words out, the doctor stopped her.

"No need, Adie. We do what must be done, yes? You have accomplished much, and . . . well, you know I'm not a sentimental man, but I am glad to see you again."

He nodded at the file folder on the kitchen table. "I think you will find the information interesting."

She looked into the eyes of the man who, when she first came to live with him, she had known so little about, other than that he was a lifelong friend of her father's. He had found her terrified, in the fort the day after her family was murdered. He loaded her into his Land Rover, while the bodies of her parents and brother lay in the back under a bloody tarp. He had ordered her to close her eyes, and not open them tell he said to. Thinking back, it didn't seem like she'd waited that long. And when she did open her eyes, only their gear was in the back of the Rover. Then they had left the place where she was born and raised, traveled by day and camped by night, nearly three thousand kilometers, and her new life began. They never talked about what had happened. Stepping forward, she embraced the man she had come to love and know as a father.

She pulled back, picked up the file, and slapped the stiff cardboard twice against her left palm. "It's time to cull an elephant herd."

CHAPTER TWENTY-TWO

December 4

As the sun came up, Adriana stepped out into the yard. Where once just a few dozen mud-and-wattle huts stood, now shelters cobbled together from old cardboard and scraps of rusted corrugated metal, all amidst a sea of cheap nylon tents in an array of sun-bleached colors littered the landscape. Open trenches, filled with raw sewage, completed the sensory shock.

"It looks the same?"

Startled at first, Adriana relaxed as Mama Bulala fell into step with her.

Seeing the look of disbelief on Adriana's face, Mama Bulala said, "Yes, I know, child. Ever since the grandfather of Loliondo, Babu wa, came with his miracle drink . . ." Scowling, Mama Bulala waved her arm about. "Since he arrived it has been like this. And it is getting worse. It is why the AMREF decided to open a clinic here. The sick and dying, they come by the thousands. There are days when automobiles are backed up for fifteen or twenty kilometers."

The two women walked around the newly whitewashed school, where, on the backside, another rectangular building had been added. At the door to the AMREF administrative office, Mama Bulala paused. "I do not know what we are to do, child, but perhaps this is why you have returned."

* * *

"We must be constantly aware," the director of AMREF's Loliondo clinic, Kathryn van der Hoch, said. "Never put yourself in a situation where you are alone. Make sure you work in teams, and always try to have at least one of the guards with you."

Kathryn slid a small stack of papers across the desk. "I need you to sign and date these forms, and we can get you started."

Adriana pretended to read the disclaimers that would relieve the African Medical and Research Foundation of any liability should she get kidnapped, raped, murdered or catch a deadly disease. "I didn't realize you had a terrorism problem here," she said without looking up.

"Well—this is not common knowledge, and AMREF and the government of Tanzania will deny it—but . . ." Her voice lowered. ". . . there are rumors of groups affiliated with Boko Haram. Although Nigeria is nearly five thousand kilometers away, the sentiment that life should be lived according to the strictest interpretation of sharia law exists here as well. There is a man, Kgosi Egwu."

Sliding the signed papers back to Kathryn, Adriana casually asked, "*Who is that?*"

Checking the forms, Kathryn replied, "He was once an enforcer for the ANC, the African National Congress, back in the early 1990s. For the last five years, he has been providing security to groups of investors looking for opportunities in this part of East Africa—Tanzania, Kenya, Uganda, and Congo. Many of these investors are from the Middle East and Asia. I'm told many of his clients are Muslim—as is much of Africa."

Kathryn stood. "Come. I'll show you around and introduce you to the staff."

* * *

BECAUSE OF HER LAB EXPERIENCE and her "sharps" skills, Adriana was assigned to one of the groups that dressed wounds and provided injected antibiotics and vaccinations. With an endless queue of sick, supervision was cursory at best.

People traveled hundreds, sometimes thousands, of kilometers to get here. At first, it was for a drink of Babu wu Loliondo's twenty-five-cents-a-cup magic juice, but when that didn't work, they turned to real medicine. Kathryn told Adriana that at any given time, at least thirty thousand people were queued up for the "cure." *That's a lot of quarters,* Adriana thought.

CHAPTER TWENTY-THREE

December 4, Mexico City

AT NINE IN THE MORNING the front gate buzzed. Peter sat at the kitchen counter reading *El universal,* Mexico's leading daily broadsheet newspaper. He laid the paper aside. That had to be Adriana. He had been anticipating—and dreading—this meeting. Part of him, the part that was lust and sin, hungered for her. He had even broken his rule and left her a voice message. But the other part, which was faithful and obedient to God, prayed that he would have the strength to do what must be done once this, their last time together, ended.

Peter had dismissed the staff for the next two days. He wanted Adriana all to himself. She had a natural healthy beauty and a confidence in her intellect and sexuality that set her apart from all the other women he had ever known. It wasn't so much that she let him do whatever he wanted to her. It was that she *wanted* him to do things to her, *encouraged* him to do things to her in ways he thought about in only the most carnal recesses of his mind. His anticipation nearly uncontainable, he walked to the screen mounted in the wall and looked at the monitor. It showed a van at the gate. He thought it strange. Adriana was to come by car, but this was Mexico. He hit the call button.

"*Una entrega para el Doctor Revant.*"

A package for him? Doctor Revant? "*¿De quién es el paquete?*"

There was a pause and a slight rustle of paper. "National Microbiology Laboratory," said a deliberate voice.

That's where Adriana worked. He buzzed the gate open and met the overnight delivery van in the driveway, where he took receipt of three medium-sized packing boxes.

Inside, he placed the packages on the glass and steel dining room table. Where the hell was Adriana?

The boxes looked official. They had NML labels identifying them as emergency medical supplies. The two largest ones had **KEEP REFRIGERATED** on them. They were addressed to Dr. Peter Revant at this address. He had only given it to three people, and he had seen two of them, the señor and señora Gutiérrez, three days ago. Each box had a packing slip attached. With his fingernails Peter tore them from the boxes. Inside one was a sealed letter-size envelope. He sat on one of the dining room chairs and opened it. When he removed the letter something square fell out onto the table. Picking it up, he saw that it was a yellowed and edge-curled picture of Adriana and him. She had just turned 18 a month before. He was 24. They looked so young! He had first met her when she was 15, and up until then their relationship had been nothing more than a schoolgirl crush on a handsome, wealthy young man. But that year, when this picture was taken, she had shown him that she was no longer a schoolgirl and that what she felt and how she expressed it went way beyond a crush. Setting the picture aside, he unfolded two handwritten pages.

My Dearest Peter,

I am sorry, but you and I shall not be meeting. We both knew this day would come, when our lives would take different paths. We also know that for one of us, a last meeting would end badly. I will always be grateful and will cherish the times we spent together. It is in your arms that I came alive again.

As I promised, I have sent the items we spoke of. In two of the boxes are the placebo vaccines. Keep these refrigerated. I decided to make them Vitamin B12 injections. This way, not only will the contagion have a direct point of entry, but your subjects will get the benefit of a boost in energy and an increased sense of general well-being. In the box with the patches is the breakdown of their contents. They are color-coded. Anyway, I digress.

Do you remember what Dr. K. used to say about how the predator-and-prey relationship works on the savannah? Let me refresh your memory. He would say that during the rainy season, when water and feed are plentiful, the relationship between hunter and the hunted is one of harmony, one in which the prey gives up its life almost willingly. But when the waters dry up and the savannah turns to brown, the relationship becomes what it really is: a brutal struggle of life and death that plays out as the strong take from the weak and the old.

Well, my love, for you and me the Serengeti has turned to dust, the water holes to mud. Good-bye, Peter. It is time for me also to take care of some unfinished business. Who knows? I may be able to draw some attention away from you. I hope life gives you all that you seek, and remember, hunting is hunting only because the prey does not know that it is the prey.

Love,

Adriana

Peter read and reread the letter. How could this have

happened? How could she have known? Well, she was the most capable woman he had ever met, and her instincts were honed by life circumstances beyond his experience.

He had been looking forward to one more day and night with her body. He prayed and read from the Quran. He believed that sharia law should govern the lives of all people, and that women should be subservient in every way. But for all that, when it came to Adriana, he could not resist her.

He picked up the picture and stared at it, remembering the young girl he had met while on a Tanzanian safari with clients. He had been so taken with her and her guardian, Dr. Jonathan Koch, one of the most renowned large animal veterinarians and wildlife managers in all Africa, that he returned with wealthy clients two, sometime three times a year to the exclusive lodge. It was during those visits that Peter learned the details of Adriana's life. Details that confirmed she indeed met the criteria to be classified as the rarest of warriors.

Although a non-Muslim, a fire burned inside Adriana, not unlike the most committed Islamic jihadist. She had an edge, honed from personal tragedy, and wielded by an unwavering hand. Beyond their undeniable physical attraction, this is what drew him to her.

Peter needed fighters for his holy war. He easily recruited from the ranks of the young, and impressionable; those who could be coerced into giving their lives for Allah. As ISIS proved daily, there existed an ever-growing number of disenfranchised youth who harbored some romanticized idea about joining a cause that required extreme self-sacrifice and hardship. Even in America.

Adriana represented the most sought-after type of warrior. Her cause had nothing to do with faith, doctrine, or a holy text. Her mission had a single focus: revenge, at any cost. Not motivated by money or personal aggrandizement, she desired only for those who took from her to pay the price. But being the most sought after made her alliance the hardest to hold onto.

For days he had prayed to Allah to watch over and guide him—to give him the strength to end this indulgence. Instead of feeling relieved he felt cheated that this one final indulgence was not to be—would Allah forgive that?

* * *

WITH A KITCHEN KNIFE HE cut the packing tape on the three boxes. As Adriana had said in her letter, two Styrofoam cold boxes each contained two hundred fifty single-dose syringes of vitamin B12. The third box held two rows of individually wrapped square adhesive bandages. Peter removed a folded piece of paper and read it:

Red: H7N9 Avian influenza 200 doses

Blue: MRSA—Methicillin-resistant

Staphylococcus aureus 100 doses

Green: *E. coli* 100 doses

Yellow: Listeria 100 doses

He looked in the box and saw bandages in light shades of red, blue, green, and yellow. Taking one out, he held an inch-square package, much like the round Band-Aids that nurses put on people's arms after a shot. Peter stood and fought the urge to send the boxes and their contents skittering across the living room floor. He knew he shouldn't feel this way—as if somehow he had been cheated—but in the moment even his faith could not cool the fire his lust left burning inside

CHAPTER TWENTY-FOUR

December 5

Arturo Valdez waited at the gate. His sister had insisted that he come and meet with this *mayate,* (nigger) and Isabel could be very persuasive. Well, if not for her, he would have died in the slums of Mexico City a long time ago instead of driving a Ferrari and earning more money than 99.9 percent of the population.

Arturo hated this neighborhood, not because it was dirty or rundown, but because it was just the opposite. Every player in Mexico City felt he had to live here. The joke was that *Bosques de las Lomas* had more guns and private security per square meter than anywhere else in the whole country. Arturo doubted this, but the idea of people whose livelihoods depended on exploitation and other less-than-legal endeavors all living in the same neighborhood and trying to one-up the rest, well, it just seemed stupid.

* * *

At the door Peter met a man of average height with a black mustache and goatee, his dark hair slicked back and held in a ponytail. A gold cross, similar to the one Eduardo Gutiérrez wore, hung around his neck. Stocky, and in jeans, he had on a pair of ridiculous cowboy boots with silver-capped toes that extended and curled up.

Arturo removed his mirrored glasses. *"¿Es usted el señor Revant?"*

His tone was dismissive, and it was clear to Peter that whoever he was, he didn't want to be here. *"Sí. Y usted, ¿quién es?"*

"I am Arturo Valdez," he said in Spanish-accented English.

Isabel had not said who she would send, but this made sense: her brother. "Yes, I am Peter Revant. Please . . ." Peter held the door open.

Inside, Peter had everything organized on the dining table.

Arturo walked around the table, picked up one of the wrapped syringes, set it back down, and ran his fingers over the Band-Aid packages. "Why are they different colors?"

"Just packaging—they are all the same." Only Peter would know what the patches really held.

"So you want to move five hundred Mexicans into the United States?" Arturo asked as he continued to examine the stuff on the table. "Generally, Americans are more interested in moving them the other direction."

"Let's say I want to make a statement about a failed immigration policy."

Arturo looked up from the coffee table. "That's bullshit, amigo. Now, either you tell me what this is really about or I'm out of here."

Peter thought a moment before responding. "Arturo, it would be best if you and I sat down and worked out the plan. As I'm sure you know, a considerable transfer of funds took place three days ago. Also, I don't believe you have the authority—or the *cojones*—to walk out of here."

Arturo held his ground and stared at Peter, then, feigning disinterest, sat down heavily in one of the chairs. "Let's get this over with."

Peter picked up a file and set it in front of Arturo. "I know what I'm asking is a bit unusual," he said, still standing. "But for the fee I'm paying, unusual should not be a problem. The biggest issue is logistics." He paused, hoping he was staying within his guest's English vocabulary. "I know that somewhere around three thousand Mexicans cross into the United States illegally every day. Of that number, about two thousand get caught. I need as near five hundred as possible to safely get across in three days. So it would seem that the normal means of smuggling them across might not work."

Arturo looked bored as he opened the file and thumbed through it. "Well, we need to send them from border cities. There are at least fifty thousand trans-border workers who cross every day. You would think that with the Internet crash and America's predictable reaction— closing the borders—these laborers wouldn't be able to cross. No, their strong backs and willingness to do any job has them in demand more than ever."

"That's good," said Peter, impressed. "This is more than just crossing into the U.S. for day labor, though. I need them to disperse and stay for at least two weeks—hopefully much longer."

"Isabel said something about vaccinating them for the flu?" Arturo asked as he again picked up one of the wrapped syringes.

Peter moved closer. With a syringe in one hand and one of the Band-Aid packages in the other, he said, "Yes, we are at the beginning of the influenza season and I need everyone healthy."

Arturo pushed back from the table, leaned back in his chair, and put his boots up on the glass top. "We will use *Tijuana, Nogales,* and *Juárez.* There are thousands who, with a little incentive"—he rubbed his thumb across his fingertips—"would gladly stay in the U.S. for a few weeks, maybe longer. And as you said, for what you are paying, an investment on our part of, say, a thousand dollars per head will be just a drop in the bucket." He smiled.

Peter was caught off guard. He had assumed that he would have to walk Isabel's man through the plan, step by step.

They spent another hour going over the timelines and reviewing the instructions for the shots. Peter intentionally spent a lot of time on the use of the syringe, and made the application of the Band-Aid just that—a Band-Aid over an injection site. He would have preferred to give specific parameters for the use of each type of contagion: listeria for pregnant women, MRSA for those with visible scrapes or cuts. But then again, as long as people got sick, that's all that mattered.

CHAPTER TWENTY-FIVE

December 8, Beginnings Ranch, British Colombia

MARCUS ENTERED OPS. ALTHOUGH JUST a little before five in the morning, the colonel, J. T., and Glen were already there. That didn't surprise him, but the other man with them, FBI Deputy Director, Nathan Reynolds, did.

"What, you checking up on us, or you just miss my smiling face?" Marcus said as he shook the deputy directors hand.

Nathan smiled. "Well, I thought I'd come see the "digs" for myself. The truth is, something's been bothering me. I spoke with the colonel a few days ago." He glanced toward the man standing next to him. "He suggested I come out for face-to-face. Something you once promised me would happen."

It was Marcus's turn to smile. "So what's on your mind, Nathan?"

"The attack on the Internet. The damage, although substantial, could have been so much worse."

"You're wondering why they didn't just blow up the buildings? Maybe even use tactical nukes?"

"The thought has crossed my mind. I mean, if they used, as we suspect, some type of Electromagnetic Pulse Generator, they most likely assembled the devices on site. Figure a generator about the size and shape of a torpedo. Well, that engineering and design could just as easily have been a bomb." Nathan looked up at the screen where J. T. had posted pictures of EMP generators. "So why not take down the buildings? Kill thousands? Completely destroy all the data servers, not just twenty percent?"

"Right," Marcus said. "And if it were a nuclear bomb, irradiate ten to twenty square city blocks? So what was the question?"

The colonel spoke. "I think the deputy director would like to hear what we, you, think about the attack on the Internet. What was the purpose?"

"You know what I think, Sam. Why didn't you just tell him?"

"I think it might be better coming from you."

Marcus paced as he talked. "Okay. The attack on the Internet was a big thumbed nose. You can't terrorize dead people. Besides, every terrorist knows what kind of response you get if you blow up a building in the United States. Anyway, all they need to do is stir the pot, then sit back and watch us come apart at the seams. They don't need to kill people. We come unglued and kill each other. Terrorism's stock in trade is the creation of panic. Play on two of the most powerful human emotions: Fear and Hatred. One begets the other. What no one seems to have figured out is that the terrorists, whoever they are, Al Qaeda, ISIS, take your pick, for them to exist, to survive, they need *us* to hate *them.*"

As Marcus talked, J. T. choreographed with pictures, video and information. "You ever wonder why they do such outrageous shit, like live-feed Internet beheadings? Rape, torture, and kill aid workers? Kidnap and enslave young girls? And they do it all in plain sight." Marcus looked hard at the second most powerful man in the FBI.

"As far as the attack on the Internet, they've accomplished all they could have hoped for. Panic! Again, like the attack almost two years ago, every person across the country has felt the impact. People don't trust that their government can keep them safe. The fact that within another few weeks the Internet will be back up, is that not possibly also by design? What was once a loosely regulated form of information exchange is going to be overloaded with governmental oversight. Where once the smartest people on the planet ran the show, now we'll have a whole bunch of second-rate bureaucrats making up the rules. And you know what? Just like the enactment of the Patriot Act, which is still very much in use, we, the everyday citizens, are happy to give up some of our 'freedom' to feel safe. But make no mistake, it's a feeling only.

"Look at what's happening in Western Europe. They've been shamed into opening their boarders to hundreds of thousands of refugees from Syria and Iraq. Now it's the right thing to do. But you don't see America opening her arms to ten, twenty thousand of these war-displaced families. Why?"

Marcus stopped pacing and stood in front of Nathan Reynolds.

"Fear! We're afraid every Muslim is an American hater, a potential terrorist," said the Deputy Director. "We even have presidential candidates out on the stump recommending we ban all

Muslims from coming into the country. Like Muslims wear a sign around their necks."

"If you already knew all this, why are you really here?" Asked Marcus

"Sometimes it's just good to know that you aren't the only one who thinks a certain way. You're right about government oversight of the Internet. As we speak, both houses of Congress are in emergency session to come up with a framework to regulate and monitor the "New Internet." He made quotation marks with his fingers.

"I guess the Executive Branch is going to get a "Kill" switch after all," said Marcus. "Now the president can decide if 'going dark' is necessary. Panic at its finest. You ever feel like you're being led by the nose, Nathan?"

The room was silent for moment. Then Nathan said, seemingly thinking out loud, "How do our reactions become less predictable?"

Up on the monitor came a view from the cameras that covered the main compound of the ranch. Marcus saw the distinctive red Maple leaf of an inbound Royal Canadian Mounted Police helicopter.

"My ride," the deputy director said. "Thanks for the insight, gentlemen."

As Glen escorted the deputy director toward the door of the command bunker, Marcus said, "You can't fight this battle from high atop the ivory tower. You gotta think and act like they do, Nathan." At the door, the deputy director turned. Marcus said, "You gotta get into the dirt, and there ain't gonna be nothing pretty about it."

* * *

WITH THE DEPUTY DIRECTOR GONE, Marcus focused on the purpose at hand. He stood next to J. T. and prepared for the team's morning briefing. At the top of the monitor wall was a picture of Yakov Anatoly Dementyev and, beneath it, photos of the five men who attacked the ranch. Below them a number of other smaller photos, with biographical information under each. It looked like some sort of unsavory family tree.

Marcus studied the pictures as he had been doing every day for the past week. Force 10 knew the identities of the five men who attacked the ranch. Over the last week J. T. and Glen had connected all of them with World Wide Employment. They used their businesses for laundering money and as fronts for trafficking in young women, girls, and boys. They also used World Wide Employment to supply enforcement muscle whenever they required specialized intimidation. The bottom row of pictures represented the enforcers J. T. had been able to track down. A nasty bunch. Most had some military training, but more importantly, all had served time in Russian prisons. The puzzle was coming together, and this morning, Marcus, with J. T.'s help, thought he had it figured out.

* * *

J. T. TOOK THE LEAD IN the morning briefing. He held up a small vial. "This is how they tracked the boys, more accurately, Garrett. I wondered why they didn't seem to know about Bodie when he crawled out the back entrance of the hide. This..." he shook the vial, "is Tritium, a low level radioactive isotope. It emits a weak beta particle. In this diluted form it's completely harmless, but it can remain detectable by infrared for weeks. God's Eye, as well as a few other spy satellites, can pick it up if the search area can be refined. I gotta say, it's pretty slick."

"How did they get the isotope on Garrett?" asked Jamie.

Up on the screen came a playbill for a troupe of Russian performers.

"This group performed at the school in Merritt right before Thanksgiving. They do interactive skits where students participate. It's impromptu. The kids get to wear costumes complete with makeup, beards and mustaches. " Chaya examined Garrett and Bodie with a Geiger counter. That's when we found the isotope trace on Garrett's scalp. Turns out Garrett played the part of Russian fur trapper. Had to wear a beaver hat. All it takes is a couple of drops. They probably did it when they put the hat on him."

"Okay, so how did they know which one was Garrett?" Sit asked.

Marcus took over. "This is where things get a little strange. We're all agreed that finding us wasn't that hard, especially considering we didn't really do anything to hide our whereabouts."

J. T. chimed in. "Some of the best computer hackers and programmers on the planet come out of Russia and the other former Soviet republics. For the most part, they work with a high degree of impunity. And even when the U.S. detects an intrusion, the best we can do is shut them out—that is, until they figure a new way to hack in. It's not as if the FBI can call up its counterpart in Russia or Ukraine and have these people arrested. I should note that more governmental regulation is only going to make the hackers' job easier."

"So when Adad just vanished off the face of the earth, almost a year ago, his partner Yakov there"—Marcus tilted his chin at the man's picture—"got curious. Then, when he had limited access to information and billions of his assets were all of a sudden frozen, he got a bit aggravated. So he hooked up with a few of these guys." Photos with short bios began to pop up below the enforcers' pictures. "And they went to work, doing exactly what our own J. T. here would have done."

J. T. said. "I've narrowed it down to a handful of people. Whoever did this needed satellite access, and not just for a few hours. To establish patterns, analyze imagery, and develop a timeframe for their mission, they had to get surveillance over the course of several weeks. That kind of access and talent is rare."

Marcus turned away from the screen. "When Yakov couldn't reach Adad, I think it's safe to assume that he reached out to Adad's father, Sheikh Nazir al-Mohmoud, or someone very close to him. From there, he got my name. God knows, I pissed the sheikh off. It wouldn't take a genius to track down my family and find them all gone from their various places of residence and employment. And, if you recall, during the FBI's hunt for Annie, pictures of the boys and me were all over the news." Marcus paced back and forth, relaxed but focused.

"If Yakov has the kind of money we do, then he has access to the same kinds of resources. They profiled me, figured out what makes me tick—my likes and dislikes. They would have been able to find out if I had traveled commercially, used a credit card, things like that. When all that came up negative, well, the red flags would be waving like hell—hard to miss. Go ahead, J. T., tell them."

"If it was me—and this is highly speculative—I would have taken Marcus's profile, looked at the number of people he was trying to protect. Then I would have narrowed down three or four geographical regions in which he might likely hide. I would start looking into high-dollar, under-thirty-day-closing real estate transactions for properties big enough to accommodate that number of people. But more than that, I would have concentrated on *cash* deals where substantially more than market price was paid."

Marcus stopped walking. "I mean it's not like we did anything to cover our tracks. We offered so much money for this place no sane person could have turned it down. Who does that? We didn't create new identities, and we don't have a lockdown on my brothers and sisters, their husbands, wives, and kids. Maybe we need to." Marcus looked around at the team and got the collective, *Yeah, when pigs fly*, look.

"Here's the bottom line. Those men came here for the boys. It's clear that if they couldn't abduct them, they were to kill them. They didn't have Bodie tagged, so they assumed both were in The Hide. So if anybody is still beating themselves up about what Bodie did and the help you gave him, get over it."

CHAPTER TWENTY-SIX

A KNOCK ON THE DOOR awoke Marcus. Nighttime sleep eluded him but he seemed to have no problem napping. The door opened and Bodie walked in slamming the door shut behind him. Marcus crawled out from under the covers and walked into the bathroom.

"What's up, bud?" Marcus asked as he splashed cold water on his face.

Hearing no reply, Marcus turned, shirt in hand, to find Bodie standing in the doorway staring at the ropy purple scars that covered his father's chest and back. Marcus had a bad habit of forgetting about them—at least how they affected Bodie and Garrett. For Marcus, they were a part of him now, but for the boys, they served as a shocking, in-your-face reminder of all that had happened in the past year and a half. Pulling on the long-sleeved thermal undershirt, Marcus approached his son and looked into the sky-blue eyes, flecked with gold. Both boys had these eyes, their mother's eyes. And every time he looked into them, he felt a stab of guilt that he hadn't been able to save her.

Bodie had grown. From the day his mother went missing, he had become, in many ways, his bother's keeper. Instead of letting her death crush him, and his little brother, he found strength beyond his years. And although still a few inches away from Marcus's height, it was this maturity that put father and son eye-to eye.

Annie and Marcus had been hauling the boys on backpacking trips since before they could walk. In the mountains, they knew the routines and the rules. But beyond that, they shared a bond forged by love and sustained by trust. They knew their strengths and weaknesses, and in the pecking order, there was no question about who was in charge when it was just the two of them. But lately, Bodie seemed more annoyed than understanding with his little brother. So Marcus reminded himself daily that this was how young brothers normally got along: they didn't.

Marcus rummaged through a pile of clothes. Pulling on his

gray wool socks, he said, "Something on your mind?"

Bodie walked across the plank floors and plopped down on the edge of the unmade bed. It was out of character for him to be so quiet, even when he was in one of his moods.

"Hey, man, everything okay?" Marcus asked. "Did something happen?"

Bodie looked at him as if to say, *You have no clue.*

"What?" Marcus held his hands out. "I do something wrong?"

Again the look, but this time it said, *You want me to make a list?*

Marcus looked closely at his son. He knew that he could come off as a little thick and less than attentive, particularly to those closest to him.

Annie always accused him of being so single-minded that he wouldn't see a burning building unless he was inside it."

And for him that was the point. When Marcus focused on something, he locked in and the world around him pretty much faded to gray—or to nothing. It had always been Annie who attended to the boys' needs for sensitivity and understanding. But now Annie was no longer with them and Marcus knew he was doing a crappy job of picking up the slack.

He leaned over and fished his boots out from under the bed, put them on, and began to lace them up. Bodie got off the bed. At the dormer, he knelt on the cushioned window seat and stared outside.

Marcus walked over and stood behind him, putting a hand on his shoulder. Bodie stiffened at his touch. But then, before Marcus could say that he had just about had it with the silent treatment, Bodie said, "You see that?"

Marcus leaned forward and peered out the window. Garrett and Chaya walked hand in hand over the snow-crusted ground along the riverbank.

As Marcus watched, they stopped at the river's edge. Garrett bent down and scraped through a patch of crunchy snow with his gloved hand. Pulling off his glove, he picked up a stone and skipped it across the smooth, calm stretch of water. A soft haze of steam rose from the surface. He bent down again, picked up another flat rock, and handed it to Chaya. In the animated way of young children, Garrett mimed a sidearm throw. Chaya nodded and tossed the rock, only to have it splash into the water and sink without a skip. From Garrett's body language, Marcus could tell he was laughing as he picked up another stone and sent it skipping across the water. After a few more attempts, Chaya finally got a stone to skip. She turned to Garrett, knelt and raised her hand, and Garrett slapped it with a high five. Then he wrapped his arms around her neck.

Bodie pushed back off the cushion, breaking contact with Marcus's hand on his shoulder. Marcus looked at Bodie as he began to pace, moving his hands in and out of his jeans pockets. As he spoke, Bodie stabbed his finger in the air at the window. "Do you see that? Do you see how happy he is?" Bodie tilted his head toward the window and came to stand in front of his father.

Marcus didn't move. Father and son shared this trait where something built up inside until it came out in a rush of emotion. Bodie held the fingers of his right hand tightly with his left, tears building in his eyes.

"You and Mom taught Garrett and me to love, because we can," he said, "Not because we should. That we needed to love every chance we get. We almost lost him. Oh God..." The words came clear and hard through Bodie's clenched teeth. Reaching out, he grabbed his dad's hand and pulled him to the French doors that opened onto a small deck. "Come here! I want you to see something—really *see* it." He opened the door and led Marcus out into the cold December morning.

Garrett and Chaya each had a handful of stones. In unison they skipped them out into the river.

Marcus stood with hands on the wrought-iron rail, feeling the cold metal bite his palms. Bodie stood next to him, and when he spoke again, a tone of calm and reason had returned to his voice. "He loves her. I love her, and I think you . . . well, Mom would never approve of the way you've treated her."

"*Treated* her? I haven't . . ."

Bodie held up his hand. "Exactly. You haven't done a damn thing. She cares for you . . ." The tears streamed down his face, the tone of a sad, hurt child in his voice. "And you know that. I don't know all that happened when you left when we went to Uncle Glen's in Australia, but I do know that if it wasn't for her, you wouldn't be here." Bodie shifted from one foot to the other and pushed a shock of long blond hair out of his eyes. "Garrett still talks to Mom almost every day. And do you know what she asks him about?"

Marcus had a pretty good idea. He couldn't define, at least not in words, the connection between Annie and Garrett. Even before his birth, they shared a special connection that only the two of them really understood. Their connection transcended even the power of a mother-son bond, as if a piece of each of their souls resided in the other.

Marcus watched Bodie, whose attention was focused on his brother and Chaya. In the four months he had been back with his sons, they had not spoken of what he went through in any detail. The boys knew only that their father had suffered a terrible beating, and they could see the scars he would wear the rest of his life. But Bodie was right about Chaya: she had saved Marcus's life, and he did have feelings for her.

"She has more pain in her than the three of us combined," Bodie said. "I don't know what happened to her, but Mom told Garrett it was really bad. According to Garrett, Mom says *we're* the only ones who can help her heal."

Marcus started to speak but, again, Bodie held up his hand. "Let me finish, Dad, jeez! I know this whole thing with Mom—us talking about her like she's still here—is a little weird. But all I know, weird or not, she's with us, and if she's ever going to find peace, there are things she needs us to do."

Bodie nodded toward his little brother and Chaya. "No matter what we do, he's going to love her because Mom needs him to love her. And . . . I think she needs us to love her, too." Bodie headed for the door, opened it, and then turned back toward his father. "He only wants one thing for Christmas. Hopefully, you've figured out what it is."

As Bodie swung the door behind him, tears welled in Marcus's eyes. Bodie had just done what he had been taught to do his entire life: take care of his little brother.

CHAPTER TWENTY-SEVEN

After Bodie left, Marcus stood for several moments gazing out the window at Garrett and Chaya. He had intentionally kept his distance from her. They met on Marcus's first morning at the Force 10 compound in Australia when she doctored the self-inflicted gouges on his legs and back—from repeatedly crawling through the barbed-wire section of an obstacle course wearing only shorts and tank top. Their attraction, although awkward, started then.

Six years younger than Marcus, Chaya, like Annie, had a natural beauty that confident, athletic women seemed to exude. It had been a year and a half since Marcus was with a woman, and he had no idea what it would be like with someone other than Annie.

* * *

Marcus softly shut the door to his sons' room. Each could have had his own bedroom but they weren't ready to be alone yet, and Marcus trusted that they would make that decision when the time was right. From his first night at Beginnings, he and the boys had slipped seamlessly back into the same routine, with Marcus reading aloud to them—as he had almost every night, even while they were in Annie's womb. The current tale was Louis L'Amour's *The Rustlers of West Fork*.

Marcus walked down the hall toward the staircase. Standing on the bridge that looked out over both sides of the great room, he saw the condensation cloud from someone out on the front courtyard. Norma was in the kitchen prepping for the morning—that left only one other person.

Grabbing a jacket from a hook behind the antique bench by the front door, he zipped it up and walked out onto the stone courtyard. The night air, cold and heavy, smelled like coming snow. The thick gray cloud cover held the dim glow from a hidden moon. Chaya stood thirty feet away with her jacketed arms crossed on the iron rail. Leaning forward so that her chin almost rested in the crook of her arms, she stared off into the night shadows toward the river. If she heard the door open and close she made no show of it.

Marcus had avoided this for too long. He owed her more than he could ever pay. Since he arrived at Beginnings he had been acting like an insensitive, uncaring idiot, as Bodie so bluntly pointed out just this afternoon. With his hands in his jacket pockets, he cleared his throat and approached.

Straightening up and stepping back from the rail, Chaya looked at him. Despite everything they had been through, all the time they had spent together, it all had been about the past, about what had happened—nothing about what was *going* to happen. Chaya smiled. The wall light behind her cast a soft glow on her olive skin and high cheekbones. Her face spoke of sorrows endured and happiness desired.

Drawing close, Marcus made a silly smile of the sort a boy might make after screwing up the courage to talk to a girl he liked. "Chaya, I'm . . ."

She reached out and put the tip of her finger on his lips, holding it there for a brief moment, her eyes locked on his. Removing her finger, she took Marcus by the hand. Without a word, she led Marcus into the house and down the main hall. She opened a plank door into a bedroom with flat ceilings, decorated as it might have looked a century ago, and led him inside.

Trance-like, Marcus stared at the bed of glowing embers in the raised stone fireplace. The quiet click of the door latch startled him back to the moment. Chaya remained silent as she took off her jacket and laid it on the old wooden steamer trunk at the foot of the bed. Then she unzipped his jacket and laid it next to hers. She unbuttoned Marcus's plaid flannel shirt. Moving her hands up his chest to his shoulders, first one side then the other, she slid the shirt off and let it fall to the floor.

She paused and ran her fingers slowly over the thick scars on his chest. Then, leaning in, she wrapped her arms around him, letting her fingers trace the scars on his back as she laid her head on his chest.

Marcus just stood there feeling like a teenage boy who, having gotten this far down the path he had dreamed and fantasized about, found himself too stunned to move. Eyes closed, he brought his hands up and lightly caressed Chaya's hair, inhaled the scent of shampoo and skin cream and woman.

Pushing back, she let go of him and pulled the pale blue cashmere sweater over her head. Standing there before him in a white lace bra and panties, she smiled again and this time held her finger to *her* lips. Chaya slid her arms from the shoulder straps, and the bra fell onto the small but growing collection of clothing on the floor.

Marcus became acutely aware that he hadn't seen a woman's breasts in a very long time.

Chaya looked down at his feet. Crocs with socks—something the boys never failed to razz him about. A no-brainer. He kicked them off and shucked the socks.

Still looking him in the eye Chaya unbuttoned his pants and slid them, boxers and all, to the floor.

"Remember the last time you stood naked in front of me?" she said softly.

Marcus nodded. How could he forget?

"Remember what I said to you?"

Marcus was gazing at Chaya's full breasts, when she laid her palm on his chest.

"Remember what I said to you?" She stepped back a bit and put her hands on her hips.

Marcus couldn't think. "Well . . ." Suddenly self-conscious, he said, "You said . . . 'think of me like I'm your mother.'"

A smile broke across Chaya's face as she stepped into his arms. "Well, I'm not your mother."

* * *

MARCUS AWOKE WITH CHAYA SPOONED into him. Gently, he rolled onto his back. As Chaya let out a soft moan and burrowed into the covers, he reached down to the floor and retrieved one of the pillows, and put it behind his head. He looked over at the sleeping form next to him, breathing, slow and deep.

Chaya stirred and opened her eyes. Reaching out, she pulled Marcus to her. And in that moment, he knew that the promise he had made to Annie—to live his life well—was in his grasp.

* * *

FOR THE FIRST TIME SINCE arriving at Beginnings, Marcus dreamed of Annie. He found himself back at their high mountain cabin in the Eastern Sierra near Yosemite. It was night, and the dimly lit space took a moment to come into focus. In the corner, by the wall of windows that looked out at the twelve-thousand-foot peaks across the narrow canyon, Marcus saw Annie, bent over, stoking the wood stove, wearing a pair of faded jeans and fuzzy pink bunny slippers.

"I was wondering when you were going to show up," Annie said as she swung the cast-iron door shut and dropped the latch. She turned toward Marcus who stood on the stone floor by the dining table. She smiled, her blond hair pulled back in a ponytail, her oversized blue-and-cream checkered flannel shirt tied at the waist, and Marcus couldn't help thinking how much she looked like the girl he had met twenty-five years ago.

"You look good, Marcus." Annie tilted her head and gave him an eager look, like a dog that wants its belly rubbed. "So you finally manned up, I see. I was wondering how long it would take Bodie to help you pry your head out of your ass."

Marcus just shook his head. This Annie, his dream Annie, was so direct, so unfiltered, so *him.* In life, she had always been the yin to his yang, the calm eye of the storm. And even though, in the dream version, she was this blunt, get-to-the-point presence, she still kept those qualities of the flesh-and-blood Annie. But in these dream encounters, she had a raw, indelicate sense of humor, no subject off limits. Then there was the small issue of Marcus not being able to talk to her. No matter how hard he tried, it was as if his mouth were frozen, the words trapped in his brain and unable to escape.

"Still haven't figured how to talk to me, huh? Well, that's okay. Come, sit with me for a minute." Annie beckoned seductively with her finger as she moved to the sofa. "Come on. I won't bite," she said, patting the cushion.

Marcus walked over and sat next to her. He caught the scent of the lavender lotion she always used, and the hint of cinnamon from her favorite tea. He smelled chicken soup. He looked to the gas stove and saw steam rising from a big stainless steel pot.

"It's so cold and stormy out, I thought, *Soup weather.*"

His senses seemed to be coming online one at a time, as if someone flipped one circuit breaker and then another and another. He could hear the howl of the wind through the big mountain hemlocks that surrounded the cabin. Outside the big windows the snow swirled.

Annie tucked her feet up under her. One of the ears from her bunny slippers hung out, and she reached down and absently rubbed the soft fluff. Her other hand reached out and took Marcus's. He could feel her flesh on his, its warmth. Letting go of the plush bunny ear, Annie brought her other hand up and caressed his cheek, making goose bumps rise on his skin even though the cabin was warm. Her eyes focused on his. "You've healed up pretty well." Annie's cute, precocious girl smile faded and her voice became somber. "Physically, anyway, but what about in here?" She tapped her heart. "She's a wonderful woman. She loves our boys as if they were her own, and that is truly something. If I'd been given the chance and had to pick someone to take my place, I couldn't have chosen better."

Marcus squeezed Annie's hand, and a tear streaked down his cheek. She wiped it with the back of her finger and brought the wet finger to her lips. "So here we are, you and me. What are we gonna do? Oh, yeah, that's right . . ." Annie stood. "You can't say, so I get to decide." And just like that, she went back to the half-crazy, wholly irreverent dream persona he had come to know and love, as she stood, danced and twirled into the kitchen.

Marcus watched as she grabbed an oven mitt and a big, long-handled spoon from the counter, lifted the lid from the pot of soup, and stirred. "So I'll tell what you're gonna do . . ." She glanced over her shoulder to make sure he was listening. "You're gonna love her. Bodie was right, you know. I do need you to love her. But more than that, *you* need to love her, for your own sake. You need someone in your life to help you find your way." She turned, spoon in hand, and looked at Marcus.

Annie spoke, her tone serious. "Marcus, tell Bodie . . . God, he's growing into such a handsome young man!" Her voice cracked. "That I'm with him every day, and when he needs me, *really* needs me, I'll be there to guide him and talk him through it."

Setting the spoon down, Annie lowered the gas on the burner and put the lid on the pot, then turned to face Marcus. "I can't see things clearly yet, but—and I know you know—this journey is just begun. Can't say it's what I ever imagined you and the boys doing, but . . . what is it you always like to say?" Annie paused a moment and struck a pose of being deep in thought. "Deck shuffled, cards dealt, play the hand you're given." She made a fanning motion with her hand. "Marcus, would you crack that window just a little? It's hot in here."

He rose from the sofa, walked over to the double-hung window by the wood stove, opened the latch and, with a tug, broke the air seal and lifted the window a few inches. A blast of cold air rushed in and hit Marcus like that first gulp of breath after being underwater for a long time. When he looked back, everything vanished: the cabin, Annie. Only he and the darkness remained.

* * *

"MARCUS. MARCUS, WAKE UP." A soft voice said.

He opened his eyes. It took a moment to orient himself. The cold breeze blew though the room from an open window. Getting out of bed, he walked naked to the window and pulled the drapes aside. In the soft glow of a yard light, he watched the snow falling in a swirling white haze. He closed the window. *That's weird.*

Marcus crawled back into bed, and Chaya leaned over him, the soft satin of her black camisole—which he had no recollection of her ever putting on—brushing against his chest.

"Did you see her, too?" she asked.

Marcus looked at her, the question written all over his face.

"Annie," Chaya said. "Did you see her? She was here."

He shook his head to clear his mind. Annie? *Here?* She hadn't been here, not really.

Chaya's voice shifted from concern to pleading. "Marcus, Annie—your Annie—I dreamed of her. She sat right here on the bed next to me. Held my hand." Chaya held her hand out as if that confirmed it. "I tell you, I felt her hand holding mine. It was so warm, and I could smell her: lavender and cinnamon."

Now fully awake, Marcus focused on the expression of hope and fear painted on Chaya's face.

She pulled the quilt up to her neck, pushed the pillows against the headboard, and propped herself up on her side, facing Marcus. "We talked about the boys . . . and you."

"You talked to her? Actually said *words* to her?"

Chaya looked at him. "I'm not speaking Hebrew." Her voice held an edge.

Marcus stared back. He had never discussed with Chaya—or anybody else, for that matter—his conversations with Annie, let alone the fact that he could only listen but couldn't talk to her. Sure, his family and Force 10 all knew that Annie and Garrett had a thing. But Marcus had never told anyone that since Annie went missing, he too had been having dreams about her. And never did he tell anyone that many of the risks he took, especially when he put his very life on the line, were because Annie promised him that she would see him through them. He had trusted her, acted without hesitation, not once thinking he wouldn't survive. And how could he explain to anyone that he was putting his fate in the hands of his dead wife?

"Marcus, she sat right here and told me . . . she thanked me for taking care of her boys . . . and you." A tear slid from the corner of her eye and rolled down past her nose and onto her cheek. Marcus reached out with his finger, wiped the tear away, and brought it to his lips.

* * *

WHEN MARCUS AND CHAYA WALKED into the kitchen at 6:00 a.m., the rich smell of baking bread filled the air. Chaya sat on the wooden bench facing the roaring fire and leaned her back against the dining table's edge. Marcus went into the kitchen, filled two mugs with coffee, and added cream and two sugar cubes to one. As he stirred, Norma walked past and gave him a pat on the shoulder. "What, no walk this morning?" she asked as she opened one of the wall ovens and removed a rack holding six golden-crusted loaves of bread. "Too cold and stormy for you?"

Marcus gave her a look and raised his eyebrows.

"That's what I thought. I was beginning to wonder if I was gonna have to take you out behind the woodshed." Marcus raised his eyebrows again. Norma shook her head in wonder. "When you arrived here, I told you, nothing but love in this house. I never said that I wouldn't kick some ass if just plain stupidity stood in the way of that happening. Now, go on. Don't make that beautiful woman wait."

Marcus picked up the mugs.

To his back, Norma said, "I think you've made her wait long enough."

* * *

TWENTY MINUTES LATER BODIE AND Garrett wandered into the kitchen. Their looks seemed to say, *You're not as smart or as sneaky as you think, Dad.* They each walked up to Chaya and gave her a good-morning hug and kiss, then gave Marcus *the* look. No mistake about it. They knew he hadn't spent the night in his room. Then, just when he thought they were going to hug him, they ducked into the kitchen and hugged Norma.

Their mom would be so proud of them, Marcus thought.

Always Annie first, then anyone else who might be around, then Marcus. It was their way of messing with him.

Returning with mugs of hot chocolate and napkins that held pieces of fresh-baked bread slathered with butter, the boys came to the table. Garrett put down his mug and bread, sat on Marcus's lap, and gave him a two-armed, throw-your-whole-body-into-it hug. "Thank you," he whispered in his father's ear.

Bodie sat next to Chaya, and when Marcus looked over at him, he smiled and winked. "Morning, Pops."

Sitting there on the bench with the three of them, it struck Marcus that this was as close to *whole* as this family had been in a year and half. Listening to the boys and Chaya talking, he realized how much he had missed this, how much the boys had missed it: interaction with the most important woman in their life. But then again, the boys had been interacting with Chaya from the get-go. *He* had been the only holdout. That Garrett, at ten, and Bodie, just barely a teenager, understood the man-woman dynamic seemed strange, as if it should be beyond their grasp. But then, they had managed to deal with something no child should ever have to confront. Taking a sip of his coffee and listening to the laughter and giggling, seeing the unabashed smiles of pure joy—this was the song and dance of life. Then, from somewhere deep in his mind, he heard Annie's voice: *"Deck shuffled, cards dealt, play the hand you're given."*

CHAPTER TWENTY-EIGHT

December 11, Centers for Disease Control, Atlanta, Georgia

Jennifer Halston sat in her cubicle on the seventh floor staring at the numbers on her screen. She had run the computations a dozen times, always with the same result. Even though her information was coming out of Africa, which often meant skewed data, her source was completely reliable. She had known Dr. Jacquard for fifteen years. They met while she was working as an administrative assistant for Médecins Sans Frontières (MSF). It had been at the doctor's suggestion that she ended up taking her analytical skills to the Center for Disease Control.

She printed the report and headed up to the ninth floor and down the wide corridor to Eldon Forshire's office. Eldon was head of the CDC's statistics division, which was second only to the infectious-diseases division in size and budget.

Usually, protocol mandated that Jennifer send the report via internal e-mail. But, once in the system, a red flag would go up, thanks to some key-word protocol, and a whole flurry of time-wasting measures would automatically go into effect. And besides, it was a good excuse to see her husband.

She paused at his door—always open unless he wasn't in. *Eldon is brilliant—almost as smart as me,* Jennifer thought as she watched him, absorbed in a report, his reading glasses hanging low on the bridge of his nose.

Her soft knock startled him. Looking up, he smiled, took off his glasses and laid them on the desktop and waved her in. She sat down across the desk from him.

"To what do I owe the pleasure?" he asked.

Smiling back at the man who had stolen her heart with that very same sincerity, she said, "We might have a problem." She slid the report across the desk.

Eldon put his glasses back on and studied the single page.

When he looked up, Jennifer said, "I know. That's what I

thought. The reports are from the African Medical and Research Foundation's clinic in Loliondo, Tanzania. Dr. Jacquard of MSF spent a few days there and had them forwarded to me.

"In Loliondo, there's this retired Lutheran priest they call 'Babu wa Loliondo.' Claims he can cure anything from cancer to HIV with a concoction made from the leaves, flowers, and berries of *Carissa edulis.* It's related to the black currant bush. According to Jacquard, there's absolutely no evidence that drinking the stuff cures anything. But we all know what happens when there's a miracle for sale.

"He said people line up by the thousands. That there are all these spin-off cures—people who've set up their own little stands. Anyway, he was talking to the director from AMERF who told him people have been showing up in just the last few days with flu-like symptoms: vomiting, diarrhea, fever. Also several people presented with open lesions that wouldn't heal. So he decided to stay a few days. His preliminary findings are in the report."

Eldon absently ran his tongue over his lower lip—something he always did when contemplating. "Okay, so what do you think?"

"I've run the numbers over and over. If Jacquard is right and we're looking at three, possibly four, distinct contagions all at the same time, mathematically it's a long shot that this could be a natural occurrence—even in Africa."

CHAPTER TWENTY-NINE

December 18, Loliondo, Tanzania

For over two weeks, Adriana worked from before the sun rose until well after it set. She kept *her* bandages in the pocket of her smock. She saw several hundred people a day, mostly children and women. She had no problem tagging a hundred a day with *her* band-aid over an injection site. It didn't bother her that some would get very sick, and that some would die. One of the first things she learned in her years living with Dr. Koch was that the very nature of Africa required a certain amount of death to ensure a certain amount of life. In truth, with scarce resources, and too many people, by her hand or not, in terms of the numbers, these people would die anyway. So why shouldn't she at least get her redemption?

Besides providing basic medical care, AMREF actively encouraged families to return to their own villages. To this end, AMREF had nonmedical staff working with groups from particular regions, organizing transportation to get them home. These patients, who got treatment and then loaded on buses back to their villages, were the ones Adriana focused on to receive *her* patches.

The information in the file that Dr. K gave her the day she arrived put Kgosi Egwu in either Uganda or Kenya. The whole Boko Haram thing that Kathryn van der Hoch, AMREF's director of operations, spoke of, was clearly just a cover so that Kgosi and his men could kidnap, rape, kill and sell into slavery girls and women as they saw fit.

Adriana knew it would take four to six days for the flu bug to infect its host, and then it would spread like wildfire. For the past several days, the clinic had been receiving reports of possible influenza outbreaks, and a few symptomatic people had been through the clinic already. Just the day before, AMREF had received a report from a village four hundred kilometers north, near Subugo, Kenya, of a confirmed influenza outbreak. In a few days, it would hit Nairobi. In a country where people lived in close quarters and traveled practically on top of one another, it wouldn't take long before someone with resources came looking for a flu shot.

As Adriana trudged through her days, she ran through her mind one scenario after another of how she would get Kgosi Egwu by himself once he showed up. She also knew that this influenza outbreak would only make the already overcrowded and unsanitary conditions in Loliondo worse.

All the AMREF staff had received vaccinations before coming here, and local support personnel were vaccinated when hired. AMREF had also supplied vaccinations to many of the longtime Loliondo residents, including Dr. Koch and Mama Bulala and her family. But just because people were vaccinated didn't mean they wouldn't get sick. Moreover, in a land plagued by HIV/AIDS, malaria, and a host of other dire diseases, flu was nowhere near the top of the list of health threats. Still, Adriana was counting on the virulence of the strain and the existence of a vaccine for it to draw her quarry to her.

* * *

KATHRYN VAN DER HOCH RAN all the way from her office through the tent city to the open-air clinic. She had just received a call that a group of armed men would be arriving in Loliondo in less than an hour. Gathering the staff, she began her briefing in a strident but controlled voice.

"We will remain composed. These men are coming for the flu vaccine. We will give it to them." She looked around and settled her gaze on Adriana. "Do you think you can administer the vaccine?"

Adriana moved from the back of the covered area that served as the clinic. "Yes, I can do it. Why don't we be ready when they arrive? Disarm them, so to speak, so they don't have to put on a show of force."

Kathryn smiled. Adriana had turned out to be a wonderful addition to the team. She could outwork any two other staff members and always had an even disposition, and even as children died by the dozens, Adriana remained calm and focused.

"Okay, that's as good an approach as we can hope for."

Turning to the armed guards, she said, "I want you to move the crowd back. Tell them we are preparing for the arrival of a shipment of supplies. If you are calm, they will stay calm."

To Adriana, she said, "Set up away from the front. There could be ten or twelve men. They're going to be looking for anything of value, so let's move out everything but the necessary supplies."

The entire exercise was orchestrated with precise and practiced movement. Soon, little remained of the clinic but a collection of dilapidated tables and mismatched plastic chairs and a patchwork canvas canopy held up by poles and tied down with ropes.

* * *

KGOSI EGWU RODE IN THE passenger seat of the forty-year-old military Land Rover. Twenty kilometers from Loliondo and he could see ahead the road clogged with cars and trucks at a dead stop. He motioned for his driver to head off-road, toward the west. No way a man of his position would ever queue up and wait for days.

He and his men had been working a job in Kenya. The past three years had seen an influx of small-scale gemstone miners as well as groups of geologists searching for oil and gas reserves throughout East Africa. It was a combination of small-time fortune seekers and large-scale international concerns; both needed guides, translators, and protection. Paid in cash for his services, Kgosi operated with little or no governmental oversight and he and his men freely took what they wanted from the villages they passed through.

* * *

ADRIANA SAW THE CLOUD OF dust coming in from the west—the opposite direction of the road that led into Loliondo. As the plume drew closer she could make out two faded turquoise bush trucks through the shimmering waves of heat rising off the plain.

Looking around, the faces of the staff, and even the guards, showed fear and worry. *And rightly so,* Adriana thought. Especially considering that throughout Africa abduction, robbery, rape, and murder happened every day, and never warranted so much as a mention in the news.

A battered Tanzanian flag as well as a banner with the AMREF logo hung limp from a tall pole outside the clinic. The men would not have to hunt for their destination.

The trucks pulled to a stop. As their dust caught up with them, Adriana watched the men pile out, each with an ominous-looking firearm slung over his shoulder. For several moments, they stood in a group, their attention focused on a figure Adriana couldn't quite make out. Then the men parted into two columns, and a tall, bulky man got out of the first truck. He adjusted the rust-red beret he wore, pushed his mirrored aviator sunglasses up the bridge of his nose, and smoothed his short-sleeved khaki shirt, then walked toward the clinic.

Adriana came from the table in back and met the man, who ducked under the canvas awning.

Many things seemed smaller now than in Adriana's childhood memories, but not Kgosi Egwu. The man stood at least six feet four and weighed well over 250 pounds. He had to be in his mid-fifties, and although he had put on weight, he looked every bit the homicidal bastard she remembered.

Adriana stood before Kgosi as he looked around the clinic. She kept her eyes lowered. He expected submissiveness and would forcibly extract it if he didn't receive it.

"This is the clinic?" Kgosi asked in heavily Afrikaans-accented English.

"Yes, *mwalimu,*" Adriana said, using the Swahili term of respect for someone of the Muslim faith.

"You are South African, girl?"

Raising her eyes, Adriana saw that Kgosi had removed his sunglasses and was staring at her. Many things had changed, but not those reptilian eyes.

A demure smile graced Adriana's lips. "Yes, I was raised in South Africa, then went to America to study and now have returned to help the people."

"The people!" Kgosi spat. "They don't need help. This is Africa." He turned away and looked out at the thousands of people living in squalor. "She will give and take as she sees fit.

"I am Commander Egwu, an important man in Africa. I have come with my men for the vaccination to the flu. We have come from Kenya, where thousands are sick, many dying. I was informed"— turning back to face Adriana now—"that you have a supply."

"Yes, Commander, we do—a small supply, but I would be glad to provide it to you and your men straightaway."

Adriana could tell that Kgosi had been expecting at least some resistance. He had probably been looking forward to flexing his muscles a bit. When he didn't respond, she said, "If you would call your men and have them step to that table . . ." She pointed at a small wooden table behind her.

Adriana spoke to the two other staff members with her. It had been decided that only a few staff would stay, just in case things got nasty. She gave scripted instructions, and the two men went to set up.

Seven of Kgosi's men filed into the clinic, followed by four burka-clad women— or perhaps girls. Adriana hadn't seen them when the men arrived—they must have been lying down in the back of the trucks. They walked behind the men, their heads bowed.

Adriana assumed that Kgosi would go first, but instead, he waved his men and the four women to go in front of him. As she arranged the alcohol swab packets and the syringes, it occurred to her that he probably had people taste his food, too.

The men lined up and rolled their sleeves up to expose their upper arms. Adriana stood in front of the table and, one by one, swabbed each arm, injected the vaccine, and pulled a bandage from her smock and placed it over the injection site. Her years of lab experience had taught her to be methodical, efficient, and, most importantly, observant. She had only two contagions left: MRSA and *E. coli.* Several of the men had visible scrapes and cuts, and a few looked a bit sickly, as if they might have eaten or drunk something that disagreed with them. Regardless, she just wanted them to get sick—the sicker the better.

After the seven men had been vaccinated, the women stepped forward. They were timid, and although she couldn't make out their ages or any physical details, as she took the first women's arm at her wrist, she felt the unmistakable tremors of fear.

"Do not worry. This won't hurt," Adriana said in Swahili as she slid the baggy sleeve of the dark gray burka up to expose a thin, young arm.

Finally, Kgosi Egwu stepped up to the table and rolled up his sleeve. Adriana gave him the influenza vaccine and put a *regular* Band-Aid over the injection site.

CHAPTER THIRTY

IT WASN'T UNTIL ADRIANA TOOK the job at Canada's National Microbiology Laboratory that she realized that Dr. Koch had been preparing her for this day since he picked her up dirty and afraid, from her home after her family's murder. Since her arrival in Loliondo she and the doctor had spent much time discussing how she might draw Kgosi to her. As far as what she would do once she had him, as Dr. Koch never tired of reminding her, "In the bush, nothing is as you expect and everything is more than you could possibly imagine."

It was late afternoon, and the director of the Loliondo clinic invited Kgosi and his men to stay the night. She felt that establishing a bit more goodwill couldn't hurt. *Brilliant!* thought Adriana. And she hadn't even had to suggest it. The last thing she wanted was for Kgosi and his men to load up and take off. She needed to get him by himself, away from town.

An early dinner of rice with roasted goat was served in the main assembly room of the school. They set up cots in two of the classrooms. Kgosi ordered the females Adriana now knew to be teenage girls to be fed and confined in one of the classrooms. It was just three in the afternoon. The sun wouldn't be down for another three and a half hours.

After the meal, Adriana returned to the hut she shared with Dr. Koch. They sat at the table and through the open door could see Kgosi's men milling about, smoking and drinking bottles of Castle Ranger, a popular Tanzanian beer. The men stayed within the confines of the original village because they wanted as little exposure as possible to the sickness and disease that surrounded Loliondo.

Dr. Koch got up and began collecting gear and arranging it on the table—a digital camera, a high-powered rifle with a scope, a rifle that shot tranquilizer darts, three canteens of water, and his leather-holstered pistol. Picking up his canvas rucksack, which contained a first-aid kit, emergency food, and ammunition and darts, he slung it over his shoulder. "Load that gear in the back of the truck." He handed her one of the canteens. "Hide yourself under the tarp."

Adriana watched as the doctor walked out of the hut and approached the men, his manner friendly and confident. She couldn't hear them, but she had spent enough time with the doctor to know he had a plan. She smiled and remembered one of the first lessons he had taught her. "The idea of a plan implies a set of anticipated circumstances. There is no such thing on the savannah. Out in the bush, a plan must be formulated in the moment, and if you are to survive, you must be ready to change it in an instant."

Behind the hut, Adriana loaded the truck, putting the rifles in the rack mounted over the back window. Then she climbed into the bed and nestled in amid the gear covering herself with the tarp.

* * *

ADRIANA LAY IN THE TRUCK and waited.

"If you follow me, I will show you where to turn off," Dr. Koch was saying. "It is thirty kilometers or so. I think you will find Nani Hill very private, and there is a spectacular view down to a rock escarpment frequented by a pride of lions. You may even be able to watch them hunt."

"Thank you, Doctor. It is safe?"

"Yes, yes, I have permission to be there. No one will mind."

Adriana heard a vehicle door open, then a voice, not the doctor's. *"Kry 'n baie wees."* Afrikaans for "Get in and be quiet."

Then the door of the truck opened. Doctor Koch said in a low voice that came from just above her covered head, *"Sobohla manyosi."*

Adriana smiled. It was a Zulu proverb, one of her father's favorites. Literally, it translated as "The honey will end," but it really meant, "What you have will end one day."

* * *

ADRIANA SETTLED IN. SHE HAD waited all her life for this day. That some lived and some died—and that at times she would decide which—well, that was a responsibility she had been taught to shoulder. As the truck rambled over the dirt track, she recalled the time when this lesson imprinted itself forever on her consciousness.

She had just turned 13 and had been spending more and

more time with Doctor Koch as he made his rounds from camp to camp across the Serengeti. At that time, four main elephant herds lived in the district. But because of years of drought, there wasn't enough food or water to support them all. She and Dr. Koch had been tracking and cataloging the herds over the course of three months. Early one morning, they observed two of the herds approaching the same water hole. Even as a young teenage girl, it was clear to Adriana that the mudhole, no bigger than ten feet in diameter, did not hold enough water for even one group.

She and Dr. Koch watched the elephants move in, the matriarchs, managing their groups. Like good mothers, grandmothers, and aunts they began to push the young toward the mudhole.

"So, Adie, what do think we should do?"

Everything about her time with the veterinarian was a lesson, so before answering, she considered the question.

"We could cull from each herd—take the old and the weak—but then we would still have four herds in distress. The grief would be overwhelming for the surviving family members, and in the end, we would accomplish nothing. Indeed, we might doom them all. We must remove one herd completely."

"Which one?"

Adriana remembered the conversation as if it were yesterday. There had been no emotion, no inner conflict, as she watched the two herds, over one hundred elephants in all. These two herds were in the worst shape. And even if they removed one, many members of the remaining herds would die over the coming dry season. They had labeled the herds 1, 2, 3, and 4. At the moment, they observed 1 and 4.

"We need to cull herd four. They're in the worst shape and have the largest numbers of young and old. Tomorrow we need to bring in the rangers as well as the outfitters from the closest safari camps. We need pros to make this happen as fast and painlessly as possible. Could take a few days."

Adriana could still see the doctor's eyes when he looked at her. When she came into his life, he was already a confirmed bachelor, a man who had no intention of ever marrying, let alone having children. But that day, the proud look of a father shown in his eyes.

The truck began to slow. Peering through the edge of the tarp, Adriana could see the sun beginning to set. The doctor always headed out at this hour, one of the best times of day to observe the Serengeti's apex predators: lions, leopards, and hyenas.

The truck stopped and the doctor got out. "This is the top of the rise. Just drive down half a kilometer and on your right you will see a thatched hut. There is a bench to sit on. *Het 'n goei nag.*"

After bidding a good night to Kgosi Egwu, the doctor got back in his truck and proceeded down the road. A few minutes later, the truck stopped.

"It's okay, Addie, you can get out," the doctor called through the open window.

Climbing out of the truck bed, Adriana grabbed her pack and the canteen. Standing next to the truck, the doctor handed her the tranquilizer-dart rifle, along with a case of five darts.

"Do you remember this place?"

Adriana looked around. When she came to Loliondo, the doctor brought her here a couple of times a week at first, then more often, until they came nearly every day. Her introduction to the East African bush, and her interest in biology and ecosystems took root here. She smiled at the slight man.

She took the rifle. "If I never told you, thank you for all you have done for me."

The doctor reached out and laid his callused hand on her arm. "You know what to do. You've always known. I'll you meet you in Mound Town."

* * *

ADRIANA MADE HER WAY OFF the road and returned in the direction they had just come. She was less than a kilometer from where Kgosi should be. For the briefest moment, it occurred to her that he might not be there, but then she put the thought out of her mind. Of course he would be there, because, like all hunters, he was a predator of opportunity and habit.

In ten minutes she was on the bluff, fifty yards above the thatched hut. Kgosi's truck was there, but she couldn't see anyone. Then, off to the left, she saw movement. It was Kgosi. He seemed to be alone. He must have walked down the road to the next rise just to make sure no one else was around. He walked up to the passenger door, opened it, and pulled the gray-robed girl from the truck. Roughly he walked her to the back of the truck, where he put down the tailgate. He said something, but Adriana was too far away to make out what.

Hesitantly, the girl removed her head covering and then dropped her robe to the ground. She stood in the light of the setting sun, naked.

Adriana knelt and loaded a dart into the rifle. She didn't need to question the dosage. The doctor had a legendary knack for estimating an animal's weight, so that the dosage would knock it out quickly, but not kill it.

Through the scope, Adriana could see a tall, thin girl, with a long neck, high cheekbones, and small breasts, trembling. 13 or 14, maybe, her black hair cropped close. Her big doe eyes filled with fear. From her body type, Adriana thought the girl might be Maasai. If so, getting her back to her people would be a bit easier, since this was their territory.

Kgosi pushed the naked girl up against the tailgate, unbuckled his belt, and let his pants fall around his ankles.

Adriana slowed her breathing and gave herself an imaginary pat on the back for going to the indoor range at least a once a month during her studies in America and while she worked in Canada.

Kgosi lifted the girl off the ground as if she were nothing more than a sack of grain, and sat her down hard on the tailgate. With both hands, he forced her knees apart. Grasping the girl by both wrists, he leaned his weight into her, toppling her onto her back. As his bottom came into view, Adriana fired the dart.

There was a momentary pause, and she hoped he wouldn't penetrate the girl before he passed out. Then, as if on cue, Kgosi slumped forward, his full weight on top of the girl.

Adriana had to rein in the urge to run down to them. She couldn't let the girl see her. Then, like a tiny dik-dik antelope that has miraculously escaped the lioness's crushing jaws and flesh-rending claws, the girl squirmed and wriggled free. Without hesitating, she picked up her robe and ran naked up the road.

The dosage would keep Kgosi out for at least a half hour. She wanted to give the girl time to get far enough away—quite possibly, already with the doctor.

Adriana waited a few minutes, then made her way down to the truck. Working quickly, Adriana removed a few things from her pack, set them on the tailgate, and stored her gear in the cab. Jumping into the back of the truck, she grabbed the cable of the come -along that was mounted to the roll bar against the back of the cab and used for pulling large game up into the bed. She secured the cable around Kgosi's wrists and, with both hands, winched his body up into the truck so that he was up against the cab, hands above his head, pants still around his knees. Then, with a roll of duct tape, she secured his legs. The whole operation took just a few minutes. She looked at her watch. The man would be out for another fifteen or twenty minutes. All she needed was five.

Adriana headed down off the bluff. Once on flat ground, she drove west and there, right in front of her, was Mound Town.

* * *

Adriana weaved through an alien landscape until dozens of conical earthen mounds that looked like miniature volcanoes, surrounded the truck.

She came to a stop, taped her pants at the ankles, rolled her long sleeves down, did the same at her wrists, and got out of the truck.

In the back of the truck, Kgosi began to stir. Out of her pack, she took a hard plastic case about the size of a paperback book, opened it, and got out a syringe. Holding it up, she tapped it a few times with her finger, more out of habit than anything else, and crawled into the back of the truck. Kneeling, she injected the contents of the syringe into the base of Kgosi's neck. Then she stepped down off the truck bed and, leaning against the tailgate, took a long drink of water from the canteen. She wiped her mouth on her shirtsleeve and waited for Kgosi to come fully awake.

His first movements were sluggish. As his eyes came into focus, Adriana made sure he saw her first.

It took him a moment to realize he was tied up. His voice had the tone of someone accustomed to giving orders, and more importantly, having those orders obeyed without question. "Girl, you untie me this instant!"

Adriana stared at him. Being this close to him bothered her more than she had expected.

"Did you hear me? Free me!"

Adriana held up the empty syringe. "Tetrodotoxin."

"What?"

"Tetrodotoxin, the poison of the puffer fish. Perhaps you do not know what a puffer fish is?"

Kgosi was struggling now, moving his taped-together legs. The more he moved the more the steel winch cable bit into his

154

wrists.

"The more you struggle, the faster the poison will take affect." She held up another syringe. "If you want to live, the antidote must be administered in . . ." She made a show of looking at her watch, ". . . five minutes."

Adriana stood back and watched the man who had changed her life—who, in fact, had led her to this very moment. He began to move his lips as if he had just eaten something very sour.

She stepped closer to the truck. "You can feel it? This is just the beginning. Soon you will be completely paralyzed. So here is the deal: You want the antidote? I need five hundred thousand Euros. Now, we have only a few minutes before the antidote will no longer work."

Adriana climbed into the truck bed, Kgosi's satellite phone in her hand.

This was one of the many contradictions of brutal gangsters who operated in the remote regions of the world: despite the primitive nature of the land and of their own actions, they were right up there with drug cartels, human traffickers, and heartless dictators when it came to sophisticated schemes for hiding money.

"What is the speed-dial number of your bank?"

Kgosi moved his head slowly from side to side. Maybe she shouldn't have injected him in the neck.

"Your time is wasting."

"Number three." Kgosi grunted, the poison clearly beginning to affect his throat muscles.

Adriana hit the number and held the phone to Kgosi's ear. "You'd better hope your banker is in."

She listened as her captive began to speak into the phone, first answering security questions, then giving his account number. From her shirt pocket, she withdrew a piece of paper, unfolded it, and held it up. Thankfully, Kgosi still had enough voice control to rattle off the long list of bank routing numbers.

With the last number spoken, Adriana took the phone away. "Now, before you can no longer move your head and while we still have a bit of daylight, I want you to take a look around."

With visible effort, Kgosi moved his head right, then left, then looked out of the back of the truck.

"I see you know what they are. That's good."

"I did . . . the money . . . Give me . . . the . . . the shot."

"Oh this?" She held up the empty syringe. "There is no

antidote."

Adriana knelt in front of him, no longer afraid. "You don't know me, but I know you. I watched from inside an acacia bush hideout as you murdered my father, then my brother. Then I listened to my mother scream as you and your men raped her and then murdered her as well. You think Africa is only for blacks, that whites have no place here? I was born here, just like you, as were my father and mother, and their parents before them. You . . ." she paused, the anger and hatred welling inside like a wave ready to crash on the beach. "You decided to take all that from me, and today I am taking everything away from you.

"In just a few minutes, you won't be able to blink or speak. Now, if I guessed the dosage right, the paralysis should stop just short of a complete respiratory shutdown."

By this point, Kgosi could barely hold his head up, and the muscles in his face couldn't form any recognizable expression. His eyes still held her, but the rage seemed to be gone, replaced with terror.

Adriana stood and released the winch. Kgosi's hands fell to his lap. She undid the cable as his eyes stayed focused on her face. "I am going to drag you out of this truck and leave you on the ground. It's almost foraging time for the ants."

Adriana got out of the truck. She tied a length of rope around Kgosi's ankles, and attached the other end around the trunk of a baobab tree just beyond the ant mounds. She drove the truck forward about ten feet until she heard the limp body of Kgosi Egwu thud onto the dry earth.

She removed the rope and the tape and stood over him. The look in his eyes was just as she had hoped it would be: pure unadulterated fear. A few of the ant colony's soldiers were already crawling over his pants.

"Unlike when you and your men raped my mother, I won't have to listen to you scream. Imagine what it's going to be like: feeling everything, knowing everything, and being able do nothing about it. Now, as you feel those little creatures eating your eyes, stinging your most delicate parts, and carrying you off, one tiny bite at a time, maybe you will have some sense of what I went through."

Adriana cleaned up, making sure she left nothing. Getting into the truck, she drove a short way back up the bluff. Then she got out and climbed onto the bed, laid the rifle over the top of the cab, and peered through the scope. There were only a few more minutes of fading daylight; the sun already a sinking orange blob on the horizon. She could see Kgosi. His clothing looked alive—and in a way, it was. She had no idea how long he would last or whether the toxin she had injected him with would eventually paralyze his diaphragm and suffocate him, but she did know that for at least as long as her mother had suffered, so would he.

She would leave the truck back at the hut on Nani Hill. It would be found tomorrow, and all kinds of theories would be put forth about what had happened. As for Kgosi, what the ants didn't eat, the hyenas would—bones and all.

CHAPTER THIRTY-ONE

December 19, Ciudad Juárez, Mexico

At five in the morning, Santiago and Matías Cruz waited in line on the Mexico side of the Stanton Street Bridge, which would take them across the border into El Paso, Texas. The youngest of five siblings, Santiago, 20, and Matías, 18, had been living with their mother and an aunt in Juárez for the past two years while working as construction day laborers in El Paso.

Santiago shuffled his feet and shifted the small pack on his back. Matías looked at his brother and smiled. They were used to standing in this line, feeling tired and desperate, but today was different.

Matías reached up and rubbed his arm through his jacket. The shot he had gotten an hour ago still ached a bit.

The line stretched ahead and behind them as thousands queued up for the trip. Literally only a few hundred feet, it could take three hours round-trip on a good day, and as much as eight on a not-so-good one, which they all seemed to be since the Internet crash in the U.S. Santiago leaned over toward his brother and said in a mix of Spanish and English, "*No* worries, *mi hermano.* Tomorrow *vamos a Colorado.*"

* * *

December 20, Nogales, Sonora, Mexico

Rosaura Díaz sat on a plastic lawn chair with her nine-month-old son, Francisco, in her arms, in Pesqueira Street Plaza. Her other children, 11-year-old Emilio and 7-year-old Sofía wandered nearby through the outdoor crafts market. Poor and three months pregnant, for her and the children, this tourist destination was their only entertainment. Her husband, the children's father, was a drunk, a good-for-nothing *aplanacalles* who, it seemed, every time he forced himself on her, reeking of *mezcal* and sweat, left her with another child in her belly.

As the children ran around, she sat on a folding chair when an older woman struck up a conversation. Wearing a simple dark dress and worn leather *huaraches*, she seemed nice. They spoke for a few minutes when the woman asked in Spanish if Rosaura had ever lived in America.

Rosaura shook her head, no.

"Would you like to?"

Of course she would. Who wouldn't? But she did not answer.

"What if you and your children could go to America and live? Would that not be wonderful?"

"*Sí*, wonderful," said Rosaura.

"You speak English?"

"Yes. I work on the other side." She nodded in the direction of the United States and patted her just barely showing belly. "When I'm not having children."

"Do you have family there?"

"Yes. Not in Arizona, but I have a sister and a brother in Nuevo México."

A sparkle came into the woman's eyes.

"What if I could give you and your children the opportunity to go and stay in America? Would you be interested?"

Of course she was interested. But she had no money.

The woman scooted her plastic chair closer. She leaned in and spoke quietly. "I will give you money: one thousand dollars for you and five hundred for each of the children. And tomorrow you will cross to do some Christmas shopping. Will your sister or brother come pick you up?"

Rosaura was listening, but she had to concentrate. She might be poor, but she wasn't stupid. She had heard the horror stories about mothers with young children who were offered a life in the States, only to end up in unspeakable circumstances, sold into slavery, and worse.

The woman reached out and patted her hand and said in Spanish, "I tell you before God"—she made the sign of the cross—"what I say is true. You think about it, and if you want, meet me at the *Taquería Panchito* tomorrow at six in the morning, with your *hijos*." The woman patted her hand again, looked deliberately at each of the children, then ran her hand lightly over Rosaura's belly. "This could well be the only chance you and your children may ever have for a better life."

***

December 21

EARLY THE NEXT MORNING AS her husband snored, Rosaura woke the children, dressed them, grabbed what she could carry in a shoulder bag, put what would fit in Emilio's small backpack, and headed for the *taquería*. When they arrived, she found the place busy and the woman she had met the day before speaking to another mother with children. She noticed Rosaura, and held up her hand indicating that she would be just a few more moments.

Rosaura and her children sat at a table in the back. A server brought scrambled eggs, soft *queso,* and fresh, hot tortillas. "Eat, please," the woman said to the family. "I am glad you decided to come." Withdrawing an envelope, she counted out two hundred dollars in twenties, and twenty-three crisp hundred-dollar bills and laid them on the table in front of Rosaura.

Rosaura made no move to touch the pile of money—far more than she had ever seen.

"Now, there is one formality we must complete, and you are on your way."

Rosaura looked at the woman, a sudden wariness in her expression.

"You have heard of the flu, *la gripa,* they have in America?"

Rosaura nodded, although, she really didn't know.

"I have a flu vaccine for each of you." She held up a wrapped syringe.

Rosaura looked at the money and thought about her brother who had left New Mexico yesterday and would be waiting for them in a store parking lot a short distance from the border crossing. The whole thing was beyond comprehension—so much money! If they wanted to give her and the kids a vaccination for the flu, why not?

***

AS ROSAURA AND THE CHILDREN approached the Morley pedestrian gate to cross over into Nogales, Arizona, she saw the familiar face of Ernesto Sanders, an American Immigration and Customs agent.

"Rosaura, good morning," the agent said as she and the kids

stepped forward.

Rosaura handed over her green card and the copies of the kids' birth certificates, which she always kept in her purse.

Ernesto looked at Emilio. "Are we going to do a little Christmas shopping today?" he asked the boy, with a sly look that implied the lad was old enough to understand about Santa.

"Yes sir," Emilio answered with a friendly smile.

The ICE agent scanned Rosaura's green card, which kept a digital record of her crossings, and handed it back to her. "Enjoy your day, and if I don't see you, *Feliz Navidad.*"

* * *

December 21, Tijuana, Baja California del Norte, Mexico

JOHN MORALES HAD BEEN IN *Tijuana* a week. For the past year, he had been living with his father midway down the Baja peninsula, in Santa Rosalía. The French copper mine the town had been built around, stood fenced off, contaminated, and abandoned. Although right on the coast, with rocky, coarse sand beaches, it was far from a mainstream tourist destination. *Pretty much a shit-hole,* thought John.

He had lived in California, just north of San Diego, from the time he was two months old until just after his seventeenth birthday. His father came home from work one day and told him he had lost his job and they could no longer afford to stay in the United States. John had to leave school at the beginning of his senior year. John's father had a friend who said he could get them both jobs at the newly opened el Boleo copper mine outside of Santa Rosalía.

John hated every day of it. As he stood in line at the *Puerto México el Chaparral* crossing that would take him into San Ysidro, California, just north of the border, he stared off in the direction of the country he called home. What a difference a mile could make! On one side, clean streets, clean water, and unbroken sidewalks; on the other, a place where everyone seemed to be on the hustle, and begging was an accepted way to make a living.

He inched along in the line and felt his anger lift. After all, he was an American. It certainly wasn't his fault his mother had brought him to the United States when he was just a baby to join his dad who had been there nearly a year. Or that, before he turned three, his mother had left with a Bible salesman and was never heard from again. English was his first language. And his name was John, not Juan. It had *never* been Juan.

In *Tijuana* it had taken only a few hours to find a group of young people just like him. They were here to find a way back home. Yesterday, he had been hanging out at the beach with a group of other young people when they met a young man and woman. *Gringos*—Americans, John assumed, but it turned out they were Canadian. Over a few beers the topic of the border came up. For a while, the conversation was light, the Latino kids lamenting that they hadn't been raised in Canada, but then the man suggested something that sounded crazy.

The man explained that he was part of a group trying to make a broad statement about the disastrous immigration policy of the United States—something John and the others had strong feelings about. He went on to say that for a limited number, if they were ready to step up now, he would give a green card and a thousand dollars. All they had to do was get a flu vaccine.

It sounded simple, and a bit odd. But, hell he'd get a dozen flu shots if it would get him across the border.

CHAPTER THIRTY-TWO
Anaheim, California

Jabril al-Mohmoud pulled away from his mother's grasp and ran toward Mickey Mouse. "Mickey the mouse!" he cried, running up to the life-size cartoon character who stood, surrounded by a bunch of excited, smiling children at the entrance to Sleeping Beauty's castle.

His mother, Rasha, smiled as she watched her son. For the past two days, he had barely left her side despite her encouragement. It heartened her to see him finally coming out of his shell, acting like the other kids, especially on their last day. Tonight the park, all lit up, looked like something from a fairy tale.

Diar and Murad, the bodyguards, kept a discreet distance, uncomfortable in their dark suits and not exactly blending in. Rasha dressed like any suburban mom in jeans and casual canvas slip-ons had brought her child to Disneyland during the park's most magical time: Christmas.

* * *

From the bridge that led into the tunnel of the castle, Tajo Alano Zambrano, known as Taz, shadowed Jabril and his mother, as he had for the past two days. This was the first time the boy had left his mother's side. With his phone, he took a picture of the boy, then of the two bodyguards, and, finally, one of the mother, and forwarded them to his crew, waiting on the other side of the castle. There, on Main Street U.S.A., the Christmas Fantasy Parade would begin in a half hour. *What a cakewalk,* thought Taz. The easiest money he had made in a while. He had five men in position. They'd brought their wives or girlfriends and kids along as cover.

Taz watched as the woman took pictures of her son, all smiles and waves, standing with Mickey's white-gloved hand draped over his small shoulder, against the backdrop of Sleeping Beauty's Castle. He followed as mother and son made their way through the castle and out onto Main Street U.S.A. Decorated from pavement to treetop, every building and lamppost strung with lights, the huge Christmas tree at the far end of the street beckoned.

Taz stayed well back as Jabril, Rasha, and the bodyguards maneuvered through the throng to a point midway up the street near the edge of the sidewalk, where they could get a good view. Over the PA system, a cheery voice announced the beginning of the parade, and with Christmas music playing behind a scripted narration, the entire ensemble of Disney characters, along with Santa, the reindeer, and dozens of elves came dancing and waving down the street. The onlookers smiled excitedly, pointing and taking pictures.

Taz meandered through the crowd until he stood directly behind Jabril and his mom. Glancing around, he saw the rest of his crew nearby. Their children, eleven in all, had moved up and flanked Jabril on both sides. As the parade made its way up the street, hundreds of kids jockeyed for a spot where they could get a hug and maybe even a picture with their favorite character.

Taz looked around and spotted the two Syrian bodyguards. A solid mass of parents and kids stood in front of them as they watched from twenty feet away with their backs to one of the curio shops.

As Santa and his sleigh approached the kid inched out onto the road. Jabril seemed a bit tentative, holding tight to his mother's hand, but as the other kids pushed forward so their parents could get a picture of them with Santa, so did he. The atmosphere was electric. *And why wouldn't it be?* Taz reflected. The Disney people were the consummate pros with a tried and true business model: happy children meant spending parents.

Taz's son, David, was the one keeping track of the brood of kids. Even though he was only 12, the boy knew the ropes. His father ran the El Paso operation for the Barrio Aztecas, and the family's nice house and cars, and David's private Catholic school education came from the money his dad made. As the kids moved along with the parade of characters making their way toward the big Christmas tree at the end of the street, David made sure Jabril stayed in the group.

* * *

RASHA WAS APPREHENSIVE, BUT JABRIL was finally having a good time. When the kids moved off the sidewalk onto the apron of the street, she figured she was close enough. Glancing over her shoulder, she saw Diar and Murad still with their backs to the storefront. She began taking photos. One of the older kids, who had been standing next to them, was pointing out to Jabril the characters dressed as two -legged reindeer.

He was saying their names and pointing. "It's Donner, Blitzen, and hey, look, there's Rudolph!"

Even though the names meant nothing to Jabril, she could see that he was caught up in the excitement, and every time he glanced back at her, her heart swelled to see him so happy. Things had been difficult for him since his father went missing.

Even though Adad had been away much of the time on business, he always made sure to speak with his son at least once a week. The last contact anyone had with him was almost four months ago, when he spoke with his father, Sheikh Nazir. Within a few days of that conversation, Rasha and Jabril moved into the al-Mohmoud family home in Damascus out of fear for their safety. As weeks turned into months and with no further contact with his son, the sheikh became increasingly attached to Jabril. Then, as the civil war continued to escalate and living in Syria became too dangerous, Rasha and Jabril had gone with him to Amman.

As Rasha watched Jabril, she glanced around at all the families—*all the women!*—and marveled that she and Jabril were here. Her married life had been a traditional Muslim one. As dictated by the Quran, Adad had the absolute right of supremacy over the family, in all things. Her role was strictly as caregiver to Adad's son. Rasha was not allowed to drive or go out in public uncovered, and although highly educated, she had no say in her husband's business, and little real knowledge of it. The truth was, if Adad were still present in their lives, this trip would never have happened—at least, not for her.

The more time Rasha and Jabril spent with the sheikh, the more indulgent the old man became with his grandson. He let the boy watch TV—almost exclusively animated Disney videos—and Jabril had grown obsessed with Disneyland. The whole idea of coming to the United States had not been hers but, rather, the sheikh's. Then the Internet crash right after Thanksgiving happened, and the United States locked itself down, and it looked as though the trip wouldn't happen.

Looking around again, Rasha envied how easily Americans moved past tragic events. Arabs, by contrast, seemed to harbor a deep and lasting sense of personal injury when something tragic happened in their countries.

After the Internet crash, it had taken a couple of weeks for limited private air traffic to resume. Even with the heightened state of alert, and most commercial air travel restricted, those with means could still manage. The sheikh's private jet had no problem landing at John Wayne Airport in Orange County.

Rasha watched as the reindeer came to the edge of the street, to where Jabril and the large group of children stood. Cameras flashed as kids jumped around and laughed. She looked over her shoulder again and saw their bodyguards still there. Jabril and the group with him began moving up the sidewalk as the parade procession continued down Main Street U.S.A. The crowd also started to move in that direction, growing denser as it neared the big, lit-up tree. Rasha got up on tiptoes and tried to peer over the heads of other anxious and excited parents. She could see the group of kids a dozen paces ahead, but she couldn't make out Jabril.

In the next instant, Rasha found herself hemmed in by the crowd. Panic began to set in. Long minutes passed before she could get close to the tree. There was no sign of Jabril, nor did she see any of the children who had surrounded him. In British-accented English, she cried out, "Jabril! Jabril!"

* * *

IN THE RUSH AND EXCITEMENT, Jabril found himself off Main Street and near the entrance to the Jungle Cruise. He looked around and tried to figure out from which direction he had come. He noticed that some of kids near him had been some of the same ones with him on the sidewalk when he was last with his mother. The biggest one, the boy who knew the names of the funny deer characters, bent down and said, "Hey, man, you lost?"

Jabril nodded and began to cry.

"Don't worry, I'll help you find your mom. My name's David. What's yours?"

"Jabril," he said between sobs.

David knelt. "She's probably looking for you right now. There are lots of people who work here, and their job is to help lost kids. There's my dad." David pointed to a man standing on the sidewalk, speaking to some other men and women. "Let's go talk to him; he'll help."

Holding on to his new friend's hand, Jabril walked up to the man.

"Dad, this kid's lost. Can you help him?"

Taz said a few more words to the people with him. Then he turned to the two boys. "Sure, I can. Hey . . ."

"His name's Jabril."

"Jabril . . ." Taz reached out and took him by the hand. "Let's go sit down, get you something to drink, and wait. I'm sure your mom will be right here."

Jabril had no point of reference for how he should act in this situation. In his world, the idea that a stranger might harm him meant nothing. There were no strangers in his life.

The three of them found a bench near a stand that sold kettle corn and soft drinks. Leaving David and Jabril, Taz bought three sodas, one of which he put the contents of two Benadryl capsules in.

Jabril took the offered soda hesitantly.

"Your mom don't let you drink soda?" Taz asked.

Jabril looked at Taz, then at the soda.

"It's okay, I'll tell her I gave it to you. Go ahead! Have a drink; it'll make you feel better."

Jabril took a sip. It did taste good, and he was thirsty. His mom probably wouldn't be too mad.

* * *

ON MAIN STREET, RASHA, DIAR, and Murad were in a heated, though whispered, conversation, being careful to speak English.

"Where is he? Where is Jabril?" Rasha demanded.

"We don't know," the bigger of the two, Murad, said. "One minute, he was with the other children, surrounded by those ridiculous creatures, and the next . . ."

"You should not have let him out of your grasp," Diar hissed. He looked at his watch. Less than five minutes had passed. "You stay here in case the boy comes back. Murad and I will each go a different direction. If we cannot find him in five minutes, we will notify the authorities."

Everything about the situation screamed to Rasha to find Park Security. She had read somewhere that it was protocol in cases of a missing child, to have the park locked down, but she couldn't argue with Diar. He was in charge; her father-in-law had been very clear on that point.

* * *

"Hey, finish up your soda," David said.

Jabril was sitting on a bench between David and his father. He looked tired and was slumping over—not an unusual sight in a place where kids, hyped up on excitement and sugar, went a hundred miles an hour and often ran out of gas.

Taz put his arm around Jabril's shoulders. "Hey *hijo*, what do you say we go get someone to help us find your mom?"

Jabril nodded, his eyes heavy.

Taz stood, took off his jacket, and handed it to his son. "Come on, I'll carry you. It's not far."

Jabril set his empty soda cup on the bench and reached his arms up as Taz lifted him from the bench.

After less than a minute of the gentle up-and-down walking motion, Jabril was sound asleep, his head on Taz's shoulder, his face turned toward the man's neck. David handed his father his jacket, which he draped over the sleeping boy.

At the exit, Taz looked at his watch. Fourteen minutes, and the gate was still open.

On their way out, the attendant said, "Looks like someone had too much fun."

Taz nodded and walked out to the parking lot, where the rest of his crew was loaded and ready to go. David opened the back door of a waiting Cadillac Escalade, got in, and helped his father lay the sleeping boy on the seat and cover him with a blanket. Taz got in the passenger seat. They had a long drive ahead of them.

* * *

Rasha, Murad, and Diar stood in line at the Disneyland City Hall on Main Street U.S.A. They were not the only people seeking help finding a lost child. By the time they got through the queue, Jabril had been missing for half an hour. After several more frustrating minutes speaking with a customer service representative, the three were led to a private office. It took another fifteen minutes to explain the situation, with Diar doing most of the talking. By the time they put the gates on monitored exit and a search for Jabril began, an hour had passed.

THIRTY-THREE

December 22, Beginnings Ranch, British Colombia

J. T. HAD A SNIT ON, as the team filtered into Ops.

"This just came across the secure network I set it up with Sheikh Nazir last year when we did the transfer of funds, mostly for me to keep tabs on him. To be honest, I never thought he'd use it."

The screen showed several lines of a script unrecognizable to most of the team.

Hamal "Ham" Kamal, Force 10's only native Arab speaker, rose from his chair and came to stand next to Marcus.

As they stared at the flowing calligraphy on the screen, they both had the same look of confusion.

"When the full light of night shines on *Tadmur,* at the temple of the king of Judea, pray with me to Allah for wisdom and forgiveness as the road to redemption and peace," Marcus said aloud.

"What does it mean?"

Ignoring Ham's question for the moment, Marcus said to J. T., "When's the next full moon?"

It took J. T. a couple of seconds. "In two days."

"Can you put up a picture of the ruins at the oasis of Palmyra? In Arabic, the word is 'Tadmur.'"

As his fingers moved over the pad, J. T. gave Marcus a baffled look.

"It's from Nazir," Marcus said to Ham.

"How do you know?"

"He and I walked through those ruins." Marcus nodded at the high-resolution picture on the monitor. "There, see the four columns and the ruins behind them? When I was there it was a large stone-walled chamber that the sheikh said was built by King Solomon, a thousand years before the Romans ever arrived. ISIS blew it up, claiming it was a symbol of Christianity. That's bullshit. They did it for shock value. Anyway, when we parted, I told him, 'May you and I both see wisdom and forgiveness as the road to redemption and peace.' I've never shared that with anyone.

"What are our options for getting to Palmyra?" Marcus asked of no one in particular.

Chaya walked past him and said, her tone deadpan. "Considering that between ISIS blowing the hell out of it and the Assad regime trying to regain control, the oasis has been turned into a war zone, it could be difficult. But let's see. " She sat at one of the computer consoles against the back wall, put on a headset, and began entering commands from the keyboard.

Still thinking out loud, Marcus said, "And why in the hell would the sheikh want to see me?"

J. T. said, "I think this might have something to do with it." A broadcast from a local Los Angeles news program appeared on the screen. The female reporter, standing in the parking lot of Disneyland, was saying that an 8-year-old boy had been abducted the day before.

Marcus looked at J. T., not getting it.

"I almost missed it. In the Amber alert, they used the mother's maiden name, Anika. Had Vanessa . . ." J. T. seemed to catch himself in an uncharacteristic moment of self-consciousness. ". . . not cross-referenced it. Anyway, I hacked into the LAPD and Disneyland's security office and got copies of the missing-person reports. Also, here are the pictures from the mother's camera."

J. T. posted them on the wall.

"The boy's name is Jabril al-Mohmoud."

Marcus spoke. "I met him—well, not *met*, exactly, but saw him . . . when I was at Palmyra, meeting with Nazir. He had a small boy with him, and I assumed he was Adad's son."

"Do you think Sheikh Nazir suspects you of having a hand in the boy's abduction?" the colonel asked.

"No, I don't think so," said Marcus, pacing again. For a few long moments, no one spoke.

"When did this happen?"

"Yesterday evening," said J. T.

"And they have no idea where the boy is or who might have taken him?"

"If they do, they're keeping it real quiet."

Marcus looked at the colonel.

"I'm on it," the colonel said, moving past Marcus to the console next to Chaya.

"Okay, J. T.," Marcus said, "work backwards. Let's take the

time his mother said she last saw him, and the time the park went on heightened alert, and use that as our window. Can you pull up the security footage from the exit gate?"

J. T.'s fingers flew over his touch pad as he spoke other commands to Vanessa. "Okay, here we go."

The team watched the video footage. But in truth, no one had a clue what to look for.

Marcus rubbed his hand over his unshaven face as he stared at the monitor. In the video footage, it was night, just about an hour before the park closed. People exited in a steady stream. Many had small children, lots of them being carried, others tucked away inside strollers. They faced a classic needle in a haystack, with one very big-ass haystack.

Marcus rubbed his eyes. "Go back! A little further. There! Stop! See the guy with the kid in his arms? Zoom in on that boy standing next to him. There—freeze it."

A boy of 10, 11, maybe 12, was in full view. Marcus walked over to the counter and grabbed a tablet. "J. T., give me the pictures from the mother's camera."

Standing in front of the screen, Marcus scrolled through the pictures of Jabril. Several showed him and Mickey. In others, crowds of kids surrounded Jabril, all against the backdrop of a Christmas parade. Marcus paused on one picture that showed Jabril, his attention flowing in the direction of the pointed finger of an older boy standing next to him. Marcus showed the tablet to J. T., who put the picture up on the big screen next to the paused frame of the video footage.

"It's the same boy. Zoom in on the man holding the kid. Can we get the child?"

J. T. played around for a few seconds. "No, the kid's face is turned away, and besides, the jacket is covering so much I can't even tell if it's a girl or a boy."

Marcus glared at the man holding the covered child. "Find out who he is."

* * *

"Meet Tajo Alano Zambrano, aka 'Taz.'"

Full-face and right- and left-profile mug shots of a Latino man in his late twenties stared out at the team. He had a thin face and short, spiky black hair. He wore a trimmed close-cropped goatee.

In the left profile, the man's neck had a tattoo of a scorpion.

"This guy's a piece of work. Robbery, drug trafficking, domestic violence, assault, grand theft auto, and that's all before he turned eighteen. He went to prison for statutory rape in Texas at twenty. Did a two-year stint in Amarillo's Clements unit—hands down, one of the worst prisons in the country.

"When he got out, our boy here had been recruited by the *Barrio Azteca*. This bunch is one of most violent gangs operating in the states. Their base of operation is El Paso, Taz's hometown. He's done quite well for himself."

The team stared at pictures of a nice house with a gated entrance and several cars, one a black Cadillac Escalade with what appeared to be a lot of aftermarket work.

"And look."

A few pictures of what looked like the same SUV from the Disneyland parking lot.

"These are from Disneyland security footage. I'm searching traffic cameras to see if we can track their route. Anyway, according to El Paso PD, he's definitely in upper management. Besides drugs and hookers, the *Barrio Azteca* are enforcers for hire by the big Mexican drug cartels and are well on their way to becoming a major player themselves.

"The boy is his twelve-year-old son, David. Mother deceased—heroin overdose when the boy was two. While his upstanding father was paying his debt to society, an aunt, Taz's older sister, took care of him."

The colonel had walked up to stand between Marcus and J. T. Marcus studied the picture of Taz with what they now all assumed was a sleeping Jabril al-Mohmoud in his arms.

"The FBI knows very little."

Marcus said, "Big surprise."

"They're aware of the abduction. So far, it's being handled on a local level with some input from the L.A. FBI field office."

Marcus cocked his head at the screen.

"What is it?" the colonel asked.

"When we were in Virginia, Deputy Director Reynolds said they'd picked up that cell phone transmission as part of a group of calls from Mexico City?"

"Yeah, he said it was from a burner phone, so they couldn't trace the exact location of the call, but that it was in a bundle of cell transmissions snagged by NSA. He was quite certain that even though there was no GPS signature, the call originated in Mexico City."

"So how's this for far-fetched?" Marcus said. "This guy, the voice of the man who killed Annie, has climbed into bed with one of the drug cartels. It wouldn't be the first time. J. T., when you and my brother were sorting through the al-Mohmoud assets, dividing them into two equally valued chunks, you found a bunch of investments that weren't exactly aboveboard."

It wasn't a question. So instead of answering, J. T. began posting pictures of denuded patches of rain forest, trucks loaded with logs ten feet in diameter, entire mountainsides being blasted with water cannons and groups of men and boys standing in ponds of mercury-poisoned water panning for gold. Under each photo was a brief description that included the enterprise, location, value, generated yearly gross revenue, and the most interesting fact— business partners. On its face, the partners were innocuous. But J. T. had plowed through the layers of corporations, trusts, and LLCs and traced many back to crime syndicates that included everything from Mexican and South American drug cartels to Russian and Asian mobs.

Marcus resumed pacing as he talked to the room. "So here's what I'm thinking. Our faceless voice has decided to resurrect the New Islamic Dawn. He's formed an alliance with a drug cartel, and for some reason, he's decided to squeeze Sheikh Nazir. Although it certainly has something to do with money, there has to be more to it. It makes sense."

Marcus paused. Around the room, they all had the same expression: *Makes sense? To whom?*

"Sure. Either group will do whatever it takes to achieve its goals, and neither has any compunction about killing innocent people. Fear is how they keep control. Chaos is their ally. Trust, beyond their ranks, doesn't exist. Each uses the other to attain a certain end. They are beholden to the two most powerful forces on earth: God and greed."

Marcus stopped walking and asked to J. T., "Have you noticed anything strange going on with the sheikh's finances?"

As account balances and transfer amounts came up on a portion of the monitor, a voice from the shadows in the back of the room said, "Very early this morning, two hundred million in cash was wired to those banks in Abu Dhabi, Singapore, and Switzerland. Because the sheikh is tied into the database J. T. set up, we can track a lot of his business dealings. Over the last several hours, there's been some consolidation of funds. It would appear that he might be planning on other transfers."

Marcus looked to the back of the room, caught Glen's eye, and gave him a nod.

* * *

CHAYA SAT AT THE COMPUTER station wearing a headset. Behind her, Marcus was doing his thing, making cognitive leaps that defied logic.

She began speaking Hebrew into the mouthpiece. All the members of Force 10 came with their own sets of connections from the past. For Chaya, that meant Mossad. The immediate problem confronting Force 10 was how to get to the Syrian desert oasis of Palmyra for a clandestine meeting with Sheikh Nazir in less than forty-eight hours. The last time the team visited this place, known by the locals as the Bride of the Desert, the *Takbir* was holding a hundred miles off the coast of Israel, in the Mediterranean. It was well within the range of the onboard Sikorsky Superhawk. This time, they were over six thousand miles away. Although, they did have a Boeing 767 at the Calgary International Airport with enough range to go nonstop to Israel.

Chaya finished her conversation and returned to where the colonel and Marcus were standing, their attention glued to the monitor.

"Okay, we have clearance to land at Ramat David Air Base, southeast of Haifa. From there, an unmarked Blackhawk will fly Marcus and whoever else is with him into Palmyra. Things are more complicated because of the battle between ISIS and Assad's army for control of the oasis. They have already destroyed some of the ancient ruins, and the situation is tense. A Shayetet 13 team will provide backup."

Marcus gave Chaya a questioning look.

"Shayetet 13—they're like the U.S. Delta Force."

"What about a pilot to get Marcus to Israel?" the colonel asked.

"I just got off the horn with our friends in the RCAF," said Bronson. "Lieutenant Colonel Anderson's got a reservist, a commercial pilot, who happens to be on station for the next two weeks. He said he could lend us the guy as well as a two-person flight crew. Seems they could use the flight time in a big commercial jet, and since it's free, and . . . oh, yeah, he'd like a case of—his words exactly—'that scotch the colonel likes so much.'"

"Make it two cases."

Marcus knew that under normal circumstances, there would be no question: Bronson would be flying the jet. But since the attack on the ranch, the colonel put an evacuation plan into effect. Two Gulfstream G5s were fueled, ready, and waiting in the newly completed hangar at the Beginnings airstrip. If the need arose, all Marcus's family could be in the air in twenty minutes. When the colonel explained the evacuation plan to the staff, they were hell-bent on staying, no matter what, as he expected. That attitude had been a key factor when he vetted the employees to see who would stay on after the change of ranch ownership. The colonel wanted people with a well-developed sense of self-preservation. He knew a situation might arise, as the attack on the ranch already proved, when he would need those who would fight, literally, to protect their lives and those of the other people who lived on the ranch.

The command center was wired with plastic explosives from above and below. If a full breach of the ranch happened, the entire cavern behind the barn, with a remote signal sent from the God's Eye satellite, would be blown up and buried under thousands of tons of rock and earth. The trouble was, an evacuation would require two pilots: Bronson and Jamie.

"Then it's decided. We need to be wheels-up within the hour. Sit, you, Ham, and Chaya go with Marcus. Bronson will fly you to Calgary and then return to the ranch. There's to be no fucking around." Everyone knew that the colonel's last comment was directed solely at Marcus.

* * *

While Ham, Sit, Chaya, and Marcus waited for Bronson to finish his preflight, the colonel stepped inside the jet's cabin. "You might need this."

He handed over Marcus's backpack—well, not precisely *his* backpack. This was the pack Marcus had taken, a year and a half ago, from one of the young men he and the boys had found ransacking their campsite on the day Annie went missing. It was battered and worn. Duct tape covered a half-dozen holes and tears. Marcus hadn't seen it since his arrival at the ranch, when he tossed it onto the closet shelf in his bedroom. He hadn't even bothered to unpack it.

Taking the pack from the colonel, Marcus recalled how this bedraggled piece of nylon and padding had been, on many occasions, like a magician's magic top hat—as if a wand had been waved over it and a few incantations uttered, each time Marcus reached in, he would pull out exactly what was needed for him to continue on his journey.

"You get what you need and get out. Christmas is in a few days and *you will be here!*"

"Yes sir," Marcus said as the colonel turned and got off the jet.

CHAPTER THIRTY-FOUR

December 23, Ramat David Air Base, Jezreel Valley, Israel

Stepping off the jet, a man dressed in a powder-blue cotton shirt, unbuttoned at the collar, with a small gold Star of David around his neck, met the team. In his mid-forties, the man's curly dark-brown hair seemed to Marcus a bit long for someone in the military. With a beard and mustache trimmed short, and dark sport-style sunglasses, he had a rugged, untamed look that Marcus liked.

Chaya was first on the tarmac. A smile spread across her face as she stepped into the man's open arms. "Eitan . . ."

They hugged for a moment, then the man held Chaya at arm's length. "*Shalom Malakh*. It is so good to see you again."

Listening, Marcus translated the Hebrew words: *peace angel*. It had been decided on the flight over that he would keep his language skills to himself, at least initially.

"I am happy to see you, Eitan. Your family is well?"

"Yes, Chaya, thank you."

"Eitan Ben Zeev, meet Marcus Diablo, Stanley, and Hamal."

Eitan gave each a cursory nod. "Now we must go. Our timeline is critical."

* * *

Marcus and the team loaded into a Hatehof Wolf, the Israeli version of the Humvee, which took them across the airport to a secure hangar to meet the leader of the Shayetet 13 team that would be their escort into the Syrian desert.

The division commander, Brigadier General Harel Shiloh,

wore a light-green beret and unmarked desert camo fatigues tucked into khaki canvas lace-up boots. He strode up to the team and greeted Chaya like an old friend with a warm embrace and a kiss on each check. Then he introduced himself to each member of the team, shaking hands. He stopped in front of Sit.

To Marcus, the two men appeared to be sizing each other up or having some kind of stare-down to see who might blink first. Then a broad smile spread across Sit's face as he gave the much smaller Israeli officer a bear hug.

"Harel, how goes the fight, my friend?" Sit asked. "I take it she still shoots true?"

"True as the day you gave her to me, Stanley. It is nice to see you again. And I must say, I am relieved to see that Chaya has chosen such fine company."

The general turned his attention to Marcus. "In our profession, friends are treasured, and to be reunited is a gift from God. He is a great teacher," he said, nodding at Sit. "You are an interesting man, Mr. Diablo. Mossad and Shin Bet—along with, it seems, your own intelligence agencies—have not quite figured you out. But if Chaya and Stanley stand with you, then so do we."

Stepping away from the team, Harel walked over to a table set up in front of a large monitor. Marcus and the team sat in folding chairs as the general began his briefing.

"This is the route we will fly." A map showed a red line from their current location to Palmyra. "We will refuel in Yontan." He pointed to a small dot in the Golan Heights. "It is a very small settlement of about three hundred and fifty. We maintain a discreet fuel depot there for just such situations, and even though the rest of the world refers to this area as 'disputed,' there is no dispute. It is our land."

The screen image shifted to a detailed topographical map of the area that encompassed Palmyra. "From Yontan, we are almost three hundred kilometers to our LZ. Flight time, if we don't encounter any trouble, is about ninety minutes. We'll enter from the north, using this ridge to mask our approach, and set down here, behind this hill," he said, following the ridgeline on the map with his finger. "It puts us one click from the ruins of Palmyra." Turning his back on the screen, he said, "We'll be flying a modified H-60 Blackhawk—quietest bird made."

Sit raised an eyebrow.

"Like the one your Seal Team Six had to destroy in the middle of the compound when they took down Bin Laden."

The general shifted his attention to Marcus. "We will have a maximum of one hour on the ground. Say, fifteen minutes to get from the LZ to the ruins each way—that gives you a half hour to get this meet-and-greet over. You will be designation Alpha. Sit and I will be providing long-range cover from this ridge. We are Echo and four of my men, in two pairs, Bravo and Charlie, will move in to cover you from closer range, here and here." The general pointed at two locations that would give each team a good view of the temple ruins from a couple hundred yards out. "You're going to be in among these walls and columns. You keep that in mind and try to stay in the open. Chaya, Ham, and the last member of my team, call sign Delta, will be in position here"—he pointed at a wall at the edge of the ruins—"to move in if everything goes to hell. We will all be wearing earbuds hooked into a secure frequency. If I give the go call, we go! Are we clear?" he asked, looking directly at Marcus.

Marcus glanced at Chaya. Well, it stood to reason that she might give her contact a heads-up about his sometimes-impulsive behavior. "Yes sir. Crystal!"

"Good. We are wheels-up at . . ." he looked at his watch. ". . . fourteen hundred hours. Our target ETA at the LZ is eighteen hundred hours at the latest—two hours after sunset. Now, I don't need to go into detail on the mess that's going on in Syria. We will have high-altitude cover from a squadron of F-16s, but—and I want to be clear—my country has no interest in getting any more involved with the ongoing conflicts in Syria than we already are. What is it your Colonel Webb likes to say? 'Get in, get the job done, and get your asses out.'"

* * *

AT 17:47 HOURS, THE BLACKHAWK set down at the designated landing zone. Everyone unloaded, geared up, and prepared to move into position. Marcus stood on the hard-packed desert floor, backpack in hand. He knelt and opened it. He removed the very same *djellaba*—a hooded simple full-length robe— he had worn the last time he visited this place. Shaking out the wrinkles, the garment smelled dirty and musty—all the better. He put it on over his drab gray wool *salwar kameez*—a coarse tunic and loose-fitting pants. It was much colder this time than on his last visit, in the hundred-degree August heat.

As Marcus was putting his empty pack back in the chopper, General Shiloh came up to him. "Here is your earbud. You will be able to hear only me, Sit, and Chaya. We don't want the rest of the chatter to distract you."

Marcus looked at the small hollow, flesh-toned device, in the palm of his hand about the size of a pencil eraser. He had seen this type of earbud before. Designed to fit into the ear, the outside had a tacky, soft membrane that formed to the shape of the ear canal and attached to the skin.

The inside was more rigid so as to inhibit natural hearing as little as possible. Inside the sphere's shell a series of microscopic receivers and transmitters operated from the body's electrical current.

"We have a contract of sorts with J. T.—have had for many years now. Oh, I'm sure he tells you that all his best stuff's been stolen and shelved. That boy loves a good conspiracy."

"I'm sorry about your wife. We have a Jewish proverb that says, 'When you have no choice, mobilize the spirit of courage.' That is what she did."

Marcus just nodded as he carefully worked the device into his ear. Millions of people had seen Annie die, and the general was right: if dying with your head held high, without a single note of begging in your voice, counted for anything, well then, Annie deserved a whole mountain of admiration.

Marcus stood with Chaya just below the rise of the hill. "You and I have to come to an understanding," he said. "For what you've done for me, for the boys, my words can't express my thanks. But you have to trust me like I trust you."

Chaya started to speak, but he held up his hand and then brought it to her cheek. "You and I, we're gonna figure this all out. I promise." Marcus lightly brushed his fingers down her cheek to the nape of her neck, then turned and walked over the hill.

* * *

THE FULL MOON IN A cloudless sky cast ghostly shadows over the desert, as Marcus made his way down the dune. In the light of day, this place would be a sea of sunstruck sand and rock, a vision of blotched yellows and golds on a rough-textured canvas. But at night, the colors faded to the ashen pallor of death. The ancient ruins, some of the most extensive in the world, represented a tradition of Greco-Roman architecture that spanned millennia and predated Islamic Arabia and the birth of Christ. Walking toward the crumbling sandstone walls and pillars that rose like broken and twisted skeletons from the harsh, barren earth, Marcus thought it looked apocalyptic and haunted.

Beyond the ruins lay the oasis. Marcus could see twinkling lights through the palm trees, and knew that near the water, in normal times, would be a collection of colorful Bedouin tents. Many Arabs, like the sheikh, considered a physical return to their historical past nothing less than a yearly obligation to Allah. Now, however, ISIS used the destruction of the historical ruins as another way to incite the West. And Assad used the fight against ISIS to show the world he had been unfairly labeled by the West as a tyrannical dictator. It was all crap Marcus didn't have time to worry about.

* * *

CLEARLY VISIBLE IN THE MOONLIGHT, the rubble that had been the ruins of the Temple of Baal Shamin, lay before Marcus's eyes, and it saddened him. When the sheikh had shown Marcus this ancient Christian temple, as they stood under the grand double-colonnaded portico, he spoke with such respect. It struck Marcus then that the sheikh spoke not so much as a Muslim, but more as just a man of God. At the northwest edge of the ancient city Marcus saw the six-columned entrance to the new meeting place—the Funerary Temple. Two of the four stone walls still stood, offering some privacy, especially in the dark. Although, as Marcus headed toward the temple, he thought how much longer it might be until it too was completely destroyed.

Approaching the temple, the voice of General Shiloh spoke in Marcus's ear. "We have at least five armed men around the temple. Proceed with care."

Marcus tapped his fingers just below his earlobe to confirm that he had received the message. Cautiously, he made his way across what was once a grand avenue. Stepping up the broken steps and peering between two of the columns he saw a robed man prostrate, his forehead pressed to the prayer rug he knelt on. Looking closer, Marcus saw another prayer rug next to the man and, to the left, what appeared to be a bowl with a folded towel beside it.

Marcus removed his shoes and let out a deep breath. Then he stepped into the ancient temple. Without speaking, he knelt on the rug over the dirt-and-stone floor. Seeing the bowl filled with water, he dipped his hands and went through the Wudu washing ritual in preparation for the Isha, the last of the required five prayers of the day. When he finished, he dried his hands, bowed his head, and prayed to Allah.

* * *

THE SHEIKH WAS FIRST TO rise. Marcus waited another minute, then got up, rolled up the rug and put it under his arm, and walked out of the temple. Standing beneath the colonnade, the two men looked at each other.

With his hands held together and his head bowed, Marcus said, "*Assalamu Alaikum.*"

According to custom, the sheikh replied in a greeting greater than had been given him. "*Wa Alaikum assaam wa rahmatu Allah.*"

The formalities complete, the sheikh said in heavily accented English, "Let us walk in this place of God while some of these magnificent ruins still stand." He set his rug down on top of the broken stone wall, gestured for Marcus to do the same, and, with his hands clasped behind his back, walked down the rough steps.

Marcus walked beside the sheikh, the father of Adad al-Mohmoud, the man responsible for setting fire to America and for Annie's death. For what seemed an eternity, the only noise was their feet moving over the rough ground, and the cold, dry whistle of a breeze that sounded to Marcus like the moaning of thousands of restless souls. Stopping next to a sandstone block the size of a bathtub, the sheikh sat.

"My grandson, Jabril, has been abducted. You may remember the young boy who interrupted our conversation last time we were together here." For the first time, the sheikh's eyes met Marcus's. "You know of this?"

Taking a seat next to Sheikh Nazir, Marcus said, "Yes, Sayid. I found out just before we received your message. Have you been contacted by those who took him?"

The sheikh stared down the length of ancient road. "My people say that he was taken by dealers in drugs, and they want money for his return."

"You do not believe this?"

"I have found that money is rarely the only purpose."

"You have paid money?"

"Two hundred million, but this is only an . . . what is the word? Ins . . ."

"Installment?"

"Yes, that is correct."

"So why did you contact me, Sayid?"

The sheikh shifted on the stone to face Marcus. "I did so against all advice. When we last spoke, you left me with an impression that you are not only a capable man but also a man of honor. I find myself an old man without a son, and now without my only grandson, and I must do all I can to save him."

"Who was with Jabril?"

"His mother and two of my best and most loyal bodyguards."

"I would like to speak to them."

The sheikh made a motion with his hand, which startled Marcus. Then, in his ear, he heard, "A group is moving toward you from the west. There are three, who are now being joined by two of the five we identified before."

Marcus casually brought his hand to his face and tapped his index finger under his ear, as he rose from the stone.

Moments later the group of five stood in front of Marcus and the sheikh. Four were men dressed in black, wearing body armor and carrying AK47 rifles. He could see earpieces, and small microphones attached to their collars, and assumed that the sheikh must also be wired. The fifth person wore a robe, head completely covered. Smaller than the black-clad men, *this must be the mother,* Marcus thought.

In Arabic, the sheikh said, "Diar, Murad, this is Marcus Diablo."

Marcus decided that the polite greetings could be skipped. He slowly pulled his robe up, keeping his free hand in clear sight, and took a photo from the pocket of his pants. Holding it out, he said, "Do you recognize the boy in this picture?"

The man named Diar took the photo from Marcus and shined a flashlight on it. "Yes, that is Jabril," he said in British-accented English.

"No, the other boy, the bigger one. Do you recognize him?

Diar and Murad had their heads close together, studying the photo. They spoke in hushed whispers; then Diar said, "Yes, he was in a group of boys and girls who were near Jabril."

Marcus took the photo back and turned to the figure in the robe. "Are you Jabril's mother?"

The woman nodded but did not speak.

Marcus turned to the sheikh. "I need her to look at the photo as well."

"There is no need—" Diar began.

"I was not speaking to you," Marcus said in Arabic, keeping his attention on the sheikh.

The sheik nodded and the woman stepped forward, pulling her *hijab* aside.

Marcus looked at the bruised and battered face, her right eye swollen nearly shut, and her lip split. Marcus looked at the sheikh, then at Diar and Murad. Holding back his anger, he handed the photo to the woman.

Diar grudgingly handed Marcus the flashlight. As he shined it on the photo, the woman broke into tears.

"Do you recognize the boy?"

Though sobs, she said, "Yes, yes. He was with a group of other children, and he was friendly to Jabril. I thought he was just . . . a nice American boy."

Marcus instinctively reached out to comfort the distraught mother, grabbing her hand. In that instant, guns were pointed at him. Gathering himself, realizing that he had violated a law of fundamental Islamists—that a woman shall not be touched by any man other than her husband or father, and certainly never by an infidel—Marcus decided he could use his oversight to push some buttons.

Ignoring the angry men pointing their rifles at him, Marcus addressed the sheikh. "Is this how one treats a guest who comes by invitation to his home?" He was speaking slowly in Arabic. "If your men do not put their weapons on the ground immediately, they will die." Marcus waited. "I will not ask a second time."

In a voice laced with anger and unease, the sheikh ordered the four men to lay down their guns.

Still choosing to ignore the men, Marcus went on. "I will help you find your grandson if I can. But when he is returned, his mother will be there. But, if from this moment, any further harm comes to her, those responsible will pay with their lives."

Marcus turned to face the two bodyguards. *"These are Allah's limits, and whoever obeys Allah and his messenger, he will cause him to enter gardens beneath which rivers flow, to abide in them; and this is the great achievement. And whoever disobeys Allah and his messenger and goes beyond his limits, he will cause him to enter fire, and he shall have an abasing chastisement."* Stepping close to Diar, Marcus said,

"As far as you are concerned, I am the messenger of Allah. If you touch her, I will make sure you suffer. Do you understand?"

If looks were bullets, Marcus's body would have been riddled. "Say it," Marcus snarled through clenched teeth.

Diar looked to the sheikh, who gave a slight nod. In a voice filled with disdain, he said, "I understand."

Looking at his watch, Marcus noted that his time was up. He turned to Jabril's mother, reached out, and took her hand again. "I will do what I can to find your son. Continue to pray and seek guidance from Allah."

To the sheikh, he said, "You are right. I am a man of honor, and from those I agree to help, I demand the same. You would be well advised to explain that to these men." And with that, he turned and walked back the way he had come.

* * *

ON THE RIDGE, A KILOMETER away, Sit and Harel watched though night-vision scopes as Marcus made his way down the hill to the ruins of Palmyra. They lay side by side on the hard ground, covered by desert camo ghillie suits that blended into the landscape on the off chance that the sheikh, too, might have snipers in place. Each was shooting a Soviet-made Dragunov SDV, which fired a 7.62 x 54R round.

"Alpha in place," Harel said softly. "Bravo? Charlie? Delta?"

"Bravo set."

"Charlie set"

"Delta, two minutes out."

The two snipers watched as Marcus entered the ruins and made his way to the temple, then disappeared inside.

"We've lost the target. Do you have eyes on him, Bravo?"

"Negative."

"Charlie?"

"No visual."

"Delta, can you see him?

"No, but I have two thermal signatures inside."

Listening, Sit made a mental note to make sure the next time he found himself in this situation he had God's Eye and J. T. wired in.

Harel turned his head toward Sit. "Nice scope. One of the new ones?"

Sit gave a slight nod. "I'll make sure you get one for Hanukkah. Glad to see you've taken good care of her."

Over the comm they heard a noise.

Harel looked quizzically at Sit. "Sounds like water. Wudu? Is he getting ready to pray? What the hell . . . ?"

Sit whispered, "I told ya, he's complicated."

Eight minutes later, the two robed men came out of the temple and stood silhouetted in the light of the full moon. From the ridge, standing beneath the ancient portico, shadowed in hues of gray, they looked like ghostly apparitions.

"We have three more hostiles. I repeat, three more joining with two of the original five. Four armed, and one in a robe with his head covered," came the message from Bravo team.

"Acquire and await my go," said the general.

Sit watched as Marcus and the sheikh walked, without speaking, along a grand avenue of ruined pillars. After a few minutes, they stopped by a large stone with a flat top. First, the sheikh sat, then Marcus. The team listened as the two men spoke about the sheikh's grandson, Jabril.

"I should not have let them go. I was foolish, an old man trying to be the light in a young boy's life, and now . . .

Marcus asked to speak to the two bodyguards and Jabril's mother. The sheikh raised his hand. Instinctively, both Sit and Harel let out half a breath, held it, and prepared to shoot.

"We have five approaching the target," said Delta.

When the woman removed her hijab, Sit said, "Oh, shit. Everybody, stay tight."

The two snipers watched Marcus reach out and take the woman's hand, and as four AK47 muzzles swung up, they readied to take their prearranged shots: Sit would take the two on the left; Harel, the other two. Sit knew that Marcus might have done it instinctively, without thinking, but he would instantly realize his error and start figuring just how to use it to his advantage. Then, when Marcus said that if the men didn't put their weapons on the ground they were dead, rifles clicked to hair-trigger mode. Both men watched the four targets lay their weapons on the ground.

With his scope still on his targets, Harel told Sit, "Remind me never to play poker with him."

They listened as Marcus threatened the bodyguard. Then, when he reeled off the long Quranic scripture, Harel asked, "Who *is* this guy?"

Finally, Marcus started back toward the ridge. When he was walking up the slope, Harel gave the order for Bravo, Charlie, and Delta to retreat. Then he said to Sit, "Really knows how to make friends, doesn't he?"

As Marcus stepped over the ridge to safety, Sit rose and said to Harel, "As for who he is, he's like nobody I ever knew. As for knowing how to make friends, yeah, he does."

CHAPTER THIRTY-FIVE

December 27, Aurora, Colorado

Manuela Cruz took the damp washcloth off her brother-in law Matis's forehead. The boy had not felt well since he and his brother, Santiago, arrived from Mexico, over a week ago. The vomiting had stopped but his fever was worse. On top of that, her son and two daughters weren't feeling well either.

Her husband Enrique stood at the bedroom door.

"We have to take him to the doctor, Enrique. Right now." Manuela said in Spanish to her husband.

Enrique and Santiago carried their barely coherent brother to the car. At the emergency room at the University of Colorado Hospital, Manuela had to go inside and get help to bring him in.

* * *

Dr. Michael Carrick looked at the patient in Bay 7. Picking up the chart, he scanned the information: temp 105, heart rate 132. Using his penlight, he lifted the young man's eyelids one at a time. Then he stepped out of the room, pulled his cell phone from his lab coat pocket, and made a call.

Ten minutes later, Dr. Arthur Limm, an infectious-disease specialist, stood beside Dr. Carrick. Matis lay naked covered in cool wet towels on a bed.

"It's influenza, I'm certain. We need to identify which strain, but I think I already know.

A nurse came in and reset the beeping IV monitor. When she left, Dr. Limm said quietly to his colleague, "We need to get him into isolation right away, and we need a list of everyone he's had contact with. Get the family who brought him in, and put them in the room as well. We need to call the CDC. If this is what I think it is, we have a problem."

* * *

Albuquerque, New Mexico

ROSAURA DÍAZ CLUTCHED HER STOMACH. Doubled over from cramps she knelt on the bathroom floor at her brother's home. The whole trip to the United States had been easy! And it hadn't cost her a dime; in fact, she had *made* money. But ever since she arrived, she had felt sick to her stomach. She had not been sick like this with any of her other pregnancies, so that surely wasn't it. Probably just some bug she picked up from being worn out. The trip and the decision to leave Mexico and her husband had been stressful and she hadn't been sleeping well.

For a few days, she had a low-grade fever, nausea, and diarrhea. Now she hurt all over, especially her stomach, and the headache felt like a hammer pounding from inside her skull. As she tried to rise from the floor, a wave of dizziness came over her. The next thing she knew, her son Emilio's frightened face stared down at her.

* * *

EMILIO WAS GLAD AND EXCITED to be in America. For him, it was a grand adventure and he wasn't going to miss his drunk father, who spent all the money and beat Emilio and his mother. But now the boy was worried. Since they arrived in el Norte, his mother had been sick. And when he heard the loud crash in the bathroom, he found her on the floor, shaking, with saliva and foam coming out of her mouth. With his uncle and aunt at work, it was only him, his sister Sofía, and his baby brother, Francisco, in the house. He didn't know what to do.

"*Mamá, mamá,*" Emilio said, brushing the sweat-soaked hair away from his mother's face.

In a moment, the convulsions stopped and she lay limp. Slowly, she started to come around and her eyes opened and focused on Emilio.

"*Llama a tu tío, Emilio. ¡Ahorita!*"

* * *

WHILE IN THE ER WAITING room, Rosaura went into another

convulsion. She slid off the plastic chair, hitting her head hard on the vinyl floor.

Within minutes, hospital staff had her on a gurney. The ultrasound revealed that her baby was not alive. They induced labor and an hour later she delivered the dead fetus.

***

San Diego, California

John Morales awoke in a cold sweat and fumbled around the nightstand to find his cell phone. Since his arrival back in the States, he had been staying in the basement of his friend Shaun Larson's house. They had known each other since middle school and often, when John's dad had to work late, sometimes all night, John would stay at Shaun's.

Like John, Shaun was an only child and his parents had always welcomed John into their home. In fact, when they found out about John and his father planning to return to Mexico, they had offered to let John stay with them. In the end, John's dad couldn't bring himself to part with his son.

While in Mexico, the two stayed in touch and when John arrived at the border crossing in San Ysidro, Shaun came to pick him up. It was Christmas break, so John had spent those first few days hanging out and catching up with old friends. For the past three days, he had been sick. His first thought was the flu, but he dismissed that self-diagnosis because he had gotten a flu shot before crossing the border. If not flu, what? His throat hurt, and he had a cough and lots of chest congestion. Maybe it was just a bad cold.

He looked at the clock on the nightstand: 5:00 p.m. What day was it? He heard the door from upstairs open. "John? John, are you awake, honey?"

It was Becky, Shaun's mom.

"Yes," he croaked.

"I'm going to turn the light on and come down."

John squinted against the bright light that shone through the open door into the guest room. Propping up on his elbow, which took all his strength, he looked into Becky's concerned face. He felt embarrassed because the room smelled of his sweat and vomit.

Becky laid her hand on his forehead.

"My God, John, you're burning up, worse than this morning!

We need to get you to a doctor *now*. Honey, listen, you don't have to worry about being sent back to Mexico," Becky said, though she didn't know whether she could prevent it. "I won't let that happen. Now, you need to get dressed. I'll have Shaun come help you."

* * *

IN THE EMERGENCY ROOM AT Sharp Memorial Hospital, John could barely hold himself up in the chair. Becky, her husband, and Shaun sat with him. Looking around, John saw another boy about his age, sitting in a chair against the opposite wall. Head hurting, shivering from chills, he rubbed his bloodshot eyes and looked again at the boy. He looked familiar. Then it struck him. The boy sitting slumped against the wall had been in their group in Tijuana, with the Canadians who had given them the flu vaccine, a work pass to get over the border, and some cash to tide them over till they got work.

The boy's vacant eyes looked back at him, without any sign of recognition.

* * *

DR. RYAN ECKERT EXAMINED JOHN in one of the curtained bays of the ER. As he listened to his heart and looked into John's eyes, ears, and down his throat, he asked questions.

"How long have you been sick?

"Almost three days."

"Vomiting? Diarrhea?"

"Both."

"Have you been out of the country lately?"

John grimaced and caught Becky's eye. They had talked about this.

"No."

"You haven't been across the border, by chance, into Tijuana?

"No."

"Okay, John, I think you have a type of flu, but we need to draw blood to be sure. For now you need stay in the hospital."

Turning his attention to Becky, he said, "I see here you're not John's mother."

"No, you see . . ." Becky motioned with her head for the doctor to move away from John.

This, too, Shaun's family and John had talked about. Becky

gave Dr. Eckert the rehearsed story about John's mother abandoning him, and his father's struggles with drug and alcohol addiction, and that he had been living with them for the past two years.

It wasn't an unusual story and the doctor seemed satisfied. Then he said to Becky, "We've had an unusually high number of cases like this over the past few days. John is the twenty-seventh person we've seen today. I asked about Mexico because some of our patients have recently crossed over the border.

"Has anyone else in your household been sick and has anyone received a flu shot?

Becky paused a moment. Just this morning, her son and her husband had mentioned that they were feeling a bit off, but they weren't sick—not like John. "My son and husband were feeling a little puny this morning, but no one's been throwing up or running a fever, and no, none of us have had the flu shot."

"Okay, we're going to keep John here, at least overnight. I would suggest that you get your family in to see your primary care physician right away and keep a close eye. If your son or husband's condition worsens, get them to the hospital. Don't wait for them to get better."

CHAPTER THIRTY-SIX
Beginnings Ranch, British Columbia

Colonel Webb focused on the big screen in Ops, looking at the face of Deputy Director Nathan Reynolds, who was in the FBI's version of the same room.

"All right, Colonel, consider the message received and understood."

For the past two days, the colonel and the deputy director had been wrangling over just how the Force 10/FBI/CIA joint investigation into what had begun as an attack on the U.S. Internet system was going to work. As usual, the feds insisted that it be a one-way street, with all threat-assessment data and other information going their direction.

Something was up, but so far, the colonel and J. T. had yet to figure it out, although both were sure the other shoe had dropped. As the last attack on the United States—when forest fires erupted from one end of the country to the other—had shown, just when you thought you'd seen the worst, you were apt to be wrong.

Two days ago, the deputy director had contacted Force 10 with a request to expand the search parameters for those responsible for the Internet attack, to include "collateral opportunities." To the colonel, the bureaucratic doublespeak meant, "See if you can find what we think we've already found." Not happy, the colonel got on the horn with his friend General Kittredge recently appointed to the Joint Chiefs of Staff. The shit quickly rolled downhill, and now the colonel stared at the FBI's second in command. He looked like a man primed and ready for a come-to-Jesus meeting.

"I want to be clear, Deputy Director: if you hold back—ever—this arrangement between your agency and Force Ten is over. The only reason that has not already happened is that I made a promise to General Kittredge."

"And here I'd thought it was Marcus who had rubbed off on the rest of you. Now I see I had it wrong."

"I'll take that as a compliment, Deputy Director. Now, can we get down to business?"

"Yes sir. For the purpose of this briefing, the participants think you are the man tasked with helping to prepare the emergency response action plan should military involvement become necessary. To ensure the best use of resources you are to serve as liaison between the civilian infrastructure and the military."

"Wow, that was quite the mouthful. You come up with that on your own?"

"Sorry, Colonel, that would be the general," Reynolds said. "Now if anyone should have the connections to check you out, they will find that Colonel Samuel Webb, retired, has been appointed by the President of the United States for just such a task. It certainly pays to have friends in high places, doesn't it, Colonel?"

"Well, Deputy Director, that depends on what those friends want."

* * *

THE SCREEN DIVIDED INTO THIRDS. In the center was the deputy director, on the left, a woman, and on the right, a man.

"Colonel Webb, I'd like to introduce Dr. Jennifer Halston from the CDC and, to my left, Dr. Baxter Ryan from Stanford University Medical Center."

The colonel nodded to each.

"I'll begin," said Reynolds. "As of 10:00 a.m. Eastern Standard Time, we have 1204 confirmed cases of H7N9 avian influenza—the latest strain of bird flu."

He moved left so that all the participants had a clear view of the screen behind him. Everyone looked at a map of the United States with red, yellow, and green dots scattered throughout. Along with every dot, the city or town's name appeared in black boldface.

"The red dots indicate more than a hundred cases. The yellow dots are fifty to ninety-nine cases; the green dots are one to forty-nine. As you see, San Diego, El Paso, Tucson, and Albuquerque are the only red dots so far. One scenario is that the original hosts carrying the infection originated in Mexico. Besides the geographical proximity of the first and highest-infection zones to the border, nearly three-quarters of confirmed cases are Hispanic."

As the colonel listened and watched, four new green dots appeared, and one of the yellow ones—Aurora, Colorado—turned red.

"Okay," the deputy director said. "I'd like to start with Dr. Halston.

"Good morning, Colonel," the woman said. "I work in the analytical and statistical division of the CDC in Atlanta. Our job is to develop models of probability based on a variety of variables. To clarify, I'm not an MD. My field of expertise is determining whether an outbreak is a natural occurrence or has been caused by some external input. To do this we use complicated mathematical formulas that give us a statistical probability. It's important to note that what we do is not an exact science.

"Over two weeks ago, we found a similar presentation of an H7N9 outbreak in Tanzania, East Africa. That in itself is not especially unusual. However, along with the influenza outbreak, three other contagions presented: *E. coli, Listeria,* and MRSA. In Africa, any one or even two of these present regularly. After all, between contaminated water and food and a tropical climate, intestinal disorders are commonplace. At the time they occurred, the outbreaks fit into our models, although they were nearing the point where we might consider some external stimulus. But we are seeing the same three contagions here in the western United States, mixed into the same zones with the H7N9 outbreaks. The statistical probability that an external agency is at work here is above ninety-five percent."

Colonel Webb listened. For thirty years, he had taken part in briefings like this, where such phrases as "external factors," "high rate of probability," and "similar presentation" were used as a clever way to talk around what the experts really thought. It was a way to ensure a degree of deniability should they be wrong. It made him appreciate all the more what Marcus had brought to the team.

The conversation shifted to the doctor from Stanford. "Colonel Webb, I'm Dr. Baxter Ryan. My background is in emergency medicine. I was an ER doc for fifteen years. For the past ten years, I have been working and teaching emergency response and preparedness. We run scenarios involving widespread infection—epidemic and pandemic situations."

As the doctor spoke, someone came into the field of view long enough to hand him a piece of paper. The doctor looked at the paper. "As of twenty minutes ago, we have another two thousand cases in Southern California, from the border up through Los Angeles. So in the past two hours, we have almost three times as many cases. What is it you call this, Dr. Halston— 'doubling the penny'?"

Doctor Ryan saw the colonel's perplexed face and said, "If you double a penny and keep doubling the amount every day, by the time you get to day twenty-eight you have over 1.3 million dollars. In very simplified terms this is how an epidemic, a localized outbreak, turns into a pandemic—a countrywide or worldwide outbreak. There is no doubt that we are in the beginning stages of a pandemic."

In the short time the colonel had been listening to Doctor Ryan, the dots on the map had more than doubled.

"Although most of the dots are now green," said Dr. Ryan, "they will all be red, I assure you."

"So, Doctor, what are the first steps we need to take?" the colonel asked.

"My team has been working on a model that breaks response protocol down to the micro levels. We need to reach out to mayors, city councils, ward or parish aldermen, and get them to identify those in their communities who have received the flu vaccine and those who are symptomatic. Many will be first responders, cops, firefighters, EMTs, doctors, and nurses. There will also be a significant number of older people who have received the vaccine. This actually helps us, because older people are more likely and willing to help out those in need. Ironically, the younger and more affluent are less likely to help and more likely to isolate themselves and their families and actively defend that isolation. They are also less likely to have been vaccinated.

"Once this is done, basic triage procedures can be set up for those who are sick and those who are symptomatic. Then they can establish support in terms of food and hydration. If this can happen, we should see areas clearing within two to four weeks.

"Initially, the most difficult task will be keeping people at home, away from work, schools—any form of travel at all. Small, cohesive regions with strong values and significant church populations will have more success. Urban areas are going to be the big challenge."

The doctor took a step closer to the camera transmitting the feed. Dr. Ryan was a big, barrel-chested man, and with his gray hair, bushy beard, and wire-framed glasses on a round face, he looked like a blend of Santa Claus and Ernest Hemingway.

"Urban areas are where the military may be necessary to quarantine fairly large geographic areas. I want to emphasize that this should be a last resort, but again, the last resort could be upon us in a matter of hours, not days.

"That was the good news. Ready for the bad?"

The colonel didn't bother responding.

"Normally, we would use social media to get the word out, to appeal to people, to build networks, but because of the crash of the Internet system, a widespread, multi-focused campaign just isn't possible. Critical networks, like police, fire, and essential infrastructure systems, are still up, so we can get plans out to them, but we are going to need to rely on television and radio to get the word out to the general populace. In truth, Colonel, as scenarios for pandemics go, we have a perfect storm brewing.

"As for the H7N9 strain, up until the outbreak in Africa and now here, it was local to China and Malaysia. Most people who contract it are going to be really sick with the typical nasty flu: vomiting, diarrhea, body aches, and chills. Some are certainly going to die—thousands, possibly. The big issue is going to be how many people are sick at the same time. We're talking millions. We must anticipate a complete shutdown of services, and in areas where winter is in full swing, people are going to be on their own. On top of that, this has already spread well beyond our borders. Do you get the picture?"

"I'm afraid I do, Doctor. I need to speak with Deputy Director Reynolds. Then we need to mobilize every military asset available. Thank you both, and may I please ask you to remain available?"

Both Halston and Ryan agreed and their feeds went dark.

* * *

Marcus and the rest of the team came from the back of the room where they had been listening, out of view.

"Make sure you've all been vaccinated," said the deputy director.

"Already done," said Chaya.

Marcus looked at the colonel, "Is it just me or does it seem like the one common thread we have here is Mexico? The voice of the man who killed Annie came from Mexico. Jabril al-Mohmoud's kidnappers are employed by the drug cartels—again, Mexico. And now this, what by all accounts is intentional infection, is suspected of originating in . . . drum roll, please . . . that's right, folks: *Mexico.*"

"We have every resource at our disposal looking at that angle and have reached out to our Mexican counterparts who have been very cooperative," said Reynolds.

Marcus walked up closer to the monitor and stared at the deputy director of the FBI. "What? Am I missing something, Marcus?"

"Well, doesn't it seem a bit odd that everything points to Mexico? I mean, the cartels are heartless, violent organizations, but at the end of the day, what advantage do they gain from shutting down their primary source of income? If people can't work, can't travel, they can't buy drugs. If the financial markets are shut down, where do the cartels funnel the millions in cash that they launder though legitimate enterprises? Remember when I was talking about 'false motion'? Well, whoever's behind this has got that offense figured out, and it's not the cartels. Now, I'm not saying they aren't involved—they almost have to be—but they're just a player."

"All right, Deputy Director," the colonel broke in. "We'll help put together an action plan, but you need to mobilize every resource you can scrounge up. I'll talk to the general as soon as we're done here. We need some time to look at this. Make sure this channel stays open."

"Thank you," Reynolds replied.

"Feels like you keep swinging, but no hits, doesn't it, Nathan?" Marcus said to the man on the screen.

"Something like that."

"Well, you know what they say: 'Hitters hit.' All we can do is step up and keep whacking away."

CHAPTER THIRTY-SEVEN

December 30, Beginnings Ranch

AT 4:30 IN THE MORNING Marcus sat behind the antique oak desk in the office on the main floor of the big log house. Steam rose from the coffee mug cupped in his hands as he stared into the flames of the fireplace. The sickness, as Dr. Ryan predicted, was spreading like wildfire. Even though everyone at the ranch had been vaccinated, some were sick, including Garrett and Norma. If there was a silver lining, it was the Internet coming back on line. Although knowing from minute to minute the growing numbers of sick and dying... maybe it would be better if it remained down.

The bigger matter on Marcus's mind was Little Ed Rojas. Big Ed Rojas managed the ranch's alfalfa and timothy hay production— no small task for an operation with twenty thousand head of livestock.

When they arrived home from their Christmas trip to Colorado Little Ed was very sick. None of them had been vaccinated and now it was too late. Chaya had been with the boy since they got back, doing her best to keep his temperature down. She had him on an IV drip to keep him hydrated, but his fever wasn't breaking. To complicate the situation, his parents and sisters were all exhibiting various symptoms of the flu, although nothing like the severity of Little Ed's.

Force 10 received multiple updates daily from the deputy director as well as from Drs. Halston and Ryan. The flu pandemic continued to worsen. The colonel hadn't left Ops in nearly forty-eight hours. True to his word, he stepped into what was originally presented to be a made-up role, as General Kittredge had no doubt known he would. With J. T.'s help, he outlined a preparedness plan that served as a guideline for those in charge of military and law enforcement personnel. Troops, regular and National Guard, had been mobilized in every major city in the country. Borders were closed; airports, trains, and bus lines shut down. The president had been on TV several times urging that all nonessential car and truck traffic stay off the roads. The whole thing felt like a recurring bad dream.

Dr. Ryan had also been right about smaller towns. They were holding the spread rate of the infection down and were beginning to see a light at the end of the tunnel, but they were also actively and forcibly isolating themselves.

The news, which every day grew more desperate and a little less polished, was horrific. As well as flu, the pockets of *E. coli, Listeria,* and MRSA outbreaks acted like salt on an open wound. But the H7N9 outbreak was the number one problem. With over three million people sick, nearly five thousand influenza deaths, and, as of this morning, several hundred deaths that had nothing to do with sickness at all, it was like watching a tidal wave of panic sweep in off the ocean and cut a swath of fear through the landscape. No amount of human will or ingenuity could stop it.

Marcus reached for his mug when the front door opened. Chaya came rushing in, tears streaming down her face. Marcus stood and held her in his arms. He knew that the worst of what was going on out in the world had just made landfall at Beginnings.

* * *

Chaya had seen plenty of sick children, especially during her two-year residency at Harper University Hospital in downtown Detroit, and seen many die. But that had been in another life, and she had not treated a child in a long time—certainly not one she knew.

During the Rojas' stay at the ranch in Colorado, several of the hands had come down with a nasty flu—especially a young man who had just arrived from Mexico. At the time, there still had been no official word about this specific outbreak and it wasn't until Ed got his family home that he realized just how serious it was.

Chaya sat in the bedroom bathing Little Ed's face and torso with a cold rag. His temperature was near a dangerously high 106° and he was barely conscious. They had been on the phone with a doctor at the small hospital in Merritt. Just this morning, the CDC had issued an official statement about the H7N9 outbreak, along with an advised protocol for containment. It wasn't that they couldn't get Little Ed to the hospital—a flightworthy helicopter was always on-site at Beginnings. Rather, the hospital and the town wouldn't risk having him. And anyway, Chaya was doing as much as the hospital could. With no medicine for the flu, his body would have to fight through it, if it could.

Complicating matters was Little Ed's asthma. The respiratory effect of this particular strain of influenza put him at added risk. Chaya had him on oxygen and was prepared for intubation. But she was losing him. She knew it and so did Little Ed's father.

* * *

MARCUS SAT ON THE EDGE of the bed and ran his hand over Garrett's forehead. The boy's fever had broken during the night, and he rested peacefully. Slowly Garrett opened his eyes and smiled, "Daddy."

"Hey, buddy." Marcus reached out and laid his hand on Garrett's forehead. "Your fever's gone. You look like you're feeling better."

"Yeah. I'm hungry. How's Little Eddy? Is he better, too?"

Marcus had promised his boys he would never lie to them. Tears welled in his eyes, blurring his vision with the heartbreak of a family's lost son and a boy's lost best friend. He closed his eyes tight, and when he opened them tears streamed down his cheeks as Garrett crawled out of the covers and fell into his arms.

Garrett sobbed. "No, Daddy! No . . ."

Marcus had no words that would console his son, so he held him while they both cried.

* * *

CHAYA STOOD AT THE DOOR, holding onto Bodie's hand. She watched Marcus as he sat on the edge of Garrett's bed. The death of Little Ed ripped though the ranch like a harsh Arctic blizzard.

She wanted to go to them, but Bodie squeezed her hand. "It's our thing with Dad," he said. "We each need our time with him. This is Garrett's. He needs to find his strength and that's what Dad's good at."

Chaya turned to Bodie. "What is it with the Diablo men that you take such care of each other, yet push each other so hard?"

Bodie wiped his eyes with the back of his hand, but when he spoke his voice was clear. "For us, taking care of each other means that sometimes we have to go though some hard stuff alone. Mom would always say that's what Dad's job was: to make sure that me and my brother had the strength to get through bad times so that whenever we were on our own, we'd be okay."

Chaya gazed at the teenage boy who stood taller than she, with his sparkling light-blue eyes and long blond hair. Before she could say a word, he put his arms around her and whispered in her ear, "We love you, and I know we're probably not what you expected, but we need you." He stepped back and held her at arm's length. "And you need us."

* * *

Marcus left Garrett with Chaya. He and Bodie walked down the half-log stairs where Colonel Webb waited. The two men shared a silent moment.

As Marcus walked to the front door, he said, "Get the team together, Sam. It's time we move." At the door, he caught himself and turned. "Sorry . . .

Already moving to follow, the colonel said, "I told you before, don't ever apologize for doing what comes naturally to you, because the day is coming."

Marcus smiled at his friend. "Okay, deal. As long as today's not that day."

As they moved out onto the patio in the dark of early morning, the colonel said, "No, not today, but you should know, I have been giving some thought to dog names."

CHAPTER THIRTY-EIGHT

In Ops, the FBI deputy director's face filled one half of the screen, General Kittredge's the other.

General Kittredge began. "I'm sorry about the boy, Sam, but unfortunately, we don't have time for that now. Thanks for the help with the action plan. I know I kind of dumped it on you. Anyway, we're doing well in the more rural parts of the country, as anticipated. We're seeing some gains in the Pacific Northwest as well, but the rest of the country is a mess, and it's only going to get worse. As of 0-six-hundred, the death toll is over ten thousand with at least four million sick, and that's just here in the States. There are outbreaks across the globe, and the finger pointing's just begun. It's a shit show for sure. Part of me wishes the damn Internet was still down. It would at the least give us some control over the release of information and maybe keep the panic manageable. After the fires last year people lost faith in the government and doubted it could protect them. We were just beginning to restore some confidence, and now..." He trailed off.

It was Deputy Director Reynolds's turn. "Everything points to Mexico as the source of the infection. We are trying to coordinate with the Mexican government, but it's slow going. We have some assets south of the border. We're putting them into play as we speak."

* * *

Marcus listened to both General Kittredge and Deputy Director Reynolds. His mind processed recent events, the U.S. Internet crash, the kidnapping of Jabril al-Mohmoud, the attack on the ranch, and now what appeared to be a biological attack. Trying to connect the dots, he struggled to find the common thread. He couldn't escape the feeling they were missing something. Then came the moment of clarity that most would see as a wild-assed leap into the realm of half

-craziness.

"Deputy Director, you need to have your people stand down. You know as well as I that as soon as the FBI starts throwing its weight around, all the bad guys are going to ground."

"All right, then, Marcus, what exactly do you suggest the Bureau do?"

The DD's tone was equal parts weariness and sarcasm.

"Well, let's see. We're in the midst of an all out pandemic. Besides the millions sick, the whole social fabric that is supposed to hold us together is unraveling. I would think the FBI has plenty to keep itself busy. You need to let *us* come at this thing. We can move… let's just say, in a less restricted manner."

"For a man who once lectured me on my willingness to throw the rule of law and due process to the winds, you sure are singing a different tune."

"Fair enough, but if you recall, then, we were talking about *you* accusing *me* of being responsible for Annie's disappearance. Now, we're talking about terrorists."

"Maybe I'm not seeing a huge difference."

With a grin and a chuckle Marcus said, "No, I suppose not!"

"Are you two about done sparring?" the colonel broke in. "Marcus, get to the point."

At Marcus's direction, J. T. put the pictures and info of Taz up on the screen.

"Okay, the Internet thing was just a distraction , albeit a damn big one. The kidnapping of Jabril is the key. We find the man who took the boy, he leads us to the man who killed Annie, and, if I'm right, a whole lot more."

If anyone else had said it, challenges about the logic used and the conclusions drawn would have been pouring in from the members of Force 10. Marcus had a roundabout way of looking at the world that made sense only to him. But his track record spoke for itself.   "Colonel, got any connections in El Paso?" Marcus asked.

Colonel Webb moved across the room to the long counter holding several desktop consoles. "I might know a guy."

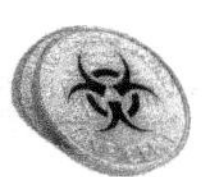

CHAPTER THIRTY-NINE

January 2, El Paso, Texas

THE THREE BLACK SUBURBANS DROVE through an opened chain-link gate whose black-lettered, metal sign read "**Alamo Freight**." They drove between two warehouses and entered one through an open garage door that closed after the third SUV rolled in.

Because of security risks at the ranch, the colonel had to split the team. He had the *Takbir* secure and docked in Vancouver. If the flu outbreak got any worse, it might be necessary to evacuate Marcus's family and anyone else from the ranch who wanted to leave. If isolation became a necessity, the middle of an ocean was hard to beat.

On this trip to El Paso, the colonel had Marcus, Weathers, Sit, Jamie, and Liam. Chaya needed to stay at Beginnings. Garrett was still recovering and both of Little Ed's sisters were pretty sick. The colonel brought in a thirty-three passenger Boeing Business Jet so if they had to evacuate the ranch, Bronson could get most of the people, maybe everybody, out in one haul. Pete and Ham, also stayed behind to maintain security and put in place an action plan for Marcus's family and the ranch staff should another incident occur.

A tall, forty-something, brown-skinned man with a few days' growth of beard and a shaved head, met the team as they got out of the SUVs.

"Colonel." The man said, extending his hand.

"Gunny. Thanks for helping us out. Domingo Márquez, this is Marcus Diablo. The rest I believe you know."

"Marcus, the devil himself. It's a pleasure to meet you."

Marcus shook the man's hand.

Domingo greeted the members of Force 10, stopping first at Sit.

"What's it been, Iggy—four, five years? Mamma asks after you every time I talk to her."

"That's 'cause she's looking for a son to replace you."

He moved down the line, stopping finally at Liam.

"Well, I'll be dammed. If it isn't Mickey in the flesh. I figured some Irish redhead would've had you digging potatoes and raising a brood of brats by now."

"Maybe someday. So how's my favorite spick?"

"It's good to have the Mickey and Spickey Show back in prime time," Domingo said, embracing his old friend.

"All right, gentlemen, I know you didn't just pop into El Paso for the tequila and poontang, so let's get to it," Domingo announced.

As everyone took a seat inside the building's conference room, five tough-looking men came in from another room.

Several pictures of Taz came up on the HD screen. "Tajo Alano Zambrano, aka 'Taz,' and the Barrio Azteca."

Unlike the earlier security photos of a father holding his exhausted "son" in his arms after a full day at Disneyland, these showed him in his element. If anyone expected a gangbanger spotting tats and wearing a wife beater, they got a surprise. This Taz was impeccably, but casually dressed, his short hair styled back, goatee neatly trimmed. He wore dark sunglasses or else had them pushed up on top of his forehead. In some of the photos he was standing by a gleaming black Escalade, in others by a silver Audi. There were pictures of him entering an upscale, pale yellow stucco home with a Mediterranean tile roof and hibiscus blooming in the front yard. In some photos, he was standing outside an office building or sitting in a restaurant or outdoor café with other well-dressed Latinos.

"Looks like a businessman, which he is." Domingo continued. "But when business doesn't go his way, people die. The Barrio Azteca, besides being one of the most ruthless prison gangs in both the U.S. and Mexico, are muscle-for-hire by the cartels to take care of issues and to move product on this side of the border." Domingo stood ramrod straight. "And by 'take care of issues,' I mean disappear dead; and by 'product' I mean three things." He held up his hand and raised fingers, one at a time, starting with the pinkie. "Drugs, women, and children.

"As luck would have it, he operates out of a warehouse much like this one less than two miles away. Many of the most visible members of the Barrio Azteca are legitimate business owners—by all appearances, upstanding citizens. They make sure to donate to all the right causes: the Boys and Girls Club, local soccer teams, health clinics— regular good Samaritans."

Domingo gestured at the new pictures on the monitor. "Now, our boy Taz owns *Para Ti*, a mobile Mexican grocery store. He's got a couple dozen trucks cruising, from early morning to late night, in the Mexican neighborhoods selling fresh tortillas, tamales, you name it. If Mexicans eat it or cook with it, he sells it. He's got operations that cover most of West Texas, and, if the rumors can be trusted, soon to be in New Mexico and Arizona." Domingo sounded like the announcer in a TV commercial.

Up on the monitor a picture showed the front entrance of Taz's warehouse. Painted about the door was the logo of a tortilla with Para ti scrawled in the center.

"Simple yet catchy. For the past three years, my group has been providing security for American companies doing business in Juárez. Mostly, it involves providing a safe show-and-tell to a white-bread exec who wants to come and press the flesh with the brown worker bees." Domingo shared a look with the colonel. "Not that much different from what you did in Iraq. Think of it like this: El Paso is the Green Zone; Ciudad Juárez is Sadr City. Here we have a reasonable expectation of safety, but once you cross into Juárez, you're in enemy territory."

Domingo stepped away from the screen. "So, Colonel, what is it we can help you with in regard to señor Zambrano?"

The colonel nodded, and Marcus stood up. "Well Domingo, lets' see if we can't get a better view of *Para Ti*." Marcus pulled his secure communication device from his back pocket and touched the screen. A few seconds later J. T's face was looking out at them from the monitor.

"Mingo," J. T. said.

"You boys are just full of surprises," Domingo replied. "So don't tell me, you found something that could hold your attention for more than a few months?"

J. T. smiled, and to Marcus he looked like a proud 20-year-old who had just been patted on the back by a rock-star idol rather than an egotistical genius in his mid-thirties.

J. T.'s face disappeared, and like a camera dropping from the sky, Para Ti zoomed into view. The high-resolution picture clearly showed the pits and pocks in the stucco façade on the front of the building.

Domingo's face was a question mark.

"We've got a few tools that are pretty slick," Marcus said. "J. T., got any heat signatures?"

The view moved in close to the building, and five yellow-orange figures grouped together toward the back, just inside a large roll-up door appeared. The view moved over the building and picked up a signature in the front and three others scattered about the warehouse area behind the main office.

"Any way to get sound?" Marcus asked.

"Give me a second." J. T.'s voice said.

A minute later, they heard the voices of men, as if in conversation on a speakerphone. A combination of English and Spanish, after a few moments, it became clear that one man was doing most of the talking.

Marcus eyed Domingo.

"That's Taz," Domingo said, "but—?"

"I turned on one of the guy's cell phones." J. T. said.

The colonel rose and walked over to the screen. He pointed at the heat signature of the group inside the roll-up door. "If we were to get these guys in this spot and get them to open that door, where would be the best places to provide rifle cover to, say, two men?"

"Let me get this straight, Colonel," Domingo said. "You're proposing that two men are going to walk in, like they were invited, and have a little sit-down with Taz?"

"If I may, Colonel," Marcus said.

As he spoke, Marcus made eye contact with each member of Domingo's team. "A boy was kidnapped by Taz and we need to know where he is. Now, we could fuck around and try and get Taz by himself, but my guess is, he's pretty cautious. So instead of us trying to draw him out, we go to him, on his turf, in a place where he's confident about his security—maybe *too* confident."

"What about leverage?" Domingo asked. "What's going to get them to open the door?"

Marcus studied the real-time picture provided by the God's Eye satellite. The five images at the back of the warehouse were still in the same place, but in the far right corner of the yard, the image of another person came into and out of view— perhaps one of the workers, Marcus thought. "Hey J. T., you see that figure in the southwest corner of the yard? Zoom in."

The picture shifted to a boy riding a skateboard back and forth over what looked like a homemade plywood ramp some twenty feet long and curving upward on both ends. It was the boy in the pictures with Jabril: David, Taz's son.

"There's our leverage," Marcus said.

* * *

It was 11:00 a.m. when Domingo finished laying out the plan, establishing sniper locations and explaining where he and his team would be to provide backup. "This whole flu pandemic is actually going to work in our favor. Right now, on both sides of the border, first responders have their hands full. Also, traffic between countries has really fallen off. That means we have a bit more open time. But the deal is, if we are talking casualties—them, not us, and I see no way around it—that limits how much time you get with Taz. Once we're inside those doors, fifteen minutes, tops. We'll all be wired, and I'm sure we're all using the same ear bud, although," Domingo paused and looked upward, as if J. T. might be floating above. "J. T., I'll be expecting a new batch of the latest generation, when this op is over." His attention was back on his audience. "Now we just need to figure out how we get to the kid."

Marcus spoke. "J. T., Taz's boy has to have a cell phone. You can tap into it, obviously."

"No problem," came the faceless reply.

"All right, find the text messages that have been sent to him by his dad. When you were zooming in, I thought I saw what might be a food truck a few streets over. Find out which ones prowl this warehouse district. There can't be more than a few. At 11:30, send our young friend a text—from his dad of course—to go pick up lunch."

"What if the kid has no money?" Asked Domingo.

"There's no way that Taz, and by association, his son—doesn't have good credit. We just need him outside those gates for a few minutes."

"Not to be a naysayer, but, what if this doesn't work?" Domingo asked.

Marcus smiled. The man was playing devil's advocate, as any good operation commander would. "Domingo, my friend, if that happens you get to embarrass me with a brilliant Plan B."

CHAPTER FORTY

Sit, Liam and Colonel Webb watched from their position on the rooftop of the warehouse adjacent to Para Ti. Each equipped with a Knights SR-25 rifle, mounted with a Trijicon reflective red-dot scope. At 100 yards, range wasn't an issue. Jamie and Marcus, being in such close proximity to at least five well-armed, happy-to-shoot-first gang members, was. Weathers would be running cleanup. A native New Yorker of Sicilian descent with olive skin and a short, stocky build, wearing baggy jeans, an oversized T-shirt, a do-rag, and tatted-up shoulders and forearms, he would pass as someone from the neighborhood on his lunch break.

Domingo and his crew prepped. They had a well-established cover as recognized, Latino employees of Alamo Freight. Alamo Freight served primarily as a transfer agent—getting freight from various warehouse locations, mostly small operators, to larger interstate freight companies. The cover required only a building with a loading dock, a forklift, and three box vans with lift gates.

Domingo sat in one of the Alamo Freight trucks in the yard of the warehouse across the street from Para Ti, eating his lunch as a food truck pulled up and parked just outside the gate to Para Ti.

He watched as Marcus and Jamie approached the food truck and ordered something. Just as Marcus had scripted, a boy came out of the gate and walked up to the food truck. By the friendly way the woman inside the truck greeted him, it was obvious they knew each other. Then Domingo heard Marcus's voice in his earbud.

"Hey, kid, you know a guy named Taz?"

The young boy, a bit on the husky side, looked up at Marcus. "What you want with Taz, man? He know you?"

His voice had that "I'm a badass cholo-boy" tone that Domingo was sure he never used at the private Catholic school he attended.

"You, like maybe, some old, long-haired narc?"

Marcus laughed. "No, man, I just want to talk to him about a business opportunity. You know where I can find him?"

The kid reached up and took the brown paper sack from the lady inside the truck. "Fuck you, man," he said as he walked back through the gate and pulled it shut with his free hand.

* * *

COLONEL WEBB WATCHED AS THE boy approached the closed roll-up door. Taz's son had his phone in his hand and was banging it on his leg. J. T. had jammed the boy's phone after sending the text from his father to go get them something to eat.

Looking back to the wheeled chain-link gate, the colonel saw Jamie and Marcus slide it open a few feet and walk through. Looking back to the boy, he saw the door roll upward and there stood Taz. J. T. transmitted the conversation still being picked up from one of the men's hacked cell phones, to the earbuds everyone wore.

"Hey, *mijo,* lunch? What a sweet boy!"

The boy looked at his phone. The message his father had sent was gone.

The two walked inside, and David went to press the button that would close the door when his father said, "Leave it, *mijo.* The fresh air is nice."

The colonel, Sit, and Liam now had an unobstructed view of full pallets and stacked crates. They could also see a table with a microwave on top of it, a sofa, and several worn upholstered armchairs. They had reviewed the plans and knew this was just a loading area at the very back of the warehouse. The building also had large refrigeration and freezer areas as well as a *tortillería*, where a machine produced corn tortillas by the hundreds of dozens. Two offices and a small reception area occupied the front.

"We're in position, Colonel," Domingo said. "Alpha just went through the gate."

"Copy that, we have eyes on them. You want to come and take a look? Might find it interesting."

* * *

DOMINGO DID A FINAL CHECK of his men. He had three on foot, the two others in vehicles nearby.

Domingo used a key and entered the warehouse where the colonel, Sit, and Liam had taken up position on the roof. It amazed him that this warehouse had been for lease less than an hour ago, and now, somehow, the colonel had executed a year agreement and the keys had been delivered to Alamo Freight's office. Although he still had no idea how Marcus Diablo and the youngest member of Force 10 were going to get Taz to give them the information they wanted, let alone walk in without getting shot all to hell.

Domingo made his way cautiously up the ladder to the roof and moved up to a position beside the colonel. All three men had their eyes to their rifle scopes as Domingo pulled a pair of binoculars from his cargo pocket. As he scanned Marcus and Jamie making their way across the yard toward the open garage door, he went through a mental checklist of what would be required to move this operation from providing backup to body recovery.

* * *

"J. T., I NEED A COVER fast. How about a medium-sized produce distributor with no connection to *Para Ti?*" Marcus said quietly.

A few seconds passed as Marcus and Jamie, standing near the food truck, finished up their carne asada tacos.

In his ear, Marcus heard J.T.'s voice. "Adam Becker, Imperial Produce, Austin, Texas. Grosses about three mil a year but has been on a little expansion over the past six months."

"That'll work. What's his wife's maiden name?"

A pause, then in a *What the hell* tone, "Ferguson."

"Okay, we're gonna move. Filter my comm so it's only you and F-one. Leave F-nine open to all communications.

"You ready for this?" Marcus asked Jamie.

"Born ready, mate," Jamie replied. The two men shared a, *you're so full of shit* grin.

They walked through the yard, looking a little hesitant—just two guys obviously in the wrong neighborhood looking for directions.

As they walked down the side of the building approaching the open roll-up door, Marcus called out, "Hey, anyone here?"

Just before they stepped into view of whoever was inside the warehouse, in a whisper he said to Jamie, "If I guessed wrong, I'm sorry."

* * *

"THAT'S HIM," DAVID SAID TO his dad, pointing at Marcus. "That's the guy who asked me about you when I was getting lunch."

The four other men had already moved to stand an arm's length away from each other, in front of Marcus and Jamie, making no effort to hide the firepower they carried. Although the pictures of Taz portrayed a well-dressed, well-connected businessman, these four guys were straight-up gang muscle: mustaches with goatees, long thin sideburns that wrapped in under their chins. Prison muscle, their life histories tattooed shoulder-to-wrist and up onto their necks. Two had teardrops inked under the corner of one eye. All had shaved heads and dark, hard eyes. Two had AR-15's slung over their shoulders and cradled comfortably in their hands, the other two held Mac 10s with magazine clips that extended ten inches below the base of the grips.

Marcus held up his hands in front of him, palms out, and stepping into character as Adam Becker, produce distributor from Austin with a Texas twang. "Hey, hey, easy there, fellas. Maybe I got the wrong place."

None of the armed men spoke. Taz set his taco, wrapped in a crumpled piece of waxed paper, on the table and stood up. "Go ride your board, *hijo.* I need to take care of some business."

As the boy scurried out he gave Marcus a look no 12-year-old boy should have in his repertoire.

Taz wiped his mouth with a napkin as he casually approached. The four men parted so that Taz had a pair on either side of him. "Gentlemen," he began as he wiped his hands with the napkin, wadded it up, and tossed it, missing the trashcan five feet away. "This is private property." His tone was even, controlled, and without a hint of an accent.

Marcus lowered his hands, and in a nervous voice that was no act, said, "Sorry, I was just looking for a guy who goes by the name of Taz. I tried to find him online but..."

"There's no Taz here," Taz said.

"Well, then that's my mistake," Marcus said hoping that J. T. was on his game. "My guy musta' been wrong."

He began to turn when Taz commanded, "Stay where you are. What guy you talking about?"

Over the comm Marcus heard, "Benito Gonzales. Supplies cilantro, parsley, and a variety of peppers. Also does some business with Becker. If they check I can intercept and cover as long as you don't stretch this charade into multiple acts."

"Benito González, he told me about your mobile grocery trucks, and anyway I came to see if you had ever considered expanding to Austin."

"You see this," Taz said addressing his men. "These white guys come here into our house, like we would be interested in doing business with them."

His turned back to Marcus. "What's your name?"

"Adam Becker, I own Imperial Produce. We cater to a largely Hispanic clientele. This is my nephew—wife's sister's kid, Sandy Ferguson."

The name Marcus gave Jamie got five stares. "Oh, he's from Australia, Sandy is a manly name Down Under."

Before speaking again Taz nodded to one of his men who stepped away from the group and pulled out his cell phone.

"Well, you know what, Mr. Becker, I have no interest in doing business with *you.* But what do you say to you doing business with *me*? Say, seventy-thirty, me being controlling partner of... what was the name? Imperial Produce."

"I think maybe—"

"Shut the fuck up. You come walking in here all full of yourself and think I'm some wetback who will roll over and piss on his belly to do business with you? Let me tell you something. I think I'll take you up on your generous offer. Let me just get my lawyer over here. That will give my boys time to make you and your curly red headed nephew here their bitches. What do you say to that?

"What, no witty retort?" Taz said as Marcus stood mouth agape. "Well, it would appear that I just made a very shrewd acquisition. Surprised I know such fancy words?"

Marcus took a deep breath, the moment of truth had arrived and he and Jamie were still upright. He smiled and let out a little laugh.

"I fail to see what's so funny, Mr. Becker."

Marcus spoke, forcing his voice to remain calm; "I find it funny how sometimes things appear one way, yet they are exactly opposite. You know what I mean?"

Taz looked at Marcus as if he were crazy.

"It's true. Trust me!" Marcus said.

* * *

FROM UP ON THE ROOF of the adjacent warehouse the colonel, Sit,

Liam and Domingo listened as Marcus and J. T. concocted a cover story in less than thirty seconds. Domingo glanced at the colonel.

"He flies by the seat of his pants," the colonel whispered. "But it's why it works— or so we hope."

Domingo wasn't quite sure how to take the colonel's remark as he shifted his attention back to the scene playing out below.

As Marcus and Jamie entered the gate the colonel said, "Okay, F-ten, you take care. We have all five targets acquired and locked. What's the go sign?"

"Trust me," Marcus said as he tapped his right fist twice on his chest.

* * *

No sooner had the words left Marcus's mouth than the four armed men dropped dead, the colonel and Liam each taking one, and Sit the other two. As Taz reached for the pistol in the waistband of his pants, Marcus said, "I'd stay very still if I were you, *cabron*." Three red dots danced on Taz's white shirt.

"Now, the fingers training those dots on your chest—they don't have near the understanding and patience I have."

Jamie had already moved and retrieved both AR-15s and had them cross-strapped over his shoulders so he could readily grip one in each hand if necessary. He was dragging a metal armchair, which he placed behind Taz.

"Sit," Marcus hissed.

When Taz didn't move, Marcus shoved him in the chest with both hands.

As Taz slammed down in the chair, Jamie zip-tied his wrists and elbows to the chair. Then he duct taped his torso to the chair back, and his legs, at the ankles and knees, to the chair legs.

Marcus stood in front of Taz, who glared at him.

"So refresh me—who's the bitch here? Oh, right, that would be you. This is how it goes. I want to know what you did with the boy you kidnapped a few weeks ago in Disneyland."

"I didn't kidnap no boy," Taz growled. "But I'll tell you this, you and your family are as good as dead."

Marcus squatted down in front of the chair so that he looked Taz eye to eye. "This is the last time I'll ask. What did you do with the boy?"

Taz stared at Marcus with dark lifeless eyes and spat in his face.

Without flinching, Marcus's right arm shot out, his fingers and thumb locked around Taz's Adams apple.

Taz threw himself back in the chair, but Jamie was standing behind it so it wouldn't topple.

Small drops of blood appeared where Marcus's fingernails cut into the soft skin. The droplets beaded up, held for a moment, and trickled down Taz's throat forming crimson streaks on his white shirt. He made helpless choking noises as he struggled against his bonds.

Marcus stayed in his squat but made no move to wipe the spittle dripping down his face. He set his free arm on top of Taz's bound hand and, through clinched teeth, said, "Now you're going to answer my question or you'll never speak again, because I'm going to tear your voice box out with my bare hand, and as your hot blood drips through my fingers, you're going to look at it for the last few seconds of your sorry-assed life. Then I am going to rip through your organization and your family, including your boy, who is already in the company of some very scary people. And in the end, whether you're alive or dead, I'll get the information I want."

Marcus had been holding Taz for almost twenty seconds and the man's face was red, his lips starting to turn blue. "You want to live long enough to see your boy grow into a man?" Marcus released his grip just enough for Taz to suck in a shallow breath. Then without taking his eyes off Taz, he raised his left hand in a beckoning motion.

Weathers stepped into the open doorway with David kicking and squirming in his arms. He stayed only long enough for Taz to get a glimpse and then moved out of view.

Marcus put one knee down and came up close to Taz's face. "You want to see him grow up? Nod your head. Good. Now, are you going to answer my first question?"

Taz nodded again.

Marcus released his grip and wiped his bloody hand on Taz's shirt.

Taz was gasping, trying to draw air through his bruised windpipe.

Marcus gave him a moment and then squatted before him again.

In a raw and raspy voice, Taz said, "I delivered the boy to a... guy in *Juárez*."

Marcus gave him a questioning look.

"I..." Taz tried to clear his throat and grimaced in pain, "...only know him as *el Capullo*...met him at...a whorehouse off *Mariscal* Street just off *Avenida de Juárez*, called *la Crisálida*. I delivered the boy and left. That's all I know."

"What did this man look like?"

Taz shook his head, still struggling to get full breaths, as the fingernail cuts on his neck continued to ooze blood. "Five-ten, on the heavy side, hair in a ponytail, and these..." He coughed, "...boots, with silver toes that curled up at the ends."

Marcus stood and looked out the door and up to where the team was. He glanced at his watch, time up. He raised his hand, index finger extended, and made a circle in the air. In a few moments two of Domingo's men came inside.

Pointing at Taz, Marcus said, "Bag him. The boy too."

In his ear, Marcus heard the colonel ask, "What's up?"

"I don't know; I just have a feeling we may need our friend Taz at some future point."

CHAPTER FORTY-ONE

Up on the roof, the team watched the final minutes of Marcus's encounter with Taz. *Impressive,* thought Domingo. Even though the whole thing had been adlibbed, it played out like a meticulously rehearsed operation.

Two of Domingo's men wrapped up Taz and got him loaded into a van with his son. Two others secured the front office and the warehouse staff. As they walked toward the ladder that would bring them off the roof and into the warehouse, Domingo told the colonel, "You take your team in the van and return to Alamo Freight. We need to doctor up the scene and make this look like a gang thing. Could take two or three hours. You guys sit tight."

* * *

Three hours later, Domingo and his team returned to Alamo Freight. Domingo picked up a remote and pointed at the flat-screen monitor. On the television, a local news reporter stood on the street in front of Para Ti, a couple of El Paso PD squad cars as well as an ambulance inside the gate. According to the reporter, initial information held that the Tejas Syndicate, a rival of the Barrio Azteca, to which Para Ti's owner, Tajo Alano Zambrano, allegedly belonged, had raided Para Ti, killing at least four and kidnapping several others.

The reporter went on to say that since the flu outbreak, violence had continued to escalate as competing gangs, taking advantage of the general fear and social unrest, tried to maintain, and if possible, increase the range of their territories.

The colonel said, "Not bad."

"Well, you aren't the only one with tricks up his sleeve, Colonel. But now, I assume you are thinking of going over the border."

The colonel gave a faint nod.

"Well, then, we have a whole new ballgame on our hands." Domingo walked up to the front of the room. "First off, we need to keep Taz and his son on ice, until you—"

"Already taken of care of, Gunny," the colonel said. "We have a good connection in the FBI. They're transporting father and son to a secure location as we speak."

"All righty then," Domingo said. "Let's discuss *Ciudad Juárez.*"

* * *

THE MONITOR SHOWED *LA CRISÁLIDA'S* location on a street map. Domingo discussed crossing the border. Going in wouldn't be a problem, but getting out might be. The difficulty depended in part on how much hell the colonel's people raised on the other side and partly on what happened with the escalating flu pandemic. He also explained that he had a safe house where they could lay low if the need arose.

"Remember earlier when I said this place is like Iraq? Well I meant it, but there are a few very important differences." He became more animated.

"Keep in mind that these thugs on the other side are *not* insurgents. They are not a rag tag bunch of illiterate, religiously brainwashed, backward-assed goat herders. They're well funded. They have the same weapons we do, and they not only know how to use them, they haven't the slightest compunction about killing. The other thing is, for this to work we need a very structured plan with a drop-dead timeline, no exceptions. So we need to know what you're after. Because I can tell you one thing, if that boy is even still alive, there is no way in hell he's anywhere near *Ciudad Juárez.*"

The colonel explained who the boy was and went on to describe some of what had happened over the past year and half. This gave Domingo's team some context, especially when it came to Marcus. Besides, for the colonel, all missions operated on a policy of full disclosure. With a full explanation and Domingo's team accepting the parameters of the mission, the colonel said, "From this point on, Domingo has ops. We are following his lead." He looked directly at Marcus.

"What?" Marcus said, a big boyish smile on his face.

Domingo took over. "We'll cross the border at dark. We'll take two vehicles—just a bunch of pals looking for cheap booze and cheaper women. This place won't start hopping until after ten, and even though we have this state of mass chaos exploding around us, where we're going, chaos is an everyday fact of life." Domingo pointed at the satellite picture of *la Crisálida.* "Mickey, you and Red,"—he cocked his head at Jamie—"are perfect: young, foreign, and by that I mean, not American. You both have those accents that women drop their panties for and men, for some reason, find disarming. So you'll run point. You'll need cash—U.S. dollars, a couple grand each will do, small worn bills." Then he paused and said, "Colonel, can I have a moment please?"

* * *

THE TWO MEN WENT INTO a small office set up with cots in the back of the warehouse.

"What's on your mind, Gunny?"

"The big man, Colonel. I think you might want to leave him behind on this op. He can run support from here."

The colonel didn't have to ask for an explanation. Domingo's demeanor said it all.

Domingo sat on the edge of one of the cots, his right leg sticking out, hands in his lap, eyes on the floor.

"Sit and I came up together, through basic and then on to sniper school at Benning. His family lived in Tennessee, mine in Odessa, Texas. Anyway, whenever we had leave, we'd head to see his mama and sister." Domingo looked up at the colonel. "Did you know he had a sister? Her name was Janelle. She was four years younger than Sit. She had troubles. Wanted more than some small Appalachian hill town could provide. Sit sent money and talked to her as often as he could. One day, he gets a call from his mother. We were almost at the end of sniper school. Janelle had gone missing, been gone almost three weeks. We'd been on a field deployment most of that time." Domingo rose and blew out a deep breath.

"We went to our CO, got three-day passes, and headed for New Orleans. On the second night, we found her. I've seen some things, but this was bad." Domingo paused. "She was in this shit-hole of a hotel, lying stark naked on a filthy bed, needle tracks on her arms and between her toes. They'd been using her like a piece of meat, one man after another. She smelled rancid; there was foam coming out of her mouth, and she was unresponsive. Sit picked her up. If you could've seen him holding her...the anguish on his face. She died in his arms and he went nuts." Domingo sat back down on the cot. "He

221

tore through that place like it was made of paper. I mean he went through doors and walls like they weren't there. And anyone who got in his way, he dropped 'em where they stood. To this day, I don't know how we made it out of there and back to base. But we did. Got Janelle's body back to her mama and never so much as heard a sneeze about what happened.

"Up till that day, Sit and I were pretty much head to head on the range. But when we got back, we had to certify at a thousand yards. Sit shot a silver dollar five times consecutively. That's a near-inhuman feat. And my guess is he still shoots that good, and then some. I'm just saying this place we're going... What they do to girls, women, and boys it's..."

The colonel had listened without interruption. He stood in front of the man. "It's what makes you such a good leader, Gunny. You know your men and the situations you ask them to go into, but you also know me. You're partially right. I did know Sit had a sister, deceased, but nothing about how she died. If he's been carrying this inside all this time, well, it needs to be addressed. Besides he's Marcus's guardian angel, of sorts. Where one goes, so does the other."

CHAPTER FORTY-TWO

Back in front of the teams, Domingo began. "We're on the move at twenty-one-hundred hours. This is a recon mission, but if you run into resistance, do not hesitate—neutralize it. We are after information, but I have no idea where to begin. There will most certainly be a madam. Probably the best-dressed and least fucked-up woman in the place, but don't count on it."

Marcus was staring at the building from the satellite feed on the screen. "Hey, J. T., you there?"

Seconds later, J. T.'s face filled the screen.

"What can you tell us about this building?"

"Not much. Building records, for the most part, aren't in a digital format in Mexico. I can give you dimensions and a guess as to a basic floor plan, but that's about it."

"Domingo, you ever been inside?"

The former gunnery sergeant looked to one of his men and nodded.

"Well sir," said a lean man in his mid-thirties. "I've been inside on the main floor only. Had a client a few months back who insisted on seeing the raunchiest place in town."

"Not a client of ours anymore," said Domingo.

"The room inside the doors is maybe forty feet deep and the width of the building. About two thirds of that space is open to the floor above. There's a long bar on the back wall. There are cheap tables and chairs, a stage to the right, and a staircase on the left. The whole place is dingy, and smells of tequila and puke."

Marcus addressed Liam and Jamie. "So it's either behind the bar or upstairs. My money's on behind the bar."

In one voice both men said, "What are you talking about?"

Marcus grinned. "The name of the place is —*la Crisálida,* the Chrysalis—the tough, ugly wrapping around a soft gooey insect. But it's what you don't see: the beautifully delicate butterfly developing inside. What better cover for a discreet whorehouse that appeals to the most discerning and perverted of customers than a first-rate shit-hole? So the question is, where's the butterfly?"

Both men looked back at Marcus as if he had a third eye.

"You need to find the butterfly, gentlemen."

"And how might we do that, mate?" Liam asked. "And for that matter, how will we know when we've found it?"

"Oh, you'll know it. Just make sure to let us know before you two decide to sample the wares."

Liam let out a huff, feigning offense, which set the whole room to laughing.

* * *

Ciudad Juárez, Chihuahua

LIAM AND JAMIE, EACH WITH a *Pacifico* in his hand, got into a cab outside the hotel *María Bonita Consulado Americano*. They would be entering unarmed and without identification. Each carried a couple hundred dollars in his pockets, and the balance of two thousand tucked inside socks and money belt. "Exactly where they will assume you are carrying extra cash," Domingo had said.

As he pulled the back door of the cab shut, Liam said, his Irish brogue making his attempt at Spanish sound especially odd. "*La Crisálida, por favor.*"

The cab driver turned in the seat. "*¿Crisálida? No Bueno, mis amigos. El Edén es mejor.*"

Jamie leaned forward. "*Habla ingles?*"

The cab driver smiled, "*Un Poco.*"

"We hear la Crisálida is special...*especial. ¿Verdad?* That's where we want to go. *¿Comprende?*"

"*Sí, sí, la Crisálida,*" the cabbie said, shaking his head as he pulled away from the curb.

* * *

SIT AND MARCUS SAT IN AN old van parked on the street a few blocks from *la Crisálida* when the faded yellow Nissan cab drove up in front of the brothel and Liam and Jamie got out.

Marcus said, "Okay, boys, have a good time. Have a shot for me."

Without looking away from the brothel's entrance, both men

224

casually tapped twice below their ear, using the middle finger.

Despite the flu pandemic and the horrific rate of violent crime, the neighborhood sidewalks bustled. Outside the numerous cantinas and clubs, men and scantly clad, heavily made-up women gave out handbills offering a variety of freebies—a beer, a shot, a margarita—as enticements to come in and peruse their wares. Amid the locals, a fair number of adventure-seeking Anglo tourists mingled. Blending in would not be a problem.

* * *

AT THE ENTRANCE TO LA *Crisálida* stood a big, heavyset Mexican man, arms crossed. He greeted Liam and Jamie. *"Hola, amigos.* Looking for a good time?"

Both nodded.

"Well, you have come to the right place. We have a cover charge."

Liam and Jamie each went for their wad of cash in their front pockets, with all the eagerness of horny young men with pussy and booze on their minds.

Seeing the healthy wad of tens and twenties each held in his hand, the big man said, "I can see you two know what you want." He uncrossed his arms. "For you, no charge tonight. Just make sure to tell the girls that Churro said to take care of you."

Peeling off two tens, Jamie reached out to shake the man's hand. "You're a mate. Have a few *cervezas* on us."

The man smiled and took the money. *"Gracias, mis amigos."*

Stuffing the money back in their pockets, Liam and Jamie walked into la Crisálida.

Inside, they saw the room that Domingo's man had described. The front part was open to the upper floor with a staircase on the left and a bar along the back wall. A mishmash of chipped, cracked, dirty tiles made up the floor. The once lime-green walls had faded and stained to a nauseous brownish turquoise. The jukebox blared some Mexican pop tune neither of them had ever heard.

The lighting was brighter than they had expected. Just after eleven in the evening, and the place was hopping, the bar stools full. Only a few empty tables remained. Along one wall, two stark-naked women, a good ten years past their prime, gyrated and jiggled about around a pole on a raised stage.

A busty woman, in a bright pink tube top and a short, tight

miniskirt, wearing a pair of stiletto heels that seemed too small for her chubby feet, came up to them.

"*Bienvenidos, amigos.* Welcome to *la Crisálida.*" She looked old enough to be Jamie's mom. She rested her manicured hand on Jamie's shoulder, the fire-engine-red nails dragging lightly down his neck.

With a huge smile on his face, Jamie flipped his baseball hat around and did his best doe- eyed boy.

"*Me llamo Muriel.* You want to buy me a drink?" Without waiting for an answer, she took Jamie by the arm, beckoned Liam to follow, and led them to an empty table. They sat as Muriel, still standing, said, "*Tequila, ¿sí?*"

As she went to the bar, Liam described out loud the inside of the building, identifying visible doorways and any obvious security personnel. From the satellite imagery and the intelligence provided by Domingo and his team, they knew that the two-story building was about 60 feet wide and 150 feet deep. The room they sat in was square, so that meant a lot of space existed behind the bar and that much more upstairs.

At least forty customers and a few dozen women who had seen hard roads and better days crowded the bar. Five tough looking men—two standing, backs to the wall, on either side of the bar, one near the staircase and two roaming—plus two male bartenders, made up the complement of muscle.

The clientele appeared to be mostly local, not a lot of white guys, although a few looked like college boys on an alcohol-fueled adventure. The whole place floated in cigarette and cigar smoke that helped mask an underlying bouquet of beer, tequila, sweat, and vomit.

Occasionally, men, alone or in small groups, always accompanied by one or more of the women, would go up the stairs, but not before being patted down by security.

Muriel returned with a tray holding three glasses of amber liquid, a small bowl of salt, and another with sliced limes. She put the tray on the table, sat in the empty chair, and crossed her legs.

She picked up one of the glasses and waited until Liam and Jamie each had done the same, "*Salud.* You know what they say, what happens in Mexico..."

* * *

MARCUS AND SIT LISTENED FROM their car. They formed a mental picture of what had been described. The question still hadn't been answered. Where was the butterfly inside this cocoon? Behind the bar or upstairs?

Both agreed that behind the bar seemed the most likely, especially from a security and escape standpoint. They also noted that everyone Jamie and Liam talked to spoke decent English.

CHAPTER FORTY-THREE

January 3

Muriel reached under the table and ran her hand up Liam's leg to his crotch and gave a gentle squeeze. "What you want?" she asked running her tongue slowly over her upper lip.

Liam rested his hand over the top of hers and said, "Lass, no offense, but me and my pal were thinking more along the lines of a shag with a younger, less road-traveled gal, if ye get me meaning."

Muriel's eyes lit up at his smooth Irish delivery as she turned her attention to Jamie.

"Bloody right, señorita. Me and my mate are mucking about for a couple of shelias with nice tight bums and big yavos." Jamie cupped his hands palms out and wiggled them side-to-side.

"Not *Americanos?*" she said.

Liam put his hand around Jamie's shoulder. "Ireland and Australia, señorita, and we've come a fair bit to see the best o 'Mexico. Can ya fix a fella up?" He pulled out his roll of cash and peeled off two twenties.

Scooping up the cash and stuffing it into her tube top, Muriel got up, not the least bit offended that she was not the preferred hunk of flesh. She went to the bar and spoke with one of the bartenders and the man standing by a door to the left of the bar.

"Looks like we're in," said Liam, as if speaking to Jamie.

* * *

"Okay, stay focused," said Marcus. "If we lose you for any reason, the cavalry is coming. We need information. In about two minutes, these people are going to know that the two of you are flush, so you need to come off as the advance team for a bunch of buddies arriving over the next few days who are looking for a place to party and drop a wad of cash. Just play up the exotic-accented, not-too-streetwise, thinking-with-the-little-head tourists."

Next to Marcus, Sit remained silent when a knock on the window drew their attention.

Domingo stood with two of his men, red Solo cups in hands, pretending to speak to each other. As Marcus and Sit listened through the open window, Domingo said, "We've got two guys for sure, working outside as spotters. We'll take care of them and hope that by then Mickey and Red will have what you need." Domingo made eye contact with Marcus, then Sit. "Take care, big man. In and out, no bullshit."

* * *

A THIRTY-SOMETHING MAN WITH a mustache, goatee and slicked-back hair, wearing a western style shirt came to the table and sat. In his hand, he held a bottle of tequila and a shot glass. "*Amigos*, a drink," he said holding up the bottle. I am Beto. *¿Como se llaman?*"

Reaching his hand out, Jamie said, "I'm Jamie. This is me mate, Liam." He patted Liam on the shoulder.

"*¿Hablas español?*" Beto asked, no doubt already knowing the answer.

With his thumb and forefinger almost touching, Jamie said, "*Un poco.*"

"No problem, *mis amigos*. Muriel says you are looking for something more...youthful."

"Oh yeah, mate." Jamie nodded in agreement.

Beto leaned in and spoke quietly. "You have come to the right place, but my friends, what you are wanting is *muy caro*—very expensive." He rubbed his thumb over his fingertips.

Liam and Jamie looked at each other. "How much?"

"Five hundred to start."

Domingo had warned them about this part of the process. They would be expected to negotiate and had to be cautious about readily agreeing with the first prices offered, but on the other hand, they also needed to maintain the image of naïveté.

Liam let out a breath through pursed lips. "Seems a bit on the steep side, mate. That the best ya can do? Ya see we have a group of mates joining up for a bash. Eight of us—*ocho hombres*. The whole gang'll be here tomorrow. My mate and I have been tasked to find a place we can call our own for a few days."

Beto poured three more shots and sat back in his chair, glass in hand. He smiled. "I can see you are businessmen. I can do four hundred."

"Make it two hundred and you have a deal, *amigo,*" Jamie broke in.

"Call it three hundred. I assure you, the girls will not disappoint you."

Both eagerly agreed.

Raising his glass, Beto said, "To your new home in *Ciudad Juárez.*"

They drank, and Beto stood up from the table. "Follow me, my friends. Paradise awaits."

They stopped at the bar where Beto asked for the three hundred from each of them. He explained that, depending on what services they finally settled on, it could cost more. He made clear that it was a pay-before-you-play arrangement. This, too, they had discussed with Domingo. Liam excused himself and went to the restroom. It was expected. It would confirm that like most *gringos,* Jamie and Liam thought that by hiding their money they could keep it safe. But actually, it only confirmed that they had at least six hundred dollars and probably much more. Domingo made the point over and over that they had to give the impression that the head driving their decisions was not the one resting on their shoulders.

Liam returned a few minutes later with a wad of worn bills.

Beto took the money. "One more small thing, and you are done with my ugly face. I must search you to make sure you are not carrying any weapons."

They stood still, feet apart, arms held out to their sides, as Beto patted each of them down. Satisfied, he nodded to the man standing with his back to the wall, and a hidden, knob-less door opened.

Electronic magnetic latch, Jamie thought. Peering in, he saw that the space behind the bar was much darker.

Beto patted them each on the back as they stepped though the open doorway, into the hazy red glow. "Enjoy, *mis amigos,* enjoy."

* * *

WHEN THE DOOR SHUT BEHIND them, it took a few moments for their eyes to adjust. The red glow, filtered through a haze of cigar smoke, came from lamps and wall sconces with glittering black fringe hanging from the bottoms.

Heavily textured dark walls and thick carpet on the floor gave this part of the bordello a more up-scale feel than the front. A bar stood in the center of the room surrounded by dark round tables and black leather-and-chrome club chairs.

A tall, thin woman came up to them. She wore a low-cut white shirt and the exposed cleavage revealed a monarch butterfly tattoo on the inside of each breast. Her face was pale, with high cheekbones, and a sharp nose. She spoke with an accent, but it didn't sound Hispanic.

Standing between Jamie and Liam the woman took each by the arm. "Gentlemen, let me show you to a table and get you some refreshment."

She guided them to a booth against the wall. At a wave of her hand, a topless Latina in a turquoise G-string came to the table holding a tray with glasses and a bottle of tequila.

Before the op, Liam and Jamie had each taken a dose of Dihydromyricetin, a compound extracted from the Japanese raisin tree. It would allow them to drink much more alcohol before some of the classic signs for drunkenness, such as slurred speech and impaired motor skills, became an issue. They definitely needed all the help they could get. Obviously lowering their inhibitions— and lightening their pocketbooks—with the help of shots of tequila was the approach of choice.

As glasses clinked and refilled, the woman with the butterfly tattoos shook her straight black hair out of her face. "What is your pleasure? Girls? Maybe boys? Women perhaps?" She ran her long black fingernails down between her breasts in a motion suggesting that she, or others like her, might be on the menu. "Take a moment; look around. See if anything catches your eye. I'll be back, and then we will get your evening started."

She walked across the room and stopped at a booth filled with what looked like middle-aged Mexican businessmen. In the briefing, Domingo had made it clear that this city was not, by any stretch, a tourist destination. Rather, it was a place with a distinct reputation among a certain demographic of sexual adventure seekers. More importantly, it was at the top of the hit list for international perverts and pedophiles. According to Domingo, no perversion, no matter how base or horrific, couldn't be catered to in *Ciudad Juárez.* Its proximity just across the border made it perhaps one of the easiest, most convenient, most economical place in the world for those who needed to keep their proclivities and perversions discreet. Consequently, at any given time the city crawled not only with Mexican gangs and drug cartels, but also with scum from all over the globe out to prey on women, girls, or boys.

Jamie and Liam described every detail of the room for the teams outside. In the back was a hall down which groups of customers were occasionally led. There was definitely a system, and Miss Butterfly Bosom was running it.

Jamie and Liam kept up the charade of sex-besotted boys out on the town. They clinked glasses, licked salt, threw back shots, and sucked lime wedges. They knew that when their hostess returned, she would expect to see a noticeable dent in the bottle of *Sauza Hornitos.*

* * *

OUTSIDE, DOMINGO HAD GOTTEN INTO the back of the van. With Sit and Marcus, he listened as Liam and Jamie described the inside of the building.

Domingo said, "It's a great setup. The front half is the shit-hole you'd expect—cheap and dirty—and the back half is a more upscale version. In one side, you wallow in the visible slime. In the other, you get a few layers of window dressing, but in the end, it's just a splash of fancy perfume on the same pig."

Listening to Domingo, Marcus had to agree. He glanced over at Sit. The big man, usually quiet, had been downright silent since they had set up watch.

Over the comm, one of Domingo's men murmured, "Bravo to lead, you copy."

Domingo responded, "Copy, Bravo. What've you got?"

"Around back, a parking lot, with three guards, and an exterior staircase with another guard at the door up top. Seems like an entrance, complete with valet parking. For the more discreet clientele."

"Copy, I'm on the move. Stay tight until I get there."

Speaking to Marcus and Sit, Domingo continued. "We'll neutralize the threat outside. You need to get one of the fancy boys to open that door at the top of the stairs."

"I can hear ya, mate. I know yer mum raised ya better."

Domingo laughed. "So sensitive. Just get the door open. Out."

To Sit and Marcus he said, "You wait for my go. Then you have ten minutes to get in, get the info you want, and get out. Go for

232

the butterfly lady."

* * *

MARCUS WATCHED AS DOMINGO MADE his way around the side of the building and out of their sight. A moment later, Marcus heard Domingo's voice in his ear. "Alpha, you are a go in two minutes."

Without taking his eyes off the front of the building where a steady stream of men flowed in and out, Marcus asked Sit, "You ready for this?"

When Sit didn't answer, Marcus faced him. Sit was staring out into the night, but to Marcus it appeared he wasn't focused on anything in particular. "You okay?

Sit nodded.

* * *

WHEN SIT AND MARCUS ARRIVED at the back staircase all the guards were gone and the door at the top of the stairs was ajar.

Sit went first. They both wore body armor under large, loose-fitting shirts. They entered the dimly lit hall and smelled the bouquet of cigarette and cigar smoke and cheap perfume. Inside, they stood still taking in the layout.

Through their earbuds they heard Liam's voice. "Madam Butterfly, first door on your right. She's not alone—two, maybe three. Good luck, lads."

Sit whispered to Marcus, "I got left."

Each carried a Walther P22 with Silencerco Sparrow silencers. Sit had chosen the small caliber for close quarters, accuracy. With virtually no recoil, moving from target to target would be fast and easy.

Knocking on the door while fiddling with the locked knob, Marcus said in loud, drunken, badly accented Spanish, "*Señorita, abierto la puerta, por favor.*"

Getting no answer, he knocked again, repeating his inebriated plea. At the sound of someone coming to the door he stepped to one side. Sit did the same on the other side.

The door opened a crack and Marcus said from behind the door, "*Bueno, bueno.*"

The door opened further, and in a blur, Sit had the man by his collar with his left hand, pistol in the right. As he barged into the room using his captive as a shield, his pistol fired twice. The two men on the sofa died instantly.

Marcus came in behind him, moving to the right and dropping to one knee.

The office had no windows. Madam Butterfly sat behind a big wooden desk. Sit rammed the head of the man who answered the door into a bar cabinet along the wall. He crumpled into a heap, dead or seriously concussed.

Marcus kept his pistol trained on the woman. When she went to pull open a drawer, Marcus said, *"Ya by ne propusti."*

The women froze at the warning, *Don't even think about it,* spoken in Russian. She stared at Marcus moving toward her. Marcus had guessed from listening to the woman's accent in her conversation with Liam and Jamie that she was Slavic, perhaps Russian.

"What brings you so far from home?" Marcus asked.

The women glared at him. "Whoever you are, you are dead. And everyone you know—all your family—"

That was as far as she got before Sit clamped his huge hand around her delicate neck, picked her out of her chair as if she were a house cat, and held her at arm's length a foot off the carpeted floor.

"My friend has no patience," Marcus said.

She tried to kick out, but Sit tightened his grip, pushing her up against the wall, blocking her legs with his body.

"Keep it up and he'll break your neck. Now I need some information; then I see no reason why you can't go back to running your business."

This got Marcus a raised eyebrow from Sit.

Slowly, Sit set her feet on the ground and maneuvered her around the desk. As he released his grip, he pushed her hard so that she plopped in a heap on the sofa between the two men with small round holes in their foreheads.

From his cargo pocket, Marcus produced a picture of Jabril al-Mohmoud.

He handed her the photo. "Have you seen this boy?"

She took it and gave a cursory glance. Sit took a menacing step toward her, and she studied it again.

"Maybe, maybe not," she said rubbing her neck.

Marcus stood in front of her. "I'm sorry, was that a yes or a no?"

Marcus watched her eyes as she contemplated the lie.

Sit knelt and placed his hand on the pale skin of her bare thigh and squeezed.

"Yes, I have seen him. But he is not here."

"When?"

"Two, three weeks ago."

"When you saw him, was he well?"

"Well....I don't..." Her face grimaced as Sit squeezed harder. "Yes, yes, he was well."

"Now, here's the tricky part." Marcus glanced at his watch, five minutes left. "You tell me what happened to him, who took him, and where they went, or this big man here is going to rip your arms off."

Eyes accustomed to being in command now held pure fear. "The man who owns this place took him."

Sit squeezed.

"I know him as *el Capullo*." Sit squeezed more, eliciting a pained whimper from the woman. "All I know is, he is part of the Gutiérrez cartel. I think he might be part of the actual family."

Sit squeezed harder still.

"That's all I know. It is the truth, I tell you."

"Okay, so where did this *el Capullo* take the boy?"

The woman's eyes darted to Sit, then fell on Marcus.

Marcus pressed his advantage. "I see that you wear his mark. Are you his property?" He pointed at the matching butterfly tattoos, then realized that one was slightly bigger than the other. The bigger one had a black patch on each hind wing. Male and female?

With her long, black-nailed fingers, she caressed the two colorful tattoos. "Once, when he had been drinking too much, he mentioned a place called *Mariposa*. He said one day we would go there. That he had a cabin built of logs, like in the American West. He fancies—"

The door opened and Liam came in while Jamie stood in the doorway.

"Hope you have her sorted. Almost time to go."

Sit lifted his hand from the woman's leg and stood. He walked past Liam to the door, said something to Jamie, then disappeared.

Marcus didn't have time to worry about Sit. He needed the rest of the information.

With his hand, he motioned for her to go on.

"*El Capullo* imagines he is a cowboy, a wilderness man."

"What is *Mariposa?*"

A hint of confidence had returned now that Sit was gone. Marcus stepped forward and put the pistol muzzle against her forehead. "I'm not fucking around with you. Tell me or die."

"I don't know. You must believe me. All I know is that it has something to do with the butterflies."

Marcus listened. He believed that she had told him all she knew, but he didn't want her to think that. "For your sake, I hope you have told me everything. Because if you haven't, I'll be back, and the time for pleasant conversation will be over."

Liam gagged her and tied her up. The man whose head Sit had banged into the wall let out a low moan, but made no effort to get up.

Marcus, Jamie, and Liam left the room and went down the outside back stairs. At the bottom, Domingo said, "Where's Sit?"

Marcus shrugged.

Jamie said, "When he walked by me he said he had to check something out and he would meet us outside. I thought it was something Marcus knew about."

Marcus and Domingo shared a quick look.

"Okay, give me two minutes, "Marcus said. "I'll get him." Turning, he ran back up the stairs.

CHAPTER FORTY-FOUR

MARCUS WALKED DOWN THE HALL, past the door to the office where they had left Miss Butterfly tied up. At the end, he turned and saw a man slumped on the floor. He wasn't moving and ragged white bone protruded from his left bicep. In the wall, he saw a seam of light. Reaching for the edge, Marcus pulled back the hidden door.

On the other side was the upstairs of the front of the building and another long hall. Whereas the upscale side was dim and sultry, this side was bright and raw. Making his way cautiously down the hall, he passed a room, the door hanging askew from its hinges.

Flimsy partitions along each wall divided the room into small cubbies, each with a bed, nightstand, and lamp. At least six shirtless boys, wearing tight boxer briefs, sat huddled into one of the spaces at the back. Marcus paused. A mix of Latino, Asian, and Caucasian, not one could have been over 16, and a few looked as young as 10. Then Marcus saw two naked white men, sprawled unconscious, maybe dead, on the floor behind the door. He held his forefinger to his lips and moved along.

Across the hall the same scene, but instead of boys, this room held young girls, bunched together trying to hide their nakedness. Marcus stared as his mind painted pictures of something worse than a parent's worst nightmare. Then he heard a primal shriek.

Holding his pistol in both hands, Marcus rushed down the hall. Out of one of the rooms ran a fat middle-aged Latino, blood streaming from his nose that had been relocated to his left cheek. Marcus hit him hard in the throat, dropping him in the corridor. At least two male voices yelled from downstairs. In Spanish they ordered everyone who didn't work there to get out. Domingo's men?

Marcus entered the last room. This one not partitioned. A bed took up nearly half the small room. Five men, some white, some brown, lay sprawled about. And by the positions of their heads and limbs, they had to be dead. Sit stood by the side of the bed, blocking Marcus's view. He walked around to the other side.

On the bed lay an unconscious young black girl. One wrist handcuffed to a rail of the metal headboard. She was naked, with dirty, matted hair, and needle tracks up and down each arm.

In the distance, Marcus heard a siren, then several more. Walking around the bed, he approached Sit.

"Hey."

No response.

"Hey, we gotta go."

Sit made no sign that he even knew Marcus was in the room. Marcus grabbed the big man's shirt collar at the neck and pulled hard. Sit's eyes fell on him, but they weren't the sparkling root beer color he had come to know. The face Marcus beheld was a black hole: the eyes held not a glint of light.

"Sit, this is not the time. We have to move, now!"

The man's eyes didn't even blink. His body was in the room, but his spirit had departed. Letting go of Sit's shirt, Marcus slapped him hard, once, twice. Before the third slap landed, Sit's hand caught Marcus's wrist in full swing.

Without squeezing, he held Marcus's arm in an unbreakable grip.

Marcus spoke, his voice low and forceful. "Sit, we move, now. I'm on your six, and don't think for one second I won't pop a round in your ass to keep you moving. Now go!"

* * *

AN ABANDONED AND BOARDED-UP hovel in the *Granjas de Chapultepec* neighborhood—one of the poorest in this city of one and a half million—is what Domingo called their Juárez safe house. It sat at the top of a hill accessed by a rough unpaved road. A few large white cedar trees stood on the back side of the dilapidated block-and-stucco house, providing cover for the two dented and rusted older-model Suburbans they had driven across the border earlier that evening.

Inside, Domingo went to the hidden fuse box and turned on the electricity. Three bare light bulbs hanging by wires from the chipped ceiling came to life. A few cots with thin mattresses, a rickety wooden table, and a half-dozen mismatched chairs, rounded out the furnishings. At the back of the house was a small room that had once been a kitchen.

Sit had not spoken a word since he and Marcus emerged from

the whorehouse. Upon entering the safe house, he stripped off his shirt and then his vest, pushed one of the cots against the far wall, and sat down heavily on it. The lightweight frame creaked under his weight.

In the small back room, the colonel and Domingo went through the debrief process that was as natural to the both of them as breathing. Marcus paused at the doorway, not wanting to intrude.

"What's on your mind?" the colonel asked.

"Just wondering how long we're gonna be here."

"Well, considering the ruckus we caused, we need to wait for daylight," Domingo replied. "It'll be safer then."

"Then I've got an idea. We've already filled the pot; how much worse could it really be if we gave it another stir?"

* * *

Marcus approached Sit, who still sat shirtless with his back against the rough plaster.

"Hey, you okay?"

"I'm not in a mood for your bullshit, Marcus."

Marcus stuck his hands in his pockets as he stood in front of his friend. "Just thought you might be interested in seeing if we couldn't give those kids at least half a chance at a better life."

He had Sit's attention. "The colonel, Domingo, and his team are on board. I just got one question: Is the big dog ready to hunt?"

In a surprisingly quick move for a man of his size, Sit was on his feet in one fluid bound. Shirt in hand, he walked past Marcus. "What I'm gonna do ain't called huntin'."

* * *

Both teams gathered around the table as Domingo laid out the op. "Now, me and my boys are going to run interference, provide auxiliary support where required. Liam's with us. I've called in some favors, and we'll have medical support and transportation for the girls and boys. The older women will be fine. But what about the tattoo lady?"

Marcus spoke up. "Jamie and Weathers, you clear the back half. Get everybody out. Anybody puts up a fight, drop 'em. As for Butterfly Breasts, tag her." Marcus pulled a small aerosol can from his pants pocket and tossed it to Weathers. "Same type of shit they used on Garrett. Although J. T. says his formula is an improvement. Just spray it on her and we'll be able to track her for days."

Weathers gingerly turned the can in his hands.

Marcus laughed. "Don't worry, there's not enough radioactivity to make your hair fall out. Now, your balls might shrink up a little..."

Everyone laughed.

Sit stood up. "Okay, Marcus and I are going in the front." He turned his attention to Marcus. "You stay on me. I'll clear the path. You convince those kids..." his jaw clenched. " ... to get out."

Domingo took over. "All right, we move in one hour. Fifteen minutes after we breach, our help will arrive. We have a little distraction arranged on the other side of the city, set to go off in about..." he looked at his watch. "...thirty minutes. It'll keep the *policia* and the *federales* busy for a few hours. That'll give us a good hour, but let's try to make it happen in forty-five!"

* * *

THERE WAS NOTHING STEALTHY about Sit and Marcus's entrance into *la Crisálida*. To their advantage, it was 3:30 in the morning and most of the clients had gone. And of those remaining, most were blind drunk.

Sit burst through the door, slamming it into the wall. If the sight of a six-eight, three-hundred-pound black mountain of muscle and rage wasn't enough to put the fear of God in everyone, the two AR 15's with thirty-round clips that sprayed the mirrors behind the bar and sent chunks of concrete and plaster flying off the walls did the rest.

"*¡Todos afuera!*" Marcus shouted. It was all the encouragement anyone needed to bolt for the door.

Sit ejected the spent clips and slapped in new ones as he pounded up the steps.

At the top, two guards dropped their pistols and put their hands in the air. Marcus ordered them out.

As Sit cleared the rooms of clients and guards, Marcus went from room to room, speaking quietly and reassuringly to the young boys and girls. Marcus organized the able bodied to help those who couldn't walk out on their own.

Finally, he came to the room where the young black girl was cuffed to the bed. Sit was staring at her from the doorway. Marcus pushed past him and went to her side. There was a sickly yellow foam crusted around her mouth. He felt for a pulse, her skin was cold. Marcus looked back at Sit and shook his head. "There's nothing we can do." He rose to leave.

"That girl's gotta mama," Sit said as he turned for the door and continued down the hall.

Marcus heard the colonel's voice over his comm. "We got you covered. Bring her out."

Marcus produced a handcuff key from his vest, unlocked the dead girl's wrist. Reaching down, he picked her up in his arms. She weighed maybe eighty pounds. Carrying her down the stairs, tears stung his eyes.

* * *

OUTSIDE, SEVERAL AMBULANCES AS WELL as pickups and cars waited. Marcus laid the body on the ground atop a blanket. When he stood up, a thin, middle-aged man with a few days' growth of beard wearing a clerical collar said, "Thank you. We will see that she is taken care of. What you all have done is a blessing. Domingo is always looking out for the poor."

"*De nada, padre.* Thank *you.*"

Marcus looked around and saw groups of the girls and boys being helped into trucks and cars. Others assisted those needing more help into ambulances.

Domingo walked up and touched Marcus on the shoulder. "Hey, these are good people. We'll do what we can. The colonel has promised resources, which will be a great help. It seems he has some connections. We'll start getting these kids across the border in the morning. It was a good plan. Here…" he handed Marcus a small black box about the size of a computer mouse. "It's a gift for the big man."

Moments later, Sit came out the front, holding Butterfly Breasts by the scruff of the neck, her hands still bound behind her back. As he propelled her in Marcus's direction, Weather's voice came over the comm. "Back all clear. Target tagged."

Then one of Domingo's team said, "Front clear."

When Sit got to Marcus, he stopped, still holding the woman's neck.

Marcus looked at her. "I have no idea what a Russian is doing as a madam of a whorehouse in Mexico, but I'm going to find out. I would suggest that before I do you head for home, because if you and

241

I meet again, it will be the last time.

"Cut her loose. Let her go," Marcus said.

Marcus could see that Sit didn't want this filth walking the earth one minute more, so he added, "My friend here doesn't like you. So heed my warning and, as fast as you can, get far away from this place."

Reluctantly, Sit released her and she slunk off into the night.

Over the next ten minutes, all the kids and samaritans disappeared.

Marcus and Sit walked away from the entrance of la Crisálida. When they were up the street, a good two hundred feet away, Marcus tossed the box Domingo had given him up in the air in front of Sit.

As if by instinct Sit's hand shot out and caught the box just above his head. He looked into the palm of his hand and, as he flipped up the safety cover with his thumb, said, "You gotta love the Irish."

Sit pressed the button, and behind them, the den of exploitation, enslavement, and perversion imploded in a cloud of dust.

* * *

FOR THE SECOND TIME THAT night the teams returned to the Juárez safe house. The colonel and Domingo talked in the back room. At the sound of conversation Domingo looked through the doorway. He watched as Marcus went man by man to his team. Not just a handshake or a thank you—no, he made a personal connection with each of them.

Still watching, he said, "If I didn't know better, I'd say he's been doing that his whole adult life."

"Well, I believe, in a way, he has," the colonel said. "I've never met anyone quite like him. He has this way of getting under people's skin."

Domingo turned back.

"Anyway, Gunny, that reminds me; I'd like to talk to you about a new job."

With a sweeping gesture of his arms, Domingo said, "What, and leave all this?"

His voice turned serious. "I really appreciate it, Colonel, but..." Reaching down, he pulled up his right pant leg to reveal a prosthetic leg inside a boot. "I don't think I'm quite up to Force Ten standards. Fuckin' IED's."

"Don't sell your skills short, Gunny. I'd have you on my team in a heartbeat. But the job I'm talking about's more important than Force Ten." The colonel nodded at Marcus, who was still holding court with Domingo's men.

"That man comes with a substantial bit of baggage. And to be perfectly transparent, I've got some personal interest in this offer as well."

The colonel explained about the attack on the ranch. "So, you see, I've had to split the team, but from here on I'm going to need all hands on deck. I want you to run security at the ranch. You'll have complete control—anything you need. I know how people like to throw around the term, 'money is no object,' but in this case it's true."

"When would this need to happen?" Domingo asked.

The colonel paused for effect. "Now, I'm afraid. I know it's short notice, so I'll make you a deal: two hundred and fifty grand, just to go take a look, and another two hundred and fifty for your team. For all the help."

"You don't have to pay me or the team, Colonel. It was an honor to help out."

"Noted, Gunny. But the money is absolutely the least of my worries. You see, he has a big-ass family—a whole slew of brothers and sisters. A hardheaded, opinionated, self-directed bunch. On top of that, he has two sons who have that..." The colonel looked out the door towards Marcus. "And then some.

"Then there's the matter of the ranch staff. It's like we have our own village, and that's no shit. And there's this gal."

Domingo's eyebrows rose in comprehension.

"Well, I've been reminded quite often lately that old soldiers need to know when to hang it up if they ever want to be old men."

"Sounds great, Colonel, but I have a wife and a two-year old daughter."

"All the better. Family is kind of a prerequisite when it comes to Marcus. As far as your team, they and their families are all welcome. But I'll leave that up to you."

* * *

MARCUS KNOCKED ON THE WALL, not wanting to barge in on the conversation. "Come on in," said the colonel.

"Domingo, I need to tell you, that's a fine group you have," Marcus said, reaching out his hand. "We couldn't have done it without 'em. I'm in your debt."

"Well, sir, write a check." He smiled.

Marcus said to the colonel, "So is he going to take the job?"

At Domingo's accusatory look, the colonel put up his hands. "I swear, Gunny, we haven't talked."

"Well, we'd be privileged to have you, all of you," Marcus said as he left the room.

"I want to warn you, Gunny," the colonel said, "this is a life-changing adventure. And I can promise you, it's never dull."

CHAPTER FORTY-FIVE

January 3, Loliondo, Tanzania

ADRIANA LEHRER LEANED AGAINST THE back wall in the office of the director of AMERF's Loliondo clinic, Kathryn van der Hoch. The cracked wooden blades of the ceiling fan creaked and warbled, while doing little to mitigate the stifling heat. From behind her desk, Kathryn glared at the assistant to the Tanzanian Ministry of Health. His printed *"Madiba"* shirt drenched in sweat, the short, thin man perched on the edge of his chair, looked uncomfortable, and perhaps not only from the heat. One hand dabbed his face with a wrinkled handkerchief; the other clutched at the arm of his chair.

Kathryn explained the situation. "Since December 11, when we confirmed the first case of the H7N9 virus in Loliondo, there has been, as expected, an exponential increase in the number of cases. We are now seeing hundreds afflicted every day, and the death toll, especially among the very young and very old, is in the thousands— and that's just in this region of Tanzania." Kathryn's voice trembled with frustration as she slapped down on the stack of documentation she had been sending daily to the Ministry of Health.

With another thump of her hand on the desktop, Kathryn said, "Tell me what the Ministry intends to do?"

Shifting in his chair and mopping his face with a now damp rag, the man stammered, "Ms. van der Hoch, we at the Ministry realize how difficult your position is. We have done some looking into this outbreak. As you know, until recently, this virus has been restricted to Malaysia and other parts of Southeast Asia."

Kathryn shrugged her shoulders and said, "So what?"

Nervously he went on. "China has huge investments in Tanzania and throughout all Africa. As a consequence, there are many Chinese who have traveled here. It is our position that the virus arrived on our continent from China."

"It is not my concern how the virus arrived, but rather, what are we to do now that it is here and killing Africans!" Kathryn didn't try to hide her anger.

"That is a somewhat more complicated problem. Since there is no cure, those who are infected must let it run its course. And we must also be concerned with preventing additional Ebola outbreaks."

Kathryn stood abruptly. "Do not speak to me as if I were a child. I am well aware of what we can cure and what we cannot. As for Ebola, the H7N9 virus has already killed many thousands more. Due to the sheer numbers, it is impossible to quarantine, and unlike Ebola, it spreads easily—and very fast. What I am talking about is vaccinating wide swaths of the population that are not currently symptomatic. What is being done on that front?"

"I cannot speak to that. Vaccination programs are not in my department. But the logistical difficulties, considering the limited availability of vaccine and the need to keep the serum refrigerated, pose some real difficulties."

Kathryn walked around the desk. "Again, I am aware of the issues, but the AMERF has secured a supply of the vaccine and is ready to begin flying it in. Also—"

The Ministry official held up his hand as he rose. "Those are matters that must go through the proper channels. But now that this virus has spread around the world, especially in America, I would not put hope in Africa being a priority. I suggest you and your staff make the best of it." He strode out of the office and into a waiting air-conditioned car.

* * *

ADRIANA HAD LISTENED. SHE KNEW that the Chinese had substantial investment in Africa. In fact, she had seen growth projections that put the population of Africa, by the end of the century, as bigger than China's and India's combined. For her, it was hard to imagine, not because of the lack of resources—for Africa was perhaps the most resource-rich continent on earth—but because the lack of infrastructure seemed an insurmountable obstacle. Then again, the Chinese had a way of producing massive infrastructure projects from the ground up, and in timeframes that defied conventional thinking.

For a time, she and Kathryn talked about a strategy going forward. The full-blown flu pandemic would continue to spread. Kathryn had the AMERF staff working in two shifts around the clock—a pace they simply could not sustain. With security becoming more tenuous by the hour and their already limited resources nearly exhausted, abandoning the clinic was becoming a very real possibility.

As Adriana walked back to the clinic, she mulled over two astounding bits of knowledge that had come out of the meeting. One concerned the ongoing Ebola crisis. Although the death toll was in the thousands and projected by the World Health Organization to reach perhaps twenty thousand or more, this disease, although deadly in about half the cases, was not especially virulent. It could be contained by quarantine and had a proven, relatively straightforward treatment protocol. But give the world a vision of a hemorrhagic fever, and Africa was in the spotlight on the twenty-four-hour news stations. New drugs that normally took years to get through testing and regulation suddenly had official sanction for use. Massive resources were spent transporting a handful of aid workers to specialized treatment centers in America. Meanwhile, in Africa, over ten thousand people died every day from manageable, curable diseases.

The other thing was the whole China angle. She had never considered it, but here it was. And the governments of Africa had fingers pointed and conclusions drawn. She imagined that it would only be a matter of days before other nations too, found ways to blame China.

CHAPTER FORTY-SIX

Amman, Jordon

YOU HAVE TO APPRECIATE COUNTRIES where money is king— where for a price, anything can be had—where the roles of man and woman, rich and poor are clearly defined, Peter Revant thought as he boarded a private jet in Rio de Janeiro. He left Mexico City the day after meeting with Arturo Valdez. If his agreement with the Gutiérrez cartel went south for some reason, he didn't want to be in the direct line of fire. Besides, he had good contacts in Brazil, particularly in São Paulo's well-established Muslim community.

Peter debated the value of returning to Amman to see the sheikh. It could all backfire. If the sheikh found out about his involvement in Jabril's kidnapping, his grand jihad, not to mention his life, would be over. But something pushed him. He needed to know what the sheikh was doing besides paying ransom in his efforts to find Jabril. And if the cartel did decide to double cross him, a possibility he could not discount, no matter how much money he had paid, being in the land of the one and only true God might be his salvation. Then there was Adriana. Even though he prayed to Allah to forgive his weakness, he could not get her out of his mind.

* * *

A BODYGUARD, THE ONE CALLED Diar, who had been sent to protect Jabril, led Peter into the large modern library. A tall bank of windows, which looked out on the mix of ancient and modern that was the city of Amman, filled the room with light. Peter had paid little attention before, but now it struck him that this modern Jordanian estate was a stark contrast to the sheikh's Damascus home located within the "Old City's" al-Shaghour neighborhood. Where this place was all sharp angles and clean lines, the home where Peter and Adad spent many weeks every year, although spacious and filled with paintings, sculptures, and rugs of incalculable age, was otherwise like a comfortable, well-kept farmhouse.

The sheikh tried to stand from a chrome-framed, pale-green armless chair. Diar rushed to his side and helped him to his feet. The sheikh brushed him off and in Arabic, angrily told him to leave the room.

He smoothed the wrinkles from his simple white robe. If Peter thought the man he saw in October was an old wolf about to be turned out from the pack, his man had been pushed out and stood alone without the ability to hunt or protect himself.

Peter approached him, bowed his head, and said without looking up, "*Al salamu alaikum.*"

The sheikh reached out and pulled Peter into a weak embrace. In a voice on the verge of a sob the sheikh whispered in Peter's ear, "They have kidnapped Jabril."

Feigning shock, Peter took the sheikh's arm and led him out to the patio where they sat side by side.

The last time he was here, the sheikh had seemed defeated, resigned that his only son was dead. But now he was downright distraught. His grandson, Jabril, had been kidnapped. He had already paid out two hundred million U.S. dollars and still the boy had not been returned, nor could he even be certain that Jabril still lived.

Peter listened with all the attentiveness of a concerned surrogate son. The money that the sheikh had paid—and would continue to pay, if things went according to plan—would help finance and sustain the wave of fear and panic being visited upon America, and now, thanks to Adriana, around the world. Yet Peter could see that the sheikh needed his *support.*

Peter reached across the table and rested his hand on the sheikh's. A common enough gesture in the West, but one reserved for only the closest of family amongst the faithful.

"We must remain steadfast in our faith, *alab.*" Peter said.

The sheikh put his other hand on top of Peter's. "Yes, *ibni,* yes," he said, responding in kind, using the familial word for "son."

Peter poured tea from a simple clay pot and handed a cup to the sheikh.

When the tired, grief-worn old man mentioned Marcus Diablo, Peter stood and turned away to hide his shock. Walking a few steps toward the pool, Peter composed himself. How could it be that this man kept coming up in conversations with the sheikh? The sheikh told Peter how he had contacted this Marcus Diablo. How he felt compelled to do anything he could, even contacting the enemy, an unbeliever, if it might help return Jabril to him.

Turning back to face the sheikh, Peter's face wore the mask of calm composure. He wanted revenge for Adad's death, but he had had more important things on his mind. Now it seemed that the sheikh might very well have dropped the opportunity to rid the world of this bothersome infidel right into his lap.

Before taking his leave, Peter vowed effusively before God to do all he could to help the sheikh find Jabril, although they both agreed that prayer was the best course. He had been in touch with Isabelle Gutiérrez and knew she had the boy. He needed to get back to Mexico.

CHAPTER FORTY-SEVEN

El Paso, Texas

At the Alamo Freight warehouse, the men gathered again in front of the whiteboard. Domingo said, "Well, that was interesting. So the question is, now what?" He turned to the colonel. "How do we proceed from here?"

"So, Marcus, what'd J. T. find out?" the colonel asked.

The colonel's question surprised Marcus. How did he know that early that morning, Marcus had contacted J. T. and asked him to begin a search for *el Capullo*? Inwardly Marcus chuckled. *That's why the colonel was, The Colonel.*

Marcus asked Domingo to turn on the monitor. A few moments later, J. T.'s face filled the screen.

"Whatcha got?" Marcus asked.

"I don't know how you managed it from what little bit our Russian madam said, but sure enough, I think I found what you're looking for."

On the screen was a satellite picture of a simple rectangular log cabin, surrounded by mostly coniferous woods. It was the kind of scene you might find in any number of places in the United States. While the real-time picture showed the cabin and the area surrounding it from multiple angles, J. T.'s voice narrated.

"The cabin's about twelve by twenty, with a rusted metal roof and a shed-style covering over the front porch. This ain't Montana, boys. It's Angangueo, in the state of Michoacán, Mexico, the home of the Monarch Butterfly Biosphere Reserve. It's a small mountain town of ten thousand. Elevation is high, about eighty-four hundred feet. Anyway, I found pictures of the cabin, as you suspected, Marcus, on both Instagram and Snapshot." J. T.'s face was back on the screen. He was shaking his head, "Sometimes you scare me, man.

"We're en route on the *Takbir*, but there's no way we'll make it into the Gulf of Mexico in time. Everybody's aboard, except the ranch staff and Glen. We left Vancouver early yesterday. We'll be off the coast of *Puerto Vallarta* in twenty hours. That puts us seven hundred kilometers from *Angangueo,* within range of the Sikorsky."

Marcus listened. He had been so focused on finding *el Capullo* that he hadn't thought through the logistics of getting the rest of the team here, or how they would be able to provide support and evacuation if necessary, not to mention, keep his family safe. But the colonel had.

"Now, Colonel, all we need to get a team into *Angangueo* is a cover story."

"Okay, J. T.," said the colonel. "I need you to find Hector Peralta. Start your search in the Southwestern U.S."

* * *

"Hector?"

"No, this cannot be," said the smooth Spanish-accented voice. "Colonel Samuel Webb? I heard a rumor you had retired. Decided it was time for a life less…complicated. One perhaps with a dog." A deep laugh reverberated over the line.

"What is it with the dog?" the colonel said, more to himself than to the man on the phone. "How's the family, Hector?"

"All well, thank you. The children are grown with children of their own, and are out into the world, and as always, Oihane is keeping me in line. So, my old friend, you tracked me down to reminisce? I'm flattered."

It was the colonel's turn to laugh. "Not a chance. I was hoping you still had some connections south of the border."

They had spoken only a handful of times since the 1980s.That's when then Captain Samuel Webb was part of a covert tactical team under General Hector Peralta, working to stem the tide of cocaine flooding from Colombia into the United States. It was like nothing the colonel had ever experienced. The Medellín Cartel, operated by the Vázquez brothers and Pablo Escobar, was the most violent and ruthless bunch of hoodlums he had ever seen. As it turned out working with Peralta proved to be the experience that laid the foundation for him to rise through the ranks and become one the most effective black-ops commanders in the U.S. Army.

"I still keep up with what is going on. But, between friends, other than the United States' disastrous immigration policy, I didn't know America had much interest in what goes on in Mexico these days, except maybe to blame them for this sickness that is everywhere."

"I take it you and your family are…?"

"Yes, yes, thank you. But many are not as fortunate."

"My interest has nothing to do with the Army, Hector. It's of a more, um, personal nature. I need a cover for a small team to go into *Angangueo, Michoacán*, and maybe a suggestion for a nearby operational location. I need only forty-eight hours on the ground."

The colonel heard a chuckle. "Not asking for much, are you?"

He could hear what sounded like fingers on a keyboard.

"You are in luck, *coronel*. There is a research project being operated by the Swiss and the Australians into the effects of global warming on the monarch butterfly habitat. The project started four years ago. The reserves are remote, so despite the pandemic and the fact that they couldn't fly out even if they wanted to, the research is ongoing."

"Can you get two of my guys in?"

"Send me their bios, and I will see if I can get your toes through the door. But, Sam, don't dally. These days, there is no respect for old soldiers like us. Perhaps the dog is not such a bad notion."

* * *

"Okay, Gunny, this is where we part company," said the colonel. "I'm glad to have you and your team on board. Marcus's brother Glen, he's a very capable man. He'll get you lined out once you get to the Ranch."

"You know, Colonel, I've spent a career preparing for the unexpected but this takes the cake."

"Tell me about it. Anyway, get your team and their families settled. Whatever you need, you got! Just keep the people on that ranch safe."

Domingo heard the note of concern in the colonel's voice. "You can count on it, sir."

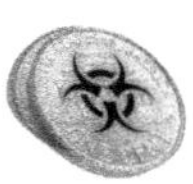

CHAPTER FORTY-EIGHT

January 5, Angangueo, Michoacán

THE MORNING AFTER SECURING TRANSPORT and supplies in Mexico City, the Force 10 team made the two-and-a-half-hour drive to Angangueo. Hector had provided research credentials for Marcus and Jamie. The research project was primarily a census but also included soil-and-water sampling. This involved a lot of walking, counting and observing, and volunteers tended to come and go frequently.

Marcus's language skills and a wild look, which allowed him to pass as a committed and possibly a bit crazy ecologist, made him a logical choice. Jamie, being graduate student age and Australian, seemed like a good sidekick. Besides, his tracking skills might come in handy.

At Hector's suggestion, using a satellite search, J. T. found several abandoned, illegal logging camps. The one selected to set up an operation post had a good landing zone for the Sikorsky Superhawk and was less than five minutes' flight time from the cabin. Piece of cake. What could possibly go wrong?

* * *

AT THE EDGE OF THE *Cerro Prieto* Sanctuary, where the Swiss and Australian research teams currently worked, Jamie and Marcus studied the cabin from a thick stand of white fir and cedar. Built on a hill, it backed up to dense forest and had a view of a small meadow surrounded by more forest on one side and an arroyo on the other.

Dressed in jeans, rain jackets, and bush hats, and wearing daypacks with butterfly nets protruding, each had a notebook and pencil in hand as they watched the cabin.

"All right, mate, you follow me and keep a lookout."

The two made their way up toward the cabin, circling around to stay in the trees. The cabin looked unoccupied.

Jamie stepped cautiously out of the trees. Two steps away from the small deck outside the cabin's back door, he stooped and held his fist in the air. He stood stock-still. He had felt, rather than heard, the small click when he set his right foot down.

A few feet behind him Marcus stopped. "What's up?"

Jamie didn't answer as he scanned the ground at his feet and near the deck platform.

"What's the matter? We not in the right place?" Marcus asked.

"Oh, we're in the right place, all right. It's just we sure as hell don't wanna be. I made a mistake, missed something..."

"What is it?"

"Sorry, mate. The bad news is, I'm standing on a pressure switch. The good news is, the wanker who set it was sloppy. His carelessness bought us one, maybe two, seconds, but you and me, we gotta take a ride." Despite the seriousness of the situation, Marcus could hear the mischievous tone in Jamie's voice. "To our left is an arroyo. Now, I can pretty much guarantee if there's a drop off, it's not much more than ten feet."

"Yeah? How do you know that?"

"Well, you told me once you would know when it's your time. Do you know that now?"

"No," Marcus said.

"Then it can't be a big enough drop to kill us—or, at least, not you. Now, I need you to move up behind me, slowly, to where you can grab my belt with both hands."

Marcus moved behind Jamie.

"All right, here we go. You might want to say a quick prayer. Grab my belt. Then, on my count, you pull me as hard as you can in the direction of the arroyo. And you stay on my ass."

Marcus grabbed Jamie's belt.

"Here we go. Three, two, one..."

Jamie shifted his weight back as Marcus pulled, and then they sprinted for the edge of the arroyo. The noise and the heat and the concussion seemed to happen all at once. The air was filled with smoke and wood debris from the blown-up log cabin.

At the edge of the ravine Marcus leaped, landing twenty feet down the steep slope. His feet hit loose, hard dirt, and he fell back onto his butt, scrambling for purchase as he slid toward a clump of tall bushes.

Seconds later, Marcus fetched up near the bottom, in a dry creek bed. He quickly checked himself for injury. Other than some minor cuts and bruises and a ringing in his ears, he seemed fine. Looking down and to his right, he found Jamie lying still.

A dagger of wood a foot and a half long and an inch thick protruded from both sides of his right thigh.

Marcus took off his backpack grabbing his secure communication device from its front pouch. No signal.

Jamie grabbed Marcus's arm. "Pull it out, mate," he pleaded. "Pull it out!"

Marcus took the first-aid kit from his pack. "Now, listen up! I pull that stick out, you'll likely bleed out right here."

With his teeth, he tore open a pack of blood-clotting granules and packed them on either side of the wound. Then he injected a pre-dosed syringe of morphine into Jamie's arm.

"Now, I need you to focus. I've got to cut off the ends of this stick, because when whoever set this trap gets here—and make no mistake, they're coming—we can't risk they'll pull it out." As he talked, Marcus used the serrated part of his knife blade to saw the stick off close to the skin. The morphine was taking effect, and Jamie relaxed. Marcus propped him upright against a large boulder, put a dressing over the wound, and scattered some pine needles over his pants to mask the injury and the first aid.

Marcus knelt in front of Jamie and pointed with two fingers to indicate "eyes on me." "Look at me. Good! We don't have a signal in this hole. So I've got to move down the canyon." Marcus glanced at the quickly graying sky. "We got rain coming. Now, when they get here, you put a sock in that smart-ass Aussie mouth. You act like a scared-shitless college boy who was offered a bunch of money to lead some crazy American into the sanctuary. You stick to the truth from there—names, whatever. You hear me? Say the words, boy!"

"Yes, sir." Jamie's voice was thick and his eyes were dilated, but he was trained and had been in similar situations before. Marcus stuffed all the first-aid gear and trash back in his pack. The kid was pale and had a worried look on his face. Before rising to his feet, Marcus said, "Now, don't you worry your curly red head. We're both leaving this place alive."

* * *

As MARCUS WAS HEADING DOWN the canyon, he could hear the sound of rocks and feet sliding down the hill. Four minutes later he had service.

"F-one, this is F-ten. You copy?"

"Copy."

"F-nine's down, critical, and about to be in enemy control. Yesterday, before we left to join the research group, in that metal shed by the helicopter LZ, I noticed gunnysacks of what looked like dried-out, prickly pear cactus. Looked like they had been there awhile. Must have been part of the food supply for the guys doing the illegal logging. We need a distraction. What if we soak them in..." Marcus felt the first raindrops, "...diesel. Will it work?"

"If we can keep from blowing up the chopper," replied J. T.'s voice.

"ETA?" Marcus asked.

"Ten minutes," came the reply from F-1.

"Okay, track on my GPS. I need F-two and F-seven. You can get close enough to the ground and let them jump. F-seven, be prepared for a possible major artery repair. Let's move, people, I need you here, like, yesterday."

* * *

MARCUS HUDDLED ON THE GROUND in the rotor wash of the helicopter. With luck, the hillside and forest, combined with the pouring rain and rolling thunder, would mask the noise. Within seconds after Sit and Chaya jumped the four feet to the ground, the chopper, with Bronson, Pete, and Liam aboard, disappeared into the dark sky.

From a clump of bushes two hundred feet away, Marcus, Sit and Chaya saw six men. Five were standing and one was kneeling in front of Jamie, who was slumped over to one side. Hang in there for just a few more minutes, Marcus said to himself, as a choke caught in his throat.

* * *

IN THE CARGO BAY OF the helicopter, Pete poured the dry, hard prickly -pear cactus lobes, most of them nearly the size of his hand, into three large galvanized tubs and then doused them with diesel fuel. The whole idea of dropping fireballs into a forest was harebrained, to say nothing of the environmental implications. But doing it from a high-octane fueled aircraft bordered on lunacy.

As they hovered at three hundred feet, Liam lit a tub of the hard prickly cactus, then began dumping them out the open cargo

257

door. As he finished one he moved to another while Pete reloaded and doused the empty tubs.

* * *

KNEELING IN THE DIRT, WITH the rain falling hard and thunder rumbling in the distance, Arturo Valdez felt anxious. He needed to find out who this man was, and then get the hell out of here. Since Peter Revant had come into his life nothing had been as it should. The Barrio Azteca had delivered a young Middle Eastern boy to him at La Crisálida, who in turn he had handed over to his sister, Isabel. Then came the call from Oksana, the nasty Russian woman who ran his whorehouse, telling him his business had been completely destroyed—blown up. Word was, the Juárez Cartel was responsible—but Arturo knew that was bullshit. It was time now for people to stop using him, and for his sister and her husband—Eduardo Gutiérrez—to acknowledge that he was not just a relative, but a significant part of the Gutiérrez cartel's success.

The young man in the bottom of the arroyo was in a bad way. He had a stick lodged in his thigh and had lost a lot of blood. Arturo had kept the cabin under surveillance since his whorehouse was destroyed and knew that two men had been there just before it blew up. Maybe the guy's partner had gone for help. Well, he would get what he could from this one, and when the partner returned, he would have a go at him as well. He instructed his men to set up a tight parameter so that if and when the other man came back they would be ready.

Arturo questioned the wounded man, and Jamie stumbled through a story about being a volunteer researcher with the joint Swiss-Australian team studying monarch butterflies. When he got to the part about being approached by an American to take him into the sanctuary, Marcus Diablo came alive in living color.

The boy was on the edge of losing consciousness when fireballs came crashing down from the sky.

* * *

SIT CHAMBERED A ROUND IN his Ruger Mini-14 tactical rifle. Chaya did the same with hers. Sit pulled an air pistol loaded with a Fentanyl dart—that would keep a grown man knocked out for several hours—from a chest holster and handed it to Marcus. Chaya would take out the two men standing closest to the kneeling man. Sit would take the three others who were spread out in a ten-yard perimeter. When the first tub of flaming cacti began falling from the gray sky, the men standing guard around Jamie began to panic. As the flaming objects continued to rain down, the men began swatting at the air as if being attacked by giant flaming mutant wasps. To their painful surprise, when they swatted the burning debris, it stabbed their hands and stuck there where it continued to burn.

On Sit's signal, he and Chaya fired their rifles. Three seconds later five men lay dead. Marcus ran, pistol pointed toward the man rising from beside Jamie's prone form. He pulled the trigger and sent a fentanyl dart into his chest.

Chaya had her medical kit out and worked on Jamie as the helicopter came into view. Bronson had located an LZ a hundred yards down canyon. He landed and left the rotor running.

Liam and Pete jumped out and hurried to help.

Chaya trotted over to Sit and Marcus. "We need to get him to a hospital—now."

"Okay, you go. Take Sit and this pile of shit," Marcus said, nodding toward the inert form of *el Capullo*. "You need to pick up the colonel and J. T. Liam, Pete and I'll clean this mess up and make our way to Mexico City. We'll hook up with you on the *Takbir* in a few days." Sit picked Jamie up as if he were no more than a sack of laundry. Marcus put his hand on Chaya's shoulder. "Take care of him!"

* * *

ON THE THIRD BODY, LIAM found a set of car keys. It took two more hours for the three men to hide the bodies under piles of rock in the bottom of the drainage. Although Jamie had the best tracking skills on the team, Pete and Liam were no slouches. Once they located the path the men had taken, they just had to backtrack. Twenty minutes later they were in a black Hummer tricked out with more bling than a rap star's ride. The tinted windows made it impossible to see in, and by the waves and nods they received as they drove through Angangueo, it was clear that everyone took them for *el Capullo* and his crew.

* * *

AN HOUR AND A HALF after takeoff, Bronson landed on the helipad atop the *Centro Médico ABC* in Mexico City. A vascular surgeon and operating room awaited their arrival. Chaya scrubbed in. Five hours later they boarded the Sikorsky, en route to the *Takbir.* Leaving the stick in place and using the clotting granules had saved Jamie's life. As Chaya monitored him, she thought about Marcus. How was it that he always knew precisely what to do? It was as if when things went bad, his mind went to some other place—a place that, in her experience, took years of battlefield experiences to hone. But he didn't have those years of experience. He had something else.

CHAPTER FORTY-NINE

January, 8, International waters, Pacific Ocean, off the coast of Jalisco, Mexico

MARCUS, PETE, AND LIAM ARRIVED on the *Takbir* a day and a half after Chaya, Sit, Colonel Webb and Jamie. Marcus went directly to sickbay.

Sickbay aboard the six-hundred-foot ship comprised three thousand square feet of the best-equipped, most technically advanced hospital facilities in the world. The lab capabilities included sophisticated blood and DNA analysis, MRI and CAT-scan equipment, as well as the latest pharmaceuticals. There was a Level 4 isolation chamber, intended to protect the original owner of the *Takbir* should his floating fortress come under a biological attack. Over the months that the *Takbir* had been in Vladivostok, every piece of equipment had been serviced, updated or replaced. The pharmaceutical stocks, including experimental drugs not yet in production, had been inventoried and restocked.

Marcus found Jamie lying in a hospital bed, his leg elevated in a sling. He looked asleep.

Chaya was hanging a new bag of intravenous antibiotic when Marcus stopped by the side of the bed.

In a whisper he said, "How is he?"

"What didja think—a bit of stick in the leg's gonna put me under?" came the response from the bed.

Marcus smiled, his hands resting on the raised rail. "Well, it's not the sticks I'm worried about. It's…"

Jamie's grabbed Marcus's hand and squeezed. "It was my mistake, mate, and you did exactly as asked."

"I know, man, but it seems that anytime you and I are together you're the one who ends up in the shit."

Jamie said nothing. He had been captured when they were in Afghanistan hunting down Adad al-Mohmoud. It hadn't been his fault then either, but Marcus was like that. He carried a huge weight on his shoulders, not because he had to, but because he knew no other way.

"Well, when you decide to stay out of the field, I guess then I'll be safe." Jamie winked.

Chaya finally spoke. "He's going to be fine. We just need to keep him down for a few more days until the stitched-up artery is healed enough to take some pressure. Now, the colonel and the team are down in the moon pool."

Marcus gave her a puzzled look.

"Oh, that's right, you've never wandered around this ship. One deck down, amidships— you can't miss it."

* * *

As MARCUS MADE HIS WAY down the companionway to the lower deck of the *Takbir*, he thought about what Chaya had said. It was true. The last time he had been on this ship, he was at death's door, having suffered a beating no one should have survived. During that time, he had restricted himself to sickbay and the private salon that sat shielded by a one-way mirror behind the bridge. Not that he couldn't have wandered around the floating palace—he just wanted as little as possible to do with anything the man responsible for Annie's death had touched.

Marcus walked down the long hall toward the stern. Midway, the hall widened and he found a set of glass double doors through which he saw the colonel, J. T., and, to his surprise, the deputy director of the FBI, Nathan Reynolds.

As Marcus stepped inside the men turned.

"Heard you made it back," the colonel said. "All good?"

Marcus nodded, distracted by the view through what, he assumed, was a wall of one-way glass.

On the other side was a huge room with a circular pool in the center, its calm water shimmering in the overhead lights. A large submersible vehicle of some sort was secured in a harness on the deck. Above was a series of gantries that could move heavy objects around the room and into and out of the pool.

In one corner, Marcus saw Sit and Weathers watching the man they had taken from Angangueo, who was lashed to a chair.

"Like the rest of this tub, that room is state of the art," the colonel said. "The hull retracts and the pool is then open to the ocean. J. T. says it can even be opened while the ship is under way. Seems that Adad was a bit—well, maybe more than a bit—paranoid. That submersible lashed to the deck has a range of a thousand miles, can be operated by a nine-year-old, and has enough food and water to sustain one person for at least two weeks. There are also a number of Remotely Operated Vehicles that can scan the underside of the ship, do repairs—even one that, apparently, can detect and disarm underwater mines."

"I don't much give a—"

The colonel cut Marcus off. "Understood. I just need you to reset. So they've been going at him hard for the last thirty hours. So far, we know his name is Arturo Valdez. Turns out, his sister's married to Eduardo Gutiérrez, head of the Gutiérrez cartel."

"So how'd you keep Sit from killing him?"

"Wasn't easy, but let's say we came to an understanding."

"What about the boy? Where is he?"

The lack of response answered the question. Marcus walked up to the window. "Is that what I think it is."

"Well if you think it's a hyperbaric chamber, then yeah," said J. T.

Marcus turned and walked back to the double doors he had entered moments ago. "This is bullshit," he muttered walking out into the hall.

* * *

TEN MINUTES LATER, MARCUS RETURNED to the moon pool control room, wearing a pair of pastel plaid shorts, a baby-blue polo shirt with the collar popped, and a pair of cream leather deck shoes without socks. In one hand he held a tall glass filled with ice and some amber liquid, in the other, a large medical bag with what looked like blood.

"J. T., can you work that decompression chamber from in here?"

"Yeah. There's also a control panel to the left of the door."

"Okay, can I talk to Sit?"

J. T. pushed a button on the console.

"Sit, I'm coming in. You and Weathers just go with it."

At the door into the moon pool room, Marcus paused and turned to J .T. "You stay with me now, okay?"

As the door closed, J. T. straightened up in his chair, "Buckle up, boys. The fireworks are about to begin."

* * *

ENTERING THE DOOR INTO THE moon pool room, Marcus roared, "Jesus Christ! I told that chrome-domed moron, Colonel Whateverthefuck, that I was to be notified as soon as this piece of equipment was up and running." Continuing toward Sit, Weathers, and the man lashed to the chair, he took a swig of whiskey, splashing some onto his shirt. Ignoring the men, he walked past them and up to the round door of the hyperbaric chamber. He set the polyethylene bag of dark-red liquid on the floor, took another gulp from his glass, and caressed the top of the door. "Time to play," he crooned.

Marcus spun around. "Holy shit! What the fuck did *you* do to piss these jarheads off?" He walked over to the man in the chair. "Let me give you a piece of advice, my friend, just tell 'em whatever it is they want to know."

Moving quickly, Marcus focused for a moment on Sit. "Jesus, you're one big *boy,*" he continued in the same redneck drawl. "Now, why don't you take your friend the pitbull there and go grab something to eat. I'm sure the chef 'ud be happy to whip ya up a batch o' fried chitlins." Marcus patted the back of Arturo's chair. "What the fuck—this poor bastard ain't goin' nowhere. I need thirty minutes to make sure my machine is working. If Mr. Army Man has a problem, you send him down, and he and I will have a lil' chat. Now go on, git."

* * *

INSIDE THE CONTROL ROOM, J. T. and the deputy director of the FBI stared open mouthed as Marcus ranted about the "chrome-domed moron, Colonel Whateverthefuck." The remark didn't seem to faze the colonel.

When Marcus suggested to Sit that he and Weathers go and get some fried chitlins, Deputy Director Reynolds said, "You sure Marcus hasn't finally gone off his nut."

"Well, we're gonna find out, aren't we?" said the colonel as Sit and Weathers stepped into the control room.

* * *

"SHIT FIRE, AMIGO, WHAT THE hell'd you do to get these hombres all up in your face?" Marcus asked as he picked up the bag of liquid off the floor.

Marcus walked up to the chair and squatted down in front of Arturo. "No speako Americano, amigo?"

He got only a sullen stare from the man.

"Whatever, dude. But you should know, these guys won't stop. I mean, they were only s'pose to be on my ship a few days, and they've been here over two weeks." Then, as if he couldn't maintain a train of thought for long, Marcus moved to another topic: "Hey, wanna see something cool?"

Arturo still didn't speak as Marcus walked behind the chair, unlocked the wheels, and rolled him up near the glass door of the hyperbaric chamber. Waving the bag in front of Arturo's face, he said, "This is a two-liter bag of blood plasma. The bag is this high-tech, damn-near-indestructible plastic polymer stuff. Okay, ready? Watch this!"

Marcus opened the door to the hyperbaric chamber, set the bag on the floor, shut the door, and pushed Arturo up close. He patted the control panel. "Now, this beauty is a decompression chamber. It's used when people dive, then resurface too fast. It's also supposed to be good for your health to breathe pure oxygen, but I'd rather use it for this. Watch! We'll set this thing at two hundred feet." Marcus pretended to play with the panel while J. T. ran the controls from the booth.

Marcus stood next to Arturo. "See how the bag's shrinking? The air in the bag is being compressed by the increase in pressure. Now watch what happens when we bring it back up to sea level." Marcus pretended to play with the panel again. He was animated, clapping his hands, "Watch, watch!"

The bag began to expand so that when it reached sea level it was swollen beyond its original size.

For the next several minutes Marcus brought the pressure on the bag up and down, each time taking it deeper. On the fourth time when the pressure went from four hundred feet deep and then up to sea level, Marcus was back next to Arturo. "Look! Ya see that?" He was tapping his finger on the window.

While staring through the door at the swollen bag of blood, Marcus drained his glass of whiskey, and with the back of his hand wiped his mouth. "The bag's been stretched to the point where the very fabric has broken down. See the drops of blood? The bag is leaking. Izzat cool, or what?"

When Marcus turned around his stupid, arrogant, half-drunk grin was gone. "*Escúchame, pendejo.* You think those two men who've been going at you for the past day and a half are crazy? Well…" Marcus knelt and jerked the arms of the chair so that his whisky-laced breath billowed out over Arturo's face, "*¡Mírame!*" Marcus yelled, "*¡Mírame en mis ojos!* This is a whole new level of crazy. This," he said, jabbing his finger into his own chest, "is a one-man band of full-blown insane!

"Pay attention! We're gonna take it down to five hundred feet." He waited a few moments as the air in the bag shrunk down to nothing. "Now we're going to bring it up as fast as we can."

When the bag exploded in a mist of red that covered the inside of the glass door, Arturo involuntarily jumped back, almost toppling the chair.

"So let me tell you how this is gonna work. You tell me everything you know about the boy, or I'm gonna put you inside this chamber, and the only way you're coming out is when they spray you off the walls. *¿Entiendes?*

"So what does señor Gutiérrez have to do with the boy?"

When there was no answer, Marcus said, "This is the last time I'll ask. What does señor Gutiérrez have to do with the boy?"

A shadow crossed Arturo's face and Marcus straightened up. "You know I just saw something I didn't like. You think I'm fuckin' with you." He opened the door. Thick, dark-red drops fell from the blood-splattered glass onto the floor. "You little lump o' *mierda*, it's not *señor Gutiérrez* at all, is it? No, it's *la señora* Gutiérrez, *tu hermana*."

Marcus walked behind the chair and rolled it into the chamber. "You know what? Don't say a word, because in about five minutes, when I've liquefied your organs and you're leaking blood from every pore and orifice like an Ebola patient, you're gonna tell me everything."

"Hey, man, hold on. I'll tell you. I'll *tell* you." Arturo's Spanish-accented voice held an edge of panic.

"I was in that shit hole you call a business. On second thought, I don't much care what you have to say. As far as I'm concerned you're a waste of good air." Marcus slammed and sealed the door. He hit the com button that allowed him and Arturo to speak. "Now let me show you some of the pain and terror you caused those children. Oh, I'm going to enjoy fucking you up."

"No, no! I'll tell you everything," Arturo yelled over and over.

* * *

WHEN THE BLOOD BAG EXPLODED, J. T. jumped in his seat almost as hard as Arturo did.

"Oh shit!"

Moments later, they watched Marcus roll Arturo's chair into the chamber. J. T. murmured, "This is getting interesting."

"Colonel, how far you going to let him take this?" the deputy director asked.

The colonel held up his hand and kept his eyes on Marcus. The man had accomplished in five minutes, what two of Force 10's most intimidating members had been unable to do in more than a day. "He's got him going. How about we let him finish putting the fear of God into him?"

Marcus continued to rail at Arturo, oblivious to the information spilling out. As he prepared to set the pressure inside the chamber at two hundred feet deep, the colonel nodded at Sit.

* * *

MARCUS STOOD OUTSIDE THE CHAMBER, punching numbers into the control panel when he felt a touch on his shoulder. He turned to find Sit standing there. In that instant, the equal measure of anger and his fear of what that anger could conjure up inside of him evaporated.

As Arturo sat inside the chamber with his back to them, Sit pulled Marcus a few feet away and in a low voice said, "Really, fried chitlins?"

With an ear-to-ear smile, Marcus said, "I considered throwing in collard greens, okra, and watermelon, but figured that might be taking it a little too far."

CHAPTER FIFTY

THE TEAM ASSEMBLED ON THE bridge as a helicopter carrying the deputy director of the FBI lifted off the deck of the *Takbir*. The last to arrive, Marcus made his way to an empty high-backed leather console chair.

Everything about the *Takbir* exemplified futuristic design. From her sleek black steel hull, to a bridge like something you would expect on a space ship, with a bank of tinted windows that looked out over an expansive foredeck.

Facing the bow and to Marcus's right, was the wall of glass that separated the bridge from what had been Adad al-Mohmoud's private quarters. This room had been Marcus's refuge the last time he was aboard this ship. From the bridge side, the glass wall served as a heads-up display screen.

"Okay, we're ready to start." The colonel stood in front of the dark glass wall.

"Here's what we know. Arturo Valdez..." As he spoke, J. T. posted pictures, bios, and other relevant information. "He's the brother of *Isabel Santiago Valdez de Gutiérrez*, wife of *Eduardo Gutiérrez*, the head of the *Gutiérrez* cartel. They have three young children."

As the colonel talked, a family tree was taking shape. "I don't need to go into how they make their money, but their net worth, from what we have dug up so far, is..." After a second when nothing appeared on the screen, the colonel cleared his throat.

Without looking up, J. T. said, "Sorry. Three hundred million, but we should assume at least double that."

Above the line of pictures of the Valdez-Gutiérrez family, a picture of Jabril al- Mohmoud popped up, and above that the face of Tajo Alano Zambrano. Above the photo of Taz was a face Marcus had not seen before.

Marcus rose from his chair, walked to the wall, and stood next to the colonel. "Is that him? The voice on the tape?"

J. T.'s voice broke in. "Allow me to introduce you to Peter Revant, once head of Global Equities, Western Hemisphere operations. I have to give it to Adad, he went to the greatest lengths to keep Mr. Revant in the shadows—and but for my superior intellect, he might yet remain faceless."

Listening to the boy-wonder, Marcus realized that this had to be the only person he had ever known who could say something so blatantly egotistical, yet not have one member of the team so much as bat an eyelash—because it was true.

"Adad set up the portion of the al-Mohmoud family portfolio that Revant oversaw under the veil of an ever-changing 'anonymous companies protocol'." This got J. T. a collective scowl that meant, *Give it to us in English, if you please!*

"It's actually brilliant. He used an algorithm like what is often used for ciphers, where a computer changes the matrix so fast and so often that the code becomes nearly impossible to crack. In somewhat simplified form, that's what he did with the list of companies that controlled the family's North and South American investments. There was a constant change of ownership, LLCs, corporations, partnerships, foundations, and, in all of it, not a single reference to, or picture of, Peter Revant. My guess is"— J. T. cocked his chin at the wall—"he never knew he was hidden in plain sight."

The room remained silent, everyone waiting for J. T. to continue.

"On a hunch, I went back to Adad. We know he was educated in London and that he controlled a worldwide investment empire, including significant holdings in the United States. I went back to several months before the fires started last year. In February, he was in New York, and then, in July, he was in Aspen."

Up on the wall, against the backdrop of the Rocky Mountains, was a picture of a large, elegant lodge-style home.

"The fires that swept the country burned that place to the ground. Ironic or intentional?"

The colonel cleared his throat again.

"Okay, right. So I went back to the curbside camera footage at the local airport. Since 9-11, all digital airport security footage is stored indefinitely in third-party information servers very much like the interconnectivity hubs that the Internet attack took out, which makes it accessible to someone of my...anyway, this is what I found."

The team looked at a grainy video of a man wearing a ball cap and dark glasses, getting into a cab. It was just a few seconds of tape, and the man's features weren't discernable. Again J. T. earned a group glare.

"You guys..." J. T. shook his head in mock disgust. "What, you think I don't have my own resources, my own friends?"

J. T. sounded almost hurt, Marcus reflected. The man could be so theatrical.

"I've got a buddy at MIT who's developed recognition software that can extrapolate facial features from as few as three measurements."

A picture of a much younger man filled the screen. "You need a little background." A picture of two older people popped. "His parents. The father a Syrian nuclear physicist working for the Russians, defected, along with his wife, to United States, in 1972. They were granted political asylum. The father taught college—nuclear physics. Peter needed a passport so the family could travel to England where Dr. Revant did a teaching fellowship at Cambridge. Both parents are deceased, car accident, or so the records say."

The parent's pictures disappeared.

"From there, all I had to do was add age, and—*bingo!* —Peter Revant. Arturo has confirmed this is the man he met when arrangements were made to move five hundred Mexicans over the border into the United States."

J. T. stood with a pad in his hand. "And get this: those five hundred were all given what Arturo believed was a flu shot. But instead, I'm certain, it was a virus. My guess is most were given the H7N9 avian flu, but some were infected with listeria, *e-coli,* and MERSA, as a way to muddy the waters. Amazing."

Everyone in the room knew that J. T. wasn't condoning what had happened; rather, he was acknowledging a devious, well-executed plan—something he was known for.

"What else we got, J. T.?" asked the colonel.

On the wall was a real-time satellite picture of a large tile-roofed house set well back on a bluff. From its vantage point, the estate had a commanding view down a valley to a large town that sat on the edge of a lake, and beyond, to cloud-shrouded mountains.

"Welcome to *Hacienda del Lago, Pátzcuaro, Mexico.* One of many estates owned by *la familia Gutiérrez.* It's over seventeen-hundred-acres—nestled in Mexico's coastal mountains. Like *Angangueo,* it's in the state of *Michoacán,* and although not quite as high, it still sits at seven thousand feet. Look at this..."

The view panned across broad, manicured lawns, a large free

-form pool with a mosaic-tile school of dolphins cavorting on the bottom and up the sides. Stands of fir and cedar, as well as gardens of geraniums, bougainvilleas, azaleas, and hydrangeas that, in the summer, would be a sea of color, surrounded the house and dotted the grounds. The view continued toward the edge of the bluff, over four tennis courts, one with a basketball hoop, then acres of trees planted in neat rows.

"Olive trees," J. T. said.

Finally, the camera stopped and zoomed in on three older-looking adobe brick buildings, perched at the edge of the bluff.

"These are the original structures on this property. They're over two miles from the big house and are situated so you can't see them from the main compound. According to Arturo, this one"— the lens focused on the building farthest back from the bluff—"has been remodeled and serves as a guesthouse for visitors who want more privacy. Now, this one"—the building closest to the bluff now filled the wall—"has been lined with something, maybe lead, that will seriously hamper thermal imaging. It could also play havoc with audio, but we'll figure something out. Arturo says it has a full cellar that is accessed from an outside hatch on the north side." The view zoomed in on the cellar entrance.

"This is where he says the boy is being held, and looky here..." The view of the cottage disappeared, replaced by a blurry picture of a man getting out of a black SUV. The picture faded back, and the face of a man standing in the driveway in front of the main house, slowly became clearer—"Peter Revant."

"When was that?" Marcus asked.

"Yesterday," J. T. replied.

"How the hell...?"

"I pirated footage off an NSA satellite that the DEA uses to monitor the movement of cartel bosses. One of the coolest features about God's Eye is that we can interface—at least until someone figures out how to stop us—with other satellites, and pirate their data stream, giving us access to a much broader real-time picture of the world."

"Do you know where he's been? Has he been in Mexico the whole time?"

"From what I've put together, he arrived in Pátzcuaro yesterday morning from Mexico City. That same jet he arrived on was in Amman, Jordan, two days ago."

Marcus's mind was moving at light speed, the thoughts piling into one another as he tried to slow down. *Amman,* he thought. "When I met with Sheikh Nazir at Palmyra, he said he and his family had left Damascus at the invitation of King Hussein and taken refuge in Amman."

The colonel took over. "If we assume that Peter Revant knows that Sheikh Nazir has asked Marcus for help in finding his grandson, what does that tell us?"

Not waiting for someone else to speak up, Marcus chimed in. "It tells us that whatever Revant's motives *were,* part of this has now become personal. Has the sheikh paid more ransom?"

"Three days ago, fifty million was wired into a numbered account in Switzerland," said J. T. "It could be just business, but I can't find a record of the sheikh ever using the account before. I spoke to Glen at the ranch. He's digging into it. Also, there's a ten-second video, sent in an encrypted file to Sheikh Nazir that I was able to...well you know..."

Projected on the wall was the image of Jabril sitting in a chair, surrounded by nothing but a brilliant light that was making him squint. His face was streaked with dirt, and he looked frightened and tired but otherwise unharmed. He held up what looked like a wide-screened smart phone. The camera zoomed in showing the time and date, then went black, without the boy ever saying a word.

"Nine a.m., day before yesterday," said J. T. "A day before Revant arrived."

Marcus walked and talked, as much to himself as to the others in the room. "We have to assume that Revant is moving into the final stage of his plan. Both events are self-sustaining now. The Internet attack has every government, financial institution, and tech company on the planet pointing fingers at each other and scrambling to come up with a more secure platform— which is an exercise in futility, isn't it J. T?" It was a question that needed no answer.

"The flu pandemic is out of control. From a group of five hundred, there are now over four million sick, over twenty thousand dead, and that's just in the U.S. One half of the world is blaming China, the other half Mexico. That brings us to the third part of Mr. Revant's plan: Jabril." Marcus stopped pacing. "The boy wasn't taken just for the money. When the sheikh and I first met, and I told him Adad was dead, I'm not sure he believed me. But at some point the notion that his son was never coming home again began to take root, and that's when the sheikh lost his will to be a part of the war against the great devils of the west. To have any real shot at long-term success, Revant needs Sheikh Nazir back in the fight."

Marcus moved back to the front of the room. "Revant knows the sheikh will do anything, spend anything, to save the boy, and if he can sell the abduction as part of some greedy plot by a group of godless drug dealers, he's golden. But when he found out that the sheikh had asked me to help find the boy, that's when the demon that Peter Revant has spent his whole adult life trying to rid himself of reappeared."

It was Marcus's turn to receive the group glare: *What the hell are you taking about?*

"Being an American! Think about it. Americans have a special sense of 'Don't fuck with me, if you know what's good for you.' No other people in the world can quite match our arrogance. Hell, look at me!"

Marcus went back to stand next to the colonel.

"Jabril is now also being used as bait."

From the back of the room, Ham spoke. "You should be careful applying American traits to a fundamentalist Muslim. I mean, we know Peter Revant was born and raised in America, but there are examples of others who have made the philosophical leap and left their upbringing behind."

"Not this guy. When he killed Annie, at that very moment, I could feel him." The words came through gritted teeth. "It was this attitude of 'I'll show you who's in control, who's calling the shots.' Forget what you think about beheading. As abhorrent as it is, as a form of punishment or retribution in the context of a culture, a religion, or a people, one can almost understand it. But when it's videotaped and broadcast for the whole world to see, that's pure garden-variety 'fuck you.' It has nothing to do with any religious doctrine."

Marcus and the colonel shared a glance before Marcus continued. "We need to work out the logistics. How do we get the team to Pátzcuaro? But more importantly, how do we accomplish saving the boy and getting Revant?"

Everyone remained quiet while Marcus finished his thought out loud. "They've had the boy for, what? Going on three weeks? What started out as a plan to extort the sheikh and get him once again fully committed to a worldwide resurgence of fundamentalist Islam has now taken on a new twist: revenge." Marcus gazed out at the most capable group he had ever known. "You think that in the last couple of days he's formulated a plan to come after me? Hardly!

But somewhere in the back of his mind, he's conjured up scenarios where *my* American arrogance brings me to him. So why don't we help him out."

"Hold on a minute," Ham said. "Did you just wait around for me to be here so you could put forth the most crazy-ass shit I've ever heard in a lifetime of crazy-ass shit? So I can be the little guy with the halo on your shoulder?"

Marcus laughed. "Okay, stay with me, Ham. Let's look at this. If Revant's goal in abducting Jabril is (one) to extort the sheikh; and (two) get the sheik's dog back in the fight, what purpose does keeping Jabril alive serve? As far as Revant's concerned, the boy is more valuable to him dead. Then he has the sheikh, his money, and his considerable influence. In fact, the longer the boy's alive, the greater the danger of the sheikh finding out Revant's behind the abduction.

"So what are our goals? If we only want Revant, fuck it. The colonel calls in some favors, and we blow Hacienda del Lago off the map. But if saving the boy is a priority—and it is for me—we have to get someone inside. So the question remains, why is Jabril still alive?"

Marcus let out a deep sigh. "I can't explain it, but I understand this guy. He has every intention of killing Jabril, but now he knows I'm involved. So his plan's changed. He's still going to kill the boy, but somehow he wants me to be a part of it. Maybe even blame the boy's death on me as a way to further ingratiate himself in the sheikh's eyes. Revant's not a fool. He's done his homework. He knows about Bodie and Garrett, about how far I'd go to keep them safe. This is where he can't escape where he was born and raised. It's a part of who he is, to show me that he has the power, that *his* God doesn't give a rat's turd about me or those I love."

Chaya stood, hands on her hips, looking defiant. "How could you possibly know that?"

Marcus smiled. Chaya's Israeli accent always got more pronounced when she was distressed or angry. He gave the only answer he had, the one he knew would infuriate her. "I just know."

The colonel held up his hand. "Okay, boys and girl, let's say that what Marcus says is true. How do we proceed?"

"J. T., I take it you've been keeping our boy Taz in play?" Marcus asked.

"How the hell..." J. T. muttered. *Glen told me that someday this would happen.*

"Well?" Marcus said.

Shaking his head, J. T. said, "As a matter of fact, I have. As far as anyone is concerned the *Tejas* Syndicate has been holding Taz. That's who Domingo and his boys framed when we ran our op at *Para Ti.* We've even done proof of life and have been sending regular demands for ransom to the *Barrio Azteca*, but, as expected, no takers."

"Here's what I think," said Marcus. "Revant just recently found out that the sheikh met with me and asked me to help him find his grandson, and that I agreed. Now he's imagining that killing me will be the *pièce de résistance* to the most devastating and successful terrorist attack ever. But unlike the rest of his plan, he hasn't filled in the blanks on this part yet. So we help him. I take it we intend to let Arturo go?"

The colonel said, "We were going to use him to confirm the location of the Gutiérrez family, but now…"

"We can still use him," Marcus said.

The colonel nodded for him to continue.

"We drop him back in Puerto Vallarta with the belief that I'm coming after him, supposing that I'm some nutcase gone rogue. Shouldn't be to hard to do considering…"

"That's no shit there, mate," mumbled Liam.

"He goes back and tells his sister and Peter Revant about this crazy man. Then we arrange for the kidnapped-by-a-rival-gang-and-escaped, Taz to deliver me on a silver platter."

Chaya was on her feet again. "That's the most stupid thing I've ever heard. You think once they have their hands on you that it's going to be a soft bed and room service?"

Marcus gazed out at the team. Clearly, Chaya was expressing a shared sentiment.

He took a deep breath. He needed to sell this, to make it seem not only reasonable but doable. "I know this sounds like a *déjà vu.* And believe me, I have no desire to have my ass beat again. If someone has a better idea, speak up." Marcus paused. When no one spoke he continued.

"No matter what we decide, the boy's time is up. If we don't go, he dies. No way around it. I can't live with that, and I don't think you can either. So let's get right to the heart of the issue." Marcus began to walk back and forth in front of the bridge windows. "From day-one, I've trusted all of you with my life, with the lives of my sons and family. Now, if this is going to work—*this* thing—you and me…" Marcus pointed at himself then at the team. "If I'm going to be a full-fledged member of Force Ten, then you have to trust me in the same way. I have no misconceptions about what they'll do to me, but..." He cocked his head and gave the team his best carny-huckster grin. "You are, after all, the best in the world at what you do, and I have complete faith that you'll have my back and get me out in one piece."

Marcus watched the colonel take a quick consensus. The assents from the team were a bit reluctant, as they should be, but unanimous, as they had to be.

CHAPTER FIFTY-ONE

ARTURO HAD HIS HEAD BAGGED as Sit led him out of the ship's hold and up toward the aft deck. Marcus waited as they stepped into the bridge hall.

"What the *fuck*," Marcus yelled at the top of his lungs. "You letting that piece of shit go? *Really?* What, you going to hold the fried-chitlins thing against me? Come on, big man. Let me have some fun and blast his ass all over the inside of the chamber. I mean, who's gonna miss him? If he's got a wife, she'll probably *thank* us! Maybe even show her appreciation in more *tangible* ways!"

"Man, you need to get some serious help," Sit said. "Crazy' doesn't even come close to expressing the depth of your fucked-upness."

Marcus winked. Sit just shook his head.

Before opening the door that would lead them out onto the aft deck and the waiting helicopter, Sit spoke to Arturo. "A word of advice, amigo. That man is loco. He's gonna hunt you, and you best pray he don't *ever* find you."

* * *

"YOU GOING TO TELL YOUR boys what you're planning?" Chaya demanded as Marcus walked into the bridge. "That you're willing to turn yourself over to drug dealers and jihadi terrorists?"

Chaya was pissed. Scared, too, and Marcus knew it as he put his hand on her shoulder only to have it slapped away.

"I'm not playing games of fun, Marcus."

Chaya had a habit of mixing up American euphemisms, but Marcus had learned that unless he wanted his ass kicked literally to let it go.

"Are you going to tell the boys this crazy plan?"

"Of course," he said.

* * *

Sitting on the sofa in the private salon, Marcus waited for Chaya and the boys. This was a big hurdle for him and Chaya. It wasn't a matter of love. Rather, it was a matter of the *cost* of that love. The boys came bounding through the door, barefoot and in shorts and T-shirts. For the past several days, the Diablo family, including aunts, uncles, and cousins, had been aboard the *Takbir,* exploring every inch of the floating palace.

Marcus stood as Chaya came in behind the boys. In a huff, she plopped down on the sofa, a wisp of hair falling across her forehead. The boys gave their dad the look that he had seen all too many times when he had been in trouble with their mother, a look that said, *Now you've done it.*

Marcus sat in one of the leather club chairs while Garrett sat on the arm. Bodie stood between the sofa and the chair with his hand in his pocket.

"Family meeting, Pops?" Bodie asked with a raised eyebrow.

Garrett moved and sat on the sofa, next to Chaya.

"Well, guys, there's something I want to talk to you about."

Garrett scooted in tight to Chaya and she put her arm around his shoulders.

Without looking at his dad, Garrett said, "You're going after that little boy, aren't you?"

Before Marcus could answer, Garret turned his face to Chaya, "Chaya, if I was that kid and there was a chance that you could save me, you'd..."

The tears formed in an instant and fell in streams down her cheeks as she hugged Garrett, "Oh, my angel, of course I'd get you back."

"It freaks people out. It freaked Mom out," Bodie said as he knelt in front of Chaya placing his hand on her knee.

She choked back her tears and rested her hand on top of Bodie's, her eyes asking the question.

Bodie smiled, the golden halos around his blue pupils twinkling. "It's the way the three of us are always on the same page—like we know what each is thinking, what the other one's going to do." Bodie leaned in and hugged Chaya and his little brother and whispered in Chaya's ear, "You'll get used to it. You just need to hang tight with us."

When the embrace broke, Chaya's bloodshot eyes met Marcus's. He held his hands up and shrugged.

279

CHAPTER FIFTY-TWO

January 11, Northern border of Beginnings Ranch

THE DAY TAZ AND HIS son were taken from *Para Ti* headquarters in El Paso, they wore blackout hoods while they were flown in a plane and then a helicopter. Hours later, when the helicopter landed and they were off-loaded, their heads stayed bagged until the helicopter took off. It was freezing cold, and both Taz and David wore short-sleeved shirts. When the bags were finally removed, they blinked and squinted. They stood in snow, under an overcast sky. An old, skinny man stared at them. He wore a pair of bulky warm pants, a worn and stained fleece-lined canvas coat, the collar turned up, and a tattered brown scarf tied at the neck. His gray hair was pulled back in a ponytail under a well-used black cowboy hat, and a thick mustache completely hid his mouth and most of his weathered face

"Name's Alvin—like the chipmunk," the old cowboy said. "Looks like you boys are in a spot of trouble." With his gloved hand, he took a pair of fence pliers from his coat pocket. As he stepped behind David and Taz, he said, "I know what you're thinking: won't be too much trouble to take this old codger." He chuckled as he snipped the plastic zip ties first from David's wrists and then from Taz's.

As they rubbed their wrists and shivered in the cold, Alvin came around in front of them.

"But you see, boys, that would be a fatal mistake. Look around. The closest other live human is almost a hundred miles away. See any vehicles? A road? Nope. All that stands between you and freezing to death is that cabin behind me. So here's the rules: I don't know who you are or what you did, and believe me when I say I don't give a great steamin' heap o' hog shit. I live out here in the winter, not 'cause I have to, but 'cause I like it. You stay here, you pull your own weight, be respectful and mindful of my home and we'll get along just fine. Don't want to do that, then our getting acquainted ends right here." Alvin blew out a cloud of breath condensation.

"Temperature's fallen—'bout fifteen right now, and I don't mean Celsius. Gonna be ten below tonight. Now, as dyin' goes, there's lots o' worse ways than freezing, so I'll understand it if that's how you want it. So what's it gonna be?"

Taz and his son shifted from foot to foot, rubbing their bare arms.

"My instructions are to keep you alive and healthy, if I can, without too much inconvenience. But if I can't, well..."

Alvin turned and walked toward the cabin where a column of smoke rose from the chimney. A shivering Taz and David followed at his heels.

* * *

FOR THREE WEEKS, TAZ AND David chopped wood, tended to the two horses, Guernsey milk cow, and a goat that were kept in a small barn. They melted snow for water, mended barbed-wire and split-rail fences, and ate better than either could ever remember. The routine was simple. Up before the sun, quick breakfast, chores till lunch, work till dinner, clean up, read or talk a bit, then bed. The only electronic device was a radio that Alvin used for emergencies and to check in with whoever had brought them here.

Then, late one night, Alvin awoke Taz and herded him out into the cold night. They walked over the frozen ground, through a stand of aspen, to a small clearing a half-mile from the cabin. Before stepping out of the leafless trees, Alvin bagged Taz and said, "You have a good boy. He works hard and listens. Now, you do as you're asked and my guess is there's a better'n even chance you'll get the opportunity to help grow him into a good man."

Alvin led him forward; two hands reached out and pulled him into a vehicle. An engine fired, rotors began to spin, and Taz knew he was again inside a helicopter.

* * *

Outside Las Cruces, New Mexico

THE VAN PULLED OFF THE highway onto a dirt road, drove for several minutes, and then stopped. Taz was jostled to his feet and guided out the cargo door. The bag came off his head, and he blinked his eyes against the sunlight.

Rubbing his eyes, he looked at the man who stood in front of him.

"Remember me? The 'bitch'?" Marcus asked.

Marcus looked at the bandages on Taz's hands. He had to give it to J. T. and the team. They had taken the ruse that Taz and his son had been abducted by the Barrio Azteca's rival, the Tejas Syndicate, to the extreme. The thumb on his left hand had been amputated at the first knuckle, and the little finger on the right, below the second. The rest of his look, Alvin had accomplished through weeks of hard work in cold, wet weather. Depending on one's perspective, Taz looked either life-hardened or abused.

Liam pulled two lawn chairs from the van and set them on the dirt. Taz looked around. The terrain looked like much of west Texas—flat, dry desert dotted with scrub brush and cacti, with mesas rising in the distance.

"Take a seat," Marcus said. "Sorry about the hands, but if we're going to sell this, you have to look the part."

Taz looked at his bandaged hands, and then held them tight to his chest as he stared back at Marcus.

From the time they picked Taz up from Alvin's, they had kept him drugged. Only this morning was he finally lucid enough to know what day it was—and to realize that he was missing two fingers.

"What about my son? Where is he?"

"Good for you, man! That's the right first question. David's fine. He's been moved to a place where there are kids his age, and he'll start school in a few days."

"So what?" Taz held up his hands. "You gonna chop me up some more?"

"Well, when you get back to El Paso, you're gonna need bona fides to prove you've been where you say you've been. We figured you'd rather lose two fingers than a hand or maybe an ear or your nose. You know how it is: if you've been in enemy hands, you'd best look the part, because once you lose trust with the brotherhood, it's a death sentence."

Marcus could tell that Taz still wasn't quite putting it all together.

"A mile down this dirt road is Interstate Twenty-five, about ten miles north of Las Cruces. It shouldn't be hard for you to get yourself into town, then on to El Paso. Now, you only have two days, so don't dick around."

Marcus opened a bottle of water and handed it to Taz. "Let

me be clear. The only options you have are: (a) do as I say, or (b) never see your son again, and most likely, get killed by the people you think of as your friends." Marcus handed Taz a cell phone.

"It's a burner with fifty dollars of prepaid service. Don't waste it. You need to make contact with *el Capullo*. Tell him that you have me. Tell him I'm a gift."

Taz kicked the hard dirt at his feet.

"Come on, Taz. You're a smart guy. You can do this! What's more you *have* too. It's the only way you get out.

"In two days, at exactly ten in the morning, I'm gonna show up at *Para Ti*. You'll be pleased to know that your staff has managed to keep things running, but a few of your buddies are definitely ready to step in and take your place. You make sure that when I get there you're alone. Don't even think about fucking with me. I'll have eyes everywhere."

Marcus got up from the lawn chair, walked over to the front of the van, and came back with a small metal case the size of a cigar box. He handed it to Liam.

Kneeling down in front of Taz, Liam laid the case on the ground and opened it. Inside, nestled into the egg-carton foam lining were two strange-looking pistol-shaped devices. One had a blue handle, the other red. Liam took out the blue-handled one and before Taz quite realized what was happening, put the muzzle to Taz's shoulder and pulled the trigger.

The gun made a *psst* sound as Taz jumped in his seat.

"Calm down; that didn't hurt," Marcus said as Taz rubbed his arm.

"Call it insurance. You've been injected with a slow-acting neurotoxin, way nastier than the flu. It takes..." He turned to Liam. "What'd the doc say?"

"Forty-eight hours," Liam said, closing the case and picking it up off the ground.

"The other gun holds the antidote, but once the cramps and twitching start, it's too late." Marcus looked at his watch. "Anyway, I'll be in El Paso in forty-four hours. Plenty of time."

Marcus stood and folded his lawn chair. "You'd best get hopping. You have a lot to do."

Taz stood and stared down the dirt road. "Who the hell *are* you?"

Marcus tossed the lawn chair into the van. "I'm nobody special. Just a guy who wants to give his kids an opportunity at a good life, and make sure the people who took their mom away from them pay."

***

AFTER DRIVING PAST TAZ WALKING down the dirt road, Marcus, Liam, and Pete headed directly to El Paso. At the offices of Alamo Freight, Marcus wasn't surprised to learn that Domingo had found another crew to carry on the work. Taz had been tagged with J. T.'s spray-on isotope GPS stuff, and they had a clone of his cell phone so they could monitor all his calls. Taz found a ride in short order. One of his contacts in El Paso had a brother in Las Cruces, and he arrived in El Paso only a few hours behind the Force 10 threesome.

Marcus was focused, but needed some rest. He knew the team was worried, especially Chaya, but that couldn't be helped. While Liam and Pete tracked Taz, he went to the back room and lay down on a cot. As he drifted off, he was feeling both anxious and guilty.

***

"HEY MARCUS, WAKE UP, BABY."

Marcus pulled the pillow from his eyes. Annie was leaning over him.

"Hey, you gonna sleep all day, or what?"

Marcus sat up. He was in their bed in the house the two of them had designed and built. The house where the boys had lived since they were born—the house he had not been back to since the day after she was murdered two years ago.

Annie rolled away from him onto her back and lay next to him, holding his hand in hers. "I love this house. We had good times here, didn't we?"

Marcus tried to answer, but no words came.

Annie turned her head toward him. Her face glowed, her blue eyes—the boy's eyes— twinkling with mischief. "And this"—she patted the covers—"God, how I love my own bed!" She stretched her arms wide and wriggled her toes, and laughed that girl laugh that was such a distinguishing feature of her dream persona.

"You don't like being here. I can tell. Too many memories?" Annie rolled onto her side, her elbow on the bed, head on her palm. "You've developed quite a habit of going to places you'd rather not be. What's that all about?"

Annie reached out, her fingers caressing Marcus's cheek. The warmth of her touch made goose bumps rise on his arms. He could smell the scent of lavender. "You need to keep your head. The team's worried about you—and about themselves. And that's on you, Marcus. You showed them what it means to care, to love, to a have a personal stake in the outcome, and now that makes what they do much harder. It makes the risks more serious. They can no longer be detached from the consequences, all because of how they feel about you.

"Oh, don't give me that look. Doubting yourself doesn't become you. This is the only way and you know it. The boys know it, and the team knows it. Now, rest—you're gonna need it."

He felt Annie scoot close, put her arm around him, and lay her head on his chest. He felt the cool brush of her satin nightgown against his skin as she whispered, "The time will come when, once again, you'll need to listen to me. I mean *really* listen, and do exactly as I say. Promise me, Marcus."

As he fell off into the deep, Marcus silently mouthed, "I promise, baby, I promise."

* * *

IN THE EARLY MORNING, MARCUS awoke with a start. It took him a moment to realize exactly where he was. Sitting up and rubbing the sleep from his eyes, he thought, *Today is the day*. If Taz had done his job, Marcus would be in the lions' den before dark.

Still sitting on the cot, back against the wall, with his eyes closed, Marcus went through a mental review. Sit, Jamie, Weathers, Bronson, Ham and Chaya had already left the *Takbir*, en route to Mexico. A long-range vantage point for Sit had been identified. Although it put him fifteen hundred yards out, he should have a clear view through the only window into the cottage where, according to their intel, Peter Revant was holding Jabril. All the planning was based on Marcus' absolute certainty that this was where he, too, would be held. Marcus knew that was an assumption that required a degree of blind trust and faith that each member of the team accepted, but was still not completely comfortable with.

At the sound of footsteps, Marcus opened his eyes.

Pete stood there. "Come," he said.

As Marcus followed Pete, he considered the ex-Russian

Spetsnaz and the point he had made just the day before while the team was still on the *Takbir*, about the extreme risks of what it meant to be bait—and that there was no mistake. Marcus, like Jabril, was bait.

Pete led Marcus to a small area at the back of the warehouse that was set up as small gym, with a heavy bag, some free weights, and a few benches. Liam was there.

"What's up?" Marcus asked.

"Well, mate, we need to tune you up a bit before turning you over to Taz."

"Tune me up?"

The punch came out of nowhere. It caught Marcus above the eye and sent him sprawling on the floor.

"What the fuck?" Marcus yelled as he brought his hand up to the side of his head. His fingertips came away bloody.

"Up," Pete said.

Marcus stayed on the floor.

"Sod it all, he'll beat your ass while you sit on the floor, if that's how you want it," Liam said, "but if it were me..."

"Up! Now!" Pete commanded.

Marcus staggered to his feet, holding his hand to his eye, which was beginning to swell. He had trained with Pete enough to know that the man never did anything without a reason. He also knew that Pete never did anything half-assed, which was suddenly a big worry.

Pete stood still, arms casually at his sides. Then he beckoned Marcus to "bring it."

Shaking off the effects of the first punch, Marcus took a defensive stance and faced Pete. "All right you commie bastard, fine—I could use a little a release right now."

Marcus came in, weight on his toes, and jabbed. Pete countered and caught him in the ribs.

"That best you got?"

For the next ten minutes, Pete and Marcus fought, and Marcus landed his share of punches. But now, sitting exhausted on a bench, he watched Pete mop the sweat from his face with a towel, otherwise showing little evidence of exertion. It dawned on Marcus that any punches he had landed were because Pete had let him.

Liam knelt in front of Marcus and assessed the damage. He opened a first-aid kit and began cleaning and bandaging. When he finished, Marcus had a butterfly bandage closing the cut over his right eye, cotton tampons in his possibly broken nose, cuts and bruises from chin to forehead, eyes that soon would be black and nearly swollen shut, and ribs so sore it hurt to breathe.

When Liam was done, Pete came over and handed Marcus a clean wet washrag.

"Suck," he said.

Marcus took the washcloth and put it to his mouth. His gums were cut and sore, and the cool wet terry cloth felt soothing.

"Show hands!"

Marcus held his hand out.

Pete took them in his and examined the raw and bleeding knuckles. "Look good."

"Look *good*? What the hell are you talking about?"

Liam spoke. "Mate, you can be a real dolt, sometimes. You think Taz can sell you to Arturo if you don't look like you put up a fight? Remember what you told Taz about his fingers? Come on. We figured it was best if *we* beat you instead of Taz. I mean, better to have your ass kicked by someone who cares about you, don't you think?"

Pete was smiling, and Marcus smiled too, even though it hurt. It also occurred to him that this was the first time he had ever seen Pete wearing an expression that might pass for happiness.

CHAPTER FIFTY-THREE

January 13, El Paso, Texas

At 10:00 a.m., Marcus walked through the front door of Para Ti. Taz sat behind the reception counter. Before setting out from Alamo Freight, he, Liam, and Pete had spoken to J. T., who used the God's Eye to scan the warehouse. As instructed, Taz was alone. Liam and Pete were in position in the warehouse across the street, ready to pull Marcus out if something went wrong.

Taz looked at Marcus. "What the hell happened to you?"

Marcus shrugged. "I tripped. So tell me, you got everything arranged?"

When Taz spoke, Marcus got the impression that the past few days had been tough. "I got hold of *el Capullo*. Man, he is seriously afraid of you. He and a few of his boys are going to meet us at the private charter terminal at *Benito Juárez* Airport at noon."

"That gives you and me time to conclude our business," Marcus said.

"Man, you got any idea what these people are gonna do to you?"

"Yeah, I think so."

Taz shook his head. "Okay, I did what you asked. Now, give me the antidote."

"What antidote?" Marcus said with a grin. "The only thing we injected you with was saline."

Taz looked confused.

"As it turns out, you do have a choice. Right now, I'm pretty sure the *Barrio Aztecas* are looking at you hard. Even if they let you back in, suspicion will always be hanging over you. And then we still have the matter of your son."

Marcus grinned. "Hell, all we have to do is put the word out on the street that you spilled your guts, and who needs a neurotoxin? So what's it gonna be? You think your boy doesn't know what his daddy does for a living? Like the big house, fancy cars, and private school somehow insulate him from the fact that you're nothing more than a drug-dealing, sex trafficking, gang member? What's he gonna do when he grows up? Follow in your footsteps? I think not."

"What gives *you* the right?" Taz spat.

"You do, and all the other people like you out there, who think that killing and exploiting innocent people is just business. I never wanted this, and I know we can't stop it. But we can sure as hell make a dent."

Marcus, his indignation rising like a pot of water coming to full boil, closed the distance between himself and Taz. "Because of your boy, I'm giving you an opportunity, one father to another, to have a good life—a chance to watch your son grow and become a man and a father himself someday. You say the word and Tajo and David Zambrano no longer exist. But make no mistake, it means turning your back on this life."

* * *

Ciudad Juárez, Chihuahua

MARCUS AND TAZ DROVE OVER the border and into *Ciudad Juárez*. At the airport Taz pulled off into the "waiting" lot and parked.

He looked Marcus in the eyes. "You gave your word, right? I leave all this, and my son and I will be safe and happy."

"Listen, man, I'm not God. I'll make sure you have the opportunity, make sure you and your boy are as safe as any of the rest of us. Beyond that, what you do with it is up to you."

Without answering, Taz started the car and pulled out into traffic. A few minutes later, they drove through an open chain-link gate and into the private charter terminal parking lot. Taz said, "I need you to limp along like you're hurt a little, which shouldn't be a stretch considering the way you look."

Taz came around and opened the passenger door, and Marcus slowly got out.

Taz stood in front of Marcus with his back to the glass front of the charter terminal building. "I gotta tell you, since the day I met you, my life's been..." He just shook his head as he took Marcus roughly by the arm and headed across the asphalt to the terminal entrance.

Stumbling, Marcus grabbed Taz for support. "Yeah," he whispered. "I get that a lot."

* * *

INSIDE THE CHARTER TERMINAL THEY walked toward four beefy men wearing sunglasses and sporting mustaches and goatees, or soul patches, standing near a seated Arturo Valdez. They had on loose-fitting jackets, no doubt to hide an array of firepower. Arturo rose from an upholstered chair. At his nod, two of the men stood at Marcus's sides while a third patted him down. Without a word to Taz, the group went out the door to the tarmac and across the asphalt to the open door of a waiting jet. Marcus's hands were zip-tied behind his back, and he was seated on the floor against the wall at the back of the main cabin. No seat belt. The door was shut and the jet taxied and took off. Less than five minutes after getting out of the car they were airborne.

Sitting there on the carpeted floor, his bound hands causing his ribs to ache even more, Marcus had to give credit to the cartel: they had their people well trained.

Arturo sat in one of the leather captain's chairs and stared at him. Then, in English he said, "If I had my way, I'd feed you to the hogs—let them eat you alive. Who knows? Maybe when the Arab is done with you? For now, though, you just sit there and behave, and think about all the ways we're going to fuck you up."

* * *

Pátzcuaro, Michoacán

TWO AND A HALF HOURS later, the jet set down, and Marcus was manhandled out and into one of two waiting Range Rovers.

Marcus rode in the backseat, with a man on each side, while Arturo rode up front with the driver. They drove for forty-five minutes, wending their way up into the foothills of the Sierra Madre. They hadn't bothered to cover Marcus's head, as if to emphasize that this was a one-way trip. As had happened many times now in the nearly two years since Annie went missing, Marcus had a moment of startling clarity about just what he had gotten himself into and how easily things might go terribly wrong.

The gravel road turned to cobblestone pavement as they approached a large iron gate, which swung open toward them. In the distance Marcus saw the big house with its red-tiled roof, but they weren't headed that way. The Range Rover made a hard right and headed past tennis courts and then the road dropped down to acres of olive trees. As they skirted the trees, Marcus wondered whether it was called a *grove* of olive trees or an *orchard.* Silently he chided himself for such idle thinking, but in the same breath, he thanked God for giving him a wandering mind.

The SUV stopped by the old brick cottage nearest the bluff, and Arturo's men unloaded Marcus, brought him inside, and tied him to a chair on a rough, unfinished concrete floor. Everyone left except Arturo. Marcus stared at those outlandish boots with their silver toes that extended six inches beyond normal, curling up so that the toe was pointed back at the person wearing them. He just couldn't let it pass.

"Where does a guy even *find* boots like that?"

Until now, the only person to have inflicted any harm on Marcus was Pete. Everything about the transfer from Taz to Arturo and the flight had been calm—too calm for Marcus's taste.

"I mean, really, do you look in the mirror and say, 'Damn, I look good!'? Because to me you look like a slightly larger-than-average Smurf."

Arturo stood in front of Marcus. Marcus lunged against his bonds, making the chair hop forward a few inches. Arturo jumped back.

"Little jumpy, aren't we, Arturo? *¿Tienes miedo, amigo? Está bien.* You should be afraid—very afraid."

Arturo looked around instinctively, as if someone might have been watching. "You're here all alone," he said. "No big-ass *hombres* to help you this time."

Marcus grinned. "Oh, those guys would never help me. I'm too wacko for them."

"For a guy tied to a chair, with no chance of getting away, you're acting pretty *bravo.*"

"It's not brave, asshole, it's a for sure. Mark my words, you're as good as dead." Marcus could tell that Arturo didn't know what to make of him.

"So why don't you go get the guy who's pulling your strings, *marioneto?*"

Arturo moved past Marcus toward the door, then spun and landed a roundhouse punch at the base of Marcus's jaw.

Marcus saw little moving dots, like a swarm of silent bees, just before he and the chair toppled to the floor.

* * *

I GOTTA TELL YOU, MARCUS, there are times when the only word that describe you is 'dumb-ass.' What is it with you and pissing people off?"

He kept his eyes closed and spat blood. The rough floor did a number on his cheek. He could have sworn he just heard Annie's voice, but he wasn't dreaming. Did this mean he was dead?

"No, not dreaming *or* dead. Now, you just lie still." A mischievous girl-laugh that was part of his dream Annie lilted in his head. "Hell, you couldn't get up if you wanted to. You do remember where you are, right?"

Marcus opened his eyes. "Oh, shit." He groaned. His face hurt. At that moment, it occurred to him that his jaw might be broken, and he considered just how much it would suck to have to take his meals through a straw for six weeks.

"Eating through a straw—*that's* what you're thinking about? Dude, you'd best worry about whether you're ever going to eat *again,* straw or otherwise. Okay, you remember what I said about listening to me? It's gonna get hairy. Things will be said. Your buttons are gonna get pushed, and you hate that, good as you are at pushing other peoples' buttons. You keep your head; keep your eye on the prize. You got a whole bunch of people doing all they can to keep you alive. Don't make it harder for them!" Annie's voice commanded.

Marcus lay on his side and wondered, not for the first time, whether he was losing his mind. As the minutes passed, he became aware of the cold. It was winter, after all, and the elevation was above seven thousand feet. Marcus was more accustomed to associating Mexico with warm beaches and cold beer. *God, that sounded good.* Then a peace descended on him. He was in the mountains. The mountains were where this whole journey had started—where he, Annie, and the boys had boarded this nightmare train. The mountains were where he had discovered just what he was made of. This was his comfort zone: cold, thin air, rugged terrain. Now he just needed to stay alive.

CHAPTER FIFTY-FOUR

SIT AND JAMIE GOT COMFY in a stand of oyamel fir. They, along with Chaya, Weathers, and Ham had arrived in Pátzcuaro early yesterday. The colonel's old friend Hector Peralta had arranged for them to be transported from Mexico City in the back of an agricultural supply truck. They had been dropped off in the dark, ten kilometers from their target sites. Bronson would be with the Sikorsky at a site Hector had procured, a ten-minute flight from *Hacienda del Lago*.

Sit had Jamie as his spotter because he was still recovering from his leg injury, and keeping him out of a possible hand-to-hand combat situation was a priority. Chaya, Ham and Weathers, who were to be joined by Pete and Liam, were at location on the hillside below the cottage. The colonel and J. T. had remained aboard the *Takbir* to run ops.

The timing for Marcus's arrival at the Gutiérrez compound was an unknown, although Marcus was adamant that it wouldn't be more than two days.

Jamie had first watch while Sit grabbed some shut-eye.

Sit stretched out his legs, his back against a fir tree, and rested his interlaced hands on his chest. As he closed his eyes, he thought about Bodie, Garrett, and Marcus. Just before he and the team left the *Takbir,* each had each sought him out.

* * *

SIT WAS IN HIS SUITE double-checking his go-bag and making sure he had his personal gear in order when he heard a light knock on the open door.

"Hey, got a minute?" Bodie asked.

"Anytime. What's on your mind, young man?"

"My dad," Bodie said, looking at the floor.

"Look me in the eye, Bodie, and speak your mind," Sit said.

"Well, you know how he is, right? Like a little dog who

doesn't know he's a little dog, and on impulse he'll just tear out after a pitbull, only to get his ass chewed off."

Sit laughed. "That's a good way to describe him. I'll have to remember that." He patted the bed, and Bodie sat. "Don't you worry, boy, I've got his back, and so does everyone else. You know he's a good man, your dad?"

Bodie nodded. "Yeah, I know, but sometimes he gets so focused he doesn't realize how far he's pushed."

They both stood up, and Sit said, "Well, then, son, you and I'll just have to make sure to keep him on track, won't we?"

Bodie clenched his jaw to keep from trembling. On the verge of tears he said, "You protect him from himself. Okay?"

* * *

AN HOUR LATER, SIT WAS on the bridge studying the satellite map with J. T. when Garrett walked in. He came and stood by Sit, looking at a high-resolution image of the site they had selected for Sit and Jamie to cover the cottage. Without speaking, Garrett walked up close to the wall. He put his finger to the picture and traced a route from the ravine, a kilometer off the road and up the gully to where J. T. had the sniper location circled in red. He cocked his head and traced his finger back down, but on a completely different line.

Sit gazed down on the little boy, who met his eyes with a big smile. "It's called 'get off the mountain'—one way up, another way down."

Sit turned back to the wall and, this time, followed the lines Garrett had pointed out. The more he examined it, the more he realized that the boy was right. In the space of a few seconds, he had spotted the best way in and absolutely the best way out."

Turning back to Garrett, "How'd you do that?"

"When we ski or climb, my dad always makes me and Bodie pick the routes in and out. He says the in-route is important, but it's the out-route that your life depends on; that there can always come a time when, because of a storm, cold weather, an injury, that you have only one choice—get down now."

Shaking his head, Sit took Garrett by the hand and led him to a console chair.

"Sit," Garrett said, holding out his fist.

Sit extended a hand the size of an oven mitt, and Garrett dropped something into it.

Sit looked into his palm. Resting there against his dark skin was a silver chain with a small medallion attached to it.

"That's my mom's Saint Christopher. Chaya helped me find a bigger chain. Here, lemme help you." Garrett took the chain back and stood on the chair as Sit bent his big frame forward.

"There," Garrett said. "Now you're ready."

Sit smiled and knelt in front of the boy.

"My dad can be hard to keep on track, but I think that you and mom'll do just fine."

Sit took the small boy into his arms and hugged him.

Garrett whispered in his ear, "I love you. Thanks for taking care of our dad."

* * *

FROM THE BACK OF THE bridge, Marcus watched Garrett embrace Sit. It struck him, seeing the small boy in the big man's arms, that he had really mucked up the works with the whole family thing, especially when it came to covert ops. The expression on Sit's face left Marcus feeling that his friend, the sniper, was thinking much the same.

Marcus stepped out of the shadows and caught Sit's eye; he had, after all, come to talk to him too. "Hey Sit. Got a minute?"

"What's up with you Diablo boys? Seems like I'm on some kinda list today."

Marcus laughed. "Come on. Walk with me. Before we leave, Chaya needs me in sickbay."

In the elevator heading three decks down, Sit said, "What is it, man? You afraid she's gonna drug you so you don't go an' do something stupid?"

"Truth? I hadn't thought about that. Probably a good thing I brought you along."

As they walked through the door into an exam room, Sit said, "You would be assuming that I don't agree with her."

"What, you need a bodyguard to hold your hand?" said Chaya. "Whatever, lay back on the gurney." She pointed.

Holding a syringe, Chaya said, "Open your mouth. Wide. The small pills we usually use for GPS tracking only last a day, maybe two, not reliable enough in this situation."

Marcus stiffened at the sharp stick, as Chaya injected a local anesthetic into the back of his mouth.

"Stay still or I'll have Sit hold you down." From a tray stand she donned a headgear with magnifying goggles. As she picked up a pair of small forceps, she turned to Marcus and put the forceps in his mouth.

"There; that should do it. I have implanted a microscopic-size GPS chip under the gum where one of your lower wisdom teeth used to be. Now sit up."

Sitting up, Marcus stared at Chaya. In her hand she held a futuristic stainless steel drill. She pulled the trigger and grinned as a high-pitched whine came from the device. Between the strange goggles and the drill, it gave Marcus the impression of what it must be like to be probed by aliens.

"You need a com device. There is a chance the normal ear buds we use might be dislodged, especially since you seem hell-bent on getting your ass beat." Her voice dripped with disapproval. "On second thought, it's a good thing you brought Sit with you. Hold his head. Tight!"

Baseball mitt-sized hands gripped Marcus' head, face to back of head. Marcus heard the sound of the drill. He felt something sharp and hot make contact with his skin behind his left ear. A pinch and pushing pressure behind his ear sent a shiver though his body. Then Sit released his grip.

"I drilled a tiny hole and inserted a com chip into the hollow space in the mastoid bone, behind your ear. This will only allow one-way communications."

Marcus rubbed the sore spot behind his ear, looked at his fingers. No blood.

"The small nano-size bit makes a hole too small for the naked eye. Plus, the speed of the drill creates so much heat it is self-cauterizing."

"So this one-way thing you were taking about?"

Sit looked to Chaya then said, "All we need to know is what *you* say. You never listen to what we say anyway. Now, we need to go; the chopper's waiting to take us all into Puerto Vallarta."

As the three made their way up to the afterdeck, Sit went on. "Marcus, you, Pete, and Liam will head on to New Mexico and pick up Taz outside Las Cruces. He is being flown from the northern border of Beginnings as we speak. Chaya, Jamie, Ham, Weathers and I, are going to take a short hop to Mexico City. We'll supply there and transport by truck to *Pátzcuaro, Michoacán*"

They approached the door to the afterdeck. Marcus nodded for Chaya to head on out to the chopper. He was never going to convince her that his plan was a good idea, even though she— the professional she—knew it was perhaps the only way to save the boy.

"You got something to say to me, Marcus?" Sit asked.

Marcus stood, silent.

"Okay then, I'll go first. You are all about trust, right? How's this for trust My group and I are on our way to some place in the mountains of Mexico to wait on your arrival, all based on your belief that you will be brought there. Now, to my knowledge, not one person has expressed any doubt. You having second thoughts?"

Marcus smiled. "Not on your life, or mine, my friend. You just make sure you all are ready when I get to *Hacienda del Lago*."

Sit put his hand on the doorknob. Marcus touched his arm. Sit turned.

"You never miss, right?"

Sit paused as if considering the question. "Not so far."

The look on Marcus's face made Sit laugh. "Not so funny when someone else gives up a smart-ass answer, is it?" Sit eyes sparkled. "You know the rule. If I have your back, it's my call. Now, you hold up your end and I, for sure, will hold up mine."

* * *

LYING PRONE ON THE GROUND in the cover of the trees, with his eye to the spotting scope, Sit located Chaya, Ham, and Weathers. They were bivouacked in dense brush a few hundred yards below the bluff on a direct line with the cottage where Jabril al-Mohmoud was supposedly being held. If all went according to plan, Pete and Liam would be joining them today.

Inspecting the terrain, Sit knew it would be a hard slog up the hill—he estimated thirty minutes—to the cottage where Marcus was so sure he would be held. The team would operate under radio silence, communicating by Morse code, using another of J. T.'s inventions: ceramic crowns that, when tapped, tooth on tooth, would send a low-frequency signal. The crowns were coded so they only worked with those of the same alloy. It wasn't nearly as good as using the secure communication devices, which looked much like a smartphone, and could be spoken into, written on, or used to send text, but they had all been in enough "dark" situations to know the drill.

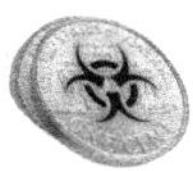

297

CHAPTER FIFTY-FIVE

Loliondo, Tanzania

Adriana said her goodbyes to Dr. Kathryn Van der Hoch. AMREF was pulling its personnel out; the clinic had to shut down. The flu pandemic was out of control and it was just too dangerous for doctors and staff, and now, with new cases of Ebola confirmed in Nigeria, the situation was unmanageable.

Before leaving her job six weeks ago at the National Microbiology Lab in Winnipeg, Adriana had laid the groundwork for this day. She had done it without anyone's knowledge, especially Peter's.

It had been the previous year, in February, when she had a surprise visitor. Although she had never met Adad al-Mohmoud, Peter had spoken of him often and she knew exactly who he was when she opened her door that late-winter night.

Adriana was instantly drawn to him. Everything Peter was, this man was more. He had a presence and confidence in which she could have immersed herself. But lovers, they were not meant to be. Instead, he wanted to talk about her work, about her vision of the world, and about, if she could, how she might leave her mark on it. They had talked into early morning, and before leaving, he gave her the name and contact information of a man who might someday be able to help her.

A week ago, she had reached out to the stranger. Her time in Africa had come to an end, at least for now. At the Loliondo airport, a small jet was waiting. Dr. K. hadn't asked a single question about her decision or where she was going. Carrying her single small bag, he walked her to the jet.

At the steps he said, "Addie, you know what separates us from all the other animals?"

"We are the only animals who can, by our very will, suppress instinct."

He smiled and hugged her. "Travel well and choose wisely."

As the jet took off she watched Dr. K. and Mama Bulala fade away. She had put the money she took from Kgosi Egwu into a trust for and to be administered by them, the only family she had.

As she soared into the sky she thought, *"I've never been to Russia."*

* * *

Aurora, Colorado

SANTIAGO CRUZ, ALONG WITH HIS older brother Enrique, his wife Manuela, and their three children, stood in the bitter cold, on the snow-covered lawn of Saint Simenon Catholic Cemetery, as Father Vince Fallon, read from the Old Testament, Wisdom 3:1-6,9:
> *"The souls of the righteous are in the hand of God,*
> *and no torment shall touch them...*
> *...and their passing away was thought an affliction*
> *and their going forth from us, utter destruction.*
> *But they are in peace.*

With an aspergillum, Father Fallon sprinkled the casket of Matis Cruz with holy water, then made the sign of the cross, as it was lowered into the dark hole.

* * *

Albuquerque, New Mexico

ROSAURA DÍAZ LAY IN HER bed at her brother's house. She had been terribly sick and had lost her baby. Although a tragedy, this was not why she seemed unable to get up. Her oldest, her son Emilio, her angel, the one who had helped her get though the beatings and neglect, who had stood by her and defended her as if were a full grown man, was gone.

She was certain that coming to America was the right thing. But how could that be if her son was dead? She had been diagnosed with listeriosis, probably contracted from something she ate. It had killed her unborn child. And Emilio had been her rock while she was so sick. Then he came down with the flu, as had her other children, Francisco and Sofia, but as the younger two got better, Emilio's condition worsened. He became so sick he couldn't lift his head off the pillow, and when they finally took him to the hospital, he had to be carried.

In the moments before he passed, he took her hand. His skin was hot, his body racked with fever and yet he said with his last breaths, "*Lo siento, mamá. Lo siento.*"

* * *

Santa Rosalía, Baja California Sur

THE MORNING WAS COLD AS John Morales and his father climbed into their truck. John had been back in Mexico only three days. The trip over the border into the States had been a disaster. His friend Shaun was dead from H7N9 virus.

When John became sick, Shaun and his parents were great, but a day after John was released from the hospital, Shaun had a fever. It began as just aches and chills, then progressed to vomiting. What John didn't know was that his friend had a mild form of rheumatoid arthritis. It rarely bothered him and, in fact, had improved greatly when he went thorough puberty, but it was still an autoimmune disease, and the H7N9 strain of the avian flu was a nasty bug, especially when it came to its effects on the respiratory system.

There was not a lot of concern those first days, but when Shaun had a seizure, things got serious. And when it hit the newswires that the suspected source of the disease running rampant across America was people who had been intentionally infected and brought over the border from Mexico, mostly through Tijuana, Nogales, and Ciudad Juárez, the interrogations began.

John had been taught to tell the truth and figured that Shaun would recover and that his parents would understand this was not his fault. But as Shaun's condition worsened, his parents had become increasingly angry, and when he slipped into a coma and the prognosis for recovery dimmed, they ordered John to leave their home.

Once the news broke, every person who looked Hispanic was at risk from fearful, bigoted citizens. There were those Americans who felt that if a person had brown skin that person was to blame. The U.S. government set up military manned safe stations where legal and illegal Hispanics could go for immediate return to Mexico. Without friends or money and with his life in real danger, John had no choice but to return to his father and go back to work in the copper mines.

As they rode in silence, John realized that what had once been his only chance at a decent life was now gone, possibly forever.

CHAPTER FIFTY-SIX

January 14, Pátzcuaro, Michoacán

JAMIE WATCHED THOUGH THE SPOTTING scope as Marcus was unloaded from the SUV. He signaled to Sit to get his eyes on Marcus.

Sit lay prone, his eye to the scope mounted on his Soviet-made, 50 caliber, Dragunov snipper rifle, that he affectionately called 'The Fat Lady'. "Pete did a real job on him." Sit said in a low voice.

They continued watching as Marcus was moved toward the very cottage he said they would bring him to.

"Did you just see that?" Jamie asked.

"No way. He didn't just wink at us, did he? I swear, that man is…" Sit trailed off.

Jamie nodded. "Yeah, he certainly is."

* * *

Aboard the Takbir, international waters off the cost of Zihuatanejo, Guerrero

"ONE MOMENT, PLEASE," J. T. SAID INTO his headset.

"Colonel, I've got an Admiral Pulver on a live feed."

Although J. T. was surprised, the colonel acted as if he were expecting the call.

The colonel nodded for J. T. to put it up on the wall.

"Admiral."

"My God, Sam, but you're one popular man."

"Nice of you to say, sir. Probably my looks."

"How the hell've you been?"

"Oh you know, hanging out, contemplating retirement."

"Cut the shit, Sam. Men like us don't retire; we just fade away into obscurity."

"Now, that's a lovely thought. So what did I do to come up on your radar?"

"Not so much what you *did* as, I suppose, what you're *going* to do. I've got a destroyer en route to you. Now don't get nervous. We're not coming after you; we've got a special delivery.

"Now, this piece of equipment is off the books. Don't ask me how, because I don't know, but somehow, it's traceable back to *los Zetas*, which my intelligence people tell me is Mexico's largest drug cartel these days. Now, what all this has to do with me, I'm pretty sure, is nothing. In fact, I've been guaranteed that if something goes wrong, none of this sticks to me or mine. Anyway, it's good to see you again, Sam, and if you really are going to retire, you have to get a dog. You got one yet?"

The colonel shook his head and laughed.

"Well, there you have it, Sam. I, for one, am glad you're still in the fight. Oh, one more thing. I'm supposed to tell you that..." He paused as if thinking of the exact words. "You're batting cleanup. I was told you would know what that means."

"Thank you, Admiral," the colonel said, and the feed went dark.

CHAPTER FIFTY-SEVEN
Pátzcuaro, Michoacán

MARCUS HEARD VOICES BEHIND HIM—two, maybe more. They spoke Arabic, but with a non-native inflection. They discussed their hosts and how they needed to finish up their business and get the hell out of here. While spilling his guts on the *Takbir*, Arturo had confirmed that his sister, Isabel, was here, though he didn't know about her husband and the children. From the conversation, it appeared that Pops and kids weren't here—one less thing to worry about.

Then, in English he heard, "Get him up, and tell those...if they touch him again."

As hands lifted the chair, Marcus had another realization: Revant didn't know that his entire beating wasn't at the hands of Arturo and his boys—that was good. Then, as his head cleared he realized that his little stunt with Arturo had landed him in a position that was out of the line of sight provided by the window—that was bad.

Marcus heard a door open and close. Then a man stepped in front of him—Peter Revant.

"Your wife was not nearly so much trouble."

Marcus sat silent and appraised the man before him: early thirties, tall, handsome, wearing jeans and a black leather jacket.

Marcus watched as he removed a pair of black gloves from his jacket pocket and slapped them in the palm of his hand.

"You know she offered to do anything if we let her go. Then it was anything if we would just speak to her." He finished gloving one hand, flexed his fingers, and started with the other. "Even though she was a bit older, your Annie was a beautiful woman. I have to tell you, I considered it."

Marcus could feel the rage building like a dammed-up creek ready to explode in a flash flood. He surged against his bonds, "You...."

In the next instant something was around his neck, choking

off his words.

Peter bent over in front of him. "These babies are slick." He waved his gloved hands in front of Marcus's face. "The knuckles are filled with lead shot."

The punch landed square on his nose and out went the lights. Then a shock of cold, wet brought him back as someone threw a bucket of water in his face.

"I think I'm going to like being a leader of the revolution against the West."

Marcus tried to slow the spinning with a deep breath, but no air would pass though his smashed nose. He shook his head; wet strands of hair clung to his face. "What, you fancy yourself the next Osama?" He laughed as blood ran from his broken nose into his mouth. "He was twenty-four when he gave up a life of privilege and wealth, and for thirty years he lived on the run, from one shit-hole to another. You think you've got that in you? I think not."

The next punch came from above—an explosion of pain in his already sore jaw. The chair would have toppled but someone held it from behind.

With his chin on his chest, Marcus groaned, "Shit! That hurt."

His head was jerked back by whoever held the rope around his neck from behind.

"You don't get it, do you, Mr. Diablo? This isn't just about me. No. The battle to restore Islamic values is being waged by many— Hezbollah, al-Qaeda, al-Shabaab and now the Islamic State. And what is America doing? Exactly what we want them to."

* * *

Aboard the Takbir, international waters off the cost of Zihuatanejo, Guerrero

ON THE BRIDGE OF THE *Takbir,* the colonel and J. T. listened as Marcus goaded Revant. Each time a punch landed, J. T. cringed and looked to the colonel. If it bothered him, J. T. couldn't tell. When the tirade began about the warriors of Islam, the colonel said only, "I'll be damned."

Several days before Marcus, Pete, and Liam had left the *Takbir,* to begin their charade with Taz, the colonel sat with Marcus in the private salon. The colonel had a routine with each member of the team before a mission. With Marcus, it was a conversation, as much for him to get things off his chest as for the colonel to judge his state of mind. In a nutshell, Marcus said the same thing that Peter Revant was ranting on about.

Marcus contended that jet and drone strikes on ISIS were exactly the response they wanted. He insisted that the jihadists wanted to die, indeed *needed* to die, at the hands of the great Satan. He said America was the only enemy that could unite the two houses of Islam—Shia and Sunni, and that for every fighter or innocent civilian killed, ten would arise. In fact, Marcus was adamant that only through this sort of action by the United States and its allies could an organization like ISIS survive and grow.

When the colonel asked him what should be done about beheaded journalists, who seemed to be the favored targets of ISIS, Marcus sounded like a battle-hardened commander.

"Just like you and each member of Force Ten, these journalists are the best. They do what they do not only because they can, but just like career soldiers or great athletes, they go into the fray because it makes them feel alive. I'm not saying we let it go. But you can't let the call to war be decided by public referendum, or because, according to some poll, sixty percent of Americans feel we should take military action. You know as well as I do, the only way to really disrupt these people is through strategic assassination—the same strategy they use."

That was days ago. Now, looking over at J. T., the colonel said, "He scares me too, sometimes."

* * *

Pátzcuaro, Michoacán

Listening as Marcus egged Peter Revant on, Chaya wondered, *Why did he have to be so antagonistic?* She was startled when, just as the first punch landed, Liam put his hand on her shoulder. "You need to let him do his thing. I know it's hard, but he's right, lass. We have to trust him."

Yeah, Chaya thought, *It's different for you. You don't love him and those boys the same way I do.*

* * *

Sit and Jamie watched the cottage and listened as the interrogation and beating started. Sit signaled to Jamie.

"I can't see him." Jamie said. "Must be standing to one side of the window."

Jamie meant Revant. They had discussed the possible presence of others in the room besides Marcus and Revant. Marcus had insisted he could get Revant by himself, but Sit and the team had a plan just in case. That plan, though, significantly reduced the chances that Marcus would come out alive.

* * *

HIS EYES CLOSED, MARCUS STRUGGLED to breathe. He focused on Revant's voice, ranting on about ISIS. He had to agree, and the confirmation that he, Marcus, seemed to think just like a terrorist gave him a strange sense of hope and satisfaction. On the edge of blacking out, he heard Annie's voice.

"You know you are a real piece of work. That little mouth-off-and get-beat-like-a-drum stunt with Arturo has you out of position. And if you're out of position, guess who else is out of position? So you know what that means?"

Marcus opened his eyes and searched the room. He tried to speak, but because of the rope around his neck only grunts came out. Revant nodded and the rope went slack. Marcus coughed, his throat raw and dry. He licked his chapped lips, his tongue felt thick and slow.

When Marcus spoke, his voice sounded strained and raspy, like someone else's. "Why don't you tell your guy to leave for a few minutes so, before you kill the boy and then me, you and I can have a heart-to-heart about your friend Adad."

Marcus saw the surprise on Revant's face at his mention of the boy. Probably he wondered how Marcus knew about Jabril. Without doubt though, the mention of Adad triggered the rage Marcus now saw on his face.

The door opened, then closed. Just him and Revant now. By Marcus's reckoning, Revant was a couple of feet away from where he needed to be to offer a clear view through the window.

Revant was breathing hard—on his way over the edge.

Marcus said, "It's okay. Adad told me all about the two of you."

The look on Revant's face told Marcus he didn't quite understand. "Hey, I'm not homophobic. As long as two people love each other..."

Revant stepped in, lowering his center of gravity, and punched Marcus in the solar plexus.

As the blow landed, Marcus threw his weight back and to his right and toppled over, landing on his side. He wanted to roll into a ball and vomit, but since he couldn't, he just vomited.

Revant kicked once, twice, three times as Marcus tucked his chin, instinctively trying to protect his face. As the pain began to overwhelm his mind, he chided himself for being a wimp. Hell, he'd seen movies where the guy took twice as many blows.

* * *

CHAYA, PETE, LIAM, WEATHERS AND Ham got a Morse message from Sit: "Prepare to move. Execute plan B."

Chaya gasped. If they breached the cottage without Sit having taken out Revant, Marcus's chances of survival were nil.

Pete got up from where he had been sitting with his back to a tree and took Chaya by the hand. "Marcus is okay," he said. "Tough. Sit just needs us ready."

Ham joined in. "If you can't do this, we understand. You can wait here."

A fire rose in Chaya's belly. "You think you're going without me, you think again."

Liam said, "The lad was just checking. Let's move."

* * *

HIS EYE GLUED TO THE Nightforce scope of his rifle, Sit thought aloud—Chaya called it "talking alone." "Goddamn it Marcus," he murmured. "You need to work some magic and move yourself a few feet." Sit could see moving shadows but no clear target.

When he spoke again he spoke to Jamie. "Tracker, change of plan. I need you to move up to below the bluff. I'm sending a text to the other group to do the same. Feel up to it?"

Jamie smiled. "No worries, mate. I was born for the fight; you know that."

Sit had never taken his eye from the scope. "Okay, boy. We're gonna get one shot at this. Let's pray Marcus pulls a rabbit out of his ass. And, Jamie, you bring him home, ya hear?"

"Yes sir."

* * *

Aboard the Takbir, international waters off the cost of Zihuatanejo, Guerrero

"COLONEL, WE ARE BEING HAILED."

On the screen a Navy Captain stood on the bridge of a ship. "Colonel Webb, I'm Captain Nolan Bard, commander of the destroyer USS *Intruder*." "Captain," the colonel said.

"Well, sir, I'm two hundred miles to your north. It just so happens that we are in the vicinity of a very large yacht, purportedly belonging to the man who replaced *Miguel Treviño Morales* as the head of the *Zetas* Cartel. Seems the rich and infamous have started taking to the open sea since this flu pandemic. Anyway, on your go, we are prepared to launch an MQ-9 Reaper drone carrying a payload of two laser-guided, AGM-114 Hellfire air-to-ground missiles. Once launched, I have orders to transfer the guidance codes to you, and she's all yours."

The colonel hadn't known exactly what the admiral and the young deputy director of the FBI had in mind, but this was unexpected. With the Reaper in the air and in J. T.'s control, he acted like a kid with new a train set. With a cruising speed around two hundred miles per hour, the drone, once at altitude, could circle for hours. With the target at an elevation of 7,500 feet, they could launch the missile, completely undetected, from 30,000 feet.

The colonel did the math. The op had a lot of moving parts— too many for his taste. But he had been in contact with Sit. The advance team, plus Jamie, was moving into position. The only problem, Sit was dialed at the distance but he still didn't have a target.

* * *

Pátzcuaro, Michoacán

EVERYTHING LOOKED FUZZY AS MARCUS struggled to regain his focus. He heard the door open.

"Everything okay?" said a male voice.

"Yes, yes. Get him up and get out," said Revant.

The chair, Marcus still bound to it, was righted. Marcus

wanted to keep his eyes closed. His face hurt but he forced himself to open them. His swelling right eye made his vision hazy. As he blinked, he realized that blood from a cut on his forehead ran into the other one.

It took a few moments, but he got his vision clear enough to see that he was now in line with the window. That was good. But now he was only five or six feet from the windowed wall, and the window was shoulder high. Thus, Sit couldn't see him. Revant, in a rage, stooped over and yelled at him, his head below the window. Sit wouldn't have a shot. That was bad.

* * *

"WHAT? YOU DECIDED TO GO this far and quit? A few minutes ago you beat yourself up for being a pussy. Now it's okay? I don't think so!"

Annie? Marcus had blocked out Revant's rant about the great cause and the role he planned to play in it.

"Jesus, Marcus. You go to all this trouble, let this piece of shit beat you like a rug on clothesline. You got people scrambling to save your ass. Now, do your part. Make him stand up."

"Can't...so tired," he mumbled.

"Can't *what?*" Revant yelled. "As for being tired, you have nothing to worry about there— you'll soon be heading for a long sleep."

Marcus opened his eye. His lips and tongue felt puffy. Revant was bent over him, his face close to Marcus's.

"You shouldn't try so hard to hide your sexuality." Revant's face was swimming in front of Marcus. It looked as if there were two of him. "Come on man, you can tell me. You didn't touch Annie, because girls aren't your thing."

The blows came raining down.

* * *

"I WILL NEVER UNDERSTAND WHAT makes you tick, or what goes on in that fucked-up brain of yours. But if turning him into a raving lunatic was the objective, well, you did it."

"Annie?"

"Yeah, baby."

The voice was soft and sweet, and Marcus felt a warmth well up inside him.

"Oh, no, you don't." The voice that had been so comforting took on a hard edge. "Now, make him stand up. Do it! Do it now, Goddamn it!"

* * *

SIT WATCHED THOUGH THE SCOPE as he listened to Marcus get his ass beat. He hated this. He had promised himself, had sworn to Marcus, that he would never stand by again and watch a member of his team take a beating, not when he had the skill, the tools and the will to stop it. But even with skill, tools and will, without a target he couldn't do shit.

He had a clear view into the window, but he couldn't see Marcus or Revant. As he lay on the ground, his heart raced. Anxiety lay below the surface, itching to get out. Both were bad. They were two things that he had spent a professional lifetime mastering, and he taught his students that these were the most important elements to understand and control— even more important than skill handling the rifle.

He took a breath, and then felt a slight pressure on the back of his neck, as if someone's hand rested there.

Sit jumped inside his skin. He didn't dare take his eye away from the scope, but he swore it now felt like someone ever so lightly rubbed his neck. Whatever it was, it felt good. It occurred to him that Marcus was finally making him lose his mind too.

Sit lay still for a long moment. He had been so focused on the soothing coolness on the back of his neck, he hadn't realized how perfectly calm he now was. This was the feeling he knew: being in the moment, visualizing the shot in his mind. Focusing on the window, he saw Revant straightening up. The face, filled with rage and anger, slowly turned to look out the window. Sit squeezed the trigger.

* * *

"ANNIE, DON'T GO. PLEASE STAY," Marcus said, his voice thick, his tone pleading.

"What the fuck is wrong with you? Your Annie's dead, I killed her."

Marcus's good eye squinted as he looked up into the sunlight shining through the window, the glare made a halo around the opening. "No, no, she's right there, in the light. Look how beautiful... Annie..."

Peter Revant began to straighten up, and at that moment, for Marcus, everything went into some ultra-slow motion movie playing out in his mind's eye. He watched as Revant turned, the glare of the sunlight through glass making him blink. Then he saw Sit, lying flat; saw the rifle recoil into his massive shoulder; saw the muzzle flash as the hand-loaded, three-inch- long .50- caliber round left the barrel; saw the bullet travel across space; saw it hit the glass and watched as the very first shard broke away. He saw a nanosecond of recognition in Revant's eyes, as the bullet struck his head above the left eye. A tiny drop of blood at first and then the air filled with a suspended spray of blood, brain matter, shards of bone and glass. The body floated through the air and landed in a puff of dust on the floor.

Marcus closed his eyes, tilted his chin up to the light, and let out a sigh. "We win, Annie. We win."

* * *

Aboard the Takbir, international waters off the cost of Zihuatanejo, Guerrero

THE COLONEL SUSPENDED RADIO SILENCE for the final phase of the mission.

"F-two, are we a go?"

Sit took a moment before answering. Should he say something about the feeling he had, like someone was rubbing his neck? Nah, this wasn't the time to come off as crazy.

"I'm a go."

"F-nine?"

"All in," Jamie replied.

"F-four?"

"In position," said Weathers.

"F-seven, your head in the game?"

"Oh yeah," said Chaya.

"Good. F-two, you have the call."

Sit spoke to the team. "When you hear the shot, breech the cottage. No one walks out but F-ten and the boy."

* * *

Pátzcuaro, Michoacán

AS THE CRACK OF THE .50-caliber echoed though the canyon, Jamie and Pete moved from one side, and Weathers, Liam, Chaya and Ham from the other. The four men with Revant, standing on either side of the door into the cottage, fell dead before the sound of the bullet that killed their boss faded.

At the door, Chaya stood with her back to the adobe wall and held up her hand, three fingers extended. When she tucked the last one into her fist, Pete burst through the door.

On the north side, Ham and Liam opened the cellar hatch. Cautiously, they went down the steep stairs into the musty darkness. With flashlights, they saw a small form huddled in the corner on the dirt floor wrapped in a filthy blanket.

Ham approached and said in Arabic, "Jabril, your grandfather sent me. I'm to tell you, 'A tree begins with a seed.'"

Jabril moved the blanket from his head, and in a small, frightened voice replied, "I am the tree."

* * *

CHAYA RUSHED TO MARCUS. HIS chin was on his chest and his face was a bloody, swollen mess.

Pete cut Marcus's bonds and eased him to the ground.

Chaya opened her pack and began working on him.

Marcus swam at the edge of consciousness. He thought he saw Revant's head explode, but now he wasn't sure. He was cold, and whatever he lay on felt hard, but otherwise, shock had set in and he didn't feel too bad. But why was Annie still yelling at him? He had done what she wanted. He made the asshole stand up, why was she still mad?

* * *

"MARCUS, MARCUS, DO YOU HEAR me?"

He forced his eye to open. Everything was fuzzy. "Annie?"

On her knees, Chaya leaned over Marcus. "Come on, look at me."

The figure looming over him came into view. Not Annie, but Chaya. He wanted to smile, but his face hurt too much. "Hey. The boy. You get the boy?"

Chaya looked over her shoulder and got a nod from Pete.

"Yeah, we got him. Stay quiet, now. It's time to go home."

* * *

Aboard the Takbir, international waters off the cost of Zihuatanejo, Guerrero

"THE CHOPPER IS AWAY, COLONEL. All aboard and accounted for," said J. T.

"Okay, bring that bird in for a closer look," said the colonel.

Using a controller similar to that of a video game, J. T. stood in front of the wall screen. One half was the high-altitude camera view from the Predator drone; on the other was the God's Eye satellite view of Hacienda del Lago.

* * *

Pátzcuaro, Michoacán

ISABEL SAT AT THE KITCHEN counter with her brother, Arturo. "This business will be concluded soon," she said. "And we can be done with the Arab. You have talked to the guards? He does not leave here, ever."

"All arranged. We will give him time to deal with Marcus Diablo."

Isabel touched her brother on the arm. "It's not like you to be so disturbed by one man."

"I can't explain it," Arturo replied. "He gets under my skin. I hate that *güero.*"

"It doesn't matter. In a few hours, the two people causing you and me worries will be no more."

As Isabel talked, they heard the echo of a gunshot.

Arturo began to rise, but Isabel reached out and touched his arm. "Leave it. Let him complete his business."

Tense and anxious, they sat in silence. Minutes later, they heard the distant sound of an approaching helicopter. Fearing that Revant might be preparing to leave the property, Isabel ordered three groups of her bodyguards to drive to the cottage. She didn't ever want this man in her life again.

* * *

Nearly a mile away, Sit still had his eye to the scope. He had gotten his shot. The team had Marcus and the boy, and he could hear Bronson coming in the chopper.

He adjusted the rifle's bipod and zeroed in on the crest of the hill. J. T. had given him a heads up about the approaching SUVs. He made corrections for windage and elevation and waited. The first vehicle crested, then two others right behind it. He took a deep breath and let out half. The old, calm under pressure, no problem this time. He put two rounds through the windshield of the last vehicle. It veered hard right and rolled, coming to a stop in the middle of the road. He switched his sights to the first vehicle. Two more rounds brought it to a stop. The middle vehicle skidded broadside to Sit's view. He shot into the gas tank, and the SUV erupted in billowing yellow flames.

Sit was packing up when Jamie arrived.

"Damn good shootin', mate. Didn't want you to get lost, so I thought I'd pop back 'round and help you out. We need to move. Bronson's due in a few minutes to scoop us up."

With his pack and the heavy rifle slung over his shoulders, Sit said, "Lead on."

* * *

Standing on the front patio, Isabel and Arturo watched as the three SUVs, each carrying four heavily armed men, sped off toward the cottages. Once they crested the rise, they dropped from view. When they heard the first two shots, the guards in the driveway moved up the steps to the patio. Three more shots came in rapid succession, then an explosion and a fireball that rose well above the crest of the hill.

With a wave of her arm, Isabel hurried her brother and the guards into the house. She ordered her bodyguards to lock the mansion down. She was glad that she had decided to give the domestic staff time off while this business with Revant concluded. No sense in giving the locals any more gossip.

In the master suite, Isabel gathered her belongings. "We're getting out of here," she told Arturo.

Black smoke came from the other side of the rise. Shots that sounded like automatic weapons rang out, then—*wop wop wop*—a helicopter approaching up the canyon.

A few minutes later, it roared off and faded into the distance.

"Let's go," Isabel said to her brother.

* * *

Aboard the Takbir, international waters off the cost of Zihuatanejo, Guerrero

"ALL RIGHT, BABY, WE'RE LOCKED," J. T. said.

On the screen, the missile streaked earthward, streaming a tail of fire and vapor. J. T. kept the drone hovering. He had one more Hellfire if he needed it. On the other side of the screen, the God's Eye satellite view through the big picture windows into Hacienda del Lago showed people moving around and stacking luggage just outside the front door.

"Getting ready to bug out." J. T. said. "I don't think so. Contact in ten...nine...eight..."

* * *

THE COLONEL KEPT HIS ATTENTION on the screen as he listened to J. T.'s monologue. The Force 10 geek didn't often get excited, but at the moment, he seemed to be in his version of nirvana. It was a relief to the colonel and the team that no domestic staff or children were on site —just Arturo, Isabel and their hired guns. The colonel understood collateral damage all too well. But when he decided to start his own private military contracting firm, avoiding killing innocent people was a top priority.

The colonel watched the screen as five bodyguards walked out the front door, each grabbing a bag or two as they made their way down the steps to the black Range Rovers parked in the driveway.

J. T. had just begun his countdown when Isabel and her brother stepped out onto the patio. Isabel put on dark glasses and turned her head toward the bluff.

In the next instant, a ball of flames filled the entire screen. When the view cleared Hacienda del Lago was a pile of rubble. Where the Range Rovers had been parked was nothing but a black, smoking hole.

Ten minutes later the satellite view showed a convoy of Mexican military trucks coming up the canyon road.

The colonel turned to J. T. and nodded.

The screen split again. The view from the camera mounted in the nose of the Predator drone was blue sky above and clouds below.

"You sure I can't keep it?" J. T. said. The colonel stared at him.

"Okay, okay." J. T. hit a button on the control console in his hands, and the drone exploded.

CHAPTER FIFTY-EIGHT

January 15, Beginnings ranch, British Columbia

MARCUS AWOKE IN HIS bed in the big house at the ranch. He hurt all over, but especially his nose and jaw. He reached up and touched his swollen lips and felt the puffy flesh around his eyes. He could only see out of the right. He could tell it was dark still. He tried to roll onto his side, but he couldn't. He reached out with his arm and touched warm flesh. Slowly he turned his head to the sleeping form next to him.

At his touch, Chaya woke. She sat up, rubbing sleep from her eyes. "How do you feel?"

"Like I got run over by a truck."

Chaya shook her head. "If you got run over by a truck, you'd be dead, so no, not a truck."

Marcus laughed and winced as he brought a hand to his sore, bandaged ribs.

Chaya turned on the nightstand light, got out of bed, and put on sweats. She went into the bathroom and returned with a glass of water. Sitting on the edge of the bed, she put a pill in Marcus's mouth and held the glass to his lips. "You are going to stay in bed for a few days. Your nose is broken, your jaw is fractured, you have four cracked ribs, and a concussion on top of all that."

The clock read 5:30 a.m. Marcus felt the pill Chaya gave him start to take effect. He was so tired...

Chaya caressed his forehead, pushing back strands of his hair. As Marcus's breathing deepened, she leaned in and kissed his split and swollen lips. "Damn it, Marcus, loving you makes me sometimes want to kill you."

* * *

January 22

Ham waited as the jet came in on approach to the Beginnings airstrip. The colonel decided that Marcus wouldn't be here to greet Sheikh Nazir and Jabril's mother. The feeling was, it would be best if the sheikh didn't see a familiar face. The more uncomfortable he was, the better.

Marcus stood at his bedroom window and looked out toward the front gate. A week had passed since his return, and only in the past three days had he been allowed out of bed for more than a few hours. The bruises were fading to a grayish sickly yellow. His eyes were still swollen, but at least he could see out of both of them. His ribs still hurt, but only when he breathed or laughed. When he saw the SUV crest the hill, he headed downstairs.

* * *

Marcus stood by himself in the driveway as the Suburban pulled up. Ham got out and opened the back door. Sheikh Nazir got out, dressed in a plain white robe with a simple white kaffiyeh held in place with a black band of woven dyed camel hair. Ham walked around and opened the other door. Jabril's mother got out. She wore Western clothing: jeans, a winter jacket, and lace-up walking shoes. Her black hair was pulled back, and she had a purple wool scarf around her neck. Her face was free of the bruises and the mask of fear that had shrouded her face the last time Marcus saw her.

No one else got out of the Suburban.

As Marcus approached Rasha, he pointed to three figures on horseback in the paddock below.

She brought her hand to her mouth.

"Jabril is going to be fine. You go with Ham. He'll take you to him."

Marcus greeted the sheikh. Both men stood, hands clasped behind their backs, and watched the reunion between mother and child.

"He who possesses sons possesses one of Allah's greatest gifts, even if they be sons of sons. Yet it is in the bosom of women that a son may grow into a good and righteous man." Marcus said.

The sheikh said, "That is not of the Quran."

"No, Sayid. It is of the book of Marcus."

As Jabril and his mother embraced, the sheikh said, "You once said to me that we must pray that our sons find a better path. I will continue to pray they find it."

"Come." Marcus said, and he started walking toward Jabril and his mother.

* * *

WHEN THE SHEIKH AND MARCUS approached, all eyes turned to them. Bodie and Garrett both said, "*As-salamu Alaikum.*"

The sheikh bowed slightly and opened his hands. "*Wa alaikum assaam wa rahmatu Allah.*"

Marcus could see that beyond his rote reply, the sheikh was put at a loss for words by these American boys' show of respect.

Marcus began to speak, but Garrett stepped in front of Sheikh Nazir and reached up and took the man's hand.

It took the sheikh by surprise, but Garrett held tight and pulled so that the sheikh had to bend. In his ear, Garrett whispered, "Would you like to meet Jabril's horse?" Without waiting for an answer, Garrett led the sheikh to the corral, where the three horses stood tethered to a rail.

Garrett released the sheikh's hand and said, while patting the muzzle of a bay stallion, "His name is Zameel. It means 'friend,' you know? Jabril choose it."

The sheikh smiled. "Zameel. That is a good name, and yes," he patted Garrett on the shoulder, "I know the meaning of this word."

* * *

MARCUS STOOD WITH SHEIKH NAZIR, Rasha, and Jabril at the bottom of the steps to their jet. "Despite our differences, we have much in common," he said. He looked back over his shoulder at Bodie and Garrett, who waved good-bye to Jabril. "If our sons are to have a chance at making our world a more peaceful place, we must first impart to them a vision of what that peace might be like."

Rasha stepped forward and hugged Marcus. "Thank you forever for bringing me my son, and may Allah smile upon you and your family."

Jabril stepped forward and tugged on Marcus's hand.

Marcus knelt and hugged the boy, then looked up at his grandfather. "Jabril is always welcome here."

As Rasha and Jabril boarded the jet, Marcus said to the sheikh, "Change begins when two agree. Let that agreement begin with us."

EPILOGUE

March 23

As the sun began to rise Marcus sat on the stone wall and sipped coffee from a thermos lid. Winter's grip was loosening. He had healed from his beating, and he hadn't had a visit from Annie since that day in the cottage at *Hacienda del Lago*, two months ago.

He had laid down the rocks on either side of the cairn built atop the rock wall that held the OLD PEACH can with Annie's ashes. The sun's first rays glinted off the can. "Good morning baby," Marcus said.

He stared down into the valley where the Clearwater River meandered through the meadow dotted with cows and the first calves of the year. This was the time of rebirth on the ranch, when everything came alive. Marcus shifted on the rock, and when he looked up again, Annie sat beside him, dressed in jeans, worn roper boots, and a green work jacket, the brown collar turned up. Her blond hair was pulled back in a ponytail tied with a baby-blue ribbon and her face glowed in the cold morning.

"Hands down, this is the best view in the world," she said. "And I get to see it every day."

Marcus smiled at her.

"It's good to see that you've healed up." She reached out and touched his face. Marcus felt the warmth and softness of her hand as her fingers traced a line down the side of his nose and over his lips. "You think maybe next time you could figure out some way around getting your ass beat?"

She laughed as she hopped off the wall and stood in front of him. "I mean, really, watching you get smacked around once in awhile does give me some small sense of pleasure, but I think you're taking it a bit too far."

"Jesus, Annie, how is that...?" Marcus paused, stunned by the sound of the words coming out of his mouth.

"Hey, don't look at me like that. Hell, you could've talked to me anytime you wanted." Annie's hands were on her hips. "For God's sake, Marcus. I'm a figment of your imagination."

"I thought..."

"Yeah, I know." Annie sat back on the wall and took Marcus' hand in hers. "You think the connection we have is though Garrett. No, baby, the connection has always been through you." The light bounced off Annie's eyes, giving her the glow of a young girl. She was on her feet again. "It's a testament to the power of love with a whole heap of Catholic guilt thrown in for good measure. You are the one who let me, the thought of me, stay alive and thrive in the boys. Now I'm a part of their imagination as well. I swear, you pack around more crap! You've really got to let some of that shit go."

"How is it that one minute you're so sweet and innocent, and the next you have all the reverence of a drunken sailor?" Marcus asked.

"What? You can't deal with me being just like you? Get over it."

Annie skipped up the first few stone steps that led to the line cabin and turned around and hopped down them. "Remember what you said to me when we first met?"

She got right up in Marcus's face and tilted her head side to side. "No?"

Hands in her jacket pockets, she kicked a pinecone and sent it bouncing across the ground. "I was sitting at that bar and you walked up and said, 'You look like an around-the-bend kinda girl.'" Annie was laughing when she looked up at Marcus. "Swear to God, that's what you said. I was thinking, *Is that the best pickup line you've got?*"

Annie's face softened and her voice turned serious. "It didn't matter what you said. Those big blues already had me.

"I know you worry about the boys, but you're doing okay. Bodie's wondering why we haven't met in his dreams yet. You let him know we're close, him and me." She shook her head. "He's just too damn much like you."

Annie came up close to Marcus again. "Chaya, Marcus. You take care with her. You need her. And so do the boys. But more than that, she needs you!" Annie rested her hands on Marcus's shoulders and stared into his eyes. "I need you...to need her...it's important."

Annie spun away and started back up the steps to the cabin speaking as she walked. "Oh, you might want to try and not dream about me when you're in bed with her. Women are funny that way." She laughed. At the top she stopped and turned toward Marcus. "You were right, though, baby. We spent our lives finding out what was around the next bend, and I cherished every second of it." She moved farther back toward the trail to the upper meadow, and just before she disappeared from his sight, she said, "I don't know what awaits, but I do know there are plenty more bends in your future."

About the Author

Mark Shaff lives in Reno, Nevada with his wife and two sons. He is anxious to be discovered as a favorite author while grudgingly holding on to his day job.

Force Ten: Doubling the Penny is his second novel in the Marcus Diablo series. *Doubling the Penny* is a sequel to *Redemption Road.* Mark like the protagonist, Marcus Diablo, is working hard to reinvent himself.

www.lrpnv.com

To find more of your favorite
titles and authors, go to LeRue Press, LLC

www.ingramcontent.com/pod-product-compliance
Lightning Source LLC
Chambersburg PA
CBHW070829190726
48292CB00006B/2165